About the 

Matt Hilton wor... ...e
security and the p... ...
Dan blackbelt and ...
with his wife and s...

Praise for Matt Hilton

'Hilton is more adept at humour than Lee Child . . . the series should be electrifying.' *Daily Mail*

'Vicious, witty and noir, Hilton is a sparkling new talent.' Peter James

'Hard-hitting and fast-paced, I was hooked from start to finish.' Simon Kernick

'Taut, thrilling, tense – I loved it!' Richard Hammond

'*Dead Men's Dust* roars along at a ferocious pace.' *Observer*

'Blood spurts and bones crunch with narrative panache' *Daily Telegraph*

'Hilton writes well . . . a promising start' *Guardian*

'Joe Hunter takes you in at the deep end . . . and never lets up . . . Breathtaking.' Adrian Magson

'This is a high-voltage, gripping read that will transfer easily to the big screen. Comparisons with Lee Child are facile, but unavoidable, and to be fair *Dead Men's Dust* doesn't suffer from the comparison. Fast, ferocious and a thrill a page, this book will have you reading into the wee, small hours. The action is non-stop, the fight scenes authentic and thrilling. The finale in particular is as good as any action scene I've read in recent years.'

Crimesquad

'The pace of *Dead Men's Dust* is a scorcher, with the action beginning right from the start and never flagging. The gritty description of physical combat rings all-too-true and the use of weapons is rough, tough and unflinching. If you like your heroes to leap off the page at you, you'll like Joe Hunter – and like me you'll look forward to the next in the series. As a story character, Joe Hunter takes you in at the deep end and never lets up. Breathtaking.'

Shots

'A dose of pure rocket fuel. Starts fast, gets faster, and doesn't quit right through to the slam bang finale. *Dead Men's Dust* is as enjoyable a thriller as you will read this year, and I do mean "Thriller"! My ears are still ringing with gunfire! I loved this book.'

Christopher Reich

Also by Matt Hilton

Dead Men's Dust
Judgement and Wrath

MATT HILTON

Slash and Burn

HODDER

First published in Great Britain in 2010 by Hodder & Stoughton
An Hachette Livre UK company

First published in paperback in 2010
1

A CIP catalogue record for this title is available from the British Library

978 1 444 70535 5 (B format)
978 0 340 97829 0 (A format)

Typeset in Plantin Light by Hewer Text UK Ltd, Edinburgh
Printed and bound by Clays Ltd, St Ives plc

Hodder & Stoughton policy is to use papers that are natural, renewable
and recyclable products and made from wood grown in sustainable
forests. The logging and manufacturing processes are expected to
conform to the environmental regulations of the country of origin.

Hodder & Stoughton Ltd
338 Euston Road
London NW1 3BH

www.hodder.co.uk

To Jacky and Val Hilton.
The best parents ever.

PROLOGUE

It was the worst year of her life.

She stumbled and fell, her shoulder ramming the bole of a tree, scraping her skin raw beneath her shirt. She cried out, but instantly clamped her teeth down on her lip to stop the sound travelling through the forest. She scrambled up and fled again, her breath catching in her throat. She wanted to howl in terror, but there was only one thing racing through her mind: Get away. Get away now.

She had to run. Leave everything behind. Everything.

But she couldn't do that. There was one thing that she had to keep safe. The only thing that would help her end the *worst year of her life*.

It had been a bad, bad year.

Her husband walked out on her in the spring and took up with a girl half his age. Summer was earmarked by the acrimonious divorce. By the time fall came round, Imogen Ballard didn't think things could get any worse.

But then came winter.

And now men were trying to kill her.

Already, blood had been spilled. Not hers, but that

simple truth was the only chink of light piercing the nightmare she'd found herself in. How long would that stay true when the men hunting her through the forest did so armed with rifles and automatic handguns? Sooner or later they would catch up with her, and then there'd be a lot more blood.

She had to run. Hide. Stay away from those hunting her with the tenacity of bloodhounds. She was at home in the woods, but she was no Lady Rambo. She didn't know if she was capable of giving them the slip, and she certainly wasn't able to fight back. Not armed as she was with nothing but a digital video camera.

She was thirty-eight years old. Not as fit as ten years ago when she was regularly competing in triathlons, but still lithe and strong. The problem was, the shock of what she'd witnessed had robbed her of much of the stamina she required to maintain her lead. The hunters were gaining.

As if to remind her, a bullet shrieked by like an angry wasp, cutting a chunk from a tree on her right.

Imogen ducked in reflex. Too late to have saved her if the bullet was on target, of course, but she couldn't stop the instinctive movement. Then she was pushing on, her boots driving through mounds of moss and twigs as she clambered over a fallen tree. Another bullet streaked past, galvanising her to push even harder.

Shouts from the men chasing her. Maniacal laughter taunting her. Another gun barked, punching the ground in front of her feet. Imogen turned down a narrow trail. The men were toying with her, enjoying her terror; that was the only reason why their bullets hadn't found her yet.

From somewhere ahead she heard a faint rumble. Her first thought was that they had called in some kind of armoured vehicle as back-up, that even now some great cannon was vectoring in to blow her to smithereens. But that thought was sheer madness. The rumble was from Great Wells, the waterfall she'd earlier scaled on her way up the hillside.

She considered running directly to the falls and throwing herself headlong to the mercy of the white water. But the falls were one hundred and fifty feet of steep cliffs. At the bottom waited not a nice deep pool, but a series of potholes set in jagged rocks. The falls offered no means of escape. In fact, they blocked her way more effectively than an electrified fence would.

She spun from the path, hurdling another fallen tree, and crashing through the lower branches of pines that grew from the steep hillside. Her only way out of here was by an unfamiliar route to her. All she could do was run, and hope that the men gave up before her flagging stamina did.

But she didn't think they would.

I

'My sister may very well be dead.'

'Don't see how I can help you, then. I'm sorry.'

'But then again, she might not be.'

It was one of those surreal conversations that you find yourself striking up with a stranger, and wondering where the hell it was leading to. I'd been taking a cold Corona on the deck of the beach house I had rented on the Florida Gulf Coast to the east of Pensacola. The woman approached me along the curve of the beach. She was walking with the devil-may-care attitude of the tourists who often walked the beach, picking up shells or water-smoothed stones and marvelling at the glory of nature. I noticed her for two reasons. She was obviously beautiful: tall for a woman and willowy of frame. She had the slim hips and broad shoulders I associated with swimmers, but she walked with a ballerina's grace. She had short dark hair and equally dark eyes; kind of Paris chic, I thought. But what struck me most – and the second reason I noticed her – was the way she called out to me like I was an old friend.

'Joe Hunter?' she said, waving a hand. 'Is that you?'

I was unprepared for visitors. My hair was mussed, I was unshaven. Worse, I was stripped to the waist, dressed only in a pair of cut-off denim shorts that were frayed along the hem. My face, neck and forearms were tanned by Florida sunshine, but my upper body still had the pallor of one not long since in northern England. Since my arrival in the US I hadn't had too much spare time on my hands; none of it spent idling in the sun. My couple of minutes on the sundeck had been an attempt at balancing the deficit.

Putting down my bottle of beer, I wiped droplets from my chin. Before answering the woman, I discreetly surveyed the beach in each direction. My first thought was, Who is she? My second, more importantly, Who is with her? In my line of work, it was important that I know those kinds of things. Judas betrayed Jesus with a kiss; a pretty woman calling my name could easily do the same to me.

But there were no enemies lurking.

She came towards me, her bare feet kicking up golden sand. I saw that a pair of sandals, slung from a loop of her shorts, bumped against a shapely thigh.

'You *are* Joe Hunter?' she asked, still ten paces out.

I looked around for my shirt, but made do with folding my forearms over my chest. My arms covered the unsightly scar next to my heart, but that was about all. Good job that I'd kept up a strict exercise regime; at least the rest of my body wasn't ugly too.

Her eyes alighted on the tattoo on my shoulder, and it was as if that one symbol confirmed my identity. Not so many people knew about the tattoo, even fewer people wore one like it. There was me and my best friend Rink. Half a dozen others who'd been in the same Special Forces team. Everyone else was dead.

'I feel at a disadvantage here,' I said. 'You seem to know who I am, but . . .'

'I'm Kate Piers,' she said, advancing to the deck and looking up at me. 'You knew my brother.'

Something in her features did ring a bell. Jake Piers was a tough, wiry son-of-a-bitch who came to our team from the Navy Seals. I was there with him when we took down a terrorist training camp in Libya, and carried him back from the raid across my shoulders after he was shredded by machine-gun fire. Jake died in my arms. He wouldn't have survived his wounds. He was shredded, his internal organs torn up. But I wasn't going to leave him behind. There was no way I was about to allow his corpse to be paraded on TV as a sign of victory for the terrorists. I carried him out of there even though it meant slowing down the extraction of my team.

'You're Jake's sister?' How could she be as pretty when Jake had been such a pug to look at?

'*One* of his sisters,' she corrected me. 'I have an older sister called Imogen.'

Wondering where all this was leading, I waved her up on to the deck and offered her a Corona.

She took the beer but declined a glass, drinking directly from the bottle. I watched a bead of amber liquid trace a line down her neck where it shivered momentarily before she wiped it away. She caught me looking and laughed.

'I bet you're wondering what I'm doing here?'

Leaning against the railing so that the sun was on my back, I ran a hand over my unkempt hair. 'Wasn't expecting visitors.'

Her eyes crinkled. She took in my beach house with a sweep of her arm. 'It's beautiful here. But lonely, I guess. Do you live out here all alone?'

'Only the last few days. That's why I'm surprised you found me.'

I *was* surprised. There were only two people who knew I had moved into the house, and neither of them was the type to give up my location without a fight. My buddy and business partner, Jared 'Rink' Rington, and Harvey Lucas, another friend out in Little Rock, Arkansas.

'You didn't get the voicemail messages Jared sent you?'

I thought about the mobile phone lying somewhere inside the house. I'd slung it aside my first night in my new home. I'd come here for some R and R: why would I want to be disturbed by phone calls? The battery would probably be dead by now.

'Rink sent you?' It was unlike him. Normally he would have paved the way first. But then I looked at Kate and decided that Rink would see what I saw. Not a threat; just a person in need of help.

'He's tied up with a case at the moment, but he said that you would be able to help. I've got a problem, Joe.

But I knew who to come to. I remembered Jake talking about his friends from his unit. He said that he would trust you all with his life. Even when he died, it was his friends who brought him home. It's why I looked up Jared instead of going to the police.'

'And Rink sent you to find me, huh?'

'Said that he was a little busy, but you'd do as second best.'

I shook my head at that.

'What else did Rink tell you about me?'

'Nothing. I already knew from Jake that you were good at your job.'

'Jake told you what we did?'

'Not in as many words. But I'm not stupid. I was only thirteen years old when he died, but even I guessed that he was more than just an average soldier. I knew that you were all part of some extra-special unit. It's because I know about your background that I came looking for you.'

'If you're looking for a mercenary, you've come to the wrong place,' I told her. 'I'm retired. Four and a half years.'

'Jared said you would help.'

'Depends what it is you want.'

'I want you to find my sister.'

'She's missing? You *should* have gone to the cops first.'

'My sister may be dead.' Kate bounced the bottle of beer in her palm.

Frowning, I put down my own bottle, turning away from her. 'Don't see how I can help you, then. I'm sorry.'

'But then again, she might not be.'

I turned around to look at her again, and she was staring up at me with her chin set with determination. She looked more and more like her brother – particularly when he grew pig-headed with stubbornness.

'I need someone to find out which it is,' she said. 'If Imogen is dead, then I have to know. The alternative is that she's being held against her will and needs help to get away.'

I owed Jake. It was his actions in saving us from the ambush that killed him. The only way I could repay his selflessness was to help his family now.

So much for rest and recuperation. I nodded at her.

'I'll get my things together. When do we start?'

'I've booked flights out of Tampa tomorrow. Can you be ready for then?'

I didn't have to look around to know that I already had everything necessary here. My SIG Sauer P228, with a half-dozen spare magazines of nine mm soft-nosed parabellums. A change of clothing. Fake air marshal documents that would get my gun past security. What more would I require?

'Where are we going?'

'Kentucky.'

Appalachia. I hadn't been there before. Mountains and valleys were just my thing. It would be picturesque this late in the year. I looked at Kate. The company wouldn't be bad either.

I asked her where she was staying and she said she'd booked a room at the Marriott. 'Unless there's somewhere else you can suggest?'

'It's handy for the airport. I'll meet you there in the morning.'

She placed the empty bottle on the deck.

'Thanks, Joe,' she said. Then she leaned in and kissed me on the cheek.

2

After Kate left, I pulled my things together. My stuff didn't amount to much; it fitted inside a single backpack. Then I went back out on the deck with another Corona, watching the sun go down over the Gulf of Mexico. It was blood-red on the horizon.

I thought about Kate's parting gesture. The kiss. I could still feel her lips on my skin. It was a nice feeling but tomorrow's calendar date was in my mind, and I brushed it away with my fingers.

The beers helped me sleep. I was up before dawn. I ran five miles along the beach, worked out, showered, shaved and dressed. Then I drove to Tampa and left my Audi A6 in a long-term parking lot. I asked for Kate at the front desk of the Marriott and she joined me for breakfast. She was still beautiful, but she didn't look like she'd slept that well; probably apprehension about the task ahead. I didn't ask too much. We could talk on the flight north.

My documents saw me through security, but a couple of questions were raised concerning a gun Kate carried. Her right to carry gave me pause for thought, but I didn't dwell on it – a number of people have special dispensation for personal defence weapons these days. It stood to reason that she'd come packing, thinking we could face danger in the days ahead. I made a mental note to have Rink check up on her background for me.

We flew into Capital City Airport, near Frankfort, where we had to take a connection flight down to a blip on the map named Little Fork. We'd been in airports or airplanes most of the day. Then it was all roads. The final leg of the journey couldn't even be called a road. A single beaten track led up from the valley, terminating in front of Imogen Ballard's house.

Imogen's house was an A-frame set on a hillside overlooking a steep valley. Behind it was a sheer rock face that probed at the nickel-coloured sky with jagged fingers. The front of the house was raised up, a wooden porch and steps necessary to gain the front door. There was no vehicle parked under the lean-to at the side of the house.

The house was lovely, and so was the scenery. Part of the Appalachian Range, it was a very mountainous region, a secluded place of beauty.

I liked the remoteness. It was the kind of place that I would feel comfortable living in. My only concern was that, for a single woman, it was very vulnerable to the wrong kind of visitors. The remoteness offered privacy and a degree of anonymity, but the location was also a bottleneck with no escape route if things became dangerous.

'Imogen lives here alone?' I asked.

'She lived here with her ex-husband, Ron, until April

this year. After that she has divided her time between here and our family's home in Maine.'

Kate had already told me about the unhappy breakdown of her sister's marriage. She'd also told me that her sister had seemed to bounce back, setting up a bring-and-buy type business via the Web. It wasn't eBay, but apparently she was doing OK. She spent most of her time hosting her site, and it seemed the remainder was spent up here at Great Wells Fall, walking and hiking in the woods. Her business passion was technical, but there was nothing in the world that could compare with the natural wonders of the wilderness.

'She likes the serenity,' Kate went on, nodding at the great outdoors surrounding us.

'Can't say I blame her.'

'She's a freelance photographer. She sidelines in wildlife photographs that she supplies to magazines and to the internet.'

We were in a rental I'd picked up at Little Fork, a Ford Explorer with 4×4 capacity and gun racks behind the front seats. Hunting – I guessed – was a passion of many visitors who came to this part of the country. Parking the Ford on the turning circle outside the house, I got out. I stood with one hand on the open door, my other creeping under the tail of my shirt to check that my SIG was positioned for a quick draw.

'Quiet here,' I noted.

Kate looked over at me and I caught a reflection of the evening sky in her eyes. She'd caught something, too: the tone in my voice.

Apart from the gentle breeze rattling the fronds of the surrounding trees, and a distant rumble that had to be Great Wells waterfall, there was nothing else. No animal calls, no birdsong.

I didn't like it.

Kate stared off across the valley. At its bottom ran the river fed by the falls but it was lost to sight by the tree cover. She scanned right, allowing her eyes to roam over the house and up the steep cliffs.

'Don't see anything unusual,' she said.

'No,' I said.

I kept my hand on the butt of my gun as we walked up the stairs to her sister's house. Kate fished in her purse. I thought she was going for her gun.

'I have a key.'

'Is the house alarmed?'

'All the way out here? What would be the point?'

Fair enough, I thought.

Kate unlocked the door and we went inside. On this floor the house had a split-level, open-plan layout with a kitchen at the far side. Open stairs led up to the second floor that extended out from the back of the house towards the cliffs. Up there were the bedrooms and the bathroom, I guessed. But I didn't have the time to check; my eyes were too busy taking in the scene of destruction.

It was as though a mini-tornado had gone through the lower level. Furniture was upended, pictures torn from the walls. A TV set and DVD player had been left smashed on the floor. Credenzas had been pulled open, drawers emptied and their contents scattered. Ornaments had been swept from the mantel over the fireplace.

'Goddamnit, the house has been burgled!' Kate fisted her hands on her hips as she surveyed the wreckage. I touched her on the back.

'Kate. Go and get in the car.'

She turned towards me, her dark eyes sparking with anger. 'Who could have done this, Joe?'

I didn't know. But we were about to find out.

The creak of floorboards from above was subtle; the shifting of a human body furtively moving into a better position. We both heard it.

Kate spun round. Before I could hush her, she called out. 'Imogen?'

I drew my SIG.

Unless Imogen was two hundred and fifty pounds and wearing boots, I doubted that the next footstep was hers. This one was on the porch outside.

I was under no illusions.

There had been no sound of an approaching vehicle, no announcement or challenge. So the man sneaking up on us probably wasn't a concerned member of law enforcement checking on the vulnerable property. Whoever was on the porch was in cahoots with the person upstairs, and they intended taking us by surprise.

I snaked a hand over Kate's mouth and pulled her close. I caught a scent of flowers on her neck. Whispering in her ear, I said, 'Get behind the counter in the kitchen.'

The men here were the ones responsible for

ransacking Imogen's house. Possibly they were the ones responsible for her disappearance. Kate struck me as being strong-willed, no shrinking violet if it came to standing her ground. But she would be a hindrance if she wasn't going to do as I said. Give Kate her due, she quickly slid out of my grip and hunkered down behind the marble-topped prep counter in the middle of the kitchen floor. She was hidden from above and from anyone coming in the front door, but not from the window or the door at the back. I could only hope that all we faced were the two I'd already identified.

Quickly glancing up, I could detect no movement there, so I swung round, putting my body close to the wall next to the entrance. The front door had been fitted so that it opened towards me.

I hadn't long to wait.

The door handle twisted violently and the door was thrust open. It was followed immediately by a large man. I saw the barrel of his shotgun first, followed by a thick arm and shoulder as he pushed inside. His mouth opened to shout a challenge.

The barrel of my SIG struck the nerves on the mound of his forearm, then I moved alongside him and the second whack of my gun was made at his collarbone. I didn't know who these people were, so I didn't have the luxury of killing them outright. My strikes were aimed to disarm. The shotgun clumped to the floor as the man's entire arm went numb. Then I had my fingers in his beard and I pulled his head down and struck him a third time on the nape of the neck.

He was a huge man and his neck was protected by a thick roll of fat, but he still sagged under the blow. I pulled him back up, jamming the SIG under his jaw. The man rolled jaundiced eyes my way, realising he'd fucked up.

'You upstairs,' I shouted. 'Come out or I'll put a bullet through your friend's head.'

Movement at the head of the stairs came immediately. But there was no sign of the second man giving up. He came out shouting a challenge of his own as he raised a rifle and fired.

The bullet struck the door lintel behind me, and I took cover behind the first man. Blindly, I fired back, but I didn't hit the man with the rifle. Testament to that was his second shot. It hit the big man I was holding in the chest, punched a hole right through him and splattered blood down the front of my jacket. Some of the spray got in my eyes and clouded my vision.

The big man dropped from my grip like a slaughtered steer, straight down in a boneless heap at my feet. Leaving me open to a third shot. I fired in reaction, but I didn't have the man clear in my sights. He must have been aiming directly at my chest.

I heard the crack of a gun. Then another, then another, followed by a veritable roll of thunder as a magazine was emptied. At the top of the stairs the second gunman danced as bullets smacked through the planks beneath his feet, making tatters of his legs.

Kate had come to my rescue. I scrubbed the blood from my eyes, spared a second to look her way. She was raised above the marble counter firing directly through the ceiling with a Glock 19, emptying the gun into the man who would be my killer.

Shit, I thought, damn good shooting.

When my eyes were clear enough to get a bead on the man, I put a single round through his forehead. The force of the bullet threw him backwards against a wall, then he bounced forwards and did a head-over-heels roll down the stairs.

Dead men tell no tales: neither of these two was going to give us any answers to what the hell had just gone on here. I glanced at Kate. She was standing upright now, looking at the men who had died so violently. There was no sign of fear in her eyes, only resignation.

She had answers to give – primarily to explain how she could shoot as well as any soldier I'd ever worked with – but they would have to wait. Hyenas didn't normally hunt in pairs. They came in packs.

'Kate. Get in the car.'

She had her jaw set in determination, but she nodded acquiescence and moved to the door. As she stepped over the dead man with the beard, she looked at me. I was crouching alongside him, quickly patting him down.

'No wallet,' I said. 'No identification.'

She stood in the doorway as I went over to the second man and confirmed he too was lacking in personal papers. From her purse she took out a fresh magazine and fed it into her Glock. She racked the slide like a pro, then went outside. I noted she was in a professional stance, her gun hand supported on her opposite wrist as she sought further targets.

'Joe,' she called. 'You'd best get out here.'

Damn it, I thought. Hefting my gun, I followed her.

Below us in the valley, racing at a speed that wasn't prudent on the narrow trail, came a convoy of three vehicles. Two were SUVs, the third a flat-bed pick-up truck. Even across the intervening distance I could make out that the men on the truck were packing guns.

For the third time in as many minutes, I said, 'Kate. Get in the car.'

3

'There's movement up at the woman's place,' said Larry Bolan, juggling a cell phone in his large hand.

The man in the designer suit looked up from his meal and pointed at Larry with a fork on which was speared a medallion of pheasant. 'Where's your brother?'

'Outside taking a smoke.'

'Get him,' said the suited man. 'Go on up there. I don't trust those other imbeciles to get the job done.'

Larry smiled at the compliment. At least he thought it was a compliment. It would have rung truer if his employer hadn't mentioned *other* imbeciles, but he didn't mind the slip.

Larry Bolan had been in the business of hurting people all his adult life. And, even if he said so himself, he was damn good at his job. In fact, there was only one man he knew who was anywhere near as good as him and that was his twin brother, Trent. Much of their ability came with the genes passed down to them from their brutish father. Their father had worked the Kentucky coal mines most of his days; his weekends he spent drinking in brothels. He wasn't happy if he didn't come home with the smell of a whore on him and men's blood on his knuckles. But Larry and Trent also boasted something that their father never had: money behind them. Their boss paid well and his influence kept the cops from asking too many awkward questions. Whereas Daddy Bolan ended his days strapped to an electric chair – soiling his pants as the switch was thrown, Larry heard – the same would never happen to him or his little bro.

So he didn't challenge his boss's turn of phrase. He only nodded, shifted his jacket so it covered the Magnum strapped to his hip and walked out of the restaurant. Other customers in the place knew Larry Bolan. They knew to get out of his way, so he had a free passage through the main dining area and the vestibule that led to the street.

He stepped out into a cool evening breeze, pushing a hand through his spiky hair. He looked along the street towards mountains looming over the small town of Little Fork. Snow capped the highest peaks. Not long now, he thought, and the entire town would be snowed in for winter. He pulled out a pack of Marlboros and lit up, took a satisfying drag on the cigarette, then flicked the remainder of the cigarette against the kerb.

His brother Trent also flicked the cigarette he'd been smoking and turned to look at his big brother. Trent eyed him in that strange way he had. Thirty-seven years they'd been together, and even now Larry found his brother's gaze a little disconcerting. It was the oddness of his eyes – one pale blue, the other dark brown – that did it. He reminded Larry of a palomino stallion he'd owned that used to look at him the same way before trying to snatch off his face with a snap of its teeth. Larry curled his lip: even Trent's damn Mohawk hairstyle looked like that crazy horse's mane.

'We on?' Trent asked.

'We're on.'

Side by side they moved across the street to where Trent had parked their affectionately named Grand Taurino. The vehicle was really a Dodge Ram quad-cab pick-up truck, but it had been adapted to match the men that drove it. It had a raised suspension and huge tyres, and was painted metallic-black with the head of a snorting animal on the hood. Flames licked from the nostrils of the beast and curled along the sides of the truck. Two huge horns had been strategically placed on top of the light rack on the cab. Like the Bolan twins, this pick-up truck was a giant bull.

Inside, the cab had also been specially adapted. Ordinarily there'd be four seats, but the rear two had been removed to allow space for the two men who collectively weighed over forty stone and stood near fourteen feet tall. Larry always drove. Being the shorter of the two at six feet nine, it was easier for him than his seven-foot-tall sibling. Not that their respective heights meant anything in their relationship; Larry was thirteen minutes older, so would always be the *big* brother.

He fired up the engine, revved it a couple of times for good measure, then peeled away from the kerb like he was a teenager again. Larry, despite his coolness, felt excited. It was always the way when he was on a job. He was good at hurting people, but more pertinently, he enjoyed it.

From Little Fork to Imogen Ballard's home up at Great Wells was a little under ten miles. Ten miles of bad road. It would take the best part of a half-hour to negotiate the twists and curves of the mountain trails. Larry didn't tell his boss, Robert Huffman, that shots had been fired at the Ballard place. Or that some bad-ass had tagged along with the woman when she'd returned home. He wanted to please his boss by delivering both their heads on a silver platter. That'd look good in that fancy restaurant Huffman liked so much.

Cell phones were haphazard round here. He knocked his brother's shoulder with his elbow. 'Hey, Trent. Make yourself useful, will ya? Get on the radio and see what's goin' on.'

Trent rolled his pale eye at his brother. Lazily he grabbed at the CB handset fixed to the dash, turning switches with fingers that weren't designed for such delicate manoeuvres. Then he called up their associates on the channel reserved exclusively for their use.

'Yo! Any of you assholes got your ears on?' he demanded.

'Trent? Trent? That you?' came back an agitated voice.

'Who the fuck you think?'

'You'd better git yourself up here an' sharp,' said the voice from the radio. 'Richie and Tom-Boy are dead, man. Whoever this mutha is, he's giving us hell!'

Larry shared a glance with his twin. Trent's pale eye sparkled. Then they both broke into mirror-image grins.

'Looks like we're in for a little fun tonight, bro.'

'You ain't shittin' me.' Larry elbowed his brother again. Affectionately this time. 'About time, Trent. I was gettin' bored watching Huffman eat.'

'At least you get to stand inside. Why'd I have to stand out in the cold, freezin' my ass?'

'You know why.'

Robert Huffman said that Trent's wall-eye put him off his dinner. Trent had killed men for less. But he wouldn't hold it against his boss. Not when opportunities like this were handed to the Bolan twins on a regular basis.

4

'Buckle up, Kate. Things are about to get rough.'

Experience has shown me that the best course of action isn't always the most obvious. We could have run. But the trail ended at Imogen's house and the only alternative was a two-hundred-yard drop through trees and boulders to the river valley below. We could have given up, put down our weapons and waited for the posse of rednecks to arrive, then thrown ourselves on their mercy. Except I don't come from that school of thought. Sometimes you just have to shock a reaction out of those trying to hurt you by taking the violence to them.

Pushing the Explorer into drive, I swung the vehicle round. The tyres kicked up gravel and dust as they dug for traction, then we were rushing down the trail. The sun was sinking, the clouds burning umber above the hills across the valley. Night would soon be on us like a fall of soot: sudden and all-consuming. But I didn't turn on my headlights. I pushed the Explorer to greater speed heading directly for the three vehicles charging up the hill.

'Who the hell are they?'

'Don't know, but they don't look too friendly.'

Even as I said it, a man on the back of the pick-up lifted a hunting rifle and fired at us. The bullet missed by a mile, continuing behind us and into the cliff behind Imogen's house.

'They'll be even less friendly when they find out we killed their friends back there.'

I saw that Kate was biting her bottom lip. Sexy, if it hadn't been for the torment in her eyes.

'You're experienced with that gun.'

'I've only ever shot at targets,' she said.

'You haven't killed before?'

'No.'

'If it's any consolation, you still haven't. It was my bullet in his brain that finished him.'

'I still shot him,' Kate whispered.

'He was shooting at us. He got what he deserved.'

Kate looked across at me.

'You saved my life, Kate. Keep that in mind and things won't seem so bad.' I reached across and patted her knee. She slipped her fingers on top of mine and gave them a squeeze.

Then there was no more time for ruminating on the morals of taking a life. We'd be dead if we didn't concentrate on the task at hand.

There was indecision in the lead SUV driver's mind. It was apparent by the way he swerved from one side of the narrow trail to the other before coming to a halt. The second vehicle had to brake to avoid hitting him, and that in turn caused the pick-up to slew to one side. The men on the truck jostled to stay upright and to swing their rifles towards us. I continued on, straight as an arrow in their direction. It was the most insane game of chicken I'd ever played.

'OK, Kate, brace yourself. We're going through.'

'They're going to shoot us!'

'They'll try,' I said.

The gap between the two SUVs was marginally too narrow for the Ford to fit through undamaged, but not enough to halt us. At the last moment I down-shifted to give us more power, pressed hard on the throttle and rammed the Ford into the front end of the SUV on our right. The SUV was shunted aside, and I continued to push through without stopping. The men in that vehicle were too busy taking cover to offer any immediate problems, but those on the left were already lifting guns.

My earlier aversion to killing these men had disappeared when the man upstairs in Imogen's house had opened fire. He had killed his own colleague trying to get at me, so I had to assume that he wanted us dead. So would those in the convoy. I lifted my gun and fired almost point-blank at the driver of the vehicle on my left. The bullet took a chunk of his skull and filled the cab with brain matter. The man in the passenger seat recoiled from the spray, his gun dipping away, and I shot him too.

Then we were past the two SUVs and the pick-up truck was now on our right. Shooting them meant firing past Kate through the window on her side. Not the ideal situation; the last thing I wanted was to risk hitting Kate. But then I saw her hit the automatic window button and lift her own gun. She fired at the pick-up, her Glock discharging noise like a string of firecrackers. Her bullets didn't hit anyone, but it made those on the flat-bed leap overboard and take cover behind the truck. The driver flung himself down inside the cab as well. Then we were past them and heading down the trail toward Little Fork.

Pursuit would come, but not immediately.

I'd killed the two men in the SUV, putting that vehicle momentarily out of commission, but they still had the use of two of their vehicles. The first SUV I'd rammed was only bashed up, not out of action. The pick-up only required its passengers to climb back on board. Our best advantage at this time was to put distance between us while they turned the vehicles on the narrow trail.

Glancing in my mirrors, I saw one man at the front of the pick-up with a mobile phone in his hand. Calling up reinforcements, I assumed.

'There could be more of them ahead,' I said. 'You'd better load your gun again.'

Kate had a dazed expression on her face. Her mind was rebelling against the horror she'd found herself submerged in. Twice in so many minutes she'd discharged her weapon at living, breathing targets, and I could tell it was not something she'd been prepared for. I had to give her kudos for even having the gumption to act the way she had. Many people would never contemplate shooting another human being, and when push came to shove they wouldn't have the presence of mind to draw their weapon, let alone fire it.

'You did well back there, Kate.'

'I didn't hit anyone.' Part of her statement sounded apologetic, but underneath it there was more than a little relief.

'You kept their heads down. That's all we needed.'

'You killed two of them.'

There was a hint of challenge in her voice, as though she was asking why I hadn't simply made them drop for cover.

'I was too close to miss.' My words were non-committal and she'd have to take them whichever way her mind was working. When men are trying to kill me, I don't generally give them a second try.

Kate dropped the Glock on her lap, her face ashen. 'Those men back there weren't waiting for us.'

'No.'

'They were waiting for Imogen.'

'Looks that way.'

'They were going to kill her. There's no other reason for two armed men to be at her house. Or why there would be a group of men waiting at the bottom of the hill to cut off her escape?' Kate was shaking as she picked up the Glock and ejected the empty clip. A new emotion shone in her face. 'But that means that she's still alive, doesn't it?'

'They wouldn't be after her if they'd already killed her,' I said. But that was assuming they were there for Imogen and not some other reason. I didn't say so to

Kate, choosing instead to allow her a little relief. I would think worst-case scenario until I knew otherwise.

'Why doesn't she get in contact with me then?' The tone of her voice said that the question was rhetorical. Kate was astute enough to come up with her own answer. 'She's too afraid. Whoever these men are, she's afraid that they'll hurt me if I'm involved.'

'But now you're involved she can come out of hiding? The problem is, she doesn't know that you're here. She's going to keep her head down.'

'We'll just have to find her, then.'

Kate took out another clip for the Glock and slid it in place.

'Looks like you've a proper little arsenal in there,' I said.

Kate's dark eyes dropped and she gnawed on her bottom lip again.

'You came prepared for trouble. What's really going on, Kate?'

'All I know is Imogen's missing and there are men who want to kill her.'

I shook my head. 'Kate. I'm not being judgemental. I only want to know the truth.'

'I already told you. Imogen called me four days ago. She said that she needed help but then the line went dead. I've been unable to get her to answer the phone since. It goes directly to her voicemail.'

'But you didn't go to the police,' I pointed out. 'You came looking for me, instead. Why didn't you contact the police, Kate?'

'They wouldn't have done anything,' she said. 'At most, some bored officer would've taken a drive up here. He'd have seen that the house was secure and Imogen's car was gone. He'd guess that she'd gone away for a few days and that would've been that. Case closed. I know how these things work, Joe.'

'That's assuming quite a lot.'

'It's unofficial cop protocol. Do only what you have to and let the rest go to hell.'

'Where'd you get your low impression of law enforcement from?'

Her answer took me by surprise. 'I *am* a police officer, Joe.'

5

The Grand Taurino made short shrift of the rutted road, eating up the miles between Little Fork and Great Wells Forest Park. Larry Bolan had driven this road on a number of occasions lately. He knew every twist and turn, every offshoot from the trail. He knew where the best places were to ambush anyone making their way down from the national park.

He chose a spot under a rock overhang. Here the road squeezed between two gargantuan boulders then swung round a long curve before meeting the layover where he'd parked the truck. He drew his Magnum and held it against one meaty thigh. Beside him Trent was shouting into the CB handset.

'Do you have to be so loud all the time?' Larry asked his twin.

'I do when I'm talking to these damn rednecks we're stuck with,' Trent yelled, banging the handset down in its cradle. 'The two pussies Huffman stationed at the house got themselves killed as well as Tom-Boy and Richie. That's four down and not a goddamn clue who the hell was shooting at them.'

'It wasn't the Ballard bitch, then?'

'Nope. Some other bitch. Guy with her shot Tom and Richie, but the woman was also armed. The boys on the pick-up had to take cover when she opened up on them.'

'So where are the assholes now?'

'Following the couple this way.'

'Get back on the radio,' Larry said. 'Tell them not to get too close. We'll deal with this.'

Trent grinned as he picked up the handset. 'Do we get to keep the woman alive for a little while, Larry?'

'Don't see why not. It's Imogen Ballard that Huffman wants. Can't see why we can't have a little fun with any other bitch that throws herself into our laps.'

Larry buzzed down the window. Leaning out, he could hear the sounds of engines on the trail above. The acoustics of the canyon made it difficult to identify how close the approaching vehicles were, but he guessed that any minute now the fun would start. As he stepped out of the truck the chassis rose by a few inches. He lifted the Magnum and stalked forwards. Behind him he heard his little brother get out the truck and follow. Trent racked a shotgun – nothing smaller than the shotgun felt worthy in his huge hands.

'We'll take them as they come through the pass,' Larry said. 'The guy's driving, right?'

'Right.'

'So make sure you shoot for him. The bitch ain't gonna be much good to us with a face full of lead.'

'Ain't her face I'm interested in.'

Larry glanced at his brother. Rape he could go along with – it wasn't as if he hadn't tasted a little unwilling flesh in his time – but Trent's suggestion wasn't something that sat well with him. Of course, his little brother probably wasn't suggesting that they rape a woman with her *actual* face shot off, but then again, who knew? There was something decidedly unhealthy going on in that mind of Trent's, and it was more than just the crazy gleam of his wall-eye that told Larry so; the ear that Trent had cut off William Devaney and now kept on his key chain had a little to do with it too.

Larry thumbed back the hammer on his Magnum. Momentarily he considered putting a bullet through his brother's brainpan. A mercy killing. His brother was getting to be a problem that maybe even Robert Huffman's money couldn't save them from.

He turned back towards the two boulders encroaching on the road. Let Trent have his crazy thoughts, he decided. They didn't harm anyone who wasn't in need of harming. Plus, that ear thing? Well, William Devaney didn't need it any more. There wasn't much to listen to in his unmarked grave up in the wilderness beyond Great Wells waterfall.

The sounds of approaching engines made a steady rumble now. Larry could even hear the catcalls of the stupid rednecks pushing the strangers towards the trap. Shots were fired. He gritted his teeth. 'Those motherfuckers better not get them first.'

'Only thing those assholes are capable of is getting themselves shot,' Trent said as he stomped across to the other side of the trail. 'In fact, after this, I think we're gonna have to smack a few heads, just to straighten them out a bit. What do you say, big bro?'

'Sounds good to me.'

'That's the only problem with shooting people if you ask me. Way too fast. I'd prefer to smash this asshole first.'

'I hear you, Trent, but we can't be takin' any chances. Whoever this dude is, he knows how to shoot. We have to take him out . . . first possible opportunity.'

'Heads up, then, bro,' Trent said as he lifted his shotgun. 'Sounds like he's almost here.'

Larry heard the vehicle coming. He thought that the timbre of the engine changed, as though slowing, but that could have been to do with the way the sound reverberated off the two boulders forming the pass. He saw headlights on the rock on the right, and now the engine of the approaching 4×4 definitely did sound like the foot had been taken off the throttle. Made sense, he thought, as the guy approached the narrow pass. It was why he'd chosen the spot for the ambush, allowing them to shoot the driver when he had to slow down to negotiate the narrow road and the tight curve that followed.

He lifted the gun in anticipation. Took a step forwards.

There it was. The blocky shape of a Ford Explorer, exiting the gap between the boulders. The headlights were flicked to full beam and Larry had to scrunch his eyes against the glare, but it didn't hinder him none. He knew exactly where the driver would be. He fired his handgun and it bucked in his hand. Purposely he aimed through the driver's side, allowing the gun to dip in line with the top of the steering wheel; just where a ducking man's head would be.

Across from him, Trent opened up with the shotgun. He fired one load into the driver's side, then followed it immediately by sending his second load into a front tyre.

The Ford dipped as the tyre exploded, then it swerved, but continued moving. The cant of the road sent the swerving 4×4 past Larry. As it did so he fired another shot into the cab. If it hit the woman, so what? She was going to die anyway, and if that meant he wouldn't be getting his rocks off tonight, then so be it. There was plenty pussy back in town for the taking. Trent could have the bitch all to himself!

Larry steadied his Magnum for a third shot, but it was unnecessary. The Ford slewed off the trail and into a ditch and then slammed into the trunk of a tree with such force that the top of the tree swayed like it was in the middle of a hurricane. Pine needles rattled down all around Larry and he had to brush some out of his spiky hair. He looked for Trent, and his brother was already crabbing across the trail with his shotgun held to his shoulder.

'You get the woman, Trent. I'm gonna make sure the asshole's dead,' Larry said.

'Watch how you go, big bro,' Trent said, a show of concern that Larry found touching. And to think he'd considered shooting his brother only moments before! He winked at Trent, flashed him a grin.

Then he moved to the driver's door and leaned in through the open window. When he glanced up, Trent's quizzical face was framed in the opposite window.

They stared at each other across the empty seats.

'Where the fuck did they go, Larry?'

6

Kate's revelation rocked me more than the collision with the SUV up the trail had.

She was a cop?

And she'd come looking for me to help find her sister?

Surely she understood that I didn't work from any law and order rule book. In fact I'm notorious for working outside the boundaries of the law – it's why I've survived the things I have. It's why some people have labelled me a vigilante, and others have even seen me as a hit man. In my opinion I'm neither, but what good is that when weighed against the opinions of thousands?

'You should've told me that you're a cop.'

'If I had, would you have still helped me?'

I gripped the steering wheel, setting my jaw.

'Would you have refused me, Joe?'

Not really sure what I was mad about, I snapped angry eyes on her and grunted, 'Of course I'd have helped. Just . . .'

'Just in a different way?'

Snorting, I down-geared, traversing a particularly steep drop of the hill.

Kate said, 'Would you have been so quick to shoot those men if you knew a cop was beside you?'

'Like I said, they were too close to miss.'

It was Kate's turn to snort. 'What do you think I'm going to do, Joe? Arrest you?'

'It just makes my job more difficult, that's all.'

'How? We both want the same thing, don't we? We both want to find Imogen.'

Sending the Explorer round a bend in the trail, I looked across at her. She looked mad, too. But her anger seemed to be directed not at me but inwards, like she was berating herself for letting her identity slip.

'There are things that I have to do, Kate, things that don't fit the sensibilities of most people. Sometimes I have to kill, yes, but I've never killed anyone who wasn't trying to kill me or wasn't hurting someone else. If that doesn't sit too well with you, I'll take you back to Little Fork and you can get a flight back home. We'll call it quits.'

'I don't want to call it quits,' Kate said, her voice rising in pitch.

'Don't you get it, Kate? How the hell do you expect me to get the job done when there's a cop looking over my shoulder?'

'What difference does it make who I am? We're in this together, aren't we?'

'You don't understand. I'm prepared to kill. If I pause for one second to worry about the repercussions, then that could be it. It'll be us who die, and I'm not willing to let that happen.'

'Joe,' Kate said. She seemed a little steadier as she leaned across and placed cool fingers on my forearm. 'Don't you see? I'm not being judgemental either. I came looking for you because of the man you are. I didn't want a by-the-book lawman as a partner. I came looking for you because I knew you'd do what needed doing *without question.*' She showed me the Glock. 'Do you think this is standard NYPD issue? I went through murder to get special dispensation to carry a concealed weapon, but it was worth it. I brought this expecting trouble, Joe. I'm not going to pull a hissy fit if you have to shoot someone who's trying to kill us.'

'OK, then.' Turning my attention back to the road, I flicked on the high beam. 'I'm pleased we've cleared up that little misunderstanding. Now, if you don't mind, open the door and get the fuck out the car.'

She blinked in astonishment as I unclipped her seat belt.

'Now, Kate,' I snapped. 'I don't have time to argue.'

I slowed the Explorer down, leaned across and pushed open her door. She looked at me in confusion, wondering what the hell was going on. Then I gave her a shove and she slid out on to the road.

Next second I went out of the driver's door.

I'd been travelling slowly enough that neither of us picked up anything more than a few scrapes, but not so slowly that the Explorer would grind to a halt between the two massive boulders partially blocking the trail.

I'd recalled the man on the road above shouting into a mobile phone. On the twisting ride down the mountainside, I'd wondered why they hadn't done more to catch us. Even the shots seemed more show than substance. Then I saw the two boulders. How the road narrowed so we'd have to take it easy going through.

Good place for an ambush.

Kate was sitting on the dirt trail with a dazed expression on her face. Then her eyes met mine, and lightning jumped between us. She was still holding her Glock and for a split second I thought she was going to shoot me.

'You OK?' I asked, moving over to her.

'What the hell was that all about? You could've killed me.'

'We were going too slowly to kill you. Anyway, I warned you my methods were unorthodox.'

'Are you insane?'

For an answer I merely pointed between the two rocks.

The sounds of gunfire shattered the night.

Kate jerked in time with each bark of a handgun, each crash of a shotgun. When the sound of our vehicle smashing into something immovable reached our ears, she was already scrambling up.

'The bastards were waiting for us,' I said. 'If we'd driven through there we'd be dead meat. Under the circumstances I think a sore ass is a fair trade.'

Kate accepted my hand as I led her off the trail and into the woods.

'We have to keep moving. Put as much distance between us and these guys as possible,' I said, taking her down an embankment and through a gap in the foliage. On our left was the rear side of one of the huge boulders. An ancient trail led between the boulder and a cliff face. The trail forked, and I pushed Kate towards the fork leading up and over the cliff with my hand in the small of her back.

Behind us came the sounds of the pick-up truck and SUVs slowing as they approached the pass. Voices were raised, men shouting to those waiting on the other side. Then came excited catcalls as the men tumbled from the vehicles in order to take up the chase. I could feel a smile painting its way on to my features. If I'd had the luxury of a mirror, I'd have recognised the grim rictus-smile I adopted when men needed hurting. There was a heat in my chest too; the bubble of anticipation building. The thing that made me feel alive.

Had I been alone, I'd have relished this challenge. I'd have grasped the opportunity to take on these men and I'd have finished them one by one or all together – it didn't matter. However, I wasn't alone. And Kate's safety was my priority.

Looking at her moving through the trees in front of me, I noticed again her athletic grace. She had exchanged the summer top and shorts of our first meeting for a beige linen jacket over a cream blouse and figure-hugging denims and boots. If anything she looked even better. Back at Imogen's house – not to mention when blasting through the roadblock – she'd shown her worth as a capable ally. However, I come from an old school where women are to be cherished and protected. It didn't matter that she was a trained police officer and could shoot better than most; I made myself a silent promise that I wouldn't allow this woman to come to harm. If that meant keeping our heads down and running away from these punks, well, so be it.

A rifle cracked behind us.

Kate came to a halt, turning back towards me with her Glock raised.

'Keep moving. They're just shooting blind. They don't know where we are.'

'Where are we going?' Kate asked, setting off at a jog beside me.

'Away from here.'

'Running away isn't helping us find my sister.'

'No, but it's keeping us alive. We can pick up the search later.'

'We could try and take one of them alive, make him tell us where she is.'

'Pointless,' I said. 'They don't know where she is. That's why they were waiting at the house. They want to find her as much as we do.'

'But they could tell us *why* they're looking for her.'

'We'll let Imogen tell us when we find her. Now, keep going along the top of the cliff. When we get to the far side, I want you to wait by that tree.'

The clifftop made a natural arch, about seventy feet at its highest point, before dipping down to the road a couple of hundred yards further on. Trees and bushes grew along the crest and there was one particularly large tree that hung precariously over the drop. Its roots had broken free of the cliff face and made a sort of natural cage among the rocks. The shadows beneath the roots were a good place to hide Kate for the short time I'd be gone.

'What are you going to do?'

'We've no transport, Kate. Unless you fancy walking all the way back to Little Fork, I'm going to have to get us some wheels. Now it's been some time since I did any wilderness survival training. Still, I remember enough to know that those clouds mean there's a blizzard on the way.' I indicated my own thin jacket and jeans. 'Dressed like this, I don't think we'd survive the night.'

'It won't take us all night to walk ten miles.'

'Not if we took the road, it wouldn't. But these guys are going to be hunting us all the way. We'd have to stick to the woods. Overland, it's more like twenty miles to town, and we don't know what other surprises the terrain might throw up. There could be rivers to cross. We get wet in a blizzard . . . forget about it.'

Her lips pinched together. She looked so much like her brother Jake that for a few seconds I was transported back a dozen years. He was a contrary son of a bitch, was Jake Piers. 'No arguments, *Officer* Piers,' I told her.

She held up her hands, the Glock hanging loose in her fist.

'Keep that handy,' I said, 'but no shooting unless it becomes absolutely necessary.'

'I won't shoot at all, Joe,' she said with the faintest of smiles, 'unless they're too close to miss.'

Waiting until she was concealed behind the twisting

roots, I leaned in close. 'Give me ten minutes. If I'm not back by then, you'll know I've failed.'

'What happens then?'

'Then you'll be on your own.'

'That isn't something I want to think about.'

No, I thought, turning away from her and down the embankment. Neither did I.

7

If he was upset that he wasn't going to have his way with a head-shot corpse, Trent wasn't showing any sign. In fact, judging by the way his shoulders shuddered he found the entire situation amusing.

'What's so damn funny?'

'The look on your face, bro.'

Larry scowled up at his larger sibling. 'You're the one with the stupid-looking face, Trent. Nothing wrong with mine.'

Trent didn't seem fazed by the slur either. He laughed in his deep rumble, as he turned to survey the pass between the boulders. Beyond them he heard the posse of rednecks drawing to a halt, uttering shouts and yells as they clambered out of their vehicles.

'The Wild Bunch has arrived.'

'Go get them, Trent,' Larry grunted. 'Organise them into some kind of search party. The bastards can't have got too far away, but every second that those idiots roam around shooting at shadows their lead is getting longer.'

'What you going to do, Larry?'

'I'll keep watch in case they try to make a break for the road.'

Trent stared at Larry for what seemed like way too long for Larry's liking. As if he was challenging his brother's authority.

'Get going,' Larry said.

The lid of Trent's pale eye slowly drooped closed, before opening again in that lazy way it had. It looked like an oyster shell opening to reveal what lay within, only there was nothing about the image that made Larry think of a hidden pearl.

'Now, Trent, before those assholes start killing each other in the dark.'

Trent finally smiled. He lifted the shotgun, ejecting the spent shells. He fed in a couple of fresh ones. Above him, the clouds finally gave up their burden and the first few flakes of snow fluttered past his face.

'You're right, Larry. In the dark, in the storm that's coming, someone might just catch movement out the corner of their eye and get the wrong idea. All it'd take would be an accidental jerk of the trigger and that'd be it.'

Trent moved quickly towards the pass before his brother had time to absorb his loaded words. But they weren't missed by Larry. He knew exactly whose finger might slip and who would end up dead. But not if he lifted his Magnum and finished Trent now; the temptation was almost too strong to deny. But he didn't lift the gun. Sometimes his brother's words only sounded like a challenge. Maybe Larry was reading too much into them, and his brother was genuinely talking about the amateurs Huffman had surrounded himself with.

If he was wrong, well, he could always kill Trent later.

Right now he was going back to the Grand Taurino and out of this damned cold. He could watch the road from the comfort of the cab as easily as he could from the roadway.

Approaching the truck, he pulled out his packet of Marlboros and shook one from the pack. Holding his Magnum made it awkward to light the cigarette, but he wasn't about to relinquish the weapon just yet. Leaning his hips against the front grill of the Dodge Ram, he hooked a boot heel over the lowest bar, and thumbed the cigarette up to his lips. The snowflakes were dropping more regularly now and he swung his gaze up to the heavens, watching the swirling flakes as they were caught in a gust of wind blowing over the clifftop. Flakes melted on his lashes, and he blinked them away.

The couple from the Ford didn't have so many options. They'd obviously disembarked from the vehicle just prior to sending it through the pass. The boys coming down the trail meant they wouldn't have retreated back the way they'd come, which in turn meant they could only have gone in one of two directions. Larry was familiar with the terrain and knew that the hills on the right were sheer and made of loose shale in most places. Chances were they had gone to the left. The nearest and most direct route came out on to the road just this side of the boulders, and Larry knew that the couple hadn't come that way. Up and over then, he decided. They're up on the ridge above me.

He considered calling Trent back. But he discarded the idea as quickly as it formed. Why give his brother any of the fun? Trent was getting too big for his boots and needed reminding just who the major force in their relationship was.

He unhooked his boot heel and wandered past the truck, making his way to the trail-end that came down off the cliffs. He lifted the Magnum, flicked away his half-smoked stub. The ember was too much of a giveaway in the darkness. Smoking kills, he reminded himself, but not always for the obvious reasons.

He was a huge man, but as fit and lithe as he was tall, and he could stalk elk with the best of them. He'd often considered going into pro-wrestling. If he partnered with his brother they'd be a magnificent tag team, but certain facts had deterred him from following such an obvious career route: for one, he liked hurting people *for real*, and second, even a superstar rating was finite. He wanted to go on hurting people for as long as he pleased, not for the duration that some greedy promoter laid on him. Besides, Huffman paid good money – the kind of top dollar he couldn't expect from the square ring.

The trail off the cliff petered out a little more than twenty paces beyond the Grand Taurino. There the steep path was hidden from view by the trees that grew all along the roadside. Larry considered entering the trail and making his way up and over the cliff to catch the couple as they fled from Trent and the others. But no. He could take them out as they came towards him.

Between two trees he found himself the ideal hiding place. He had a limited view of the trail, and the darkness would make it nigh-on impossible to distinguish one person from another, but that would cut both ways. They wouldn't see him until he stood up and let loose with his handgun. He wouldn't have to wait long. In fact, he could hear someone making their way down the trail now. Easy money!

Or it would have been if not for the cold metal that was suddenly pressed to his neck.

'Lose the cannon,' a voice whispered.

Larry grunted as he raised his hands to the sides to show the man the gun was no threat. He allowed the Magnum to slip from his palm so that it flopped upside down, hooked only on his index finger.

The man with the gun to his head quickly took the Magnum away.

'The keys to your truck,' the man went on, 'give them to me.'

'I don't have them,' Larry said, finally finding his voice.

'Don't fuck with me.'

'I ain't fuckin' with no one. I don't have the keys.'

No way was he going to give the Grand Taurino up.

Then sparks were in his eyes and he tasted metal. It took him a second or so to realise that the man had struck him on the side of the head with the barrel of his gun. Blood trickled from beneath his hair and into the collar of his jacket.

'Son of a bitch,' Larry growled.

'Last time,' the man said. 'The next head wound will be permanent.'

'Keys are in my jeans pocket. I'm gonna have to move my hands if you want them.'

'Slow and easy.'

Keeping his left hand outstretched, Larry brought his right hand to his hip. Crouching the way he was, the keys were nipped by the material of his jeans. He straightened slightly to dig the keys out of his pocket, then passed them over his shoulder to the man behind him. As the man snatched the keys from him, Larry readied himself.

The gun was pressed to the base of his skull.

'Don't.'

Larry settled back into his crouch.

'That wasn't so difficult, was it?'

Actually, thought Larry, it was fucking terrible. I should have gone for it. Now you've got my gun and my wheels. Worst thing: I don't even know who the fuck you are so's I can take them back.

'Who are you?' Larry asked.

'I could ask you the same thing, but let's not fool one another. We'd be wasting each other's time, wouldn't we?'

Larry rolled his shoulders. The blood from his scalp was making a trail down his spine. 'Guess so. One thing I do know is that you're not a cop.'

'Didn't claim to be,' said the man putting the gun under Larry's ear. 'So I've no qualms about killing you.'

Larry didn't consider himself a coward. But he didn't relish dying with a bullet in his ear or being left in the forest as crow bait. 'You're not going to shoot me, buddy.'

'I'm not?'

'No, the sound would bring the others running. I guess you're going to have to let me live.'

'For now.' The gun came down on the nape of Larry's neck. Unconsciousness wasn't instantaneous, allowing one last thought to flutter through Larry's mind. No actual words, just the knowledge that he would wake up again, and when he did he was going to make this man wish that he had killed him outright.

8

'Kate,' I whispered. 'I told you to wait for me.'

She was standing in the shadows ten feet above me, staring down at the huge man lying at my feet. Her left hand was at her throat, but I could see that the hand holding her Glock was steady enough.

'I'm a cop, Joe. I'm not used to being told what to do by civilians,' she said. 'Anyway, I could hear the others getting closer. What was I supposed to do?'

'You should have done as I asked,' I told her. But at the same time, I couldn't be mad with her. Her independent streak had actually helped me out. Her approach had kept the big man distracted while I sneaked up on him. Plus, I didn't have to backtrack up the cliff to fetch her. 'Never mind. Come on, we're getting out of here.'

Kate came down the steep path at a jog. I caught her in the crook of my elbow and she pressed her left palm to my chest. For a long second our eyes locked, before Kate blinked and turned away. She used the Glock to point at the unconscious giant.

'Who is he?'

'Don't know. But he's gonna be pissed when he wakes up.'

'He's only knocked out? Well, at least you didn't shoot him, this time.'

'Maybe I should have.'

Kate pressed herself away from me. I watched as she stooped and patted the big man down. 'No identification. Just like the others.'

When I'd killed the two up at Imogen's house the idea that they'd come without any identification had been concerning. I was worried that they might be professional hit men but I'd quickly come to the conclusion that they were rank amateurs. Looking down at this big man, I decided that he wasn't as inexperienced as the others, but he still wasn't a trained assassin. Very dangerous though. I didn't doubt that he had a way about him when it came to extreme violence.

We hurried down on to the road and I looked along the curve to where our Ford was lying among the trees. The darkness didn't allow a clear look at the 4 × 4 but I didn't think it would be much use to us now. Instead I looked towards the vehicle this man had come in. I hadn't realised what a garish monstrosity the pick-up actually was.

'Subtle,' Kate noted. 'It'll stick out like a sore thumb.'

'We aren't going to be in it for long. All we need is to get away from here and then we can ditch it for something else.'

She shrugged, moving closer to it.

'Careful, Kate. There could be others nearby.'

'I know all about approaching vehicles, Joe. It comes with the job.'

Following her, I scanned the ridge above us. The men who'd been chasing us had fallen quiet. Their whoops and yells had been replaced by the silence that men adopt when they are in fear of impending death. As far as they knew, I was hiding in the forest and could open up on them with a barrage of bullets at any second.

Kate checked out the interior of the Dodge Ram while I covered her. When she nodded that it was clear, I quickly came and clambered in. I placed the liberated Magnum on the dash and then pushed the keys into the ignition. Kate slid into the passenger seat, her eyes doing a scan of the insides. She was in full cop mode. She opened the glovebox, but found nothing interesting. Nothing of worth in the door pocket either. When she pulled down the sun visor, a small pamphlet fell into her outstretched hand.

'Look at this, Joe.' We were in shadows, so I couldn't immediately make out what it was.

'What is it?' I fired up the engine.

'A menu.'

'We don't have time to eat.'

'From a restaurant in Little Fork,' she went on, as though I hadn't spoken.

'What about it?' I spun the monster truck in the road.

'That brute you knocked out – or any of those other good ol' boys – do you think any of them are the type to dine on fancy French cuisine?'

Taking a closer look at the menu, I saw that it was

an expensive glossy brochure depicting an equally expensive and glossy restaurant. Le Cœur de la Ville. She was right: these men looked the type to prefer beer and a five-doller bucket of spiced wings, not the à la carte menu that the brochure offered. Not that the presence of the menu meant anything specific; for all I knew, the big man had fancy tastes that exceeded his bar-room brawler image.

'What are you getting at, Kate?' I glanced over to where I'd left the unconscious man in the trees. There was no sign of movement but I heard the crack of a rifle. Whoever fired at us was a pretty poor shot. Then we were round the curve and out of the line of fire.

'Last time I visited with Imogen we went to that restaurant for a meal. I told you that Imogen is very good with computers, didn't I? Well, I remember she was doing some work for the restaurant, developing a website for them, supplying the publicity photographs and digital graphics.'

I didn't see where this train of thought was leading, other than yes, it was a coincidence.

'After that visit, I spoke to her on the phone. She was really mad.'

'What about?'

'Apparently, prior to her finishing the work the restaurant changed owners. The new owner let her go, and then refused to compensate her for the time she'd spent on the material she'd developed. Imogen lodged a complaint through her lawyer.'

'I hardly think that anyone is going to try to kill her

because of a bill for ... what would it be, a couple thousand dollars at most?'

Kate considered my words. 'It was just a thought.'

'It's about the best lead we have,' I conceded. Then I slapped the steering wheel of the truck. 'Next to this thing. I'll get Rink to run it through the system and see who the vehicle's registered to. We find out who owns it, it could lead us to the person who sent him after Imogen.'

We were clear of any pursuit now, and I noticed that Kate had finally relaxed enough to put her Glock back inside her purse. I kept the SIG handy – just in case. Plus there was the Magnum on the dash if it became necessary in the future to take out anything as large as its owner.

Kate had her eyes closed. She was chewing her lip again, and I couldn't help glancing at her in appreciation.

'You did OK back there.'

'For a cop, you mean?'

'I'm not a cop hater, Kate. It's just that ...'

'Yeah, you already said: I cramp your style.'

I chose not to pursue the line of conversation. Anyway, I'd noted her smile.

'Where now?' she asked.

'Little Fork.'

'Isn't that likely to be the town where these men are from?'

'Yeah. So they won't expect us to go there. Besides, I want to find out who they work for.'

'We should go to the police.'

'Yes, we should.'

She looked at me, expectant.

'But we're not going to,' I finished.

'We have to report what happened at Imogen's house. There were men waiting to kill us, Joe. The police need to know what's going on.'

'All that will happen is that we'll end up in cuffs. Small town like Little Fork, they won't have the facilities to deal with something like this. Likely we'd be sent to Frankfort or Louisville for questioning. We won't find Imogen while we're locked up in a prison cell.'

'Where'd you get *your* low impression of the police from?'

'Experience,' I told her. 'We have the same goal most of the time. It's just our methods differ. Whenever I've dealt with cops in the past, it's been like banging my head on a brick wall.'

'You're forgetting that I'm a cop. I know how things work. I can do all the talking, Joe. They don't even have to know that you're involved, if that's the way you want it.'

'So you're going to take the rap for shooting four men?'

'Some of the bullets that killed the man from upstairs will come back to my gun. I'm going to be up in front of an IA panel whether you're involved or not.'

'You told me that the gun wasn't police issue.'

'I said it wasn't NYPD issue. It's still registered to me. All they need do is a ballistics check.'

'Not unless it was previously test fired and the rifling

marks were added to a register. If it hasn't they'd need the gun to check against. No gun, no match. Lose it, Kate. Throw it in the next river we pass.'

'No.'

'So tell them nothing. They still don't know who we are – even if they did, do you think those men intend to lodge a complaint?'

'They have to. Four of their friends are dead.'

I waved my hand at the forest. 'They'll get dumped out there someplace.'

'Like they were probably planning to do to us,' she finished for me. She sighed. 'We have to say something, Joe. We can't just let this thing go on.'

'We'll say something once we've found Imogen, not before. And the only way we'll do that is to go speak with the people responsible for making her disappear.'

'OK,' she said. 'I don't like it but we'll do it your way.'

9

'You haven't found her yet?'

'No. But I'm on it.'

'You know better than anyone what will happen if she makes this public.'

'Don't concern yourself, Wallace,' Robert Huffman said. 'Just keep signing the papers and rubber-stamping them in the correct place and *leave the rest to me.*'

The man referred to as Wallace sat back in his chair and looked across his desk at Huffman; he knew not to argue. He scowled at the man's cigar hanging idly from the hand drooping over the arm of the chair, waiting for the overload of ash to drop to his hardwood floor. The image summed up Huffman's attitude to everything. Don't worry. Everything will be fine. Leave it to me.

'We could lose everything, Huffman.'

Huffman waved down his accomplice with a gesture of the cigar. The ash still clung tenaciously to the tip. 'Stop whining. I've got the Bolans on it.'

A third man in the room snorted. 'The Bolans couldn't find their asses if you didn't give them directions.'

'They're doing more to find Ballard than your people,' Huffman pointed out.

'My hands are tied.'

'So leave the woman to me and keep your criticism to yourself.' Huffman aimed the cigar at the man. 'You do remember that I don't take criticism lightly? Or do I have to remind you?'

'I'm only saying, is all,' said the third man, folding his arms over his barrel chest like a petulant child. The colour drained from his face as Huffman stared at him.

'What about these others that have showed up?' Wallace asked. 'The Bolans didn't seem to handle them too well.'

'They were hampered by the fools *he* rounded up,' said Huffman, aiming the cigar at the third man. 'That's what comes of using amateurs. We should have left it to the Bolans.'

'If they'd handled things right in the first place, we wouldn't be in this position now,' said the barrel-chested man. 'They should have killed Devaney quietly; not tortured him to death so half the county could hear his screams.'

'That was necessary to our plans. Or have you forgotten that as well?'

'I remember. But I still think Trent's a goddamn liability.'

Huffman placed the cigar between his teeth. Then, moving so fast that he'd stood up before the barrel-chested man was aware of, he caught a handful of the man's tie. With his other hand he swiped up a cut-throat razor so it was a hair's breadth from the man's eyes. Huffman peered over the edge of the blade, chewing on the cigar. 'The way I see it, there's only one liability here.'

Wallace knew better than to stand up. 'Easy, Huffman. He's only voicing all our concerns.'

'No. He's sticking his nose in *my* business.' Huffman reversed the razor so the sharp edge touched the bridge of the man's nose. 'I've a good mind to cut the goddamn thing off.'

'We still need him.'

'Yeah, he's still a handy tool, I guess.'

He slowly released his grip on the tie and the man quickly backed away. His face was white and there was a smear of blood on his lip where he'd bitten through it.

Sitting down, Huffman replaced the razor with his cigar. The ash miraculously still clung to the tip. He seemed amused by that. Behind him, the barrel-chested man exhaled deeply, a finger searching his face for damage. Huffman ignored him. 'Just like our friend here, Larry Bolan is a handy tool. Without Trent, we don't have Larry; it's as simple as that.'

'You still trust Larry to get the job done?' Wallace asked. 'After what's just happened?'

'I do.' A smile grew. 'In fact, what happened to him is just the motivation he needs.' Huffman turned his head to regard the barrel-chested man again. 'Plus, I'm bringing in some extra help. All I ask is that you keep to our agreement and have your people looking the other way. Otherwise you – and your family – will be surplus to requirements.'

The man nodded quickly.

'Extra help?' Wallace's face turned sour. 'How much is that going to cost us?'

'Not a fraction of what it'll cost if we don't find Ballard.' Huffman reached lazily for the ashtray on Wallace's desk. He was inches short of it when the ash finally fell and landed on the prospectus Wallace had been studying prior to his arrival. Huffman smiled at Wallace's frown. He tapped the folder and the stylised image on its cover. 'Do you want to give up everything for the sake of a few bucks?'

Little Fork was a town in a state of re-emergence. Like a chrysalis, it was being transformed from within. It could turn out one of two ways: incredibly beautiful, or incredibly ugly.

The town had once been the abode of coal miners who worked the local pits. Their method was unusual, digging horizontally into the mountaintops in a way particular to this region. But the pits had died a generation ago, and Little Fork had barely resisted becoming an abandoned ghost town like so many others. Tourism had saved it. It was on the Kentucky Wild Rivers map, so had benefited from the holidaymakers swarming into the state in search of some white water action. At the end of the 1990s the population had barely reached two thousand, but now, a decade later, it was ten times that and growing. Hotels had sprung up, shopping malls, a multi-screen movie theatre, restaurants, and, to serve the growing population, huge tracts of land had been acquired in order to build new homes. In line with the magnitude of growth massive amounts of money could be made by those in a position to reap the bounty. And therein lay the ugly underbelly of Little Fork's transformation. Because where there was big money to be made, there was always the potential for violence. And murder. And a man like Huffman wan't averse to doling it out if anything got in his way.

Robert Huffman wasn't a native of Little Fork, Kentucky. He had been born and raised elsewhere. He had arrived here three years ago, an investor in the growing town. He had thrown millions of dollars into Little Fork's rejuvenation, but its return had already topped billions. He was sitting on a treasure trove and he certainly wasn't going to lose it all because of one interfering bitch. Or his accomplices' reluctance to spend a few bucks.

'My people will be here tomorrow,' he said, standing up and signifying that the meeting was over. To the barrel-chested man, he added, 'They'll be eager to get started, so make sure you keep out of their way. They don't like your type.'

IO

First order of the day was to find somewhere safe to hide while we decided our plan of action. When we arrived from Florida, we'd booked rooms at a hotel at the airport. We couldn't go back there: too obvious. Instead, we found a motel on the outskirts of Little Fork and I paid for a single room out of cash in my pocket. The small, greasy man who checked us in weighed up Kate, put two and two together and got his sums all wrong. He gave me a knowing look, then an exaggerated wink as I led Kate out.

'He thought I was a hooker,' Kate huffed as I unlocked the door to the room. She glanced down at her clothing, a small crease knitting her brows. 'Do I look like a whore to you, Joe?'

'I wouldn't know.'

She sniffed back a further complaint – probably at my ill-concealed lie – then pushed by me to go inside. There were a number of new motels and hotels in the area, but this one had been around for a while. It was just the kind of place you could rent by the hour. Our room was third along in a row of a dozen. I chose the place because it was off the beaten track, not for its star rating. It was small, little more than a box with a bathroom tacked on the side, but looked clean enough. The place would do for the few hours we'd be spending there.

'There's only one bed,' she announced. 'Where the hell are *you* going to sleep?'

'Didn't plan on sleeping,' I said, as I tucked the Magnum under the mattress for safe keeping.

Kate tilted one hip to the side and threw back her shoulders. Bit the tip of her tongue. 'We've only just met, Mr Hunter. I hope that jerk at the front counter hasn't given you any ideas?'

I didn't answer. Just stood there looking. Damn it if she didn't look great.

Kate came towards me and laid her hand on my arm. I could feel her warm fingers through the material of my jacket. Her eyes were sparkling. She'd just survived a terrifying ordeal, realised her life had been at risk, and it had been me who'd saved her. She was glad to be alive. I could see that she wanted to share the feeling. I'd seen this response to life and death situations before; it was generally misguided. On tiptoes she reached up and kissed me on the lips.

When I didn't return the kiss, she retreated. I saw colour creep into her cheeks. I'd tried to save her from embarrassment later on down the line, but all I'd done was embarrass her now.

'We had to keep up appearances, Kate. I registered us as a couple. It would've looked odd if I'd then asked for separate rooms. But don't worry, once the door's closed we can drop the charade.'

'Charade?'

'This,' I said, touching a finger to my lips. 'There's no need.'

Her face lit up with humour. But it was an act. She was humiliated and wanted to cover the shame.

'It was only a kiss, Joe,' she said. 'Don't read anything into it. It was just to say thanks.'

I lifted a hand. 'There's no need.'

'Yes, you've already made that clear.' The playfulness fell off her like a discarded cloak. She sat down on the protesting bed, flung down her purse, and looked at me with fire in her eyes. 'It would do you good to lighten up and have a little fun, Joe. Instead of being so goddamn uptight all the time.'

Her comment took me back. Uptight?

'I'm trying to keep us alive, Kate.'

'Who'd want to live if they were as wound up as you are?' she snapped.

Dumbfounded, I turned slowly away. 'I'd best go and move the Dodge. Keep the door locked until I come back, OK?'

'Yes, sir,' she said, flicking me a salute. Then she stood quickly and walked to the bathroom. The door slammed. I could hear her muttering to herself right through the door.

What the hell is eating her? I wondered. I'd tried saying the honourable thing and for some reason it had backfired on me. It was so much like my married life that it actually brought a nostalgic smile to my face. Then I recalled what day it was and the smile slipped away.

I stepped out into a biting wind.

The motel was anonymous enough, but, as Kate had earlier pointed out, the Dodge Ram with its customised paint job would bring the bad guys down on us in no time. I fired it up then drove a mile through town to another motel. I parked the Dodge under some trees so that it was blocked from the highway – making it look like we'd attempted to conceal the vehicle – but not so well hidden that it wouldn't be discovered. It was better for us if the bad guys wasted time staking out that motel than searching for us at ours. Then I headed back to the first motel on foot. On the way, I stopped off at a convenience store and purchased some snacks and juice. At the last second I added a large bar of chocolate to my groceries – a peace offering for Kate.

Out of the shop I found myself an empty doorway. Pulling out my cell phone, I rang my friend Rink.

'What the hell have you said to Kate to piss her off so much?' he asked me.

'She's already called you, then?'

'Yup,' Rink said in his anomalous Arkansas drawl. 'Passed me details of a vehicle you want me to look at. Then she started in on me about you. What's got her all bowed up?'

'Beats me. I was just being my normal self.'

'Right. Nuff said.'

'What's that supposed to mean?'

'Cool as ice is OK, but not all the time, Hunter.'

'I'm not always like that.'

'No, sometimes you're in a foul mood.' He chuckled. 'She's a fine-looking woman, don't you think?'

'For a cop?'

'Ah, she told you, then? Didn't think it would matter, buddy. Not seeing as who she is.'

'Can't believe she's Jake Piers' little sister.'

'Me neither. He was one ugly son of a bitch,' Rink said. 'I guess he got all the ugly genes and there was none left by the time Kate came along.'

'She's beautiful,' I agreed.

My silence afterwards was perhaps a beat too long.

'You got a thing for her, Hunter?'

'No.'

He laughed at my blatant lie. 'She likes you, buddy. There'd be nothin' wrong if you felt the same. You don't have to stay a monk the rest of your life.'

'I can't let things distract me, Rink. You know that. I start paying attention to her pretty face, I miss the gun pointing at her head.'

'Things getting out of hand up there?'

I told him what had happened at Imogen's house and on the drive back to town. Four men dead already and we still had no idea who we were fighting or what had become of Imogen.

'You want me to come up?'

'Not yet. You need to be in Tampa. If you fail to show up at court, the judge might throw the case out.'

Rink was tied up with the trial of Rupert Heavey.

He had spent a month gathering evidence that showed Heavey was a key player in the acquisition and supply of underage girls to the porn movie industry. There was a suggestion that Heavey tried the girls out himself. Rink's good work had closed down Heavey's outfit, and was set to put the sick-minded bastard behind bars. We couldn't jeopardise the trial with a no-show of the key witness.

'I'm hopin' that I'll be called to the stand tomorrow. Soon as I'm done I'll head up your way.'

'I'll keep you posted. Don't know where we'll be this time tomorrow. If you can get me the name of the owner of the Dodge, it could lead us anywhere.'

'OK, leave it with me.'

'Thanks, Rink.'

'No problem, man. You keep safe, y'hear? An' take care of that pretty face of Kate's.'

'I get the message, Rink. It's OK to look when there are no guns pointing at her, right?'

'There's hope for you yet.'

I hung up and lifted my sack of groceries. When I set off walking again things seemed a little better. Rink was right – as usual. It did no harm to appreciate Kate for the beautiful woman she was. I was a free spirit now. It was two years since my divorce from Diane, so I wasn't beholden to her any more. The problem was, it was also eighteen years to the day since we'd married. Something like that takes some getting over.

I was mulling that thought over when I heard the roar of an engine. Instinct made me snatch at the SIG beneath my shirt tails and I came close to drawing and firing at the clutch of men on the back of the pick-up truck. Instead I merely hung my head and concentrated on keeping hold of my grocery sack. Anyone who'd looked me in the face was already dead. I doubted any of the men on the back of the pick-up would see anything more than a guy on his way home from the store.

As they passed I took a look at the men on the back. They were young hot-bloods. If they weren't hunting me through the woods they'd likely be sitting round swilling beer and heckling the local cops. The two inside were older, but they had the same look as their younger friends, only a little more grizzled and world-weary. Not one of them looked my way.

The thought of following the vehicle to wherever they were heading skipped through my mind, but the feasibility of following on foot was laughable. The image they portrayed, I guessed that they were familiar faces in town, so I decided to wait. I could always ask around later.

Then I saw the two dark SUVs coming towards me.

The first SUV was banged and scraped all along the side: the one I'd barged out of the way when breaching their roadblock.

The second of the vehicles would still contain the blood and brain matter of the two I'd shot and I wondered who was so desperate that they'd drive such a vehicle back. Of course, there was at least one man who didn't have a ride: the big guy I'd pistol-whipped, then stolen his truck.

The second SUV was slowing as it neared me. The man had never seen my face, so I wasn't concerned that he was slowing down because he'd recognised me. Maybe he was simply looking for someone to vent his frustration on. Adjusting my bag of groceries, I quickly dipped a hand under my jacket and pulled free the SIG. Concealing the weapon behind the bag, I continued walking.

The SUV was almost parallel with me now. It was now travelling at a crawl and the driver had sent it over the central markings so that it headed directly for me. My pulse picked up exponentially. My finger tightened on the trigger.

'Hey, asshole!' a man shouted at me from the passenger window. 'You gonna move your fuckin' ass? Can't you see we're trying to pull in?'

Two things were apparent in the split second it took to relax the tension on my gun's trigger. I was standing at the entrance to an alleyway and the man shouting at me wasn't the same one as I'd brained with my gun barrel.

If it was possible, this man was even bigger and more powerfully built than the man in the woods. He had his hair shaved up the sides and back with a crest of hair on top like a grown-out Mohawk. He looked pissed at my inconsiderate blocking of the road and he'd twisted his face into a mask of rage. When he glared at me I saw that there was something unusual about his eyes. A touch of the David Bowie look.

'Don't make me get out this truck,' the giant shouted at me. 'Move your fuckin' ass!'

I gave him a weary nod, stepped up on to the kerb. I watched as the SUV swung into the alley, my eyes on the driver now. I'd only seen his face in darkness, and a relaxed state of unconsciousness, but there was no doubting that the driver and the man I'd knocked out were one and the same. Judging by the dark stain on his jacket the cut on his skull was still bleeding.

As he gave the SUV throttle and drove down the alley, I moved off the kerb and watched the vehicle's progress. The alley ran between two tall buildings. Even in the darkness I could make out a loading dock about a hundred yards down. The SUV stopped, brake lights flaring, and the big man with the mismatched eyes got out. He reached for something that I guessed was a padlock. His curses were discernible even at that distance. Then I heard the unmistakable sound of a roller shutter forcefully thrust upwards.

Serendipity.

I put down the bag, held my SIG against my thigh, then walked along the alley.

I I

When he'd wakened from his enforced slumber, Larry Bolan should have been apoplectic with rage. However, surfacing from the thick cloud of confusion with his brother patting his cheeks, he found he was only mildly annoyed. Some of the turnaround in his mood had to be down to the fact he was still alive, but even more to the fact that he would get another chance at killing this man. A bullet in the dark would have been too painless. This way he got to do it with his hands.

'Your head's split wide,' Trent remarked, helping him to his feet.

Larry touched the cuts on his skull. 'Tell me about it.'

A rifle cracked almost by Larry's ear and he flinched from the noise. Looking towards the trail, he caught a glimpse of tail lights as the Grand Taurino sped round the curve.

Larry looked at the tall youth with the smoking rifle.

Without warning, he grabbed the boy's throat between his massive fingers and squeezed. The boy was lifted off the ground, toes scrabbling for purchase on the dirt.

'The hell you doing *shooting at my wheels*, Jeb?' he

roared in the youth's purpling face. Then he tossed Jeb aside and the gangly youth cartwheeled into the nearby bushes. He landed awkwardly on his back, twisted among branches.

Larry and Trent stomped down on to the road. Looking in the direction where their vehicle had disappeared, they both stood in silence. Behind them, the rest of their friends dragged Jeb out of the undergrowth.

Larry turned and looked dispassionately at the dazed youth. 'You OK, Jeb?'

Jeb nodded in confusion, wiping at scratches on his forehead.

'Be thankful I'm not in a bad mood,' Larry told him. Then turning to the group of men surrounding him, he warned, 'Any of you motherfuckers mess up again, believe me, I'll rip your fucking heads off.'

The men all nodded in acquiescence.

'Any of you idiots got a phone with a signal?'

One man handed over his phone. 'One bar only, but it might be enough, Larry.'

'Go get the fucking cars,' Larry told the men. 'We ain't achieving nothing standing round here, are we?'

The men scattered, and only Trent was with his brother as he reported in to Huffman.

'How did he take it?' Trent asked when Larry hung up.

'In his usual way,' Larry said. 'He's bringing in some help for us.'

'We don't need help.'

Larry touched the tender spots on his head. 'No,' he said.

Before they returned to town, they backtracked up the hill. They laid out the four dead men in the living room of Imogen Ballard's house, then Trent got busy with a can of gasoline off the pick-up. Flames fought back the flurries of snow falling on the disintegrating A-frame.

Sending the others ahead, Larry and Trent commandeered Tom-Boy's SUV.

'It's full of shit,' Trent complained as he surveyed the blood and tissue sprayed through the interior.

'It'll clean up back at the shop,' Larry said.

As was the norm, Larry drove.

They caught up with the others at the pass. Trent got out the SUV armed with his can of gasoline and doused the Ford Explorer. Then there were two fires raging on the mountainside.

Good job it's winter, Larry thought, otherwise Trent'd probably burn the entire forest down. Trent's growing fascination with flames was another thing that concerned Larry about his strange sibling.

Trent grumbled all the way to town, brushing at drips falling on him from the roof.

'I ain't cleaning this fucking thing,' he told Larry about a dozen times before they reached Little Fork.

Larry didn't bother arguing. His head felt like someone was beating it with a hammer and all he wanted was to get back to their workshop where he could find something to take away the pain.

They'd left the snow up in the hills, but it was still a gloomy night. Not too many people out on the streets. The others continued on, but Larry slowed the vehicle as they approached the back alley that led to the workshop where they'd customised the Dodge. A guy with a bag of groceries was standing in the mouth of the alley, watching them warily.

'The fuck's his problem?' Trent enquired, then he leaned out the window and yelled at the man. Larry closed his eyes, flinching with every word rocketing around inside his skull. When he blinked open his eyes the man had stepped up on to the kerb. Larry drove into the alley.

'Should have run the fucker over,' Trent said. 'Inconsiderate bastard!'

'Trent . . .'

Trent blinked across at him. 'What's up, bro?'

Larry could only shake his head.

Arriving at their lock-up, Trent clambered out and set to the padlock. As Trent cursed loudly, Larry reached for his Magnum. But it wasn't there. Good job, because this time he really would have put a round through his brother's skull.

When Trent opened the door, Larry drove the SUV into the workshop. He didn't turn off the headlights until Trent found the light switch and bathed the shop with stark light. Larry climbed out of the vehicle, trailing a string of viscous gunk that clung to the sleeve of his jacket. Gross! he thought, wiping the congealed blood on the hood of the SUV.

'Jesus Christ, Larry,' Trent moaned. 'You don't have to make things worse than they already are!'

'Shut the fuck up, will ya?' Larry walked over to a tool bench arranged along the far wall. He was pretty sure he had a stash of morphine somewhere. His head was pounding, and his nose was full of the stink of Tom and Richie's brains. God knows what the hell he had sticking to his clothes. 'How could things get any worse?'

I2

'Maybe I can answer that.'

At the sound of my voice the two men turned to stare at me. They were the biggest human beings I'd ever seen, and between them they almost blocked out my view of the far wall. I'd thought that Rink was big, but next to these men he'd have looked slight. It made me feel like a child in comparison.

The difference between us was really measured by the fact that I was armed and they weren't. The SIG made me the top dog in the room.

Both men looked at me, then down at the gun.

'Either of you fancy your chances?' I brought up the SIG so that it was aimed directly at the face of the man with the odd eyes. He was the most vocal and likely to be the most irrational.

'You're the asshole who was blocking our way,' he said, pointing a hand at me. He rolled the hand into a fist the size of a Sunday roast. 'You want to fuck with me because I bawled you out?'

The other man turned fractionally. 'Trent? It's the goddamn man from the woods.'

Nodding in confirmation, I moved further into what I now could see was a mechanical workshop. There were tools arranged on the wall, a pit under the parked SUV. Perished oil made dark patches on the floor and had made its way on to the walls and furniture too.

'I recognise your voice,' said the man I'd pistol-whipped. 'What are you? English?'

I didn't bother answering. Instead, I asked, 'Why are you after Imogen Ballard?'

Both men exchanged glances. I saw something in their faces that I hadn't noticed before. It wasn't obvious face-on, but when they turned in profile I saw that they had the same shaped features. Kind of Neanderthal.

'You're brothers, right?' I said, advancing a step. 'So who's the youngest out of you?'

'We're twins,' said the man with the odd eyes. Trent, the other had called him.

'So you're the youngest then?' It was the way he'd answered, as though in defence of his pride, that told me. I turned my attention to the eldest brother. 'OK, it's like this: you tell me everything or I shoot your little brother. How does that sound?'

A strange look passed over the man's face, but it wasn't fear of my threat. 'He's big enough to look after himself. Why'd I care if you shot him?'

Trent scowled at his brother, but it was as if he saw the humour in the words and he started huffing out a laugh.

'Fair enough,' I said.

Then I shot the youngest brother.

His left knee buckled where my bullet punched through it, and as big and strong as he appeared, he still went down on the ground screaming.

'Motherfucker!' His brother lurched towards me. I brought up the SIG so he had a good look directly down the barrel.

'See,' I said. 'I knew you were bluffing.'

The older brother had come to a halt again. His face was painted with rage. 'I'm gonna rip your fucking head off for that.'

'No, big man, what you're going to do is start talking.' I moved the SIG so it was once more pointing at his brother. 'Otherwise I'll show you what a hollow-point can do to a face already that ugly.'

Some people have decried the effectiveness of the P228 over its predecessor the P226. With the nine mm parabellum ammo having less stopping power than .45 ball, some military and law enforcement officers prefer other sidearms. However, I didn't see the problem. When loaded with hollow-point ammunition, the P228 has enough power to stop a charging rhinoceros. It would easily blow the man's face apart, however huge his head was.

Taking another step, I held out my gun with both arms at full stretch in what's known as a stressfire isosceles stance. It's one of the stances favoured by Israeli Special Forces, designed for point shooting under extreme duress. It's also damn intimidating as the stance suggests that you are aiming directly at a specific target and about to discharge your weapon.

The older brother's hands came up. 'OK, OK, easy

now. I do care about my goddamn brother. What is it you want to know?'

'Start with your names,' I told him.

'Larry. That's Trent.'

'Second names.'

'Don't fucking tell him,' Trent groaned from the floor. Some of the shock of having been crippled had dissipated, but none of the agony. I guessed these men were used to pain. So I shot him in the other knee.

'Aw,' was all Larry said as he looked down at his screaming brother.

'Let's keep this conversation strictly between us from now on,' I told him.

'Bolan,' Larry yelled. 'It's fucking *Bolan*, OK?'

'Got it. Now you tell me who you work for.'

There was a little reticence in Larry's posture, so I fired again. This time into the wall behind his head. He must have felt the heat of the bullet passing his ear, it was so close.

'Robert Huffman.'

'Is he from here? Little Fork?'

'Dallas, Texas. He has offices there.'

'But he also has offices here?'

'Yeah.'

I fired another round the other side of his head.

'Let's speed this up a little, shall we? Give me the address.'

There was murder in Larry Bolan's eyes but he told me the address. Some office block in the affluent central district. Above a restaurant, he said.

'Why does he want the woman?'

Larry Bolan must have known the consequences of lying because he told me enough to make a considered guess. I shook my head in disgust: people dying for greed was nothing new.

When he was done, I saw Larry glance down at Trent and there was tenderness in his gaze not normally associated with hard-asses.

'You going to let us live?' Larry asked me.

'Would you let me live if the circumstances were reversed?'

'Sure, I would.' A smile crept over his face, and fleetingly I wondered if he'd seen something I was unaware of. Maybe a confederate sneaking up behind me.

But it wasn't that at all.

It was resignation.

'I'd keep you alive while I ripped your arms out of your sockets. I'd gut you and make you watch as I stamped your guts all over the floor.'

'Sounds entertaining.'

I knew it was coming before he even moved. I could see the tightening of his hands, the creases appearing next to his eyes, the slight dip of his body. He was coiling for the attack. Larry had realised he was going to die, but he wasn't about to give in without a fight.

Squaring my SIG on his chest, I prepared for the tell-tale widening of the eyelids.

Then my peripheral vision caught a flicker of movement. Trent rising up, his hand whipping towards me. A wrench he'd snatched off the floor spinning at my head. Despite myself, I ducked, and the wrench missed me. But it had also pulled my aim a fraction of an inch. As Larry charged and I pulled the trigger, I already knew it wasn't enough to kill him.

The bullet hit his left shoulder, too high up on the meat to even stop him. He was massive and all the power of his driving legs covered the short distance between us in a little over a second.

He loomed over me like the proverbial barn door. Only barn doors don't come equipped with piston-like limbs intent on rending you apart. He snatched at my gun with one massive hand and grabbed me round the throat with the other. It would be a waste grappling for the gun because it was a fight I couldn't hope to win. I drove my knee into his groin instead. Wind huffed out of him but it didn't stop him.

Larry picked me up, his fingers digging into my throat and wrist and he swung me and slammed me against the roof of the parked SUV.

'Bastard!' he snapped into my face. 'You should have killed me sooner.'

'Yeah,' I grunted, my back bent tortuously over the roof of the car. 'I should have.'

Larry laughed, picked me up and then slammed me down again. My kidneys felt like they'd been mashed and black flickers of non-light span across my vision. His arms were too long for me to strike at his face with my free arm, so I brought down my fingers, digging for the radial nerve in the arm holding my throat. I'd have been as well trying to sink my fingers through oak. To show me the error of my ways, Larry dug his hand into my throat. Luckily for me his hand was so large that it wasn't putting all his pressure on my trachea. If that had been the case, the cartilage would have easily popped and I'd have choked on my own blood. Still, the pressure was making me black out.

With compressed blood pounding in my skull, I brought up my knees, getting my feet wedged into his pelvic girdle. I strained, trying to push his weight away from me, using my legs to gain distance.

I was aware of Trent's voice in some recess of my mind. 'Kill him, Larry! Kill that motherfucker!'

He didn't know, but his baying was actually my salvation. It made Larry realise that he was going to finish me too soon. He'd told me he wanted me to live while he ripped me apart and eviscerated my body. That wouldn't be the case if he choked me to death. Larry picked me up so that I was over his shoulder, then he hurled me through space and I landed on the hard concrete. My head smacked the floor, my teeth gnawing a chunk out of my tongue, but that was a small price to pay in exchange for the oxygen I sucked in.

I'd also held on to my SIG.

Larry was coming at me again. I brought up the gun.

Then Trent wanted in on the action.

He threw himself across the floor at me. Grabbing my arms, he hauled me towards him, throwing his weight over my face.

Larry's feet found my exposed ribs. He got two swift kicks into me before Trent rolled further on top of me, blocking me from his brother's boots. Not that he was trying to protect me; he wanted me all to himself.

Trent punched me, his knuckles connecting with the top of my head. He had to rear up to get a clearer punch at my face.

I felt like I had a mountain on top of me, but I wasn't about to give in yet. Freeing one hand, I groped for his face. My thumb found his blue eye, and I pressed with all my might. It doesn't matter how big a man is, there are still vulnerable points on his body. The eyes are the most vulnerable of all. I felt his eye implode, and jelly-like gore pulsing over my hand. Trent pulled away from me. He was screaming again.

My SIG was now free of him and I brought it between our bodies. I jerked the trigger. Blood danced above him, some of it spattering on the ceiling. Trent groaned, and I heard Larry's tortured scream of denial. I shot Trent again – just to make sure.

As his weight collapsed over me, I shoved him aside, putting him between me and Larry. He would have to reach over his dead brother to get at me, but before he could do that I'd put a bullet in his body too.

As I searched for him, my view was blocked by the front end of the SUV.

Where the hell is he? I wondered.

Then I was scrambling out from under Trent's dead weight, looking for the other man, expecting him to be coming at me from the far side of the SUV.

But Larry wasn't up to avenging his brother instantly. The fucker was making a run for it.

Let him run, I decided. I'd achieved what I came here for. I now knew who my real enemy was and why he wanted Imogen Ballard dead. I could always kill Larry Bolan another time.

When I didn't feel like a train wreck.

I staggered to my feet.

I half-expected sirens as the local cops responded to the sounds of gunfire. But subconsciously I knew that was unlikely. The twins' workshop was in a deserted commercial strip. Metallic bangs and angry shouts were probably a regular feature of this place. Maybe screams were too.

Painfully, I made my way to the head of the alley.

My bag of groceries was still there, untouched.

I picked it up and continued my return to the motel. Kate would be wondering what had kept me. She'd probably be angry that I'd been away so long.

13

What I did, I did because I thought it was right. But I couldn't disregard the knowledge that I'd viciously tortured a man, then half-blinded him. Putting two rounds through his heart when he was trying to kill me was probably the least despicable of my actions. But that wouldn't be a factor, not when I'd been the one who'd gone into the workshop armed and looking for blood.

I've killed men before. Only occasionally in nightmares do I ever recall the faces of those men. Still, as I walked back to the motel, I was experiencing a cold sickness in my soul from what I'd just done.

Justifying my actions, the Bolan twins were trying to kill Imogen Ballard. Trent Bolan had murdered others in the past, and would have gone on doing so until I stopped him. Given the opportunity the twins would have murdered Kate and me if we'd been caught in their ambush on the mountain trail. But none of that would mean a damn thing in a court of law. Vigilantism is never tolerated, whatever the justification.

There'd be a shit storm when the deaths became

public, and – apart from my anonymity up until now – I didn't see how I could avoid arrest and imprisonment. I'd already used up all my cards, according to my old CIA contact, Walter Hayes Conrad, who'd covered for my actions in the past.

Approaching the motel where I'd left Kate, I shrugged off the worry. It was pointless being concerned about something that might never happen. I intended going after the men who were threatening Jake Piers' sisters, and there'd likely be more deaths. If I survived, I could worry about the consequences.

The drapes were drawn in our room. A faint amber light glowed at the edges of the windows. Snow began to flutter past the halogen lights in the parking lot and gather on the sloping eaves of the motel. It looked like a scene from a Frank Capra movie. I paused outside the door, my bag of groceries clutched to my chest as I sucked in a deep breath.

My hesitation was because I knew Kate would be repulsed by my actions. She was a cop. How would she react to what I'd done to Trent Bolan? In a lot of respects, that made me a cop's worst nightmare. Would she despise me? That was the last thing I wanted. I'd told Rink earlier that I couldn't allow myself to be distracted by a pretty face, and I'd meant it. But for all my best intentions, I'd failed.

Kate was very beautiful and feisty and I was strongly attracted to her. When she kissed me it had taken all my will not to kiss her back.

It took a lot to open that door.

It was best not to mention the episode yet. The fact that my throat was twice its normal size, I had a lump on my head like a duck egg, and my ribs felt like Rocky Balboa had used me for a punch bag, might give the game away. I'd admit to a run-in with the twins, but not to the outcome. She didn't need to know *exactly* what I'd done to Trent.

I stepped into the damp warmth of the room. 'Kate. It's only me, Joe.'

Kate wasn't in the living room. The bed was mussed from where she'd been lying on top of the comforter and the TV was switched to a local news channel with the volume down low. The bathroom door was closed, and I could hear a trickle of water from the shower.

Putting down the bag of groceries, I pulled out the chocolate and placed it strategically on the bed like a peace offering. I shrugged out of my jacket. There was a mirror over a chest of drawers. My face wasn't as bruised as I'd thought – Trent had punched me above the hairline – and my neck only felt like it was swollen. I lifted the hem of my shirt and studied my ribs. They were red and tender to the touch but I couldn't detect any abnormality. Thankfully, Larry had been kicking me with his instep and not the toe of his boots, so I'd escaped any broken bones. I dropped my shirt, covering the incriminating evidence.

'Kate?' I didn't want to embarrass her if she happened to come out the bathroom in a state of undress. I rapped on the door. 'Kate. I'm back.'

There was no answer, and I experienced a cold spurt of dread in my gut.

'Kate?'

I tried the door handle and the door swung silently inwards.

The bathroom was empty. Steam hung in the air, and water still trickled from the showerhead. Kate hadn't been absent long.

I wondered where she could be. She was a free spirit and not exactly helpless, so I shouldn't have been as concerned as I was. Maybe she'd gone out to a nearby store to purchase some food – neither of us had eaten since leaving Florida that morning. Even so, something about the emptiness of the room told me I was fooling myself. It was warm and clammy from Kate's shower, but there was something else.

Where was she? What had happened here? For the briefest of moments I wondered if she'd left out of embarrassment because I'd brushed her off. But I discarded that idea. A feeling lingered in the atmosphere, almost like some residual fear had been left over following sudden violence. It pervaded the air like a static charge.

Lifting the mattress with one hand, I found the Magnum where I'd left it. I shoved it down my waistband next to my SIG Sauer. The inclination that I might need the heavy firepower was strong in my mind.

My shoe scuffed against something lying partly hidden by the bed.

Kate's mobile phone.

It was one of those with a flip front and I opened it up.

The screen saver showed Kate standing with her arm round the shoulder of another woman. The second woman was a few years older, fairer of hair and slightly heavier in build. But there was no denying the family resemblance. Kate and her sister, Imogen, were mugging for the camera. They both looked very happy, caught in a snapshot of simpler times.

Ordinarily I'd have closed the phone then. A person's mobile phone is the equivalent of a personal diary these days. It is where people store all their memories. I would have felt like an interloper invading her precious space if not for one thing: Kate had left the phone for me to find it. There was a clue on the phone to who had taken her, and where I would find her.

Wondering if she'd discreetly snapped her abductor, I first scrolled through the photograph files. There were dozens of pictures, many of them of Imogen, some of Kate dressed in her NYPD uniform, smiling proudly at the camera. There were a few of friends and landscapes, one of Imogen's mountaintop home, but none of anyone who'd come uninvited to this room.

Next I went to her call register and to her dialled numbers.

I recognised Rink's number immediately. She'd called him six times over the last four days. But his wasn't the most recent number in the list. There were two above it. The first I quickly ascertained was likely to be Imogen's cell; it was no Sherlock Holmes power-of-deduction moment, the number was logged as SIS. There were a dozen or so calls made to the same number prior to Kate calling Rink and four occasions during the time they'd been in contact. She'd called Rink a little over an hour ago and then tried Imogen's number again immediately after. Twenty minutes after that she'd called the final number on the list. I selected the number and hit the 'view' button. Kate had barely been on the phone for two minutes. It didn't tell me who the call was to or what it had been about, so I hit the green call button.

'Little Fork Sheriff's Department,' announced a woman. 'How may I help you?'

It was all I needed and I hit the red button to end the connection.

'Damn it, Kate,' I sighed. 'Why didn't you do as I asked?'

But the answer was obvious. She was a cop. Duty had prevailed.

I couldn't really blame her.

It was her career at stake, after all. She was evidently concerned about what had happened up on the mountain. It would be the death of her career as a police officer if she didn't call it in. Problem was, she'd just traded her career for her life.

Larry Bolan hadn't told me *everything*. But he'd told me enough.

Robert Huffman was in charge, but one of his confederates came in the shape of Sheriff Jim Aitken. Aitken had watched while Larry and Trent had battered his predecessor to death with their fists. He hadn't even intervened when Trent had torn an ear from Sheriff Devaney's head to show him the error of not doing as he was told.

I could imagine how it had played out. Kate's call had been put through to the sheriff and he'd promised to deal with things personally. Aitken had come here and Kate had opened the door to him. Aitken had then drawn his gun and taken her away. Kate had had the presence of mind to drop her phone, warning me that I'd very likely walked into a trap.

'Shit,' I said. But that was about as effusive as I felt.

Reaching behind me, I came out with a gun in each hand.

Just as something crashed through the window trailing smoke.

No such a thing as a warning shout for me. The Little Fork Sheriff's Department meant business. The teargas canister was only the start of worse things to come.

14

There were only two options open to me: surrender or resist.

Surrendering isn't normally in my vocabulary.

But how could I resist officers of the law?

Sheriff Aitken was one of the murderous group headed by Robert Huffman, but I couldn't be sure how far his influence extended to the men and women under his command. In all likelihood, the junior officers were simply good people following orders. To them I'd be a gun-toting fugitive who'd brought violence to their town. They'd be determined to bring me to justice, and if I came out with my guns blazing, I could expect them to return fire.

I didn't want any good people to die.

To surrender meant coming out empty-handed. In approximately five seconds, I'd be face down on the sidewalk with my hands cuffed behind me. Then straight to a cell. At Aitken's mercy, I didn't doubt that some tragic accident would come my way while pent up in a cage. Maybe Larry Bolan would be my first visitor. That's if Aitken's trigger finger didn't slip the second I poked my head out of the motel-room door.

There were only seconds to decide.

The tear gas was launched with the intention of forcing me into their arms. If I didn't show quickly, they'd be following the gas into the room to take me down while I was coughing and choking on its effects. Shouted commands from outside drifted to me, but I wasn't listening. They were irrelevant to what would happen next.

The front door was covered, so too would be the bathroom window. No apparent way out. The cops had me cornered and debilitated by their gas.

Unless they'd wrung it out of Kate, they wouldn't know that I was ex-Special Forces. They couldn't know that I'd been trained to continue fighting even under extreme duress. Being exposed to tear gas, CS, PAVA, and all manner of non-lethal chemicals and irritants is standard practice for someone with my background.

The gas had filled the room.

Grabbing up my discarded jacket, I tied it round my face as an improvised mask. It didn't help my eyes, but it took away the acridness tearing at my respiratory system. Then I moved to the cupboard upon which the TV played away to itself and shoved the TV to the floor. The newscaster on the screen didn't seem aware of the tumble he'd just taken.

Using the TV as a step, I clambered up on to the cupboard. From outside I heard the scuff of feet as the assault began. I thrust upwards, throwing back the service hatch into the loft just as feet pounded towards the building. Men were shouting, identifying themselves, telling me to lay down my weapons. Then I hauled myself into the roof space, rolling sideways so that I could kick the hatch back into place. The sound of it slamming shut was covered by the crash of the room door being smashed off its hinges.

Immediately the shouts of the first officers inside filled the room below, then banging and clattering as they moved through the room bumping into furniture. They'd be wearing gas masks, but they'd still be confused by the smoke. When the living area was cleared they'd move to the bathroom. I came to my feet in the narrow attic space, moving hurriedly to my right. When the motel was built, the expense of fitting out the rooms wasn't extended to the attic area. No walls had been erected, so I had a free run to the far end of the building. Unsure of what I'd find in the room below, I hauled open the hatch and dropped through the hole into darkness.

The room was vacant. The drapes were open, and I could see the gumball lights from the Sheriff's Department's vehicles dancing on the snowflakes drifting by the window. Pulling free my jacket and shucking into it, I moved quickly to the door and opened it an inch. I could see movement at the far end of the block. It wasn't the kind of take-down you'd see conducted by big city SWAT teams. Three squad cars. A maximum of ten or twelve officers, I calculated. Most of them were in the room or covering the back. There were only two men outside, and only one I was interested in: a short, stocky man in a cop's uniform standing at the front of a liveried car.

I'd never seen Sheriff Aitken before, or even had a description of him from Larry Bolan, but I knew who the barrel-chested punk was. Like all murdering cowards, he wasn't about to put himself in the line of fire; not when he had innocents under his command who could be ordered to do so.

It'd be a matter of seconds before they realised how I'd escaped them. Give them another half-minute and they'd be conducting a thorough search of every room in the block.

Never let it be said that Joe Hunter is too rash for his own good. I could run, yes. But running, like surrender, doesn't sit too well with me. I'm more your go-for-broke kind of guy. Which was the driving force for me throwing open the door and running directly at Sheriff Aitken.

The punk didn't see me coming. He was too intent on watching the assault on the motel room. His face was a long oval, mouth open in anticipation. He was holding a revolver down by his thigh. Probably the gun he intended using to assassinate me.

Aitken was blind to my approach, but not so the deputy who was standing aiming a shotgun over the open door of his squad car. He caught my rush in his peripheral vision and his face swung my way. Surprised, he couldn't make immediate sense of the man running towards him, but his eyes blinked in astonishment at the guns I held in my hands. It took his brain a second or so to recognise the danger, to fire commands to the hands holding the shotgun. In that time I'd crossed most of the distance between us and brought up my SIG.

I fired before he did.

I aimed directly for his central mass and hit him dead centre.

The man dropped behind the car door and he stayed down.

That pleased me. It meant that I wouldn't have to kill the poor sap. I'd purposefully fired into his bullet-proof vest. The Kevlar would have stopped the bullet, but not the impact which had knocked the wind and the senses out of him.

I didn't stop my forward rush, only angled it towards Sheriff Aitken.

Now he was aware of me.

He turned, bringing up his revolver.

He was wearing a vest as well, but he deserved something a little more lethal. The only thing stopping me unloading a full clip into his head was that I needed him alive. He couldn't tell me where Kate was if I left him steaming in the frigid parking lot.

Aitken didn't have such qualms. All he was interested in was having me dead at his feet. My mad charge was all the justification he required to put me down. Who would challenge the killing when it was so obviously self-defence? With me dead, Kate would follow. Then they could get back to finding Imogen Ballard and put an end to this hiccup in Huffman's plans.

Aitken fired.

Only I was dropping under his line of fire, skidding like I was headed for first base. The snow helped my crazy attack, allowed me to slide the ten feet that separated us. Instead of stepping aside, Aitken was too intent on shooting at me. He tried to track me with his gun, but my movement was faster than his ability to follow it. Then my feet slammed into his shins and Sheriff Aitken sprawled over the top of me, his revolver sliding away into darkness. His body was on top of mine but only for as long as it took me to swing him over and on to his back. I came up from the floor with one knee on his chest and the Magnum under his chin. My SIG was squared on the door to my motel room.

The shots fired had alerted those within the room. I saw a man in a gas mask and vest come out of the cloud of tear gas pouring out the open door. He had a pump-action shotgun and it was aimed at me.

Good guy or bad, I wasn't going to let him take off my head. I shot him in his left leg and he collapsed in agony.

'The next man out of that room dies!' I roared at the top of my lungs. To add validity to my threat, I fired a couple of rounds into the room – careful to keep the bullets above their heads.

'Get up,' I said to Aitken. 'Now!'

Aitken scrambled up, showing me his empty hands. 'Easy now, son. I'm unarmed.'

'I'm not your *son*,' I snarled at him. 'Now get in the car. You drive.'

'You're making a big mistake . . .'

I cracked him round the side of his face with the barrel of the Magnum. 'The only mistake is that you're still alive, asshole. Now get the hell in the car before I decide to put things right.'

Aitken didn't need telling twice. He bustled into his squad car even as I clambered in the back. There was mesh between us, but it didn't mean a thing when I was armed.

'Drive,' I shouted.

'Where?' he asked as he reversed away from the other parked cars. I saw the man I'd shot in the chest rolling on to his knees and was gratified to see that he appeared unharmed.

'Away from here. And don't try to lead me into a trap. I'm not an idiot, Aitken. Try to set me up and I'll do to you what the Bolans did to the *real* sheriff.'

At my words, I saw his head shrink into his thick shoulders.

'Yeah, I know all about that. And everything else you've got going with Huffman.' Behind us the deputies were racing for their vehicles, planning on giving pursuit. 'Get on the radio, Aitken. Tell them to back off or I swear to God I'll kill you.'

Aitken was quick to comply. He also drove like he intended outrunning the storm that was growing stronger around us.

'Take us out of town,' I ordered.

'Where?'

'I'll know it when we get there.'

'What happens then?'

'That depends on whether you've harmed Kate or not.'

'I haven't. I swear to you she's fine.'

'So maybe I'll let you live, Aitken,' I said, 'if you tell me where she is.'

'I'll tell you! She's with Huffman.'

'Where?'

'I don't know.'

I drew back the hammer on the Magnum. The double click was ominous.

Aitken cringed. 'I swear to you … Jesus … I don't know where he took her.'

'Think.' Tapping the Magnum on the wire mesh, I warned him, 'You've got until I tell you to stop. You don't come up with where she's at, well, Aitken, that'll mean you've outlived your usefulness.'

15

'You will tell me who he is, bitch, or I swear I'm going to hurt you in more ways than you can imagine!'

Stripped to the waist, an impromptu bandage wound round his gun-shot shoulder, Larry Bolan menaced Kate Piers like an ogre out of a dark fairy tale.

Kate was sitting in a semi-dark room, propped on a folding metal chair with her arms cuffed to the back legs. Her linen jacket had been pulled off, her cream blouse torn open at the front exposing her bra and even her boots had been taken away so that she sat with her bare toes curling with each of Larry's words.

'Who is he?' Larry demanded again.

Kate just stared at him in defiance.

Larry slashed his hand across her face, his callused palm almost tearing the skin from her right cheek. Her head rocked from the blow, and her eyes momentarily lost lucidity.

'Who killed my brother?'

He raised his hand.

'Lay off, Larry,' said Robert Huffman as he walked from behind his desk. 'You're going to kill her, damn it.'

'Yeah, I'll kill the bitch . . . if she doesn't start fucking talking!'

Larry hit Kate again, and this time he saw a smudge of blood from the corner of her mouth when her head stopped shaking. She was a tough woman, a good cop, but she couldn't halt a moan of agony.

'Enough!'

But Larry wasn't finished. He grabbed a fistful of her hair and yanked her head to one side. He curled his other fist.

Huffman grabbed Larry's bicep.

'Enough, Larry,' he said. Softer this time. 'I mean it.'

Any other man laying a hand on Larry would have his fingers torn off one by one. But Huffman was another story. Larry nodded.

'Killing her isn't going to help,' Huffman said. 'It won't bring Trent back.'

'No . . . but it will make *me* feel better, boss.'

Larry had fantasised about killing his little brother more times than he could keep count. Since they were small children and he'd first considered smashing his brother's skull with a rock, the thought had plagued him. As they'd grown older, his thoughts had persisted, only now his choice of weapons had grown to include guns and knives and axes. He had dreamed up all manner of ways to end Trent's life, each more inventive than its predecessor. He had never thought that he'd see his brother die before *he* actually served the coup de grâce.

Watching the Englishman blow away Trent's knees, gouge out his freak eye, then put two holes in his body large enough for Larry to push his fists through, had never been the way he'd imagined his brother's demise. The bastard had robbed him of his lifelong wish. But that wasn't why Larry was in a cold rage.

He'd never have done anything to harm Trent, despite his daydreams to the contrary. As much as someone like Larry Bolan could love, he loved Trent. They were brothers. More than that, they were twins and shared a special bond. Sure, Trent had that twisted eye and an equally twisted mind, but he was still Larry's little bro. Being the older – and, in Larry's opinion, the much wiser – it was down to him to take care of his sibling.

Their useless mother had been no good. All she cared about was where her next drink was coming from. She ended up on some street corner up in Louisville, then God knows where after that. Their daddy – for all his anger at the world – loved his sons, but little good that had done the boys when he was carted off to the electric chair after he raped and beat two women to death when he was high on 'shine from his backwoods still. The boys were taken into the system. Wayward and violent, they'd been unadoptable, going from one orphanage to another. Juvenile detention came next, then the Big House. Throughout all those years it had been Larry's responsibility to keep Trent safe.

And he hadn't failed.

Until now.

'Alive she's of use to us,' Robert Huffman reminded him. 'She can help us find her sister.'

'She isn't going to tell us anything, boss.' Larry finally

released Kate's hair and her head lolled on her chest, semi-conscious.

'Maybe not. But we'll use her to bring her sister to us.' Huffman clapped the big man on his uninjured shoulder. 'She'll also bring this man to us. Why go to all this trouble when he'll walk right into our hands?'

' 'Cause it feels good.' To emphasise his point, Larry shoved Kate's head backwards, his fingers twisting her jaw.

Huffman stepped between them and Larry turned his face away in disgust.

'I said leave it be, Larry,' Huffman said, and this time the tone of his voice made it clear he wasn't going to repeat himself.

Larry stared at his boss. Huffman returned his gaze, and the hint of a smile appeared at the corner of his mouth. Larry Bolan was good at hurting people, but so too was his boss. Huffman hadn't always been a property developer.

Larry's eyes flickered away. He pushed a hand through his hair, felt a clot of something and wondered if it was some of Trent's blood from when the man shot him. He studied his fingers, but couldn't tell if it was Trent's or his own from when the same bastard pistol-whipped him in the woods. He was a mess. A good excuse to make his retreat without losing face. 'I need a shower.'

'Good idea.'

Larry was unsure whether he was referring to the shower, or that he'd backed down. But he wasn't about to ask. All the stories about Huffman were true: his viciousness was legendary. He wouldn't get to kill the Englishman if he gave Huffman cause to cut his heart out. .

Behind him, Huffman watched the big man leave the room. Then he turned and gazed down on Kate. The woman rolled her eyes up at him. Reflected in their wetness was the glint of the cut-throat razor Huffman held cupped in his palm. Huffman slowly slid it back into its holder on his wrist, pulled down the sleeve of his Versace suit jacket.

Huffman smiled.

He could tell by the look on her face that she wished Larry would come back.

16

'Do not – I repeat – do not try to follow us,' Sheriff Aitken shouted over the police radio channel. 'No outside interference. We must keep this situation *self-contained*.'

Aitken's commands to his men wouldn't mean an awful lot. Despite warnings not to follow, the officers would be frantic to find their leader. They would call in back-up. State troopers, or maybe even big city cops from Frankfort. There could even be a call put through to the nearest FBI field office. That would complicate matters and shorten the window of opportunity for getting Kate back.

Aitken seemed more afraid of outside interference than he was of the gun I pointed at him. He exhorted his troops to back off, then changed tactics, shouting and making threats if he even got a sniff of any form of pursuit. It saved me the problem of forcing the same commands from him.

Some police vehicles were fitted with transponders or GPS tracking devices, but Little Fork's law enforcement budget probably didn't stretch to such things. The falling snow gave cover from aerial pursuit, effectively grounding helicopters and light aircraft. The only way we'd be found was if a local spotted Aitken's car and called it in. But that wasn't very likely. The snow was now coming down in blizzard quantities and we were five miles out of town at an old mining camp abandoned ten years earlier.

The cop car was partly hidden under a lean-to next to a decrepit wooden cabin so faded with age it was almost as pale as the snow. I led the sheriff inside, getting out of the cold. The cabin had been stripped of anything of value, and all that remained was a single broken chair and an equally broken table. Setting the table top against a wall, I smashed it in two with a kick, ending up with a rough plank which I set against the wall. Then I made the sheriff reach his arms round the back of it and I used his own cuffs to link his arms together. The measure wouldn't halt a determined effort at escape, but it would slow him down.

'If that plank falls over, I'll shoot you,' I said, giving him something to occupy his thoughts. It caused him to stand rigidly to stop the plank from sliding beneath him.

Pushing my SIG into my denims, I kept the Magnum in plain view. The shiny steel gun looked more intimidating.

'It's time, Aitken. Are you still useful to me?'

'I've told you, I don't know where the woman is. I took her and handed her over to Huffman. Where they went after that, I don't know. I got the call that you'd showed up at the motel and high-tailed it back there.'

'Where did you leave her?'

'There's this restaurant in town . . .'

'French restaurant?' I asked, remembering the discussion I'd had with Kate earlier. At the time I hadn't given it much credence. However, it was obvious once I thought about it. The restaurant had been purchased by new owners. Huffman and his business partners were buying up pretty much all the property in and around Little Fork. It stood to reason that they were the buyers, and that they would set up residence at a central location. The restaurant – le Cœur de la Ville – was literally at the heart of town.

'Yeah . . .' He gave me a funny look. 'Place called le Cœur.'

'Where is it?'

Aitken described the location.

'This Robert Huffman. Tell me about him.'

'Tell you what?'

'First off: his description.'

'So you know who to kill?'

'Yes.'

He was perfunctory. Cop speak. 'White male. Tall, about your height . . . six feet maybe. Two hundred pounds. Athletic build, though. Aged early fifties. Short grey hair, well groomed. Designer suit. You know the type.'

'Right. Now tell me something about him that isn't obvious.'

'Like what? What do you want me to say?'

'While you're speaking, you're not dying, Aitken.

Think about that.' I tapped his barrel chest with the muzzle of the gun.

Seeing sense in my words – maybe even a way out of this predicament – he said, 'He first showed up about three years back. He brought big money with him. An investor in all the land development around here. He hails from Texas, heads some business outfit out there.'

'What kind of outfit?'

Aitken's face went flat.

I cocked the hammer on the Magnum.

'You know what I'm talking about!'

'Organised crime?'

'Of course.' Aitken sneered at me. 'You don't know what you've stepped into here, buddy. You're only one man: what do you hope to do against someone like Huffman?'

'What I need to do.'

'You'll die.'

'Maybe.'

'There's no maybe about it,' Aitken said smugly. 'From what I've heard, many men have tried to kill him, but he's still around. They aren't.'

'Many men have tried to kill me, too.'

The smugness dropped off him. My words must have resonated; now he was just a frightened man. 'Best thing you can do is forget all about Robert Huffman. Pack up, buddy. Go home, wherever that is.'

'First I get Kate back,' I said. 'How many men has Huffman got at his disposal?'

'Local boys? Eight or ten.' He snorted in derision. 'Did have a dozen until you showed up.'

Nodding at him, I said, 'Yeah.'

'They're just local punks. When Huffman sends real men after you, things'll be different.'

'By real men you mean the Bolan twins?'

'The Bolans? They're nothing, man. I'm talking about men who do this kind of thing for a living. The Bolans – they're just thugs.'

'Were,' I corrected him. 'Trent's dead.'

Aitken's eyes went wide. I noticed a bubble of saliva crack as his lips parted. 'You killed Trent? Holy shit . . .'

'He was trying to kill me. So were the men on the mountain.' Prodding him in the chest, I added, 'So were you.'

'You're trying to justify your actions?' Aitken asked. 'Trying to look for a way out of this, son? Maybe we can come to some kind of deal, huh?'

'I'm not justifying anything, Aitken. Just telling you how it is.' Placing the muzzle of the gun against his gut, I added, 'Just so you know what kind of man I am. People fuck with me, I fuck right back. You understand, right?'

His eyebrows drooped. 'Yes. I understand.'

'So . . . go on. Finish what you were telling me about Huffman.'

'You're going to kill me anyway,' Aitken said, his voice a hoarse whisper. 'Why should I tell you anything?'

'There are easy ways of dying or we can make things very, very hard. Larry Bolan explained what you *all* did to Sheriff Devaney. I'm sure I can be as imaginative if needs be.'

'I had nothing to do with Will's death.'

'You didn't try to stop it. That's tantamount to the same thing, isn't it?'

'It was Will's own fault.' Dejection brought his chin down on his chest. He knew how flimsy his excuse sounded. 'If he'd listened, everything would've been fine. He should've taken the money like the rest of us and then got the hell outa here.'

'He died because he wasn't about to let some criminal walk into town and take over. That was his job, Aitken. It was your job, too.'

'There was more to it than that.'

'Like what?'

'Huffman and Judge Wallace had made a deal.'

'A judge is involved?'

'Yes. The judge had to be part of it or Huffman's plan would fail.'

'Tell me what's going on between them.'

'Huffman invested in the town, got it back on its feet, but then he started buying up everything. No one else got a look in. If Huffman saw something he wanted, Wallace would rubber-stamp any applications that he sent through his office. Between them they were raking in land worth millions at resale. Will got wind of their deal and threatened to blow them both out of the water.'

'The sheriff was putting a case together?'

Aitken snorted. 'No. He was blackmailing them.'

'He wanted in on the deal?'

'Just hard cash. If they paid up, Will said he'd disappear, leave them to their scam.'

'But Huffman set him up. He sent you and the Bolans instead of the cash.'

'Wrong, again! Huffman did the deal. He paid Will off and told him to leave. Will – pig-headed fool that he was – didn't. He stayed on, flaunting his position as sheriff. Maybe he thought he had Huffman over a barrel. That's when the Bolans went to speak to him.'

'What are you getting out of this deal?'

'My family owns land down by White Rapids; Huffman wants to pay me good money for it.' He shrugged as best he could in his awkward position. 'I was also promised the position of sheriff once Will was out of the way.'

'So it all comes down to greed?'

'It's not just about the money,' Aitken said barely above a whisper. 'I have a wife and son. My boy's only twelve years old. Huffman makes a point of asking after their health.'

He stared at me pointedly, letting the silent innuendo sink in.

'You're supposed to be a cop. Couldn't you have gone through the proper channels if you were being threatened?'

'Gone to Will? He'd have laughed in my face. He was as corrupt as any of us.'

Small town politics, I thought wryly, how'd I end up bogged down in this?

'So,' I offered, 'you couldn't go to Sheriff Devaney.

Huffman's got Judge Wallace by the balls. You could've still gone outside, Aitken. The state cops would have backed you up.'

'Not before my wife and kids were paid a visit by Huffman. I don't want to go home and find my family with their heads cut off.'

Around us the blizzard was growing stronger. Wind pushed at the shingles, setting off a clatter.

I could sympathise with Aitken. But not much. In my estimation he was a coward, and I thought his fear of retribution on his family was really an excuse. If he was so concerned about them, he'd have taken them and run away. Or he would have put a bullet in Huffman's skull. No, he was waiting on the money that Huffman had promised for his land. He struck me as the type who'd willingly offer up his wife and son if Huffman came calling.

'Tell me about Imogen Ballard,' I said. 'Why's Huffman after her? She witnessed what happened to Sheriff Devaney, right?'

'Yeah, she was there. But that's not it.'

I frowned at Aitken. He must have seen my confusion as a minor victory. A way out for him. He was actually smiling as he lifted his head and stared me in the eye.

'You thought you had it all figured out, huh? Well, sorry, but you don't know the half of it.'

Standing stock-still, meeting his gaze, I said, 'Tell me.'

'You obviously know the woman, right? How she was divorced?'

I didn't bother answering.

'She got herself a new man.'

Not Huffman, I thought, please don't say Huffman.

Aitken rolled his head on his shoulders like a boxer between rounds. 'Will Devaney,' he announced. 'She was helping Will blackmail Huffman and the rest of us.'

Stunned, I could only stare in disbelief.

'She still is. To the tune of two million dollars.'

17

Twenty minutes later I was back in the driving seat of the cop car. This time I had it all to myself. Aitken's revelation had rocked me more than I liked to admit. So I drove into Little Fork with my brain buzzing.

Imogen wasn't the innocent I'd been led to believe. There was me thinking she was lying low for fear of violence from dangerous men, when all along she was as much a criminal as the rest. What had started out as a small claim against the new owner of le Cœur de la Ville had led her to uncover the scam between Huffman and Wallace. Instead of following proper channels, she'd taken this knowledge to her new lover, Sheriff Devaney. Between them they'd hatched a plot to make themselves rich. Unaware of her involvement, Huffman had ordered Devaney silenced. Imogen had then made contact with demands of her own. The twenty thousand dollars Devaney had demanded was now two million. Pay up and she'd disappear. Refuse and she'd sink them all. Huffman was sitting on an empire worth billions; little wonder he wanted her stopped so badly.

I'd come here and made war on Imogen's behalf. If I'd known the truth, I would have had nothing to do with it. Not that I'd have stood by and allowed the woman to come to harm, but I'd have handled things differently. The problem was I came because Kate had asked me to. And that was what was troubling me now. How much of the truth was Kate party to? Had she known what was really going on and was she involved in some way? It was a more believable reason for her doing this off the record than the one she'd given me. She'd known that she was going up against violent men and that's why she'd brought me along: to even up the odds.

She'd used me.

I'd been paying too much attention to her pretty face to notice the gun pointing at my own head.

The facts were all there.

Except there were huge holes in my reasoning.

If Kate was involved in her sister's get-rich-quick scheme, why had she come here searching for her? Her mobile phone had proved that Kate had been frantically calling Imogen for the last four days. Also, if she'd been party to the blackmail, she would have known who her sister's enemies were: she'd never have called Aitken and allowed herself to be captured.

Kate knew more than she was telling, but I didn't believe that she was aware of what Imogen was up to. Unwittingly she'd thrown herself at Huffman's feet. He now had leverage against Imogen that could force her to show her face. Both sisters were in more danger than ever they'd been.

To me, that meant only one thing.

Get Kate back.

Aitken said he'd handed Kate over to Huffman at the restaurant. It was as good a place as any to start.

The storm that had brought unexpected levels of snow to this corner of the Appalachians was a boon. It covered my approach to town in the distinctive Sheriff's Department car. Expecting to make it all the way through town in the police cruiser was a little too optimistic, though. I ditched the car as soon as I saw the first houses, pushing it down an embankment so that it was hidden from the road. Then I walked in. I needed another vehicle, and I knew where to get one.

The monster truck was where I'd left it.

Larry Bolan obviously had more important things on his mind than going in search of it.

The keys were still on the front tyre.

Starting the engine, I flicked on the wipers to clear the windscreen of the accumulated snow. Then I drove out the motel parking lot, swinging out of town again and retracing my route to the sheriff's car. There were no fresh tracks in the snow. I reversed the truck so that it was backed close to the cruiser, then hopped out.

Opening the trunk, I said, 'Think I was going to leave you here to die of hypothermia?'

Aitken blinked up at me from the shadows inside the trunk. His eyes were all that was visible above the gag I'd wrapped round his face. He said something but it was just a garble.

Grabbing him under one armpit, I hauled him out.

He swayed, his cramped muscles rebelling. I led him to the cab of the truck and pushed him inside. Taking a key from my pocket, I unlatched one wrist, but only for as long as it took to feed the cuff under an arm-rest on the passenger seat and then snap it back on him.

Back in the driver's seat I looked across at my captive.

'Wondering what's happening, Aitken?'

His eyes rolled my way.

'I said I'd kill you when you were no longer useful. I just thought of a way you can help.'

I started the truck and then headed into town.

Le Cœur de la Ville was situated midway up what was once the main street of Little Fork. It was a three-storey building that stood taller than the stores flanking it. The ground floor was given over to the exquisite dining experience promised by the pamphlet Kate showed me earlier, while the upper two were apparently reserved for less public affairs. The restaurant was closed for business. Maybe it had something to do with the storm and the fact that there were very few people about, but I guessed that it had shut up shop for other reasons. The middle floor was in darkness but lights burned behind shutters at the top.

'Where does Huffman have his office?'

Aitken nodded, tilting his chin at the upper floor.

The entrance doors were double-width, glass from floor to ceiling. The glass frontage extended the length of the building, tinted so that diners within could enjoy their meals without being gawked upon by the less wealthy types wandering by. There's nothing like a street person drooling down a window to put you off your lobster thermidor. I surveyed the entrance, but thought I wouldn't be going in that way.

Driving along the main street, I took the next left up a service alley and came to an intersection with the second street over. I parked the Dodge Ram and spied along the street to the rear of le Cœur. This secondary street was reserved for less ambitious businesses than the French restaurant, dominated by a strip of bars and individual family-owned stores. Light spilled from a seven/eleven at the far end, but everything else appeared to have closed early because of the storm. I couldn't see any pedestrains. Glancing at my wristwatch, I saw that the seven/eleven was due to close shortly as well.

'The staff in the restaurant, I guess they're no part of Huffman's network?'

Through his gag, Aitken muttered something unintelligible.

Pulling the gag from his mouth, I allowed him a deep breath. When he'd finished working his jaw, he said, 'Locals. They're just simple folk taking a wage. If they suspect what their employer is involved in, they know enough to keep their noses out of it.'

'What's the likelihood of any of them being inside?'

'By now? Very slim. Even the lights in the kitchen are off.' Aitken indicated narrow windows on the lower level. They were in darkness.

'That's good.'

'You're not thinking of going in there, are you?'

'Who's going to be with Huffman?'

'Don't know for sure. Trent and ... uh ... I mean Larry Bolan could be there. Maybe a couple of others.'

'What about the hicks who attacked me and Kate on the mountain?'

'They'll be long gone. Probably drinking to their friends' memory, by now.'

My mouth made a tight slash. Aitken lifted his shoulders, but it wasn't an apology.

'You mentioned *real men* that Huffman has working for him. They here yet?'

'Could be.' The way he licked his lips said otherwise. I reached across and dragged the gag back into place. Pointless talking to him when he was only going to lie.

'Can I trust you to keep quiet a minute or two?'

Aitken nodded.

'Don't suppose I can.'

I struck him on his jaw, just a quick backhander that he didn't see coming. His head rolled on his meaty chest, breath whistling through his nose.

Pulling out Kate's mobile phone, I punched in numbers.

'Kate?'

'It's me, Rink.'

'What're you doing on Kate's phone?'

'Long story,' I said. I told him what had gone on and what I'd discovered since. Then I said, 'I'm going to get Kate back.'

'I'll pack some things an' I'll be there in a couple hours.'

'No, Rink. You concentrate on putting Rupert Heavey away first.'

'Heavey can kiss my ass! I'm coming up there, Hunter.'

'The case could be dropped.'

'If it's dropped, so be it. We can always put Heavey down another time.' His words were laden; no doubt about it.

'We can't do that, Rink. He's a creep, yeah, but he doesn't deserve that.'

'You know there's more than one way to skin a cat, Hunter.'

'I can't wait a couple hours. I have to do this now. They've got Kate.' Beside me, Aitken was stirring from slumber. I could see movement behind his eyelids. 'Hold on a second, Rink.'

I gave Aitken another tap on the jaw and his eyeballs rolled up into his skull.

To Rink, I said, 'Before you hightail it up here I need you to do something for me.'

'Go on.'

'A guy called Robert Huffman's at the head of this. Apparently he has connections to organised crime over in Dallas, Texas. Can you see what you can dig up on him? Also, who he might have at his beck and call?'

'I'll do that. You still want who owned the Dodge Ram?'

'Larry Bolan?'

'You already figured that out, huh? Lawrence Grey Bolan. Bad dude, Hunter. One of twins. Trent Bolan's the brother. Extra bad.'

'Trent's gone.'

'Say what?'

I told Rink about the fight in the workshop.

'Shit, Hunter. Haven't I told you a dozen times—'

'We don't have a licence to kill any more? I know, Rink. Still want to come up here?'

'Are you kidding me? I'll be on the next flight.'

'Give me a call when you get in.'

'Just make sure you're around to answer it, brother,' Rink said.

When Rink calls me brother it holds extra significance. It means that he's worried about me. I didn't want him to be concerned; I just wanted him there with me. If there's anyone I'd trust with my life it's Rink. I have a real brother, John, but I'd be hard pushed to choose which one of them I love the most.

I hung up and put the phone back in my pocket. Along the street the lights in the seven/eleven went out. An old guy, bent against the drifting snow, locked up and then wandered away into the storm. I watched him go. There was no one else around.

I started the Dodge.

Leaning over, I slapped Aitken out of his dreams.

'Wake up. It's time to get useful.'

18

Larry Bolan could be mean in drink.

Whisky in particular brought out the animal in him.

He had anger issues when he was sober, let alone when the buzz of liquor was in his head. For that reason he had not touched a drop of alcohol in the last twelve years. Last time he'd downed a pint of JD, he and Trent had gone on a wrecking spree that saw three bars closed for renovation and six guys in hospital. One of the guys had never walked right afterwards and one lived on pureed meals for six months while his jaw went through reconstructive surgery. A cop took medical retirement – and gave up his dreams of fatherhood – when Larry flattened his testicles with a kick. It also got both Larry and Trent an eighteen-month stretch at the State Pen at Eddyville.

Drink had sent him inside. Drink had also killed his daddy. Larry did not drink again.

Until now.

Because the alcohol made him surly, he chose to drink alone. Down in the fancy restaurant he downed two fingers of Scotch in memory of his little brother.

Then he drank another two, promising Trent that he'd be avenged. His next two fingers were just for the hell of it. After that he began to lose count.

Two fingers of whisky was nothing to a drinking man, but not many of them had fingers as thick as Larry Bolan's. He looked down at his hands. He wished he'd just throttled the hell out of the Englishman, like he'd started to do. Another squeeze and his head would have popped right off. Trent would still be alive.

'And I'd be fuckin' sober.'

Larry placed his empty glass on the counter. He lifted the bottle of imported Aberlour Scotch whisky and saw that it was empty too. Eighty dollars a bottle – Huffman would just have to dock it from the blood money he'd promised to pay for Trent. Larry looked for another bottle from behind the bar. The bar was fancy. Polished walnut. Stain-free. Not at all like the bars where Larry and Trent hung out when they were younger. He didn't recognise most of the brands of liquor arranged on the shelves. What the hell was wrong with stocking some good ol' Kentucky sour mash? He stooped down, rooting under the walnut instead.

He heard the roar of an engine.

His ears were buzzing with the Aberlour.

But he recognised the sound.

The Grand Taurino.

Raising his head level with the bar top, he squinted towards the front of the restaurant. The specially coated windows made it difficult to see outside. All he could see was a wash of blazing light.

The engine roared louder.

'You have got to be kidding me!'

The windows imploded, and the roaring Dodge followed the cascading glass, throwing aside tables and condiments and flower arrangements. The monster truck wasn't held up by the furniture; it simply smashed it aside or ground it beneath its massive tyres. It came on.

Directly towards Larry.

Slowed by the liquor, he was caught in the awkward position of rising. Left or right, he couldn't make a decision, and instead could only watch transfixed as the Dodge roared at him. The headlights were thrown to full beam and light also blazed from the rack on the cab. His hands came up in reflex, but his strength was no match for a monster truck. It smashed the walnut off its moorings, ramming the board backwards with decapitating tenacity. Larry went down amidst shattering glasses and bottles, experiencing a crushing weight that took away his senses faster than any amount of strong liquor could achieve.

19

Men had died by my hand this night. I had held two men under a gun, then killed one of them when the situation degenerated out of control. I'd forcibly fought clear of a police attempt at taking me down. Shot at officers of the law. I'd kidnapped and – to all intents and purposes – tortured a sheriff. So, a little criminal damage was the least of my crimes.

Then again, the dollar value of this latest crime, plus the fact that the act could endanger life, put it firmly in the 'first degree' bracket, so maybe I was underplaying the fact that I'd just sent a vehicle through the front of a building. I wasn't driving the Dodge Ram, but that wouldn't mean a damn thing: I'd forced Sheriff Aitken into the act under duress.

Aitken hadn't argued, but he wasn't a willing driver. He only saw my crazy plan as a way of staying alive. I handcuffed him to the steering wheel. Then I jammed a wrench I found in the cab so that it wedged the gas pedal to the floor. Then I slipped the vehicle into drive, before clambering out the Dodge as it headed directly for the glass frontage like a blunt arrow aimed for the heart of

Huffman's empire. Aitken was under no illusion as to what would happen if he attempted to turn the vehicle away from its target.

Before the Dodge hit the restaurant front I was running, sprinting into a service alley between two buildings further along. I heard the muffled roar of the Dodge tearing up the restaurant. But I didn't stop. I continued sprinting so that I came out on to the street at the back of le Cœur de la Ville. Without stopping I moved directly to the rear door and grabbed at the handle. Locked; but it would be.

Using the Magnum, I fired a round through the lock. Then one where the mechanism met the door frame. When I wrenched the handle this time, the door swung open, chunks of shattered metal tinkling beside my feet. Staring into a short but dark passage, I saw another door at the far end. I listened a moment. Bangs and crashes were sounding from the front of the building. I could have sworn that the floor trembled beneath my feet, but maybe that was only my body's reaction as it was flooded with adrenalin. Freeing a hand by shoving the Magnum into my jeans, I pulled open the second door. Quick scan of the room, left, right, centre, and I saw only an empty kitchen. A muted nightlight was the sole source of illumination but it was enough. I moved into the kitchen, skirting a huge stainless-steel work surface, above which were hung all manner of pots and pans.

Aitken had described the interior well. The door at the right corner – a double swing-door set-up – let into the public dining area. I wasn't interested in that door.

The one I was looking for was in the opposite corner. Approaching it quickly, I opened the door and scanned the stairway that led up to the top floor.

There were other stairways inside the building. They were semi-public and gave access to the first-floor office space. To get to the uppermost floor, you had to traverse the offices to this end of the building and pick up this stairwell. Only this one went to the very top. Anyone fleeing the building from the uppermost floor would come down this way – particularly with the sounds of destruction emanating from the front of the building.

The truck had finally come to a halt, but not the engine, which continued screaming in anger as its forward plunge was stopped by something immovable. The crashing noise was furniture shifting as gravity fought the effects of chairs and tables being forced into unnatural positions. It made listening for anyone coming down the stairs difficult. I closed the door behind me, mounting the stairs. I kept my SIG close to my hip, barrel pointed upwards. That way there was less chance of the gun being knocked from my hand if anyone was waiting for me round any corners.

At the first landing I listened again. The noises from below were muted now. I heard the thrum of feet dashing across a floor above me. I peered up the stairwell. There was a light on at the top and I saw an amorphous shadow skitter across the wall. Someone was heading down.

A man rounded the twist in the stairs. Medium-sized man in shirt and trousers. Black shiny shoes. Short greying hair. He could have been anyone – an innocent employee of the restaurant – if not for the gun in his hand.

Seeing me, he blinked in surprise. Lines tightened at the corners of his mouth. He lifted the gun.

I fired before he did, from the hip. Because of the angle, my bullet caught him in the lower abdomen, punched out between his shoulder blades. The man's face elongated. Then he toppled head first, rolled down the stairs and ended up sprawling at my feet.

Robert Huffman's face was a mystery to me, but I knew that this man wasn't the one holding Kate. On closer inspection, his clothes were off the rack, his shoes a cheap brand. He'd died protecting a man who earned more in an hour than he could hope for in a month.

Stepping past him, I scooped up his handgun, a Glock 17. For a second the thought that it was Kate's gun had crossed my mind, but I knew otherwise. The guns were similar, but Kate's was a Glock 19. Slightly smaller: more befitting a woman's hand. The ammo was interchangeable with that for my own gun, but I didn't have the time to start transferring it across. I shoved the Glock into my waistband alongside the Magnum. The big gun was almost out of bullets and the Glock was a handy replacement.

Moving upwards, I did so with more stealth. Obviously Huffman had more than the local thugs to call on. I doubted there'd be many; it wasn't like this was the headquarters of Tony Soprano, just some minor mobster who'd seen a niche in the market. Not that it would matter. One man with a gun was enough to kill me if I made a mistake.

At the top of the stairs I paused. The door before me was shut. If anyone was on the other side, they could gun me down as I stepped through. Moving to the door, I stood to the hinged side, leaned across and pressed down the handle. The door swung away from me. No shots invaded the space where I'd be expected to be standing. I glanced around the jamb. There was an office space, tastefully decorated. A huge desk and a leather chair behind it, a lamp casting illumination over a stack of papers. Paintings on the walls. I vaguely recognised the style, but the name of the artist wouldn't come to mind: it was extraneous to my needs. Moving into the room, I checked the corners for anyone lurking inside. No one. So I headed directly across to the door in the far corner. Windows here gave a view of the street below. All I could see was a curtain of snow. I could smell exhaust fumes from the Dodge that was still revving somewhere below me. And yes, the building was trembling under its churning wheels. My senses were supercharged now. I could make out a frantic whisper from beyond the doorway. It was a one-sided conversation, someone talking into a telephone.

Could be calling in reinforcements – or the police, which would be exactly the same thing under the circumstances.

I swept open the door and stepped into the room.

There was a single man. Unarmed, I saw, apart from

the mobile phone he clutched. His clothing was of good quality, but I didn't think he was Robert Huffman.

He was a slight man in his late fifties, his face aged and lined beyond his years. His hair was more salt than pepper and was receding. His eyes had the yellow cast of someone with a kidney malfunction. There were tiny veins in his cheeks, a patchwork of broken corpuscles, making his face look like a relief map of a river delta. He held the phone to his mouth, said, 'He's here.'

Then he held the phone out to me.

Holding him under the threat of my SIG, I took the phone from him and held it to my ear.

'Huffman?'

'You have me at a disadvantage.' Robert Huffman's voice barely contained a trace of his Texan roots hidden beneath mock joviality. 'What do I call you?'

'Your death if you've done anything to harm Kate.'

Huffman laughed. 'That's a little melodramatic. Do you practise your lines by watching old Clint Eastwood movies?'

Ignoring the taunt, I said, 'Where is she?'

'Where would you expect her to be?'

'Where are you?'

'Like I'm going to tell you?' He chuckled again. 'Don't worry, she's safe. She will stay that way if I get what I want.'

'What do you want?' Inside I cringed. The first tenet of counterterrorism is that you never give in to demands. That was a rule ingrained in my psyche throughout my active military career.

'Let's start with your name.'

'Joe Hunter.'

It was pointless denying my identity; he would only force it from Kate.

'Hunter?' Huffman said. The conviviality of his tone became even stronger. 'Now how ironic is that?'

'Now who's talking clichés?' Next he'd be hitting me with the old chestnut about the hunter becoming the prey. I cut that line of conversation. 'You said you wanted something. I want Kate back. Let's deal.'

'Kate's a beautiful woman. I can see how you'd want her back. So yes, let's deal.'

'You want Imogen Ballard in exchange for Kate?'

'Exactly.'

'I don't know where she is.'

'Find her then. Hunt her down. Bring her to me and Kate's yours.'

'Where will I bring her?'

'That's good, Hunter. No whining about having to find her. No excuses. I like that. You sound like someone I can trust to get the job done.'

'Where will I bring her?' I asked again.

'That's yet to be determined.'

'You're not in Little Fork any more.'

'In a short while I won't even be in Kentucky. However, some of my associates will be. I've put a contract out on your head.'

'Thoughtful of you.'

'Let the presence of my men motivate you. If they kill you, well, it will be a slight hiccup in our arrangement.

But, Hunter, that won't stop me. I have Kate. She'll bring her sister to me and I'll have the two of them to do with as I please. If you want Kate back, I'll stand by our agreement: the quicker you bring Imogen Ballard to me the better it is for the both of you.'

'Send your thugs all together, or one at a time. It won't make a difference. I'll send them all back in body bags.'

'Bravo, Hunter. That's the spirit. I know I can count on you.'

'See you soon,' I said.

'I look forward to meeting you.' He let the implication hang in the air. Then as an afterthought he added, 'Keep the phone, Hunter. It will come in handy when you've found Imogen.'

'I'll speak to you soon, but not on this phone.'

Dropping the phone to the floor, I ground it beneath my heel.

Throughout my conversation with Huffman the sickly-looking man had not moved. He watched me destroy the phone with a look of distraction.

'Roger Wallace, I presume?'

The man blinked up at me with his jaundiced eyes.

'Where's Huffman?'

'On his way to Dallas.' He wore a look of resignation, like he'd just realised that his partner had left him to face my wrath on his own.

'I guess that you're just another misguided individual who was forced to do Huffman's bidding?'

He shook his head. 'No. I knew what I was doing. I'm dying. I've a wife and children, I have grandchildren. I want to leave them comfortable after I'm gone. Huffman has given me that opportunity.'

'You're supposed to be a judge,' I said. 'You're supposed to protect the people you serve. Instead you stand by when they're murdered. Noble sentiment about providing for your family means nothing. Not when you're lying. It's greed, Wallace. That's all it is. Greed and murder.'

'You're going to kill me?'

'No. I'm not your executioner. You'll be tried by the people who you've betrayed.' I rapped him round the side of his head and he fell unconscious at my feet. 'And I guess they'll be better judges than you've ever been.'

20

Sending Larry Bolan's truck through the front of the restaurant had been a little pointless. I'd been expecting Huffman inside, bodyguards too, and the stunt with the truck had been intended as a distraction while I made my way inside by the other route. Huffman had arranged it so that all I had to do was walk inside and take the phone from Judge Wallace. I'd killed the man on the stairs for nothing. But I didn't let that concern me; I had more important things on my mind. Primarily, who were these *associates* of Huffman and why had he warned me they were coming?

My first thought was that I couldn't deliver Imogen Ballard to him if I was dead. But it was like he said: my death was inconsequential to his plans. He had Kate, and ultimately that was what would bring Imogen to him. My value was no higher than that of any other of the men he had at his beck and call.

It didn't take much figuring out.

Huffman simply couldn't help himself. He enjoyed pitting man against man. He enjoyed the thought of blood and violence. By promising to return Kate to me, he knew that I would fight tooth and nail. His own men would be coming with the same intention. He'd warned me about them because he wanted us to fight and he was not the least bit concerned by how many of us would die.

He had no intention of returning Kate to me. If I delivered Imogen Ballard to him, both women would die. Likely he'd make sure I died too. He wasn't going to leave any loose ends.

Smashing the phone was a mistake.

I should have demanded proof of life first.

Now I had to accept his word that Kate was alive and that he'd keep her as bait for her sister. Still, to do that, he had to make contact with Imogen. That gave me the luxury of some time, none of it to be wasted here fighting contract killers for Huffman's amusement.

When we'd first arrived in Kentucky, we had booked rooms at a hotel at the airport. I had left my spare clothes and supplies in my room. That would be my first port of call. With the supplies I had fake documents that I could use to book a flight out of there.

I left Judge Wallace unconscious on the floor.

Making my way down the stairs I searched my pocket for my mobile phone. Instead, I found Kate's.

A plan of sorts came to mind.

I rang Imogen's number, not expecting her to answer. She didn't, but I left a message on her voicemail. Imogen obviously knew enough not to use her phone – it could be too easily traced – but I suspected that she hadn't cut herself off with any finality. Maybe she would access her voice messages. With some networks you could do that remotely from any landline.

'Imogen,' I said. 'I'm Joe Hunter. I was a friend of Jake's, maybe he told you about me? Kate has been taken by the men you're hiding from. I'm going to get her back. But I need your help. Ring me.'

Then I could only hope that I was right.

My next call was to Rink.

'I'm getting out of here, Rink.'

'Uh-oh.'

I told him about my conversation with Robert Huffman.

'He's put out a contract on you?'

'So he said. I have to assume he was telling the truth.'

'Unless he's only tryin' to frighten you,' he said, 'so that you deliver Imogen to him quicker.'

'That'd be a waste of time.'

'Nothin' frightens Joe Hunter, huh?'

'Plenty of things frighten me, Rink. Contract killers don't.'

'So where are you going?'

'If Huffman's heading for Dallas, so am I.'

'I'll change my flight plans,' Rink said. 'Join you there instead.'

We arranged to meet at Dallas Fort Worth Airport the following morning.

'You want me to pick up Harvey on the way?' Rink asked.

'We could do with the extra firepower.'

'Harvey will be pleased to hear that. I asked him to

dig up what he could on Huffman for you. He's been itchin' to get in on the action ever since.'

We hung up, and I felt a little better knowing that my friends were on their way. Despite my macho words, the thought of having a bunch of contract killers hunting me was concerning. If I failed, Kate would die too, and that was something I *was* afraid off. I wanted to believe that I had a purpose in this world. My protective side had kicked in and if Kate was to die, that would make me question everything I stood for.

That isn't going to happen, I promised myself.

I was back at the bottom of the stairs, standing at the entrance to the kitchen. The only sound from the public area now was the tick of the Dodge Ram's cooling engine. Someone – most likely Sheriff Aitken – had turned it off.

For a brief moment I considered going into the restaurant. Two outstanding issues needing resolving in there. First off, I had to decide what to do with Aitken. I couldn't kill the man in cold blood, so I had to leave him as I had Judge Wallace. They would be dealt with by the law of the land. Second, I needed transportation out to the airport. The Dodge was available. But the truck was too visible a target.

With the SIG and Glock 17 pushed down the waistband of my jeans, I moved over to the door I'd come in by. The Magnum I placed on the stainless-steel counter in the kitchen. It was no good to me any more.

It was still snowing.

The deserted streets were tranquil beneath the fall of

virgin snow. There was a hush, the blizzard blanketing and deadening all sound. The sidewalk looked pristine; not a footprint in sight. Pulling up my collar, I stepped outside and broke the image. My trail led away from le Cœur de la Ville.

As a rule I love snow.

But occasionally it can be as great an enemy as any other. I could only hope that it hadn't brought the airport to a standstill. Something like that could slow me down more than any number of killers.

21

Before today Larry Bolan had never been knocked unconscious.

He'd battled all his life and some of those he'd gone up against had occasionally got their licks in. But he'd always brushed off their punches, laughed in their faces, and then smashed them into the ground.

To have it happen to him twice in the same day was bordering on ridiculous. The only good thing about both bouts of senselessness was that he'd actually come out of them alive.

After he wakened in the forest, Trent had been there with him. This time, his first thought was that Trent was gone. The loss of his little brother hit him afresh. But Larry wasn't the crying type; he was the type that raged against grief. The pint of whisky he'd downed didn't help his frame of mind either.

He came up from beneath the wreckage of the bar like an erupting volcano. When the Dodge had slammed into it, he was fortunate that he had been in a crouch. At the last second he'd managed to duck his head, avoiding decapitation, and the truck had knocked the bar over and on top of him. He'd slammed his head on something hard and gone out as if a light switch had been flicked. The bar top had formed a shield between the truck and his collapsed body. The walnut board had been his saviour, but now it was only an encumbrance. He lifted it on his shoulders as he came to his feet, and hurled it aside with a roar of anger.

Then he stood blinking at the carnage.

Le Cœur de la Ville wasn't such a fancy-assed restaurant any more.

The Dodge was further along the wall from him. After it slammed the bar, the vehicle had continued to push forwards, seeking escape, but it had been nudged and bounced and had ended up jammed in a corner of the building. Its hood was angled towards the ceiling, the front wheels balanced on a pile of smashed tables and chairs.

His eyes were a little unfocussed, but Larry saw movement in the cab.

He thought it might be the man who'd killed Trent, but that didn't make sense. What would be the point of ramming the truck into the restaurant and then sitting there doing nothing?

Shards of glass tinkled off him as he pushed through the drift of demolished furniture. There were small slivers in his hair, and he could feel a powdery residue on his face. He stank of spilled liquor. A couple of minor scratches on his hands stung like crazy. The wound in his shoulder was on fire. Otherwise he was unharmed.

But his truck was bashed all to hell.

Whoever the man who killed Trent was, Larry had already sworn to kill him. Now, seeing his beautiful Grand Taurino in a state, he swore that he would do more than kill him; he was going to wipe him and everything he held dear out of existence.

'Who's there?' a voice called from inside the cab.

'Aitken?'

'Larry? Is that you?'

Larry clambered up the pile of shattered tables, his heel skidding in a pool of oily liquid, and then grabbed at the driver's door handle to pull himself upright. Peering in the open window, he saw Sheriff Aitken with a bruise on his jaw and a tiny cut on his forehead. The windscreen was starred from where Aitken's head had slammed against it when the truck rammed through the front of the building.

'What the hell have you done to my truck?'

'I didn't do this, Larry.' Aitken tried to pull his hands away from the steering wheel so that Larry could see the cuffs. 'See?'

'You could have still steered the damn thing.'

'The guy had a goddamn gun to my head.' Aitken began rattling at the cuffs. 'Get me outa here, will ya?'

'He was with you all the way inside?'

'No,' Aitken said. 'He jumped off at the last second. He was going in the back way after Huffman. There was nothing I could do, Larry. Anyway, it's just a truck!'

'Just a truck?'

Larry didn't like Jim Aitken. He was a pussy stooge if ever he'd seen one. And he knew that Aitken didn't like him much either. Plus, Aitken absolutely hated Trent.

'You could've taken your foot off the gas.'

'The guy jammed it down *with a goddamn wrench*,' Aitken shouted. Then he started pulling at the cuffs in frustration. 'Are you gonna do something, Larry?'

'Yeah, hold still. I'm gonna do something.' Larry reached inside the cab with both his huge hands.

'About time . . .'

Larry clamped both hands round Aitken's head and twisted violently. The sound of vertebrae snapping was like the discharge of a small bore rifle.

'You should've kicked the goddamn wrench away,' Larry said to the dead sheriff.

Larry negotiated his way through the furniture wreckage so that he was again on steady footing. He wiped his boot heel on the carpet, wondering what the hell he'd stood in. Probably some kind of food dressing with a name he couldn't pronounce. It didn't matter. It was of no more concern to him than the man he'd just murdered.

He took a look at the front of the building. The entire glass front was gone, most of it spread through the interior of the building. The snow was falling fat and heavy. It was a whiteout. Some of the flakes were finding their way inside and drifting on currents of air. In this neck of the Appalachians snow wasn't unknown, but it was a long time since Larry had seen a blizzard of this strength. Further along the passes would stay blocked, for a couple of days at least. The only way out of Little Fork would be by foot or by flight. So he left the Dodge where it was.

He pushed through into the kitchen area. It was in darkness, but there was ambient light nudging in through the service door at the back. That was where Trent's killer had come in. He swung immediately into the stairwell that led to Huffman's offices on the top floor. He listened but couldn't hear a thing.

He didn't know how long he'd been unconscious, but he had the feeling that the man had already gone. He climbed the stairs to the first landing. He saw Eric Conroy lying dead at the base of the next flight of stairs, a hole the size of a rosebud in his gut. Larry kicked him over and saw the rose had bloomed on his back. He checked but Conroy wasn't armed. That wasn't like Conroy, Larry thought. Huffman's fetch-and-carry boy was never without his Glock 17. Trent's murderer was amassing quite a gun collection.

He stepped over the dead man and mounted the final flight of stairs. Lights were on above him. He watched for shadows, but there was no movement so he entered the first office and saw the door open to the next room. He listened. He could hear breathing. Someone had taken a knock and was breathing raggedly. Larry was familiar with the sound: he'd knocked enough men unconscious that he recognised it.

Judge Wallace was lying on the floor. The man was sprawled out like a starfish, legs and arms splayed. His head was back and his mouth wide open. He had a bruise on his face and Larry guessed the guy he was after was getting a bit too fond of pistol-whipping folk.

Larry was no more concerned with the judge than he'd been with Jim Aitken. He stepped past him to open the next door, and saw that Huffman's office was deserted. The chair where Kate had been cuffed was empty.

Larry scowled at the open space.

Huffman had taken off with the woman.

If Huffman had still been here when the man arrived, one or the other would be dead on the floor. There was no sign of blood, no sign that a fight had even taken place.

He turned back to Wallace.

Crouching down beside the judge, Larry slapped the older man's face a couple of times. His face had an unhealthy pallor, but then again, it always did.

'Wallace! Wake up, Goddamnit!' He slapped the judge again, and this time the man stirred. His eyelids flickered repeatedly, eyes attempting to focus. A hand came up and pushed against Larry's chest. Larry grabbed the hand and swung the judge up and round and sat him in a chair.

Wallace came out of his enforced sleep bewildered. It took him a full half-minute to get his bearings. All the while, Larry stood watching him with his arms folded over his chest.

The judge finally looked up at him and Larry saw his pupils contract.

'Larry?' His voice was barely above a whisper.

'Yeah, it's me. What happened here, Wallace?'

'Get me a drink, will you?'

'First you tell me what the hell happened. Where's Huffman?'

Wallace worked his tongue in his mouth, building up moisture. He'd been sucking dry air for a while now by the look of him.

'Huffman's gone back home.'

'Dallas?'

'Yes. He took the woman with him.' Wallace tentatively pawed at the bruise on his face. 'He's dealing with the situation, he said.'

'More like he's run off and left us to pick up the shit.'

Wallace nodded. 'You know he's not interested in us, Larry. It's always been that way.'

'He wouldn't have got anywhere without us.' Larry unfolded his arms and made fists at his sides. Blood was seeping through his bandages and blossoming on his shirt. 'Trent died for him.'

'We were just a way of making money, Larry. We were just tools to him. Expendable tools. Accept it.' Wallace leaned forward, elbows on his knees, hanging his head in his cupped palms.

'My brother was no expendable tool,' Larry warned. 'And neither am I.'

Wallace waved away his words.

'Huffman has a plan. He's going to get Imogen Ballard. He's got her sister for bait. When it's all over, he said he'll be back.'

'I take it Kate's bodyguard was here? Any idea who he is yet?'

'Called himself Joe Hunter. Could have been a fake name for all I know.'

'Hunter.' Larry tested the name on his lips. Didn't like the taste, so he spat on the carpet. 'It'll do.'

'Huffman spoke to him on the phone. He told Hunter to bring Imogen to him.'

Larry didn't say anything. He was still thinking about the man he was going to kill.

'Crazy thing is,' Wallace said, 'he warned Hunter about the men he's bringing in.'

Larry looked at Wallace. He remembered when he'd told Trent about Huffman's extra firepower. 'We don't need help,' Trent had growled. Larry had agreed with him then. And he still agreed with him now.

'Joe Hunter is mine.'

Wallace shook his head. 'Stay out of it, Larry.'

'He killed my little brother.'

'Leave it to the professionals,' Wallace said. 'You can stay here and help me clear up the mess at this end.'

'What? All of a sudden I'm a fucking cleaner? And you say that Huffman thinks of us as tools?'

'Take it easy, Larry. We have to get things sorted here before news leaks out. First we have to control police involvement. We have to find Aitken.'

'Aitken's dead.'

'Dead? Hunter did that?'

Larry neglected to answer. And Wallace wasn't a judge of men for nothing.

'You killed him, Larry? Why, for God's sake?'

'Because he was an expendable tool. Just like the rest of us.'

Then he reached for Wallace and picked him bodily out of the chair. He swung round, walking towards the front of the office.

Wallace yelled, 'What are you doing?'

'Cleaning up,' Larry said. 'I'm not having a dirtball like you warning Huffman that I'm on my way to Dallas.'

Larry heaved Wallace above his head, holding him aloft for a long second, then he threw him through the window. Wallace took the glass and part of the frame with him. He dropped with the falling snow, only much, much faster.

Larry heard the dull thud.

He peered down on Wallace's lifeless form three levels below him. The snow hadn't done much to cushion the fall.

'Leave it to the professionals, huh, Wallace?' Larry said. 'The hell I will! No one kills Joe Hunter but me.'

22

Little Fork airport wasn't large. It didn't take international passengers. It was only in the last few years that any kind of passengers had flown there. Before that it was strictly freight. However, the sudden land boom around Little Fork had forced the airport to follow the times. Across the way, through the falling snow, I could make out a large building under construction. It was due to open in the spring of next year, according to messages on some massive billboards. For now, serving as the flight terminal, there was a single-storey building, low and squat and constructed from steel and glass. The only concrete I could see was on the floor. One side of the building was for arrivals, the other for departures. Everyone shared the same checking-in doors, coming or going. Security was pretty non-existent. There were only a handful of people in the departure area, and most of them were too busy watching the overhead announcement board to pay me much attention.

The flight to Frankfort was delayed.

So was the one to Louisville and to Lexington and Jackson and Hardinsburg and all the other major airports in the state. It looked like I was in for a long wait.

I got coffee from a vending machine and a sandwich from another and I sat down in a corner where I could watch the entrance doors. If this was a major airport I'd have been searched, but because it handled only internal flights, I had my SIG in its customary place in the small of my back. The Glock I'd taken from the man on the stairs at le Cœur de la Ville was buried beneath my spare clothes in my backpack. If anyone challenged my right to carry the guns, I had fake documents that said I was a US air marshal and I'd be left alone.

Back at the hotel where I'd collected my things, I'd phoned in a flight booking. I was warned there might be delays, but the blizzard was forecast to blow itself out within the next hour. That was three hours ago. It was worst-case scenario to me. I had to get moving, and sitting there was doing nothing to change that.

For another two hours no flights took off from Little Fork. Neither did any planes land. The only good thing about the storm was that it was working both ways. I couldn't get out, but neither could Huffman's hired killers get in.

I checked for messages on Kate's mobile phone. I was hoping that Imogen had got back to me, but she hadn't. The message I'd sent to Imogen's voicemail had always been a long shot, but I was still hopeful. I put the phone away. Getting up from my chair, I wandered through the terminal. All the flights were still delayed. I purchased more coffee. It was black and strong. I needed it: it had been a long day and wasn't finished yet. Not by a long way.

Back in my seat, I watched the entrance doors. I was expecting Aitken's crew to arrive at any second. He would have been released from the cuffs by now. He'd be back at the station house and coordinating a search for me. Judge Wallace would have come round as well. He'd have told Aitken my name. They'd have had the flight bookings checked. My real name wouldn't show: I was booked under a false one. But if they had any sense they'd put two and two together. They'd know that my cover was false if they ever got round to thinking about it.

Something about the no show of the police was beginning to bother me. Made me wonder what the hell was going on. Maybe Aitken and Wallace were just a little slow on the uptake, but surely one of them – or their people – would have thought to check out the airport by now? Maybe Huffman had ordered them to back off. If I was locked in a prison cell it would take away the enjoyment of having me battle his hired guns: I wouldn't be much of a challenge to them then. Plus, my usefulness in finding Imogen Ballard would be nil. Huffman wanted me dead, but he wanted Imogen more.

I was on my third coffee when the blizzard finally stopped. However it was a full two hours after that before the display boards changed and showed that a flight to Frankfort would be leaving at 09:55 a.m., which was only twenty-five minutes away. Almost eleven hours after I'd sent the Dodge Ram through the front windows of le Cœur de la Ville, it looked like I would finally be on the move.

When it came time to board the plane, I hung back to the last moment. There were only twelve other passengers. I made unlucky thirteen. I'm superstitious, a lot of military people are, and on any other occasion I'd have looked around hopefully for any stragglers who would change the number in my favour. But this time I actually wanted to be certain I was the last man aboard. It was my only way to be sure that no one was following me.

The airplane was a Beechcraft 1900 air taxi, used for commuting between Little Fork and Frankfort, and only had nineteen passenger seats. There was no galley or flight attendant, and it was down to the co-pilot to secure the doors before flight. Ten of my fellow fliers were men, the final two being an old woman and a small boy. No one on board gave me any negative vibes, and I settled into a seat at the back of the craft and closed my eyes.

Take-off was a little bumpy. But then we climbed up above the remnants of the storm and things became smoother. It was a short hop to Frankfort, and I dozed all the way. I hadn't slept since early yesterday morning, and I needed the nap.

Frankfort hadn't been touched by the snow but the skies were heavy and grey. We landed at Capital City Airport to a slight drizzle. I was OK with that. The rain wouldn't halt my connecting flight to Dallas. Disembarking the plane, I could see Boone National

Guard Center across the single runway. There was no activity at the military base. I made my way to the arrivals terminal, tagging along with the old lady and the boy. All the other men were wearing suits and ties and I'd have stood out in their crowd.

Using my fake ID, I purchased tickets for my onward journey; then I had to sit and wait until my plane was ready to go.

Capital City was bigger than Little Fork airport, but not by much. I could see the people queuing to board the Beechcraft 1900 I'd recently departed. None of them looked like professional killers, but you never could tell. Top assassins don't look like killers, they look like your average next-door neighbour. I doubted Huffman's team would be travelling the same route as I had. Likely they'd have chartered a flight direct from Fort Worth to Little Fork. I'd probably missed them by the skin of my teeth.

Part of me regretted the fact.

Maybe I should have waited for the bastards at Little Fork and killed every last one of them as they stepped out the airport. It would have changed everything. I wouldn't feel like I was running, which was never a good feeling.

An hour later I was on a corporate Jetstream 41, heading south-west for Dallas Fort Worth. We flew over Arkansas and into Texas and I exited the plane into a sunny day. It wasn't hot, just warm, but it was a pleasant change after the blizzard. Not that I could spend too much time enjoying the sun on my face. I'd just entered my enemy's territory and from now on must be on my guard at all times.

As soon as I'd cleared arrivals, I pulled out Kate's phone and checked for messages. Still none. I rang Rink.

'Where are you?' he asked.

'DFW.'

'What took you so long?'

I told him about the snowstorm.

'Cool.'

'Where are you?'

'With Harvey. We're outside the airport. Do you want us to come and pick you up?'

'No, I'll take a cab. You guys follow and see if you can spot a tail. No one knows about you yet: I want to keep things that way.'

We arranged to meet at a motel off Route 80 on the outskirts of Arlington once we were sure no one was following me.

'You ain't going to believe what Harvey dug up on this Huffman character,' Rink said. 'Very interesting.'

'I can't wait.'

23

Reunited with his Magnum .357, Larry Bolan stepped out of the rear of le Cœur de la Ville into the blizzard and saw the single set of footprints leading away up the street. The snow was coming down hard, and the prints had almost been obscured, but he could still make out the faint depressions in the snow. Hunter wasn't that far ahead. He didn't bother following him. There was only one place that Hunter would go, so he backtracked to the workshop where he'd left Trent.

Now that his blood had settled a little, he regretted killing Aitken and Wallace. His anger, and the whisky, had driven him to act irrationally. But he didn't want anyone getting in his way. He wanted revenge. But now he didn't have anyone to look after his little brother while he went after Hunter.

Trent was where Larry had last seen him. He was lying in the shadows at the back of the workshop. One knee was bent and an arm was crooked up as if he was waving, so he looked like he was in the first aid recovery position. But there was no way Trent was recovering from this. The two holes in his back were large enough to accommodate Larry's fists.

Larry crouched down and touched his brother's cheek. It was stiff with cold – maybe even rigor – and Larry drew his fingertips away. But then his hand went back to Trent's face and turned it towards him. Trent's pale blue eye was gone.

He laughed without humour. 'Don't worry, Trent, it's actually an improvement.'

Larry sighed. He closed the eyelid to hide the mess. Standing up, he looked down on his brother.

'I'm gonna get the son of a bitch that did this to you, bro,' he promised. 'I'll make him hurt before he dies.'

Then he got in the SUV they'd brought here earlier.

The stench inside was overpowering. Larry dropped the windows, deciding he'd rather endure the cold than the stink. He backed the SUV out into the loading area, then pulled down the shutter on the workshop and clicked the padlock in place. Trent would be as much at peace here as he would be anywhere. When he was done with Joe Hunter, Larry would see to a proper burial, but for now, the workshop would serve as Trent's tomb.

He drove to the airport.

He didn't go inside the departure building.

He parked the SUV in a position where he could see inside. He could look through the glass front, but anyone inside would see only their own reflection. The snow was coming down heavy, swirling in the draughts round the building, but he could still see the doors. If anyone came out, he'd spot them. He sat with his Magnum in his hand. Trent's Mossberg Persuader was on the seat beside him. He didn't want to use the guns, though. When he killed Hunter it would be with his hands. He'd only shoot him if he tried to run. Wing him in the leg, or something. Then he'd pull his head off his shoulders and crap down his neck.

Through the snow, he could see Hunter sitting in a far corner of the building, nursing a paper cup. The man had changed his clothes since their last encounter. But he would have had to: his other clothes were splashed with Trent's blood.

A hundred times he almost got out the SUV. He could walk inside the airport and corner the bastard. But a hundred times he held back. His head was still full of liquor fumes. He wanted to be clear-headed when he killed Hunter. Crystal clear.

Before leaving the restaurant, he'd pulled on a heavy overcoat. But he was cold. The wind was blowing through the SUV, carrying snow with it. He tasted flakes on his tongue. But he didn't close the windows. The stink of brains was sour in his nostrils and he could smell the whisky coming out of his pores. The cold was helping clear his mind for what was to come.

The snow stopped.

There was a bustle of activity on the runway as a plough and a truck with a heater mounted on its back set to clearing away the snow. Except for visits to a vending machine, Hunter didn't move. Neither did Larry.

Larry was shivering by the time he watched Hunter stand up and pull a rucksack on to his shoulder. Hunter disappeared through the departures door. Finally, Larry stepped out of the SUV. He left the Mossberg where it was, but slipped the Magnum inside a coat pocket.

He went up to the booking desk.

'When's the next flight to Frankfort?'

'There's a flight preparing to leave, sir,' said the airport rep. He didn't meet Larry's eyes. Larry was sure the man could smell him and was turning away to avoid the stink. The guy tapped buttons on a computer. 'There are seats free. I can book you on it if you wish?'

'How long until the next flight outa here?'

'Two hours.' He glanced up at Larry. Then his eyes quickly flicked down again.

'Give me a ticket for that one,' Larry said.

He paid cash from his billfold, took his tickets then went off to the public restroom. Inside he studied himself in a mirror. No wonder the guy had been giving him funny looks: he was still covered in dust and slivers of glass. He washed his hair and face. Then he leaned both hands on the sink and stared at his reflection in the mirror for a long time. His eyes began to go out of focus, and for the briefest of seconds he saw someone else's eyes staring back at him. One brown, one pale blue.

Trent was along for the ride. He wanted to be there when Larry ripped Hunter's heart out of his chest.

24

I was in my room at the motel outside Arlington when a knock came at the door.

I'd been sitting on the bed with my SIG on my lap. Standing up, I held the gun close to my hip as I walked across the room. I'd pulled the blinds shut on arrival, so had to peel one of the slats aside to take a look outside.

If I'd never seen the Bolan twins, I'd have thought the two guys standing outside were huge. Rink stands about six three and Harvey is a shade taller. Rink is built like Mr Universe, while Harvey looks more lithe and rangy, like a young Muhammad Ali. They were an odd-looking combination. Rink's part Japanese and has the blue-black hair and hooded eyes of his mother. His muscular build is down to his Scottish ancestry on his father's side. Harvey on the other hand was blue-black all over, from his bald head down. Rink had on a denim jacket and jeans over a white T-shirt. Harvey looked as slick as ever I'd seen him in a silver-grey suit with matching shirt and tie. Harvey had a laptop bag with him, which he'd hung from one shoulder. He was fixing his cuffs as I peeked out at them.

They were my best friends in the entire world and I was pleased to see them both.

I let them in. Harvey came in first, while Rink took a last look behind them. Harvey put out his hand and I shook with him. Then Rink followed and grabbed me in a bear hug. He squeezed me and I was reminded of the kicking that Larry Bolan had lain on my ribs.

'Easy, big guy,' I laughed. You'd think we hadn't seen each other for years instead of the few days it had been. But that's Rink for you.

'Things looked clear on the way over here,' Harvey said.

'I was hoping that we would spot a tail,' Rink said. 'After coolin' my heels at court all week I could've done with the action.'

Distracted by the fact that Kate was being held by dangerous people, I didn't care much about Rupert Heavey. If his defence attorneys called for a mistrial due to the no-show of the key prosecuting witness, then to hell with it. It was like Rink said: there were more ways to skin Heavey than by putting him through the legal system.

Shutting the door behind them, I got the preamble out of the way. 'You said you had something interesting about Robert Huffman?'

Harvey slid the bag off his shoulder and pulled out his laptop. He cabled it up to a socket in the wall. We'd chosen this motel because it advertised internet access in all rooms. Sitting on the bed with the computer on his thighs, Harvey began tapping keys. A minute later he turned the screen to me so I could take a look.

'Robert Huffman,' Harvey said. 'Entrepreneur businessman. Multi-millionaire.'

Huffman was a good-looking guy. No doubt about it. He looked fit and healthy, and dressed the part. He was wearing a navy suit, white shirt, light red tie. He had a lot of upper-body definition that the suit couldn't disguise. Long slim legs. He looked like an athlete who'd retired from competition but had kept up his training regime. He had short, immaculately styled hair. It was growing grey, but it gave him that 'distinguished look' that people talk about. His face was tanned and lean.

Whoever had taken·the photograph had caught him smiling, but I didn't buy the look. His lips were too tight and his dark eyes too cold. He had the black depthless gaze of a shark.

I stared at his photograph and I hated the bastard.

Harvey tapped keys and another shot of Huffman came up on the screen. He was younger in this shot. His hair was black. Still smiling without any emotion extending to his dead eyes. Except this time he was wearing an orange jumpsuit. There were numbers beneath his name.

'He's done time,' I said.

Harvey pointed at the name of the correctional unit. Seagoville. A federal prison on US Highway 75 to the south—east of Dallas. Not far from where we were.

'Minimum security,' Harvey said. 'Huffman did time, yeah, but it wasn't hard time.'

'What was he locked up for?'

'He cut a man's throat.'

'And he only went to a minimum security prison?'

'The charges were dropped from murder in the first when he hit the cops with a little quid pro quo,' Rink explained. 'He went state evidence against his former employers, the Texas Syndicate. In exchange for putting away the Felitta brothers, his charges were dropped to manslaughter. He did three years' soft time at Seagoville.'

'I'm surprised he made it out the other end. No one likes a grass.'

Harvey raised his eyebrows. 'No one fucks with Quicksilver.'

'Quicksilver?'

'That was Huffman's street name. He was the Dallas syndicate's top enforcer. By all accounts he was a very capable killer. No one was going to go against him.'

'Not when it was all a set-up,' Rink added.

'What kind of set-up?'

'There's an assumption that it was just a plot to get rid of the Felittas,' Rink said. 'His arrest allowed him to talk to the DEA out from under the eyes of his bosses. The Felittas were the supposed power in the syndicate, but Huffman was just bubbling away under the surface, ready to take over when he got his chance.'

'So he gave the DEA all they needed to put the Felittas away,' I said, 'with the intention of taking over where they left off? Criminals don't stand around when there's a gap in the market, I'd have thought some other outfit would have moved in while he was away.'

Harvey shook his head. 'It wasn't like that, Hunter.

The other syndicates stayed out of the way. They left Dallas alone for when Huffman could come back. His actions with the Felittas have been *forgiven* by the other syndicate heads, if you get my meaning?'

'It suited them that the Felittas were out of the picture?'

'Yeah,' Harvey said. 'The Felittas were old school: no one wanted to deal with them any more. When he was released from prison the other syndicate heads welcomed Huffman back with open arms. In some eyes his going down for three years was seen as heroic; like he's some goddamn martyr to the cause.'

'So he did his three years then walked out and into the Felittas' shoes?'

'Not exactly,' Harvey said. 'The syndicates left Dallas alone, but others had moved in. By the time Huffman came back the street gangs were running the narcotics and prostitution. But Huffman wasn't interested in that any more. He saw his future in real estate. You've seen what he's been up to around Little Fork, right? That's only one of his ventures.'

'There are others?'

'Many others.'

'So he has plenty of people in his pocket,' I assumed. 'Plenty of Bolans and Aitkens to pull on if need be?'

'My guess is that there are lots of people at his beck and call,' Harvey said. 'But they're not the ones we should be worried about. The other syndicates owe him. He did time for them. He can probably pull on any of the mobs, ask for their help. We could be going up against some of the top enforcers in the country.'

'Bring it on,' Rink said. He looked like he meant it.

'Mob enforcers aren't usually the type to work outside their frame,' I said. 'It isn't as if every syndicate in the country is going to send their best man. You ask me, there'd be way too many competing egos. They'd probably spend more time fighting each other than they would looking for me.'

'It only takes one,' Harvey said. 'If he's good enough.'

'Yeah.' It was a sobering thought.

Huffman hadn't been talking about only one man. He'd been talking plural. We really had no idea about how many men he was sending against me. But it didn't matter; if they came I'd stop them. Simple as that. I wasn't going to worry about them until they showed up. I certainly wasn't going to run and hide.

'Why Quicksilver?' I asked.

It was Rink who chose to answer. He did so in his usual drawl. 'The pussy is good with a blade. Skilled and very fast, they say. Y'know, as in quick with the silver?'

'We've been there before.' I saw Rink's fingers go to a livid scar on his chin. The scar was courtesy of Tubal Cain, a serial killer who was very good with a knife. Cain made the mistake of abducting my brother, John, and we'd hunted him down. Cain had cut the two of us – he'd almost killed me, but I'd rammed a bone from his stash of trophies in his throat. 'We'll stop Huffman, too.'

'Don't underestimate him, guys,' Harvey cautioned. 'There are stories about Huffman. Apparently his specialty is to slice the throat, but he's also been known to peel off the faces of his enemies while they're still alive. If the stories about him are true, he's as bad a dude as any you've gone up against.'

I sniffed in disdain. But Harvey was right: you should never underestimate anyone, especially when he was the top enforcer of a crime syndicate. Nobody gains that accolade without proving himself.

'Any word from Imogen yet?' Rink asked.

I shook my head.

'Let me have her number,' Harvey said. 'I'll see if her phone can be located.'

Passing Kate's phone over to him, I said, 'I doubt you'll get anywhere. My guess is that Huffman's already tried that.'

Harvey smiled. 'Huffman won't have the contacts I have.'

He handed the phone back after memorising the number. 'Keep that close in case Imogen does get back to you.'

'I'm expecting another call,' I explained, putting Kate's phone in my jacket pocket.

'Huffman?' Harvey asked.

'He's bound to press Kate for a way to contact me. He'll find out that she left her phone back at the motel and guess that I have it now.'

'Maybe we should get rid of it. He could use it to find you.'

'You said he didn't have the contacts you do.'

'And I mean it, but it's easy to find an active phone. Kate's service provider could run a search for hers. I don't doubt he has contacts at that level.'

'We don't have to worry about that, Harvey, because I'm going to find him first.'

'Assuming he's here, that is,' Rink said.

'He's here. It's his home turf; it's where he'll feel strongest.'

'Shouldn't be too difficult to find him,' Harvey put in. 'All I need do is a search of public records. See who owns what and then track back to a registered office.'

'Or we could look in a phone book.'

I picked the yellow pages off a stand by the bed and dropped it next to Harvey. It was open to a page I'd marked by folding down a corner. 'Huffman is supposed to be a bona fide businessman these days. He has his own ad right there.'

Harvey laughed. He closed down his computer and picked up the telephone directory.

'Sometimes the old ways are the best,' I said.

25

'Tell me about Joe Hunter.'

Robert Huffman had just received a status update from Little Fork, and he was surprised by what he'd heard. Hunter – as he'd already known – had been to le Cœur de la Ville. According to one of the men Huffman had sent there, Hunter had gone in with extreme prejudice. No one was left alive. Huffman's valet, Eric Conroy, was dead. Judge Wallace was dead. Jim Aitken was dead. Even Larry Bolan was missing and presumed dead. With no one left to helm damage control, Little Fork was now swarming with state troopers and agents from the FBI field office at Frankfort. His men were getting out of there and returning to Dallas.

'There's more to this man than meets the eye,' Huffman said. 'Tell me what it is.'

Kate was no longer handcuffed, but she was still a prisoner.

She was sitting in a chair with two men watching over her. Their guns were holstered, but they were an ever-present threat. Kate knew not to stand up without their permission. She only went to the bathroom if one of them went with her. She was given food and water, but the cutlery was plastic and the plates were paper.

'I don't know much about him,' she said.

Huffman was standing over her. But he wasn't menacing her as Larry Bolan had back at the restaurant. He stood with his hands folded, peering down at her with what was supposed to be a kindly smile. Somehow that was much worse.

'So tell me what you do know,' Huffman said.

'I know that you're in serious trouble. Kidnapping a police officer is possibly the least of your crimes, but it'll be the end of you. You've just attracted the attention of the FBI. They won't rest until they find me and you're locked away for life.'

Huffman laughed softly. He unfolded his hands and he showed her the cut-throat razor cupped in his palm. He didn't need to move any closer; the way Kate shrank back from him was enough.

'Who says that anyone will ever find you, Officer Piers?' he asked. 'No one knows you're here. In Little Fork you weren't acting under any jurisdiction. I've checked with a source in the NYPD: apparently you are on vacation, Kate. Your trip to Kentucky was off the books. If I cut you up into little chunks and scatter your remains over the plain out there, who would know where to look?'

'I told colleagues I was visiting with my sister. When I'm not found there, they'll start looking for me. You're the first person that the FBI will come to.'

'Why would they come to me?'

'I told them my sister was having trouble with you.'

'Ah, the unpaid bill she was complaining about?'

'Exactly. I can't believe that this is all a result of a goddamn unpaid bill.'

Kate was pushing for information herself, but Huffman wasn't about to enlighten her.

'If I'm questioned I'll feign ignorance. I've been in Dallas for the last two weeks. I have a hundred people who will swear to that.' Huffman lifted the razor and studied it. 'Now, Kate, let's not waste any more time. Tell me what you know about Joe Hunter.'

'He's just a guy I hired to help me find my sister.'

Huffman used the razor to cut an imaginary loose thread from his tie.

'Just a guy?' He thought of all the death and destruction that the *guy* had caused in Kentucky. 'How did you find him?'

'He advertises. I called him. Simple as that.'

'Please don't lie to me, Kate.' Huffman cupped the razor in his palm again. He went behind her and laid the hand on her shoulder. The steel was like a sliver of ice against her flesh. Kate tried not to shiver, but he could feel the tension in her body. 'You knew him before this.'

'No. I've just met him.'

'Where?'

'New York.'

Huffman teased a lock of Kate's hair with his fingers.

'If he's from New York, what were you doing in Florida?' Kate slowly moved her head so that her hair was pulled from between his fingertips. 'I've checked.

You flew from Tampa to Little Fork. Before that you flew from New York alone. He's not from New York, Kate, he's from Florida, isn't he?'

'He met me in Florida. He had other business there.'

Huffman clucked his tongue. 'Why are you protecting him, Kate? If he's just some P.I. you hired, why all the lies?' He plucked at the lock of hair again. 'Are you lovers?'

'No.' She wrenched her head aside. Huffman followed with his hand, and this time he gripped her hair tighter. 'I told you, I just met him,' Kate said.

'You seem angry. Is it because I'm touching you, or could I have hit a raw nerve?'

'We're not lovers,' Kate spat out. 'Why would you think that?'

'Oh, just the impression I got when I spoke to him on the phone.'

'You spoke to him?' Kate's voice was barely above a whisper. 'What did he say?'

Huffman smiled. Kate was a police officer. She'd been trained to deal with difficult situations like this. Ordinarily he'd struggle to get anything from a cop, which was why he was appealing more to her private side. He felt a tremor flood through her. He knew that there was much more to Joe Hunter than she was admitting to.

'He wants you back. Doesn't that strike you as strange . . . seeing as you just met?'

'I'm paying him to find my sister. I'm his meal ticket. Of course he wants me back.'

'Oh, there's more to it than that, Kate. It's obvious that Hunter cares for you. I think that you care for him as well. Therefore I believe you know much more about him than you're telling.'

Kate shook her head, but the movement was too rehearsed.

'I've told you—'

'That you only just met?' Huffman dropped his hand to her shoulder again. He allowed the flat of his razor to trace the line of her collarbone. 'Yes, you did tell me that. But sometimes people can't deny the attraction. Call me an old romantic, Kate: I believe in love at first sight.'

Kate didn't answer. Huffman allowed his blade to drift lower so it rested on the swell of her breasts. Turning the razor ever so slightly it snicked through a strap on her bra. The bra slipped, displaying the dark edge of an areola. Kate immediately moved to cover herself, but Huffman tapped her fingers with the blunt side of the blade. He turned to the two guards. They were hard-faced men, not the best of lookers. He'd picked them as Kate's jailers for that very reason.

'Guys,' he said, 'How long have you known the lovely Kate?'

'Couple of hours, boss.'

'Do you think she's beautiful?'

'I'd fuck her,' said one. The other guffawed and added his feelings on the subject.

Huffman returned his attention to Kate. He walked round her slowly. 'Do you see how quickly attractions can be built? Now, I know my friend, Rourke, over there was perhaps a little uncouth, but he illustrates my point.'

'He's a pig! And so are you.'

'Yes. But let's not dwell on it. Tell me about Joe Hunter.'

Kate closed her eyes.

'He's just a guy.'

Huffman placed the razor blade against her jaw. 'If I sliced off your face, would he still want you back?'

The cold steel dug a furrow in her flesh, but Kate tried not to flinch. A single bead of blood welled out. 'He wouldn't get paid. I'm sure that would piss him off.'

Huffman finally walked away from her and she tugged her bra back into place.

'Very noble, Kate,' he said. 'Protecting your man.'

'He's not my man.'

'OK, we seem to have established that. So we'll move on to the next question. Where's Imogen?'

'I don't know.'

From across the room he looked at her again. He folded his hands, and stood like he was contemplating her words. 'That's the first time you haven't lied to me, Kate. It looks like we could be getting somewhere, after all.'

Kate turned her face to the floor, refusing to look at him. Blood trickled from the shallow nick in her jaw, pooling in the hollow of her throat.

Huffman nodded at Rourke. 'What you said a moment ago: if you feel the urge, just make sure she's still breathing afterwards.'

Kate's eyes snapped open.

Huffman shrugged.

'If Hunter's not your man, then you're fair game.'

He turned his back and left the room, closing the door behind him as Kate shouted in denial. Rourke was a pig, but he would help break down the woman until she'd tell him everything. Later he'd return and if she still wasn't forthcoming, maybe he'd reintroduce her to the sharp edge of his razor.

He was one floor up in a short vestibule that led into a large living space. He passed through both and out on to a veranda, where he leaned his elbows on the veranda rail, and looked out at his surroundings: not downtown Dallas, but flat grassland. In the distance was a line of trees that marked the perimeter fence to the ranch. The trees were almost a mile away. Anyone approaching would have to traverse the open space first. He would see Joe Hunter coming.

With Imogen Ballard or without.

He relished the idea of meeting Hunter man to man.

Even if such a distraction was probably counter-productive to his business interests, he was looking forward to taking on a man who'd proven so resourceful up until now. His life as a businessman had taken away the freedom he'd enjoyed when he was the Felitta brothers' enforcer. Back then he could sate his need for violence whenever he desired. But, since he'd swapped his blade for a business portfolio, life had been a little boring. The challenge that Hunter presented made him feel *alive*.

His eyes skated towards the furthest outbuilding on his property. When this place had been a working ranch the building had been in regular use. Back then, beef had been the ranch's main product. More recently, the cuts of meat coming out of that building weren't deemed appropriate to the market and had been scattered on the plains instead. Hunter wouldn't be the first person he'd turned into chopped liver.

26

At Capital City Airport, Frankfort, Larry Bolan had to leave his guns behind. It angered him, but he had no valid reason for carrying the weapons on to an airplane. He didn't have the papers. He hired a strongbox at a nearby storage facility, intending to collect them on his return. Then he took his connecting flight to Dallas Fort Worth, to pick up the trail of the man he would kill. The Magnum would be a miss, but it wasn't an insurmountable problem. He intended killing Joe Hunter with his hands.

Still, he needed a gun.

There were others he might have to kill. Things with them weren't personal, and he didn't mind putting a couple of rounds through them if it helped speed up the process.

He caught a cab from the airport.

'Take me to the nearest roadhouse.'

'You looking for girls?' The driver was a little fat man with a pink face and nicotine-stained fingers. He watched Larry in the rearview mirror.

'Yeah, that's the kind of place I want,' Larry told him. 'Hot, dancing girls.'

'I know just the place.'

Twenty minutes later Larry handed the driver a ten-dollar tip.

He stepped out of the cab and looked across the parking lot at Minnie's. It was the kind of place that came alive at night. Garish neon signs in the shape of voluptuous women would gyrate and entice the punters. There was a rip-off of the Disney character mouse striking a pose, blowing a suggestive kiss over her shoulder, her skirt lifted to show her bare ass. The other signs were the conventional type you saw at places just like this: XXX in bright red; Girls, Girls, Girls in blue. The country music would be loud. The lot would be full of trucks and jeeps and noisy, drunk men. But right now, Minnie's was quiet. There were only two vehicles in the lot, an old Pontiac and a classic model Cadillac. The Cadillac was coffee-coloured, like the one in that old Chuck Berry song. The paint had faded in the Texas sun. Somehow, a latte-coloured Cadillac didn't have the same ring to it.

'Minnie's is never shut,' the cab driver said, leaning an elbow out the window. 'Just go on round the back, you'll get in that way.'

The cab pulled away, kicking up dust from the lot.

Larry was still wearing the overcoat. It was warm. But he didn't take off the coat: he needed both hands free and didn't want to encumber himself with carrying it. He made do with unbuttoning the jacket and allowing it to hang open. It flared out as he strode towards Minnie's.

The building was a low oblong of wood planks. The

planks had been painted black, but in places the sun had done its work on them and they'd faded to a dull grey. There were no windows at the front. No one inside wanted to shock the sensibilities of less open-minded people passing on the highway. The double doors at the front were shut. A handwritten cardboard sign was tacked to the doors, a bold red arrow pointing to the right. Larry swung that way without breaking stride. His route took him past the two parked cars. He glanced inside both but couldn't see what he wanted. His eye lingered over the Cadillac: cool car.

Round back he was greeted by a closed door and two minders who looked like tough guys – big men, muscular and tattooed. Larry Bolan dwarfed them, put them to shame. They didn't block his way. One of them even opened the door for him.

Larry stepped into a room as black as the building looked from outside. The tables were scattered at random, set round a raised stage where the strippers would dance. Across the room he saw a light above a bar. A woman was standing behind the bar, watching TV with the volume turned off. Carrie Underwood was singing her latest hit, lip-synching with the music coming from speakers round the stage. The woman didn't look at Larry.

He took in the other customers.

There were only a half-dozen guys in the room. One old man sat alone, nursing a drink. The other five were in a booth at the back of the room.

'Jackpot,' Larry said to himself.

He ignored the guy sitting alone, he ignored the woman at the bar, and he walked directly to the five men. These were the kind of men Larry had come looking for. They were all relaxed, sprawling in their chairs. Bottles of beer were scattered across the table. They watched his approach with their hard eyes like his presence didn't bother them. But Larry knew otherwise.

He deliberately stood very close to the table, looking down on them, so that he invaded their personal space.

He looked from each face to the next. They all looked back.

'Who do I speak with?'

'That would be me,' said the man sitting at the centre of the group. Larry guessed that would be the case. The leader of the group had two guards on each side, protected. He was in his late twenties, thickset with short black hair. He looked like there was Native American somewhere in his blood. The men either side of him were younger by a few years, boys playing at being men.

Straight to the point. 'I want guns.'

'Are you a cop?' asked the leader.

'Do I look like a goddamn cop to you?'

'What makes you think I have guns?'

Larry just stared.

This guy was the resident ball-breaker. Places like Minnie's always had them, men who protected the strippers from unwanted advances. Unwanted advances meaning 'free'. You wanted a private show, you paid this guy.

'How much are you willing to part with?'

'Depends on what you've got for me.'

The man looked like he was weighing up his decision, but Larry knew it was all show. Larry turned and started walking away. 'Forget it. I'll take my money somewhere else.'

'Hold up.'

Larry heard the table being moved, the legs scraping on the wooden floor. He stopped and turned. The leader was standing, his four minders flanking him. 'Let's not be so hasty, huh? You want guns, I've got them. Why go anywhere else?'

'I ain't messing around. You want to do a deal, we do it quickly.' Larry patted a bulge in his breast pocket.

The man gestured towards a door next to the bar. 'Come with me.'

Larry followed the man. The other four crowded him. Larry stopped, looked each of them in the eye. 'My business is with the man. Back off, boys.'

They were like terriers circling a bear. Alone they were no threat, but together they thought they had what it took to bring him down. They puffed out their chests, readied themselves.

Larry chose the nearest man to him. He was the largest of the group, scar-faced, with a hoop earring hanging from his left lobe and a squint in one eye. He looked like he had lost a few fights in his time. Larry grabbed him by his face and squeezed. He had the man's jaw in the palm of his hand, fingers and thumb digging into the nerves beneath each ear. The man roared in pain. Larry stiff-armed him away and the man crashed backwards against the table they'd recently vacated.

'I said back off.'

There was a moment of hesitation. Things could go one of two ways. There would be extreme violence or they'd give in and cower away. Larry didn't mind the violence. No one moved except for the woman behind the bar: she scurried away to the far end.

Then the leader barked at his friends, 'What the hell you doing? There's a guy here with good money to spend. Get the hell out of his way, will ya?'

He waved Larry after him as though nothing had happened. Larry went through the door and shut it behind him. He thought that when he opened it again, those guys, plus the two from the door, would probably be waiting.

He was in a storage area. There were crates of bottled beer and liquor, cleaning fluids and mops. Other things Larry merely skimmed over. The leader went through another door and flicked on a light. They were in a small cubicle not much larger than the prison cell Larry had once called home. A window at the back of the room was boarded over. It was furnished with a table and two chairs, cheap plastic with metal legs. On the table was a stained coffee mug. There was also a steel cabinet. The man dug in the pocket of his trousers for a chain, came out with a bunch of keys, then opened the cabinet.

'You called Tito?'

The man froze, then looked at Larry with that wary look of someone waiting for what might be coming next.

Larry indicated the coffee mug. On it were printed the words *Tito's Mug*.

Tito laughed. 'Yeah. One of the girls gave me it as a present. Grateful for my services, if you get my meaning?'

Larry was nonplussed by the sentiment.

Tito turned back to the cabinet and pulled out a wooden box, using another key from his chain to unlock it.

Larry studied the guns inside.

'The Taurus is no good to me.' It was a five-shot Saturday Night Special, too small for his hand. 'I'll take the other two.'

Tito pulled out the two semi-automatic handguns. The first was a Dan Wesson from the Pointman series in the 1911 style, seven shot, .45 calibre. It was blued steel with a rosewood grip. It was still small compared to Larry's hand, but big enough to kill so would do as a back-up weapon. But he was more interested in the second gun. It was a Desert Eagle Mark XIX. It took nine .357 Magnum bullets and had a ten-inch barrel, almost twice the size and weight of the Dan Wesson. His kind of gun.

'You have ammo?'

Tito pulled out two boxes and placed them next to the guns.

'How much for them both?'

'Two thousand bucks. I'll throw in the ammo for free.'

'I could buy them new for that.'

'You could. But then you'd have to register. Then –

assuming there's no reason you can't have them – you'd have to wait while your application was cleared. You don't strike me as the type of man who's willing to wait.'

Larry growled, then tugged out his billfold.

'Fifteen hundred. Final offer.'

Tito shook his head slowly, like he was aggrieved. But Larry recognized the greed in his eyes when he zoned in on Larry's cash. Larry peeled off fifteen hundred dollars and placed them on the table. They made a considerable stack of notes.

While Tito counted the money, Larry fed rounds into the Desert Eagle. He pushed the Dan Wesson into his coat pocket, the spare ammo into the opposite one.

'Are your boys going to be waiting on me on the other side of that door, Tito?'

Tito pushed the roll of notes into his trouser pocket.

'Not my style.'

'Shame,' Larry told him with a smile. 'I'll just have to wait and try the guns out later.'

27

I was alone in a rental car: a discreet light blue Saturn SL1, the model affectionately known as the 'gas saver'. Rink and Harvey had their own rental and were staying clear of me. They were the ace in my sleeve, and we wanted to keep things that way as long as possible.

We'd travelled north from Dallas, up toward Ray Roberts Lake, then swung east at a small town called Pilot Point. Then we'd struck out on minor roads into farm land that stretched away toward the Oklahoma state line. My car came with a GPS location finder, but it was pretty useless out here in a landscape where there were only fields and small wooded areas. The synthesised voice kept exhorting me to turn round and go back the way I'd come. In the end I switched it off. Robert Huffman's personal abode wasn't the easiest place to find.

I kept in touch with my friends via cell phone. They were on average a mile behind me. If anything happened, it could take them time to reach me. However, in most places out here on the flatlands, you could see all the way to the horizon. At any second I could be in the sights of Huffman or any of his people. One car passing through might not seem suspicious, but two in close convoy would attract attention.

Back at the motel outside Arlington, Harvey had done some digging on his laptop. From the registered business address for Huffman's property development company, he was able to track down the list of properties owned by Huffman. There were many, but one in particular stood out from the list: Quicksilver Ranch. Guessing that Huffman was the narcissistic type, it didn't take much concluding that the ranch would be a good place to start our hunt for him. The ranch was very remote. If I was holding someone prisoner, I would have chosen a place just like it. No one would hear the screams. Plus, it was easily defended. No one could approach within a mile without giving themselves away.

Harvey had Googled the location. I memorised the directions. It should have been easy: according to the map, there was only one way in and one way out. The trouble was finding that actual road. This area didn't get that many tourists. There didn't appear to be a need for road signs. The only hint that any dwellings were hidden over the horizon was the occasional mailbox fixed to a post at the entrance to a trail. Many of the trails were nothing but two lines of flattened grass. And there were sometimes miles between each.

I kept on driving.

Fields were spread out on each side of the road. The grass was turning brown now that winter was on its way.

Herds of cattle grazed in the distance. The cows had long horns, unlike the breeds I was familiar with back in England. Their horns reminded me of the set that had been fixed to Larry Bolan's Dodge Ram. I wondered what had become of the big man. But thinking of him also made me recall the way I'd killed Trent. I couldn't blame Larry Bolan for hating me; if he'd killed a brother of mine I'd want him dead too. That was something I'd have to deal with later. I didn't want him haunting me for the rest of my days.

For now I had to concentrate on getting Kate away from Huffman. The only way I could do that would be to find where he was holding her.

I stopped the Saturn.

Jabbed buttons on my phone.

'You'd better hold back,' I told Rink.

'What's up, Hunter?'

'Just stopped to get my bearings.' I stared off across the fields on my left. I knew Quicksilver Ranch was over there somewhere.

'You want me to call in AWAC support?'

Back when we'd been in the forces we'd had high-altitude spy planes and satellite technology to guide us in to targets.

'A compass would have been ample.'

'You can't be far off now,' Rink said. 'Keep going, you'll see it soon.'

Way ahead of me I noted a blur on the horizon. It looked like the tops of trees. Sometimes people fancified gateways by planting trees and shrubbery.

'Wait there, Rink, I'm going on ahead. If I don't find the entrance I'll backtrack.'

Harvey's voice rumbled in the background.

'Damn,' Rink responded. Then to me, 'Heads up, Hunter. There's a chopper headed your way. You'd better get moving. Two parked cars are going to look suspicious.'

'Is it paying you any attention?'

'Yeah. Coming in low. Checking us out.'

Rink went silent. I guessed he'd put down the phone.

I started the Saturn. Then I spun it in the road and began driving back in the opposite direction. It would be less suspicious if I was heading away from the ranch when the chopper came my way.

I could see it off in the distance, a black speck hanging above the road. From this distance I couldn't identify its type. I continued towards it, travelling at a steady fifty miles per hour. No urgency, just someone passing through. I wanted to drive much faster. Any second I expected the flash of a rifle.

But it didn't come.

The chopper banked, started skimming the land towards me.

Rink came back on the phone.

'They checked us out good, Hunter. Two guys. They weren't looking for us, but they might pay you a little more interest. We'll start heading your way. Just in case.'

'Yeah,' I said. 'But travel steady. There's no need to worry, yet.'

Ringing off, I pulled my SIG out of my waistband and placed it on the seat next to me. Then I reached across to the passenger side for a baseball cap I'd brought with me which I pulled down on my head. A more obvious disguise would probably warrant further inspection. Supposing that the men in the chopper were employees of Huffman, they would be going by physical descriptions given by Judge Wallace, Sheriff Aitken or Larry Bolan. From up in the cockpit of the chopper they'd only get a cursory look at my face. If I played things cool, it should be all right.

Keeping the pressure on the gas pedal at midway, I continued travelling towards them. The chopper crossed the distance much faster. It was identifiable to me now: a Bell Jet Ranger, grey with red flashes on its tail. There was nothing that indicated it belonged to Huffman, discounting the two men inside, who had the stern faces associated with bad men. They scrutinised me with an unhealthy amount of interest.

Playing my part, I smiled at them, waved, kept on going. Watching them in my mirrors, I saw the chopper bank left and swing round after me, then zoom up on my left. The man in the co-pilot seat stared at me. I feigned confusion. The man gestured at me, telling me to take the hat off, so I complied, showing him my fresh buzz cut. Then I frowned, opened my mouth. 'What?'

The guy seemed happy enough with that. He shook his head at me, turned to the pilot, and the chopper flew on ahead. Dust swirled in my vision, then the chopper rose up in the air and I was under it and away.

Searching for it in my mirrors, I saw it heading east, towards the copse of trees I'd noticed earlier. I guessed I'd found Huffman's hiding place.

Looking ahead, I could see Rink and Harvey approaching in their Ford Windstar mini-van.

We slowed and came to a halt so we could speak through our windows.

'I take it that Huffman's expecting you,' Rink said.

'Looks that way,' I said. 'But we've got a problem now. If I turn back that way, the men in the chopper might get suspicious. They might not be as easily put off next time.'

'So how do you want to play things? Do you want to head towards Pilot Point? We'll go on and scope out the place.'

'No, I think we've done enough for now. We'll fall back to Pilot Point. Come back again tonight.'

'They've seen us as well,' Harvey said. 'Maybe we should continue this way, loop round and come in from the north. We'll see you back at the lake house.'

Harvey's suggestion made sense. Maybe the chopper would be lying in wait ahead, watching for them. If they didn't show up in the next few minutes, the men would probably come looking for them again. Maybe this time there'd be a face to face meeting. The men from the chopper would probably end up dead. But I didn't want Rink and Harvey thrown into the mix yet. I wanted to keep them in reserve for when I went in to take Kate back.

'Easy as it goes, guys,' I said. 'Avoid contact if you can.'

Rink winked and gave me his shit-eating grin.

Harvey pulled away and I watched them go. Then I started my car and drove towards the lakeside cabin we'd set up as our base.

I wasn't too disappointed. This trip had always been a simple matter of reconnaissance. And I'd seen enough for now. The presence of the chopper meant that Huffman was home and waiting for me to arrive.

'See you later, Quicksilver,' I said.

Driving a little faster than before, I followed the same long road back to Pilot Point. To pass the time, I thought about Kate. I pictured her walking along the sand as she approached me that first time, her sandals bumping her hip with each step of her long legs. I thought of her drinking Corona straight from the bottle and how a drip had run down her chin and into the hollow of her throat. The bead of liquid had shivered in time with her pulse. As early as then I was attracted to her.

When Kate kissed me at the motel at Little Fork I'd played it cool. I kidded myself that I was being professional. I couldn't afford to be distracted. Really I was feeling a little guilty. Eighteen years to the day, Diane had kissed me in a similar way. We were standing in front of the vicar and had just said our vows. Till death do us part, we'd sworn. I suppose that in my heart there'd always be a place for my ex-wife, but Rink was right, I didn't have to be a monk all my life.

My thoughts drifted to my conversation with Rink when I'd phoned him after dumping Larry Bolan's truck that first time.

He had asked me if I had a thing for Kate. I'd denied it and Rink had admonished me. He knew exactly what was going through my head.

'I can't let things distract me, Rink,' I'd argued. 'I start paying more attention to her pretty face, I miss the gun pointing at her head.'

If I'd heeded those words, maybe I wouldn't have missed the Land Rover speeding across the field on my right now.

The first I knew of its presence was when a bullet shattered my window and buried itself in the instrument panel in front of me.

Immediately I went into defensive mode. I pressed the gas pedal to the floor and the car shot forwards. It made it all the way up to eighty miles per hour, but that was it. I'd picked the nondescript car for its ability to blend, not for speed. It wasn't known as the *gas saver* for nothing.

Behind me, the Land Rover bounced over the verge and on to the road behind me. Looking in the rear-view, I could make out two men inside it. One of them was intent on driving, while the other hung out of the passenger window aiming a rifle.

Apparently my disguise hadn't worked as well as I'd thought.

Attesting to that fact was the grey and red chopper

racing in from the right. The passenger in the chopper had an automatic rifle as well.

Superior machinery, superior numbers and superior weapons. How the hell do I get out of this fix?

28

Tito was true to his word, but Larry Bolan wondered how long that would last. When Larry came out of the back room and through the storage area into the dimly lit bar, Tito's four friends had returned to their seats around the table. They were talking among themselves. As Larry made his way across the room, passing the raised stage, the man he'd stiff-armed was scowling, but the others only watched him with mild distraction. He nodded at them and they all nodded back. The scowling man made it look like he was trying to regain face with his buddies, his nod accompanied by a curled lip.

Larry laughed then turned away. He could hear the others laughing, and it wasn't at him.

Boys will be boys.

Tito was walking behind Larry. It was as if he wanted to see the big man off the premises. He made it look like he was happy with the fifteen hundred dollars, but maybe he hadn't quite taken Larry's joke at face value, which was wise, because Larry hadn't been joking.

Larry caught Tito's reflection in a chrome surround

on the doorway. Tito was looking back at his friends and there was a lot of gesturing going on.

Larry felt for the Desert Eagle, but then let it go.

Tito stepped past Larry, pushing the double doors open with the flats of his hands. The doors banged, startling the two minders who were lounging outside. Both men came to attention, swinging into battle readiness. Then they saw who was coming out and they faltered.

Tito jerked his head at them.

'Chill out, guys,' he told them. 'My friend's leaving.'

Larry watched the men's faces. He saw a paleness creep into one of their throats, a slight widening of the eyes of the other. They were signs of apprehension, and not because they weren't going to be doing their duty. Tito's words were some sort of prearranged signal. Larry heard faint footsteps from inside. Tito came to a standstill, and Larry went on by him. Tito tapped Larry's elbow and Larry glanced back. Tito stuck out a hand. 'It was a pleasure doing business with you.'

The way they were standing, Larry would have to turn his back on the two minders to take Tito's hand. But he was OK with that.

'Yeah,' Larry agreed, taking the hand.

He'd given up his back, but the disadvantage was negated by the fact that he could now see the four men approaching from inside the bar.

Larry smiled down at Tito.

He heard the shift of feet behind him.

'You made some good money back there, Tito. You should've left things at that.'

Then he hauled Tito by the hand towards him. He pivoted, whipping Tito around and off his feet and directly into the two minders. Tito crashed into them, stalling them, and Larry threw a right cross over the top of him, crunching his fist into the face of the minder on the left. Larry felt the power in his arm as it transferred to the man's jaw. It was like an explosion of kinetic force that compressed the man's jaw up into his skull. If that man wasn't dead, he was going to be taking his meals through a tube for a long time. He dropped straight down, his upper body folding over the top of Tito and taking them both to the floor.

The second minder stumbled, his legs entangled among those of his friends. Larry reached for him, grabbing the man by his shirt, and tugged him free of the mêlée of limbs. The man was above average size, but in Larry's hands he was a child. Larry hauled him straight up and off his feet, pivoted again and threw him against the wall next to the open doors. Larry rammed his knee between the minder's legs, even as he reached with one hand and pushed the nearest door closed. From inside came shouts of dismay, and suddenly the other four were charging forwards. Larry dragged the minder with him, placing the man between him and Tito's four friends. Two of them had handguns, the other two had knives, but none of them could use them. Larry slammed the other door in their faces.

The minder was winded from his manhandling, but not finished. Foolishly, in Larry's estimation, he threw a punch at Larry's jaw. Larry dipped and the man's fist hit the side of his head high up near the crown. The man probably broke his fist, but Larry didn't wait to find out. He slammed the man's head repeatedly against the closed door, the sound echoing the frantic banging coming from the other side. Blood had spattered all over the wood by the time Larry allowed the man to slip to the floor.

There was a hasp and padlock on the door. They were probably used at night when the front doors were open to the public. Larry threw the hasp and clicked the padlock in place.

Then he turned to Tito.

He'd finally fought free from under his unconscious friend. But he'd only made it up to his knees by the time Larry leaned in and grabbed him round the throat with one big hand.

Tito's face showed that he was terrified by what had just gone down. But he was supposed to be the hard-ass around here. 'Do you know who you are fucking with?' he demanded.

'The hooker was right getting you that present,' Larry grinned at him. 'But she got the words wrong. It should have said Tito *is* a mug.'

Tito tried tugging at Larry's wrist, but he'd have been as well trying to tear a wolf's jaws from his throat. Then he went for the gun tucked in his trousers. Larry grabbed the wrist of Tito's gun hand and dragged the arm to his side. He was holding Tito in the exact same fashion as he'd held Joe Hunter yesterday. He'd made a mistake that time, and Trent had died. There'd be no mistakes now.

Twisting the gun hand, he heard the bones in Tito's forearm grinding together. The man began to scream through clamped jaws. Agony was in his face. Larry twisted even further and the bones began cracking, making sounds as if the man's arm was going through a wringer. The gun dropped from his deadened fingers. At the same time Larry squeezed his other fingers together. Cartilage popped. Blood flecked Tito's lips with each harsh gasp.

'You ain't as tough as you think you are, Tito,' Larry said. Then he hauled him up, transferring his hand from wrist to crotch so that he had Tito extended above his head as if he was a barbell. He held him there for a long three count while the man squirmed, then Larry threw him down. He barely felt a twinge in the wound in his shoulder – that was the amped-up power of adrenalin for you, he thought.

Tito hit the floor flat on his back, almost as though Larry had slammed him directly through the pavement. He didn't move. But Larry wasn't finished. He lifted a heel and stamped on the man's chest for good measure. Wind whooshed between Tito's teeth, but there was no corresponding intake of breath afterwards. His sightless eyes rolled back in his skull.

Larry leaned down, dug a hand into Tito's pocket and extracted the fifteen hundred dollars. He also picked up Tito's weapon. A girlie Glock 19, but still another worthy back-up weapon. Then he tugged out Tito's keychain and inspected the keys. He smiled.

He drove the Cadillac out of the lot just as the other four men came boiling through the front doors. Larry shouted wordlessly at them, flipping them the middle finger as he shot by. The two with guns lifted them, but didn't shoot. Next second they dropped the guns by their sides and ran round Minnie's to check on their boss. Larry wondered which one of them would be the new resident ball-breaker if he ever passed this way again. Maybe the one with the squint eye, he thought. God help us!

He drove the Cadillac east towards Dallas.

The car was a tank, but it was a reliable old workhorse and it covered the miles easily. Larry thought over what had just gone down. He was well armed now. Other than his cab fare and tip to the driver, he hadn't spent a cent. If Tito hadn't been such a greedy asshole it would have been different. But Larry had known from the second he pulled out his wad of notes that Tito wouldn't be happy until he'd taken it all away. In the end, his greed cost him everything: the guns, the money, the Cadillac, and probably his life.

He sent the Cadillac plodding north, up the 35E, and joined route 77 past Lewisville Lake and Corinth, then headed east at Denton to pick up the road that would take him up to Pilot Point and into Grayson County. He'd been there before, running shotgun with Jim Aitken. That time he'd travelled with Aitken in one of Huffman's private jets, but he wasn't complaining. The Cadillac was a cool set of wheels. He was on his way to Quicksilver Ranch. Exactly the place he expected to run into Joe Hunter.

29

I've trained in defensive driving. It's standard for any soldier engaged in counterterrorism, but on those occasions I was generally driving a bullet-proof sedan, or a hummer or jeep. In comparison the Saturn was like cheesecloth on wheels. The men firing at me could have been throwing stones and they'd have still put holes in the ten-year-old car.

The men in the Land Rover seemed more intent on putting bullets in me than those in the chopper did. They preferred to use the helicopter to bring me to a halt. The pilot kept dropping the chopper into my line of vision, forcing me – they hoped – to swerve or brake. I just aimed the Saturn directly at them; they weren't going to wait until I crashed into them – they wanted to be paid for killing me and the cash would be no good to them if they were dead too.

Eighty miles an hour turned out to be more than fast enough. Even on a smooth blacktop it's a reckless speed if you're swerving to avoid a 4×4 attempting to ram you. On this road, where there were as many potholes as there were patches of asphalt, it forced me to slow down to sixty just to stop the car flipping and rolling. As it was, the Saturn bounced along the trail, kicking up dust and gravel in its wake.

The rifleman in the 4×4 kept up a steady volley of shots. The back window was history after the first two bullets and there were holes through the passenger seat now. I should have fired back at them, but I hadn't yet.

My SIG was right there on the seat beside me, but for the time being it was prudent to keep both my hands on the steering wheel. I kept moving, heading west, trying to lead my pursuers back to an area where I could defend myself.

South Highway 377, the road from Pilot Point to Collinsville, was somewhere ahead of me, but right then all I had were fields and the occasional stand of trees. Nothing I could use as cover from the chopper or where I could lose the men in the more powerful Land Rover. I needed built-up streets and brick walls. But I had grass and trees and herds of cattle.

Risking taking my hands off the wheel, I jabbed the speed dial on my phone. My words to my friends were straight to the point, 'Guys, I need you back here now!'

'On our way,' Rink said in return, and I heard the sounds of Harvey spinning the Windstar in the road.

'I've two in a Land Rover and the chopper's back and they all have rifles,' I shouted over the roar of the Saturn's tyres on loose dirt.

That was it as far as the report went. Rink and Harvey would be coming after me now. The only problem was there were probably four or five miles between us. Even if I stopped now, it would take them too long to get back to help me. I had to do something to slow the pursuit, while keeping myself alive.

First thing I did was hit the brakes. The Saturn screeched along the road, back end fishtailing, sending up clouds of dirt. The Land Rover roared in, its front grille ramming into the back of my car. The Saturn leaped forwards at the collision, back wheels bouncing and grabbing the earth for traction, and I dropped gear and pressed the throttle to the floor. As I raced on, I searched for the Land Rover in my mirrors and saw that it was concealed in the cloud of dust. That was good, because it meant they couldn't see me. I braked again, pushed forwards immediately after. Another gout of dirt rose up into the air. Immediately I braked, twisting on the steering wheel, sending the Saturn in a sidelong skid. As soon as the car came to a shuddering halt, I snatched up my SIG and leaped out the door.

I was no sooner clear of the Saturn than the Land Rover rocketed out of the cloud of dust. I had a split second of eye contact with the driver before it hit my car. The Saturn was blasted into smithereens, huge chunks of metal erupting as though a grenade had gone off inside. Something hit me on my shoulder, spinning me to the floor. But even as I went down, I was twisting like a cat, bringing round my gun. I saw the Land Rover rise up into the air, the front wheels caught on the wreckage of my car. Then it continued upwards, and began to list to one side. The list became a full roll to the side and the Land Rover went through a complete torque before crashing to the earth. The heavy vehicle didn't stop. It hit the soft verge and rolled again, and kept on rolling. This time it was the 4×4 casting off large chunks of metal. I saw the passenger flung from the wreckage, wheeling his way across the grass, his body a series of disjointed shapes that didn't resemble a human being any longer. I couldn't tell what had become of the driver, but I hoped he'd be as dead as the rifleman.

Coming painfully to my feet, I searched the sky for the helicopter. Dust and smoke obscured my view. There was a terrible stench in the air, a mix of fuel and burning plastic and eviscerated bodies. I could hear the chopper, but I couldn't see it. That meant they couldn't see me either. Stooping, I ran for the wrecked 4×4. I searched for the dropped rifle but couldn't locate it. All I found was the driver hung up in his seat belt. Blood covered his face, but his eyes were open. He was dazed, but he caught movement in his peripheral vision and snapped his face towards me. I didn't know the man, had never seen him before, but right then we were mortal enemies. He was a professional hit man who was trying to kill me. I shot him once between his eyes. It was cold, yes, but I couldn't leave him alive.

I looked for the rifleman who'd been thrown from the wreckage. He was a steaming bundle thirty yards away. He wasn't moving. So I turned my attention back to the chopper.

I didn't have long to wait.

The chopper came roaring overhead and I was battered by the downwash of its rotor blades. Smoke from the demolished vehicles swirled round me. I used the cover to run back to the other side of the 4×4. Lifting my gun, I fired two rounds through the undercarriage. Chances of hitting the pilot were slim, but I needed them to move away from me so I could get a clear shot. Two 9 mm Parabellums through the body of the craft did the trick. The chopper swooped away, heading to a distance of a hundred yards or so before the pilot swung it round. The rifleman was now facing me and he fired a round. The bullet passed directly through the body of the 4×4. Then it continued on and I swear I felt the heat of its passing.

Rising from a crouch, I fired at the rifleman. It was a hurried shot and I didn't expect it to hit. But as the rifleman flinched back inside the craft, I scurried to the far end of the wreck. His next round went through the space I'd just vacated. I waited. I could see the chopper through a gap in the wreckage begin to drift towards me. Holding my breath, I aimed my SIG, waiting for just the right moment.

Then something happened that I didn't expect. The helicopter dropped so that it was only a yard or so above the field. A side door was thrown open and two men jumped to the floor. They immediately fanned out, then they dropped to crouches, levelling M16 assault rifles at the wreckage I was behind.

My guess was that after the first two had checked me out, they had realised I was the man they were looking for and had hurried away for extra firepower. The two in the 4×4 had possibly been out at the perimeter of

Huffman's land watching for anyone coming in that way and the chopper pilot had directed them to me. They thought that six men had more chance of taking me than two. They were probably right.

I wondered how far away Rink and Harvey were.

Too far.

Then I had no more time for idle thought because the two on the ground opened up with the assault rifles and the wreckage around me was being torn to shreds. I flattened myself to the ground, began rolling side-over-side, keeping as low a profile as possible. Hot metal churned the air. A lot of the rounds were stopped by the wreckage, but as many were getting through. Bullets punched the earth close to me. All I could do was to continue rolling and trust to some higher being to get me out of there alive.

I made it to a shallow ditch at the shoulder of the road, dropped into it, and then began crawling as quickly as I could out of the line of fire.

The two men were inching forwards, continuing to unload rounds through the 4×4. Some of their bullets must have been tearing the dead driver to pieces: that only showed me how determined these killers were to finish me. The chopper took off again, flying high, the pilot taking a look to see if I was dead before the two on the ground would move in.

Catch 22. I could fire at the chopper, or I could fire at the men on the ground. Either way I'd give up my position and the others would vector in on me. If I stayed where I was and did nothing, the chopper crew would see that I'd moved away and it would only take them seconds to find me again. Then the men with the assault rifles would move in to flank me and I'd be back to square one. Whatever way I looked at things my position was pretty dire.

Snatching a quick glance along the road, I hoped to see a Windstar heading my way, but the road remained empty. It was down to me to get out of this alive.

Pulling out the Glock 17 I'd liberated from the man I'd shot at the restaurant, I readied myself. In a situation like this, I could only hope to even up the firepower a little. I raised my head just high enough to see what was going on.

The chopper passed over the 4×4, turning slowly in place as the rifleman strafed the ground where I'd been hiding. The smoke boiling from the wreck was still my ally, but that would only last until the downwash blew it apart. Rising up quickly, I fired at the rifleman. My bullet hit him, cutting a chunk from his left shoulder. The man bobbed back inside the craft and the pilot must have grabbed at the controls, as the chopper dipped violently away.

I'd hoped to kill the rifleman in the chopper, force the pilot to keep well away from another shot, effectively halving the odds against me. But I'd only winged the bastard. Cursing under my breath, I looked for the men on the ground. One of them was hidden by the smoke, but I saw the other running at a tangent across the field, seeking to cut me off. Firing at him, I forced him to the ground. The man rolled as I'd done earlier. Then on his belly he returned fire. He looked like he had military experience. I fired again and my round dug a clod of earth from in front of him, causing him to jerk back.

Immediately I began crawling again. Worst-case scenario was being caught in this ditch with a man armed with an assault rifle at either end while a third gunman hovered overhead. Making it to a point east of where the nearest man was, I again swung up on to the edge of the ditch, firing at him. As I'd been moving, so had the man. He was ten yards closer now. He fired at me; a burst of sustained fire. The earth and grass around me exploded, dirt pushing into my eyes, making me fall back down into the ditch. The son of a bitch was a decent soldier. Quickly I scrambled away. Then I rolled on to my back. The second gunman was coming along the ditch towards me.

We both fired.

A bullet scorched my left thigh but my bullet caught him directly in his stomach. The man doubled over, his forward run bringing him closer to me. He crashed to the ground and his M16 flew from his hand. He wasn't dead yet. He scrambled to grab at a sidearm strapped to his hip. I put another round through his head and this time he fell still.

Glancing at his assault rifle, I considered going for it. But then the whine of the chopper was over me again and I heard the thump of running feet and knew that the other gunman was charging at me. I was still on my back, a prone target for either of the men bringing their guns to bear on me.

The man on the ground had more chance of killing me first. I aimed both my guns at him. It was awkward, holding the guns over my head and firing backwards, but I saw that he was forced to leap to one side. It would only be seconds until he was back though. I was seriously deep in it, I realised.

The helicopter screamed over me, and I put a couple of bullets through its belly. Then I snatched my attention back to the man on the ground. I saw him rise up, his M16 raised to his shoulder. There was a gleam of satisfaction in his eyes. He caressed the trigger. Then I saw something else in his face. Indecision. He glanced to his side. The barrel of his assault rifle swung with his gaze.

A millisecond later his head disappeared under a welter of blood as a high-velocity round tore through it.

Thank God, my friends are here at last.

The man died instantly, but his brain's last command had been to pull the trigger of his gun. Rounds blasted from the M16, but they were ineffectual as they drove into the dirt next to the road. A second or so later the man's knees collapsed under him and he pitched chest down on the floor.

Now there was only the rifleman in the chopper to worry about. The chopper was out of my line of sight, but I could hear the crack of the rifle. A gun boomed in response and there was a scream and the sound of someone falling heavily to the earth. The same gun boomed again, a steady roll of thunder, and the pitch of the helicopter's engine changed. I sat up and saw the chopper banking away, trailing smoke from its fuselage. It headed north away from my position. The chopper was losing altitude all the time, and I wondered how long it would be until the engines gave out and it plummeted to the ground. A few seconds later came a distant *whumph!* and more smoke tinged the Texas skyline.

I grinned.

I turned round, looking for Rink and Harvey.

But they weren't my saviours.

Larry Bolan was.

30

There was nothing that Larry Bolan desired more than to have Joe Hunter dead at his feet. The only problem was that he hadn't planned to have it this way. He wanted to hurt the man first. Hurt him badly. To shoot Hunter while he was lying in a ditch at the side of a field in the middle of nowhere just didn't sit right with him.

He'd driven here with no firm plan in mind. If Huffman knew he had killed Jim Aitken and Judge Wallace he'd hardly greet him with open arms. On the contrary, the men that Huffman had brought in to stop Hunter would be set against Larry if he showed up at Huffman's door. Anyone with sense would steer clear of Quicksilver Ranch.

But Larry had a good reason for heading to Huffman's place. He knew that Huffman would have brought Kate Piers here. Joe Hunter had proven to be *capable* back in Little Fork, and Larry had quite correctly surmised that Hunter would head here too.

He just hadn't thought he'd find him so soon.

Larry had seen the smoke first. Then the chopper circling like a vulture scoping out the land for food.

He even heard the rattle of gunfire over the constant rumble of the old Cadillac's wheels on the rutted road. It didn't take a genius to figure out what was going on.

Speeding along the road, he'd seen the chopper drop low and deposit two guys with machine-guns on the ground. The guys had spread out, rattling bullets through a crashed Land Rover. There was the wreckage of a second vehicle on the road ahead.

Larry had stopped the Cadillac, and, using the far shoulder of the road as cover from the men on the ground, he'd raced the last hundred yards or so towards the wreckage. The car was too mangled to be recognisable, but enough was left for him to use it as a shield to move closer. No one noticed him. They were too intent on a target scrambling along a ditch on the other shoulder of the road. Larry only got flashes of the figure crawling away from him, but he knew it could be only one man. He could feel it like a lodestone drawn to a magnet: the man in the ditch was Trent's murderer.

Larry saw one of the gunmen charge round the Land Rover and jump into the ditch. Hunter hadn't seen him. He was trading rounds with the other man who was approaching from the other side. Larry almost rose up to shoot the running gunman, but then he saw blood punch out of the man's body as he staggered and fell. Another round barked and the man didn't get up. Larry raised his eyebrows. He had to change his estimation of Joe Hunter – he was proving more than capable.

Then he decided, no, he's as easily killed as any man. The second gunman had seized the moment to aim his

M16 assault rifle directly at Hunter. Plus the chopper was racing in and another man with a rifle was getting a bead on Hunter's prone body.

Larry didn't have more than a second to decide. He wasn't about to let any of Huffman's punks have the satisfaction of finishing Hunter. Hunter was his to kill.

'Hey!'

The man with the assault rifle glanced up. He saw the Desert Eagle pointing at him and Larry blasted his head right off. The Desert Eagle was a piece of work, he decided.

The guy in the chopper snapped his gaze from the dead man, looking for where Larry crouched behind the wreckage. Larry shot him too. The Magnum load ripped a hole out of the rifleman, low down in his groin. The man's legs went out from under him and he fell screaming from the chopper. He landed, boneless, on the earth and didn't move again.

The chopper pilot got a good look at Larry. If the chopper got away, then Huffman would definitely be pissed with Larry. He fired at the pilot. But the man had pulled on the controls, swinging the chopper away. Not that it mattered: the bullet from the Desert Eagle smashed through the engine casing and the chopper lost power as smoke began blowing from the hole. Larry watched as it lost height and caromed into the field where its rotors snapped off and the body rolled over twice and then erupted into a massive fireball. The pilot wouldn't be telling tales to Huffman now.

Quickly Larry marched out from behind the wreck,

moving purposefully towards where Hunter lay in the ditch. He'd have to be careful. Hunter was armed. He looked like he was damn good with that pistol too. However, Larry had one big advantage. Hunter wouldn't be expecting him.

Larry pointed the gun directly at Hunter's head.

'Drop your weapons, punk,' Larry growled.

Hunter's face was a picture.

'Now, asshole. I won't tell you again.'

Hunter exhaled, but he didn't put down his guns.

He swung them quicker than Larry could follow so that both barrels were aiming back at him. Hunter sat up.

'You put down your weapon,' Hunter said.

Larry's smile was slow to form.

'This isn't the way I want things,' Larry said.

'Pity,' Hunter said. 'It's the way it is.'

'So what do we do now? Shoot each other?'

'Looks that way, doesn't it?'

'Sure does.'

But neither of them fired.

Larry didn't waver from his target.

'You killed my brother.'

'I did,' Hunter agreed. 'He was trying to kill me. So were you, Larry.'

Larry nodded very slightly. No getting away from it. The thing was, on those occasions he was being paid to kill Hunter. This time it was personal. He edged an inch closer to the prone man.

'I could shoot you now,' Larry said.

'Not without me shooting you.'

'Is that how you want things to turn out?'

'Personally, I'd rather kill you and get out of this alive, but,' Hunter smiled thinly, 'if there's nothing for it . . . so be it.'

'A fatalist, huh?'

'Realist.'

'So what do we do about it?'

'Start shooting or walk away, Larry.' Hunter wormed a leg beneath himself. 'Walk away and we'll do this another time.'

'You think I'm going to do that? So you can shoot me in the back?'

'That'd be the coward's way. I'm no coward. Anyway, I owe you, Larry. You just saved my life.'

'I saved you so I could rip you apart at my leisure.'

'I know that. But you aren't going to get any satisfaction if I put a slug in your head first.'

Larry considered that. Hunter was right. What if he fired and Hunter got him first? Maybe his goddamn gun would jam. What kind of half-assed revenge would that be? Personally, he didn't care if he died as long as Hunter died too, but how would he know for sure?

He squinted along the road at a low dark shape headed their way.

'Another time, then?'

'Another time.'

Larry stepped back, watching as Hunter came to his feet. He kept his gun trained on Hunter, as Hunter kept both his guns aimed at him. He locked stares with the man. Larry heard the roar of the approaching vehicle. He didn't look away, but he continued to walk steadily backwards.

'Huffman's men are coming,' Larry said. 'Don't go getting yourself killed after all this. You're mine, Hunter.'

'You've got a date, Larry.'

Back at the car wreck, Larry finally turned and jogged towards his Cadillac further along the road. Part of him expected a bullet in the spine, but a more resolute portion of his brain told him that Joe Hunter wasn't going to shoot him like a dog. There was more to Hunter than that: it was like he said, he wasn't a coward. Unlike punks like Tito back at the roadhouse, he wasn't about to try to take Larry from behind. If he'd been that kind of man, he'd have killed him that first time they met in the forest.

Larry eased into the Cadillac, twisted the key in the ignition. The engine roared to life, and Larry spun the car in the road. He looked back and could see a vehicle coming, sending up a cloud of dust in its haste.

'Don't get yourself killed, Hunter,' he said one last time.

Then he drove away.

31

Larry Bolan had been wrong on two major counts. It wasn't Huffman's guys who were driving like crazy men towards me. I recognised the shape of the Ford Windstar and knew that it was Rink and Harvey charging to my rescue. And he was wrong when he allowed his bitter desire to hurt me to get in the way of a clean kill.

I made a big mistake too. I should have shot Bolan the second he turned to run back to the Cadillac. But that isn't in me. Face to face, I'll do what must be done to any enemy, but I'm not going to put a bullet in someone running away. It's a failing for someone engaged in my line of work, but it's also something I'm damn proud of.

Holding my guns at my sides, I watched Larry spin the car round in the road. The Cadillac – a classic model with fins and chrome – was like a huge boat on wheels, and I couldn't imagine where he'd got it. He roared away in a plume of dust. So I turned and watched my friends haring towards me. I stepped out so that I was on the shoulder of the road, and I waved, letting them know I was OK.

Bringing the Windstar to a halt, both Rink and Harvey lurched out of the vehicle. Rink had a pistol-grip Mossberg shotgun in his hands and Harvey came armed with a Glock 17. Both their faces were set. Intent on killing.

'Easy, guys. It's all over.'

'The hell, you say?' Rink surveyed the scene of devastation all around us. Three vehicles destroyed and six men dead. 'We leave you alone for five minutes and . . . well . . . just look at this! You're hoggin' all the fun yourself.'

The roar of the Cadillac was still audible, even if the car was now out of sight.

'One of them is getting away,' Harvey said. 'You think that's wise?'

'It wasn't one of Huffman's men, it was Larry Bolan.'

'Bolan,' Rink said. 'Last I heard he *was* one of Huffman's men.'

'He isn't any longer. Believe it or not, Larry just saved my ass.'

'Get outa here!'

He wasn't speaking literally, but Rink's words weren't such a bad idea. We piled into the Windstar, the guys up front and me in the back. Harvey navigated the road round the wreckage of my Saturn, then headed off at speed following in the same direction Larry had gone. Back to Pilot Point.

I told them what had happened, ending with Bolan's reluctance to shoot me when he had the chance.

'So he's looking for a showdown?' Rink said.

'I suppose I owe him.'

'For killing his brother?' Harvey asked, incredulous. He caught my eye in the rear-view mirror. 'That's crazy thinking, man.'

'I was thinking how I'd be if someone had killed my brother,' I said. 'Or either of you. I don't blame Larry for wanting a one-on-one with me.'

'You don't owe him anything,' Rink said. 'There's no honour in the man, Hunter. You know that.'

'I know. But that doesn't change anything.' I laughed at the absurdity. 'Larry saved my life. I agreed to give him a chance at what he wants. You know how much I stand by my word.'

'The truth, Hunter?'

Giving him a sheepish grin, I said, 'OK. I want him too.'

'The guy's a goddamn freak of nature.' Coming from Rink, that statement meant something. 'Why'd you want to fight somethin' like that?'

I considered my reasons. It was perhaps misguided, but since Larry had manhandled me back in the workshop where Trent died, I'd been feeling a little inadequate. 'I have to prove something to myself.'

'Man . . .' Rink groaned. 'That means if he kicks your ass, I'm gonna have to fight him.'

Rink has an absurd sense of humour at times. But I wasn't laughing.

We drove through semi-rural areas where human habitation was more apparent, and picked up South Highway 377 toward Pilot Point. All along the way

I watched for Larry Bolan's wheeled warship, but apparently he'd headed off elsewhere.

We cut through Pilot Point without stopping, passing a bank infamous for having been robbed by Bonnie and Clyde, so Harvey said, then followed a minor road to our destination: a fishing cabin hidden from the road by a stand of live oak on the bank of Ray Roberts Lake. The cabin was totally utilitarian, a staging area for the continuation of our plan to get Kate back. 'Have either of you any connections here in Texas?' I asked.

Rink shrugged a negative, but Harvey bobbed his head.

What had recently gone down had spoiled my chances of spiriting Kate from under Huffman's nose. He'd be on high alert now. Our next incursion on his land would have to be planned. And it should be soon, before Huffman could marshal his forces against me.

'What're the chances of you getting hold of a couple of rifles, Harvey?'

'Could get my hands on as many rifles as you want,' Harvey said. 'But I guess you're thinking of specific types?'

I told him exactly what I would like.

Harvey shook his head. 'How soon do you want them?'

'How about right now?'

Harvey clicked his fingers like a magician. But then he smiled slowly and said, 'Sorry, Hunter. I'm good, but not that good. Leave it with me, I'll see what I can do.'

'Got a plan?' Rink asked me.

'Yeah, we give Huffman hell.'

32

Falling back to a safe position, Larry Bolan took the loop road round the city of Denton, passing the CH Collins Football Stadium, while he considered his next move.

It didn't take much debating: Joe Hunter must die in agony.

Resolute, he blinked at the scenery and realised he was now heading back west on University Drive towards Highway 35.

On his right was a burger joint – as good a place as any to stop. Not that he wanted food: he was looking for a payphone.

Pulling in, he checked out the other vehicles in the lot. There was a mix of cars and vans, but his Cadillac would stand out if left in the open. Sooner or later he would change the plates, but he was in no rush. He doubted anyone back at Minnie's would report the vehicle missing. Hell, they wouldn't even report Tito missing. Still, he parked it at the back, next to some dumpsters. There was a *No Parking* sign. Like he cared. Then he got out of the Cadillac and stretched expansively.

He was wearing the overcoat he'd brought from

Little Fork, but he was still reluctant to shed it. The coat camouflaged the guns in his waistband. He pulled it closer to his body as he walked round the side of the building and into a cool breeze. He saw what he wanted: a booth attached to the outside wall. He searched his pockets for change, fed quarters into the machine.

The telephone rang a dozen times before it was answered.

'Hello?'

'That you, boss?'

'Larry?' Huffman asked. 'Larry Bolan?'

'Yeah. It's me.'

There was a pause. Larry knew that those empty seconds were very important. At the end of them he would know if this was a mistake. Perhaps the biggest mistake of all.

'You survived?' Huffman sounded pleased, but that meant nothing. He always seemed happy and relaxed, whatever murder he was planning. 'I thought Joe Hunter had killed you along with Aitken and Wallace.'

Larry smiled. He was in the clear: Huffman was unaware of the fates of his co-conspirators. Neither had the pilot filled Huffman in before he had brought down the helicopter. Larry wasn't averse to letting Hunter take the crap for all those deaths.

'I was trapped under wreckage when the bastard sent my truck into the restaurant. I was knocked out. When I woke up I was too late to save Aitken or the judge. By the time I got my act together, everyone had already gone. So I did what I thought best: I followed Hunter.'

'You followed him here?'

'Only as far as the airport, but then I got held up by a blizzard. But I guessed he'd be heading your way.'

'You're in Texas, then?'

'Just down the road a piece,' Larry said, not about to divulge his location just yet.

'That's great, Larry. I could do with you here with me. Hunter's around.'

'You know where?'

'No, but he can't be far away. Come in, Larry. Help me. I want a good man at my back.'

'What about those others you were bringing in?'

'Yes, they're all here. I called them back from Little Fork.' Huffman grunted. 'But forget them, Larry. You know you were always my favourite.'

But you didn't care for Trent, did you, you bastard? Larry thought.

'You still want to kill Joe Hunter, right?'

'I'll be there in a couple of hours, boss.'

'That's great, Larry, just great.'

Larry hung up.

Yeah, just great, he thought. But not for you, *boss*. If you get in the way, I'll kill you too.

33

The lake looked eternal, like it was a billion years old, but it had only been created back in the early 1980s. It got its name from the commissioner who'd backed the plan to bring water to the prairie: Ray Roberts himself. I'd never heard of the man, but he got my respect. The lake was beautiful. The water was very still, the surface almost glass-like and reflecting the cerulean heavens. Oak trees hugged the shore and birds called in the treetops. The water made a gentle lapping noise, which was soothing after all the mayhem.

It was a nice place for a couple to take a romantic stroll. I wondered what it would be like with Kate beside me. Except she was enduring hell as Huffman's captive.

I stuffed my hands in my jacket pockets, as I watched a couple of youths in a rowing boat. I could hear their laughter echoing across the water. I wondered if those two boys had the same strength of friendship that I shared with Rink and, increasingly, with Harvey Lucas. If one of them fell overboard, would the other dive in to save him? I decided he would. That's what people did for their friends. I returned to the cabin, determined to get started.

The evening sky had turned to molten brass. Rink had lit a lamp in the room. Plus, Harvey was back. Between them they were lugging a large wooden crate with a pack of supplies balanced on top that they dumped on the bed.

'I couldn't get us Dragunovs,' Harvey said, referring to the cream of sniper rifles, 'but these should suffice.'

He cracked open the lid of the box and I saw two US Army M24 bolt action sniper rifles. I eyed the guns with appreciation. The stocks were a Kevlar and graphite composite, and they were fitted with Leupold-Stewens M3 Ultra telescopic sights with built-in compensators for bullet drop. I was familiar with the US Army issue rifles and knew that they could be relied upon up to a range of approximately one thousand yards. They had an internal magazine that took five .308 Winchester rounds. Good guns in anyone's estimation.

'Suffice, my ass!' Rink lifted one of the M24s from the crate and snuggled the butt against his shoulder. He swung the rifle round and aimed at an imaginary target at the far end of the room. At that distance a steel-jacketed round would punch a hole through the wall and sail off across the lake and probably still kill a man on the far side. 'I prefer these to the Russian rifle, hands down.'

'You *are* good,' I told Harvey.

'Told you I was,' Harvey said, flashing white teeth. Then, growing more serious, he added, 'I've got these on loan, guys. I promised I'd return them after we're done. Anything happens to me, I need you to get them back to their rightful owner.' He named a sergeant from the Joint Reserve Base at Fort Worth.

'The JRB is a naval air station, isn't it? Why'd they need sniper rifles on a naval base?'

'The SEALS fly out of there sometimes,' Harvey said. That was all the clarification I needed.

Our next assault on Quicksilver Ranch would be like invading a fortified military base. We'd be outnumbered and outgunned. And we didn't have the luxury of a human shield the way Huffman did. So, it wasn't going to be a head-on attack. Stealth – and the long rifles – would be our greatest assets.

But it was looking like an almost impossible task.

Then serendipity struck.

The phone in my pocket vibrated.

I studied the screen before answering. It wasn't Imogen.

'That was some show you put on earlier,' Huffman said. 'I only wish I'd been there to see it.'

I flicked the phone on to speaker so that my friends could hear. They stood very still, not giving any hint that Huffman had an audience.

'I wish you'd been there, too,' I said. 'I'd have killed you and got things over with.'

'Ah, but that would've been a let-down, wouldn't it? Where's your sense of the dramatic, Hunter?'

'I'm not the type for dramatics. I just get the job done.'

'So you have Imogen Ballard?'

I didn't need to answer. He knew that I didn't have her.

'You do still want the lovely Kate back, don't you? She's a fine woman, that one. And loyal. Do you know what it took to force her to admit that you had her telephone, and then to give me the number?'

'If you've hurt her . . .'

Huffman laughed.

His voice growing a shade softer, he said, 'The sooner you bring Imogen to me, the sooner you get Kate back. That minimises the opportunity for Larry Bolan to harm her any more.'

'Larry Bolan?'

'Yes, my big friend is here. He hates you, you know. But that's understandable. After what you did to his little brother, he wants to eat your heart.'

'Trent was a psychopath.'

'Can't deny that. He was one crazy-eyed son of a bitch. But he was still Larry's little brother. You can't blame him for hurting Kate to get back at you.'

'If you want Imogen, you'll stop him, Huffman.'

'Larry's his own man in that respect, so you'd better just find Imogen.' All the fake joviality had disappeared from his voice now. 'You have until this time tomorrow night. Bring me Imogen, Hunter, or I'll be sending Kate back to you in little pieces.'

'Tomorrow night.'

I hung up. I didn't want to listen to the bastard's voice any more.

Rink and Harvey had remained silent throughout.

Now they were all questions. Primarily why I hadn't told Huffman about Larry's part in the earlier gun battle.

'Huffman would've had him killed.'

'That's what we want,' Rink said. 'One less enemy.'

'What's more important to you, Hunter?' Harvey asked. 'Freeing Kate or getting your showdown with Bolan?'

I just looked at him, and he waved the question away.

'I didn't tell Huffman about Larry for a good reason. He was bluffing, Larry isn't hurting her. Don't forget – she's too valuable a hostage: it's Kate who's going to bring Imogen to him.'

'But why stay quiet about Bolan?' Rink asked.

'Huffman made a valid point. He said that Larry is his own man. What he hasn't realised is that Larry will put his own agenda first.' I smiled coldly. 'Whether he knows it or not, Larry's our ally behind enemy lines. All we have to do is figure out how best we can use him.'

'You think he'd bring Kate if you promised him a chance at you?' Harvey asked.

'No. Even supposing we could find a way to contact him, he'd only kill her. That'd guarantee him his chance more than anything.'

'So what good is he to us?'

'When we go to do the exchange of Imogen for Kate, Larry will be there. I'm guessing that Huffman will use his presence to intimidate me. He'll be in charge of Kate, but his mind will be focused on me. I'll play on Larry's anger and draw him out.'

'Giving us an opportunity to steal Kate from him.'

'That's leaving an awful lot to chance,' Harvey said.

'Chance *would be* a fine thing.' I held up the phone, showing him the flashing envelope symbol on the screensaver.

Chance or coincidence, Imogen had returned my call at the same time as Huffman had decided to call me.

34

As roll-calls go, the impromptu gathering of Huffman's men bore no resemblance to the kind you see in military command centres, but that was what it was. They were in the large lounge area on the upper floor of the ranch house, a group of killers who would rather be on the move than standing around waiting for orders.

There was Huffman and Larry Bolan, a select number of Huffman's usual men employed at the ranch, and five others. These five added a sense of danger to the meeting as though they could turn on each other at any second. A meeting of narcissistic minds is always a dangerous thing, particularly when each of those minds thinks themselves above the rest assembled round them. These five were not used to working as a team: each of them usually headed a group of their own and felt it was a personal insult that they were not elevated above the others. Huffman didn't give a damn: he would play on their egos in order to get the most out of them. Each one of the five would want to prove that they were the best and they would do everything in their power to demonstrate that.

Huffman was the only person seated. He was in a large wing-backed chair, a cigar cupped in his palm as his hand rested on his crossed legs. He had disdained the usual suit and tie, electing on this occasion to dress more like the other people here. He was wearing a windcheater jacket and canvas trousers that he'd tucked into laced-up boots. The clothing gave him freedom of movement, and also, being a flat sandy colour, a level of camouflage that his designer suit couldn't match. On his head was a baseball cap, the same colour as the rest of his clothes. On his hip he had holstered a Beretta PX4 Storm, a 'full size' semi-auto with a magazine capacity of seventeen rounds. Unbeknown to all gathered there, he had his cut-throat razor secreted in its pouch on his right wrist.

He was sitting in silence watching the others. One of them, Remmie Souza, was standing with his arms folded over his expansive chest. Souza was a big man, muscles the type you see in prison yards, and his stance showed off the massiveness of his biceps. Huffman wanted to laugh at him; next to Larry Bolan Souza looked like a wimp. More than once Huffman had noticed Souza casting a look Bolan's way, then frowning in self-admonishment.

'It is time to put your differences aside,' Huffman finally said. 'I have just offered Hunter the incentive to fight even harder to free the woman. He'll be coming. Unless you work as a team, I guarantee he'll beat you.'

'He won't beat us,' said a grey-haired man as he fingered the hilt of a knife on his hip. 'He got lucky with the others, that's all.'

Charles Grade was the oldest man in the room. He was in his early fifties, but he still had the body of a man twenty years younger. He was as lithe as a cat and his wide green eyes added to the resemblance.

Watching Grade from under heavy brows was the youngest man. 'He won't beat me, anyway,' Desmond Molloy said to Huffman in an accent evocative of Northern Ireland. He nodded his head in Grade's direction. 'Can't vouch for that old man over there.'

Molloy was a hard-faced man, his skin pocked with acne and more than one scar. His father, Patrick, had been an IRA hit man back when the Troubles were on, and Desmond had picked up the mantle after his father was shot dead by an undercover SAS soldier. These days he worked out of Newark and he was generally at odds with Grade who worked for a rival mob out of neighbouring Jersey City.

Grade sneered.

'This old man could still teach you a lesson, boy.'

'Bring it on,' Molloy said.

'Easy, you guys,' said Cal Burton. 'Huffman's right. You can't underestimate a man who takes out six armed soldiers with only a handgun. We need to stick together on this.'

'What's wrong with you, Tex?' Molloy demanded. 'No faith in your abilities? I didn't think you'd be the type to be afraid of one man: last I heard you claimed to have taken out three US marshals with only your bare hands. Are you telling me that was all bullshit?'

Cal Burton was a native Texan, although he was more

likely to be found in Austin than here north of Dallas. He was a tall, raw-boned man with a florid complexion and a shock of hair that looked like a badly stacked sheaf of corn. He was missing two teeth at the front and had the habit of rolling his tongue through the gap. Some people looked at Burton and assumed that he wasn't firing on all cylinders. They usually only made that mistake once.

He laughed at Molloy. 'There weren't three of them, Paddy. There were four. Plus I killed the asshole they were supposed to protect.'

Molloy sneered again, turned to Souza. 'What about you, Remmie? You afraid of one Englishman?'

'I ain't afraid of no one,' Souza said, but again his glance slid over Larry Bolan.

The last person of this unusual gathering was the most anomalous of all. It was against the norm for a woman to be an enforcer, but Ruth Wicker had proven her ability time and time again. Once she'd been a DEA agent, but she'd found working for the other side far more lucrative than working for the government. In blazer and trousers she still looked like she was on the government payroll. She was slight in build, with a face that would never be called pretty. Never had she used her feminine ways to build her career; she relied solely on her ability to deliver pain with a viciousness most men could not match.

'You should learn to keep your mouth shut, Molloy.'

'Who asked you, bitch?' Molloy snapped at her. 'You shouldn't even be here. Why'd you bring in a frigid woman if you wanted us to work together, Huffman?'

Wicker shook her head slowly and her hand crept towards the gun on her hip.

'Go on, Wicker, draw your gun. I'll shove it someplace you've never had something shoved before.' Molloy leered at the other men in the room, but no one seemed impressed by his lewd talk. He threw up his hands. 'Ah, to hell with the lot of you. I work better on my own anyway. Just keep the feck out of my way.' Turning to Wicker, he pointed a finger at her. 'Especially you, Wicker, you feckin' dog.'

'What's wrong, Molloy?' Wicker asked. 'Upset because I turned you down? Shit, it must be frustrating when you can't even score with an ugly bitch like me.'

'Feck off.'

The other men in the room laughed this time. Molloy's face reddened, and he finally fell silent. He crossed his arms the way Souza did, and glowered between Wicker and Grade, unsure which of the two he hated the most.

'Now that we've got the pleasantries out of the way,' Huffman said, 'we can get down to business. You were all asked here because your employers owe me. You were chosen to represent your respective syndicates because you're the best at what you do. But, gentlemen – and lady – I do not expect you to work for free. As promised you'll all be paid handsomely, if you kill Joe Hunter. Your best bet is to do that as a team.' He looked once at Larry Bolan before continuing. 'I don't care which one of you actually finishes him, as long as he dies. But there is one thing that you must not do.' He looked at each of them in turn, his gaze lingering for a little longer on Molloy. 'No one hurts either of the women.'

'I thought you wanted this Ballard woman dead, boss,' Cal Burton said.

'I do, but only after I've had a long talk with her. She has evidence against me that I need to get back. If she's dead she can't hand it over.'

'You think Hunter will actually deliver her to you?' Wicker shook her head slowly. 'The way he's fighting for Kate Piers, it's unlikely he'll be the type to hand another woman over to you.'

'Ballard is a stranger. She means nothing to him. But I believe that Kate is another story altogether.'

'They're sisters, aren't they?'

Huffman looked over at Souza. It was the first time the man had shown any interest other than in matching Larry for bicep size.

Souza unfolded his arms. 'He's hardly going to hand over the sister of the woman he's protecting. Something like that isn't going to endear him to his girlfriend, is it?'

'Can I ask a question, boss?'

Huffman looked at Cal Burton. The man did that infuriating roll of his tongue, saliva cracking as a bubble popped. Cal ran a hand through his scruffy hair.

'What would you like to know?'

'If it's so important that you get Imogen Ballard alive, why'd you want us to kill the man who's best placed to bring her to you?'

'He's far too dangerous to be allowed to live. If he handed over Imogen in exchange for her sister, how long would it be before we were back to square one? He'd come after Imogen with as much determination as he's already shown.'

'You said a minute ago that he didn't know or care about Imogen,' Wicker pointed out. 'Why would he come after her?'

'Because Kate would ask him to.'

'So why let Kate live?' Molloy asked. 'Why not gut the bitch and show this Hunter what'll happen to him if he doesn't hand Imogen over? Give her to me: I'll do it for you.'

Wicker turned angry eyes on Molloy.

'You're a pig, Molloy. I'd call you a misogynist but you probably wouldn't understand what I was talking about.'

'I like women just fine,' Molloy told her. 'So long as they *keep their feckin' mouths shut*!'

'You know something, Molloy,' Wicker said. 'If every man was like you I would become a lesbian.'

'Shit, I thought you already were.'

'OK, that's enough!' Huffman stood up and placed the cigar between his lips. Around the cigar, he said, 'Fighting each other, you're making it easier for Hunter.'

'Get Wicker the hell out of here then,' Molloy said. Turning to Charles Grade, he added, 'And you'd be better getting shot of that old man. He's only going to slow the rest of us down.'

'I've a better idea.'

The Irishman began to turn towards Huffman's voice, just as Huffman whipped his right hand across his throat. A silver flash at the end of his fingers seemed to caress Molloy's skin. Molloy's eyes went wide, then the flesh in his throat gaped and a flood of blood was pouring down his neck. The gash widened further and Huffman had to step away to avoid the squirt of blood from a severed artery.

Molloy realised he was dying.

He grabbed at his throat with both hands. It was pointless. He stumbled to his knees. He tried to scream at those standing immobile around him, but the razor had sliced through his larynx and all that came out was a gurgle. Blood squirted again, in time with each faltering beat of his heart. He collapsed face down.

Huffman eyed each of the others in turn. 'I've had enough insolence out of that asshole. Anyone else here who thinks they can talk to me like *that*?'

Burton rolled his shoulders in a shrug. Wicker stared down on her tormentor with a look of smug satisfaction. Only Souza looked perturbed, but not from any love of the Irishman. Grade was actually smiling.

Grade said, 'That Hunter is one bad bastard. Poor Paddy there didn't stand a chance. I'll make sure his people know he died a hero, boss.'

'Thanks,' Huffman said with a cold smile. 'Appreciate it, Grade. Anybody else see anything differently, now's the time to say so.'

Three of them seemed pleased with the outcome. Only Souza stirred, but just to cross his arms again.

'Problem?' The razor was still a pale blur in Huffman's cupped palm.

'No, boss, of course not. Molloy was a liability,' he said. 'He would've sacrificed the rest of us to get his own way.'

'Yeah,' Larry Bolan rumbled from behind him. It was the first time Larry had entered the conversation. No one else caught the meaning in that single word, but Huffman looked across at the big man.

'Do we all think we can work together now?' Huffman asked. No one declined. 'Good. Let's get started then.'

Huffman crouched down and wiped the cut-throat razor clean on Molloy's trousers. He slipped the blade up his sleeve and into its holder before standing up. Throughout the meeting his hired hands had stood silently at the outside of the ring of killers. He indicated two of his men over. 'Take this piece of shit out of here.'

'What will you do with him, boss?' Wicker asked, watching with an unhealthy interest as the two men lifted Molloy from the floor.

'He'll go where the others went. To the slaughterhouse.'

35

You can disappear for a week without really trying. As long as you don't make contact with anyone, and you don't lay down a paper or electronic trail, then you can skim along below the radar. Imogen Ballard had done just that without any great effort.

For the past seven days she'd been an anonymous passenger on a cruise ship that had taken in the Caribbean Islands, visiting Puerto Rico, St Thomas and St Maarten. She had stayed on board on an all-inclusive basis, avoiding disembarkation where she would have to show her passport or where a record of her boarding card would be kept. An imprint of her credit card had been taken when she had originally boarded the cruise ship at Miami, but until it was time to leave she'd used only an on-board charge card. No record of her transactions had entered her banking system until she was back on dry land, and even then it would possibly take days before the record was updated. The original booking had been made and paid for in cash. Only someone with access – and the time – to enter all tour operator systems would have been able to uncover her whereabouts. It was something that Huffman had not thought of.

Neither had I.

I met Imogen at Dallas Fort Worth International. When she walked out of the arrivals lounge at terminal C, I immediately recognised her. She had changed her hair since the photograph on Kate's phone was taken. She'd cut it short and coloured it darker and she was tanned from sub-tropical sunshine. Sunglasses concealed her eyes. But I knew her. She was the double of Kate. Slightly shorter, slightly heavier of build, but she would have passed as Kate's twin rather than her older sibling.

'Hi, Imogen,' I said. 'I'm glad you came.'

'If what you say is true, how could I stay away?'

As was to be expected, Imogen Ballard was very nervous. She had only my word that I was her friend and this was a woman who'd been running for her life for the past week. She studied me from behind the sunglasses. 'I remember you from Jake's funeral. It's weird meeting you again after all these years.'

'I'm only sorry that it's under these circumstances.'

'Me, too.'

Taking her luggage from her, I turned towards the parking lot. I'd commandeered the Windstar from my friends, leaving Rink and Harvey to make plans back at the cabin on the lake. I just walked, trusting that Imogen would follow.

In terms of area DFW Airport is the second largest in the United States, encompassing ground between both cities from which it takes its name. We came out from the terminal and headed off to pick up the road north for Pilot Point. We didn't speak for the first few minutes. She was jumpy; I could be another ploy of Robert Huffman's to get his hands on her – which to be fair I was, in a way – and could be driving her to him right now. She was putting a lot of faith in a man her deceased brother could no longer vouch for.

'What do you have on Huffman?' I finally asked.

'Why do you want to know?' In my peripheral vision I saw her shift towards to the passenger door, as though readying herself to leap out of the moving vehicle.

'I know you have evidence that can bring his business down, but is there more to it than that?'

She didn't answer immediately. When she did, it was with a question of her own. 'Are you seeing Kate?'

'No,' I said. Then I regretted answering so quickly.

'Oh, I thought . . .'

'I was employed by Kate to find you.'

'When I accessed my voicemail, there were messages from my sister. The impression I got was that . . . well . . .'

I gripped the steering wheel. Changed the subject.

'I'm pleased that you decided to make contact, Imogen. I know you're putting a lot of faith in me.' Taking my eyes from the road just long enough to make a connection with her, I said, 'Kate's relying on the both of us.'

Imogen pushed a finger beneath her sunglasses and I got the impression she was wiping away a tear. Then I had to turn my attention to the road. Traffic was very heavy, crawling along in all lanes. We were on the North Stemmons Freeway passing Lake Lewisville, approaching a bridge that spanned a spur of the lake. Road signs advertised turn-offs for Hickory Creek and Corinth; straight ahead was Denton.

'Where are you taking me?'

'We've a cabin at Pilot Point.'

'*We* being?'

'Did Jake ever mention another member of our team called Jared Rington?'

'You mean Rink? The Japanese guy?'

'One and the same,' I said. 'Except he's only half Japanese. His father is Scottish. Rink's there waiting for us. There's another guy, too. Harvey Lucas.'

'Don't know him.'

'He wasn't one of our team. But I wish that he had been. He's good.'

'Did Kate hire them, as well?'

'No. They came here to help me get Kate back.'

'Three of you,' Imogen shook her head disconsolately. 'Do you realise how many men Robert Huffman has at his beck and call?'

'A lot less than he started with.' I told her what had happened since Kate and I arrived at her house above Little Fork. It was my way of reassuring her that we were on the same side. But I saw horror in her face long before I'd finished.

'You killed Trent Bolan?'

'He was going to kill me.'

'What about Larry?'

'Got away.'

She pushed her face into her cupped palms and moaned.

'They're monsters. Do you know what they did to William Devaney? He was the sheriff—'

'He was your lover.'

Pushing the sunglasses on top of her head she looked at me with red-rimmed eyes. 'Yes. He was my lover. But then the Bolans beat him to death. Trent tore his ear off, Joe.'

'That's the downside of mixing with people like them,' I said. 'Devaney shouldn't have tried blackmailing them.'

Imogen made a sound of scorn. She snapped the glasses off her head, closing them and pushing them into her purse. I discreetly checked to see if she was packing the way Kate had been but saw only the usual things that accompany a woman, plus a digital video camera.

'You were there when they murdered Devaney?'

'Yes.' Her fingers went to the camera. 'I was hiding in the woods. I was supposed to record the meeting Will had with Huffman. Will wanted it to use as evidence.'

'You're saying that Devaney wasn't blackmailing Huffman?'

'Of course not, he was only building a case against him and Roger Wallace. He was going to take the money and the recording and pass them to the state police. Will knew that he was too close to them to do otherwise. He had to pretend to be as dirty as the rest of them.'

'Why didn't he bring in the state boys before then? Why use you to record the meeting?'

'He trusted me. It had gotten to the stage where he didn't know how many of his own people were involved in the scam. If he went to the state police first he couldn't be sure the word wouldn't get back to Huffman. When Jim Aitken turned up with the Bolans it proved he was right to worry.'

'Jim Aitken told me that after Devaney was killed you made your own demands.' Looking at her steadily, I said, 'To the tune of two million dollars.'

'And you believed that sack of shit?'

'I had no reason not to.' I didn't mention that I'd been torturing the guy at the time.

'He was lying.' By the way she turned her face away I knew that he wasn't the only one.

'I don't care,' I said. 'What you tried to do was wrong, Imogen, but compared to the things that Huffman and the others did, it's nothing. The only thing I'm angry about is that your greed put Kate in danger.'

'I wasn't blackmailing anyone. I only wanted what was rightfully mine. Huffman owed me money.'

'A couple of grand,' I said.

'Doesn't matter. He was refusing to pay me for work I'd done at his restaurant. I wasn't going to let him get away with it.'

'So you put your sister's life at risk because of a couple of thousand dollars? I bet it doesn't seem like such a good idea now.'

'I never meant for Kate to get involved.'

'Doesn't matter,' I said, throwing her words back at her. 'She is. She might die, Imogen.'

Her fingers went to her face again, and this time I could detect the tremor in them. That Imogen had attempted to embezzle money from dangerous men didn't really concern me. There were worse things she could have done: such as trying to demand money from innocent people.

'Imogen,' I said. 'I've laid all my cards on the table. You know who I am, who is with me. You know we're here to help you. If I had any agenda other than getting Kate back, you'd know that too by now.' I didn't say that she'd be dead, but she got the message. 'Tell me what you have on Huffman.'

She nodded, and I detected a nerve ticking at the corner of her right eye. She sucked in a deep breath. 'I was developing a website and publicity campaign for a restaurant in Little Fork.'

'Le Cœur de la Ville.'

'Yes. The owners were planning a grand relaunch. They refurbished the entire building, sank thousands of dollars into bringing it up to date. Little Fork was growing at an exponential rate. A top-class restaurant was a magnificent investment in the town.'

As she spoke, I thought of the last time I'd been in the restaurant; it wasn't such a great investment now.

'It came as a surprise when the owners announced that they were selling up. Up until that point they'd been very excited about their plans for the place. I'd reached a stage where I was almost ready to launch the publicity campaign and then the rug was ripped from under me.'

'Huffman purchased the place. Then he refused to pay for the work that you had done.'

'Yes,' she said. 'There was no warning. Practically overnight things turned sour. The owners just left and Huffman moved in. I know things like that happen all the time in business, but nevertheless there was something fishy about it. I was allowed to clear out my equipment from the office that I'd been using at the restaurant. But – and normally I would be ashamed to say this – I took more than what belonged to me. I found files on le Cœur's computer pertaining to the buyout by Huffman. They showed that the entire deal was a sham: Huffman purchased the building and the business, along with all its assets, for a miserly twenty thousand dollars. It didn't take much to realise that Huffman had forced the owners into selling. Huffman needed to be brought to book for that, so I took what I'd found to Will.'

'And this was where Devaney hatched his plan to prove Huffman was employing dirty tactics to purchase land and property?'

'Will already knew that there was something going on. He told me that he'd been conducting his own investigation into Judge Wallace and the fact that he was rushing Huffman's purchases through the system. He said that he needed more evidence, though. Something tangible that would prove their guilt.'

Our journey had taken us round Denton city limits and I had to concentrate on the roads while I picked up the spur that would take us along the northern edge of the city to the road up to Ray Roberts Lake. Imogen was silent, as though she'd explained everything. But there were still too many holes in her story.

'Aitken told me that Huffman paid Devaney off but he refused to back down. He told me that Devaney began to demand more money.'

Imogen stirred beside me. She straightened a little in her seat, but she still had the look of defeat. 'If he did, it was without my knowledge.'

'Tell me the truth, Imogen. Devaney went from being a cop to someone who saw a chance at getting rich. And you saw it as a way of getting revenge on Huffman.'

'OK, Joe, I'll admit to that. We did see it as an opportunity to take what was rightfully mine. I just wanted to make Huffman pay up. But, despite what you think, we were going to hand the money and the record of the deal over to the state police.'

'After you skimmed your cut off the top?'

'No,' Her face had become very hard. 'I was going to go through the proper channels. I'd already lodged a compensation claim against Huffman; I intended pushing that through court when Huffman and Wallace were on trial. I had more chance of winning my case for compensation at a criminal trial than I did via any other route.'

'So you set up the meeting with Huffman?' I angled the Windstar on to a turnpike, picking up the road to the north. 'Why in God's name did you do it all the way out in the woods?'

'We didn't have much time to prepare. Huffman was obviously nervous about meeting somewhere the handover could be observed. So we chose the woods above Great Well waterfall. I knew the area well; I knew all the good hiding places. I went ahead, set myself up so I could film the handover.'

'Except Huffman didn't turn up,' I said. 'Aitken and the Bolans came instead and that's when they murdered Devaney.'

'No, Joe. Huffman was there.'

'But I thought . . .'

'I don't think that the others knew, but I saw him. He came to watch and he looked like he loved every second of Will's death.'

'You got him on video?'

'Yes.'

'And you still have it?'

She touched the camera in her purse. 'Right here.'

'Have you made copies?'

'Of course I have.'

I nodded. 'Aitken said you didn't witness the murder.'

'Aitken couldn't lie straight in bed,' she said scornfully. 'He knows the truth. They murdered Will in front of the camera even though they knew I was there. They had men hiding in the woods and they expected to catch me. Against all odds I escaped them. I had to hide for a full day and night, but I managed to give them the slip.' She stopped and looked directly at me. 'Why do you think Huffman's so desperate to get his hands on me, Joe?'

'OK,' I acquiesced. 'So why Aitken's story that you then tried to blackmail them?'

'It was all I could think of to make them back off. Even if I took the evidence to the state police, it wouldn't have saved me. Huffman would've still had me murdered by one of his other men. I thought that I could buy my freedom back. I asked for an inordinate sum of money just to throw them, make them concentrate on that instead of on finding me.'

'Instead, you made things a million times more difficult for everyone. You should've confided in Kate. She's a police officer. She would've known what to do.'

'I know that now.' She couldn't suppress her frustration any longer and it came out as a series of deep racking sobs. For a second I genuinely felt sorry for her.

'You made some mistakes, but you're not the only one. From now on we start thinking ahead.'

'We go to the police with the evidence?'

'Not yet. That won't save Kate.'

'What do we do, then?'

'We end this.'

I pulled on to the shoulder of the road. Cars rocketed past, the displacement of air buffeting the Windstar.

'Are you prepared to do what must be done to get Kate back?' I asked. 'Even if it's very dangerous?'

'Anything. I'd give my life for her.'

'Good,' I said. 'Because that's exactly what you might have to do.'

36

'Sit down.'

'I need to use the bathroom.'

'Again?'

'Can't help it,' Kate said to her jailer. 'You keep giving me water; it has to come out some time.'

'Wait until Rourke gets back.'

'Why? Can't a big tough guy like you handle things on his own?'

Rourke was the man who'd been lewd towards her when Huffman had been in the room. After Huffman had left, Rourke had gone further. He had delighted in ripping off her blouse and bra and it was all that Kate could do to hold on to her jeans. Rourke had enjoyed her humiliation more than any titillation he'd gained from seeing her breasts exposed. She was glad he was out of the room. He'd gone off on an errand, leaving Nixon alone with her.

Nixon, for all he was a hired gun, didn't appear to be as cruel as Rourke, and it was he who had given her back her clothes after Rourke had attacked her. He was a big guy, with short sandy hair. His cheeks bore freckles and he had watery blue eyes that seemed large behind round spectacles. He had a wedding ring on his finger, which struck Kate as unusual among these kinds of men. She wondered if he had children, if he was a man whose conscience could be played upon.

'I can handle things pretty well,' Nixon told her. 'Now sit down.'

'I need to pee. Do you expect me to do it right here?'

'You do that and you'll damn well clean it up.'

'Wouldn't it just be easier if you let me go to the bathroom?'

'Jesus Christ!' Nixon stood up from the chair he'd placed by the door to the hallway. Coming over, he pulled out his gun. 'You go to the bathroom, but you're in and out, OK? Plus, I go with you.'

Kate nodded. Then she walked towards the bathroom with Nixon hovering behind her. During her incarceration at the ranch things had always been the same. Whenever she'd used the bathroom she'd been observed. Usually Rourke had been her chaperone, the sick bastard getting his kicks from watching her go through her very private moments. She'd gone beyond embarrassment after the second time. She'd realised that when she was up and moving it gave her an opportunity to escape. Plus, when last she'd been in the bathroom, she'd noticed something that neither of her jailers had recognised as a possible weapon. Thoughts of fighting back covered her shame at being ogled by a pervert.

'Can you undo my cuffs? I need both hands to do

this.' Kate looked down at her buttoned jeans, then across at the toilet. 'Unless you intend doing it for me?'

A flush crept over Nixon's face. 'Lift your hands up.'

Nixon unlocked her cuffs, placing them on a credenza just outside the bathroom door. He nodded at the toilet bowl. 'Go on. Be quick.'

Kate worked her wrists, promoting the flow of blood into her weakened fingers. She reached for the door, about to push it to.

'No you don't.' Nixon caught the door with the side of his foot. 'The door stays open.'

Kate sighed, turning for the toilet and unbuttoning her jeans. 'OK,' she said. 'No problem.'

Nixon grunted something. Then, allowing the door to swing partly shut, he said, 'We're not all animals like Rourke. I only want to know what you're up to; I don't need the full details.'

'I didn't think you were a sicko like him. Thanks, Nixon.'

He exhaled sharply, turning his back. Kate watched him slip his gun back into its holster.

She allowed herself a smile.

Now, she thought, to get out of here.

She'd given Joe all the time she was prepared to. If he was going to rescue her, he'd have done it by now. It was down to her to extricate herself from this predicament. She wasn't some shrinking damsel from a Hollywood movie who would sit around looking pretty until the hero came charging in to save her. She was a NYPD cop, for Christ's sake! Time she started acting like one.

Kate actually sat down on the toilet. It wasn't going to be easy. With her decision to make her break for freedom adrenalin had flowed through her body. At first she desperately needed to urinate, but not now. All her bodily functions had shut down as her body readied itself to fight or run. She had to squeeze hard just to add validity to her story. She used tissue off a roll then flushed, pulled up her clothing, and silently lifted the item she'd noticed wedged behind the toilet bowl. Nixon barely glanced over his shoulder. Kate turned to the sink and ran her hands under the water. She towelled her hands dry, stepping back towards Nixon with the towel still in her hands.

'Thanks, Nixon,' she said to attract his attention. She deliberately used his name to humanise him, and to humanise her in his eyes. She smiled. 'You don't know how badly I needed that.'

'Just finish drying your hands and then get back out here.'

'Sure.' She allowed the towel to drop to the floor. 'I'm all done.'

Nixon turned his body halfway into the room. His mouth was coming open to speak. And that was when Kate raised the canister of insecticide she'd lifted off the bathroom floor. She'd concealed it under the towel until she was close enough, had used the cloth to cover her hands while she pulled off the cap. She gave Nixon a full blast of the spray directly into his eyes and open mouth.

The insecticide was never going to kill Nixon. All it

would do was sting his eyes and give him a foul taste in his mouth, but the way he reacted was as if Kate had squirted him with sulphuric acid. He lurched away, crying out, his hands coming up to cover his eyes. His spectacles stopped some of the spray, but he was still momentarily blinded. Kate kept on spraying him, giving her all the time she needed for what she had to do next.

She brought up her bare foot and kicked as hard as she could directly in the juncture between Nixon's legs. She hurt her instep but her pain was nothing compared to what Nixon experienced. He groaned, his hands now going between his legs. He crumpled forwards as his knees gave way. Kate reached across him, snatching at the metal cuffs on the credenza. Then she tried to push past him, to get clear of the bathroom. Nixon grabbed at her, one hand catching at an ankle. Kate kicked loose and she managed to swing round him and bring up the cuffs at the same time. These cuffs were the rigid type with a solid spacer bar between the two hoops of steel. Kate slammed the cuffs down on Nixon's head. He yowled, one hand coming up to protect his skull, the other reaching for the gun in its holster. Kate slammed him a second time, cutting a chunk out of his scalp.

Nixon tried to turn towards her, but Kate danced around him, catching hold of the hand he had on top of his head. In the next instant she had the cuff on that wrist and she snapped it in place. The advantage of rigid cuffs was that once one of the hoops was in place a person inferior in strength could control a much larger opponent by way of leverage and pain compliance. Kate twisted the cuffs, straightening Nixon's arm against his elbow, then she tugged, pulling him down and flat on his face. She quickly knelt against his shoulder to stop him getting up then grabbed at his free hand even as she twisted the cuffed arm round. Nixon howled, tried to resist, but she just twisted the rigid bar and he howled again. Then she managed to jam the other cuff in place.

Nixon's gun was partly out of its holster. Kate grabbed it.

Nixon was face down, but he could still fight back or shout for help.

Kate only had a second to decide. She brought down the butt of the gun on the nape of his neck. Nixon swore. Kate struck him again and some of the fight went out of him.

'Damn it,' she whispered harshly. 'Just black out will you, Nixon!'

She'd seen Joe knock out that colossal monster, Larry Bolan, by hitting him across the back of the skull. Why wouldn't Nixon just go to sleep so she didn't have to keep on hitting him? She didn't want to crush his skull altogether, but it looked like she was going to have to. Then she changed her grip, caught the gun by its barrel, brought it down like a mallet and this time Nixon did flatten out. He exhaled loudly, then fell into a regular rhythm of shallow breaths.

Kate stood up, her entire body trembling.

She glanced round the room, looking for her boots. They were nowhere in sight. She doubted that they'd even been brought from Little Fork. Barefoot she'd be at a major disadvantage but she wasn't going to let that stop her. She moved quickly to the door to the hallway, checking Nixon's gun as she went. It was a Glock 17, bigger than the model she was used to.

Expertly she ejected the magazine, checked the load and saw it was full. Reinserting the magazine, she racked the slide placing a round in the firing chamber. She flicked off the safety. She was trained never to carry a gun with the safety mechanism disengaged, but she had learned from Joe that the time you wasted flicking off the safety could mean the difference between life and death.

Thinking of Joe, she paused in her flight. What if he'd been killed?

She fought the idea aside. It wasn't something she wanted to contemplate. Not now. Not ever. Huffman had tried to force information from her by playing on her feelings for Joe. She'd lied, said they were merely engaged in a business partnership, but Huffman had been nearer to the truth than he could ever have guessed. Kate had indeed fallen for Joe.

Enough, she thought. She wasn't going to get out of this fortress going all weak-kneed over a man. She had to stand firm and do what must be done. There'd be no warning shouts. No warnings at all. She must shoot to kill whether her enemies were too close to miss or not.

She pulled open the door and spied along the hallway. There were closed doors to her left, a long narrow hall to her right. Double doors opened into some sort of lounge area further along. She listened but could hear nothing of the low murmur that had filtered from that same room earlier in the day. She stepped out into the hall, feeling her bare feet skid on polished planks. She sucked in a breath, lifted the Glock and headed for the lounge.

Except for when she'd been brought here and bundled up the stairs gagged and blindfolded, Kate had spent all her time in that one bedroom under constant guard. She had no idea of the layout of the building or of the number of people here. She knew that she was on the upper floor of a large house but she hadn't realised just how big the place was. It was by definition a ranch, but was more akin to the plantation houses of the Deep South. When she came into the lounge she saw wide French doors leading on to some sort of balcony. Beyond the doors a prairie spread to the horizon, tall grass burnt yellow by the sun and wind. It was heading for late afternoon and the sky had paled, turning a light shade of grey along the skyline.

Glancing back over her shoulder, she looked for another way out. The stairs, she guessed, must be further along the hall. For all she knew they'd take her directly into the midst of Huffman and his men. Her gun would give her a fighting chance, but she wasn't deluded; she knew exactly what the odds against fighting her way through a group of killers were.

She moved through the lounge, skirting a tall wing-backed chair, her feet squeaking faintly on the boards. Then she came to a halt. A stain marred the floor. A dark fan like a crow's wings, only this crow must have been massive. She identified the stain without having to study it in any great detail. Blood had seeped into the grain of the wood. Someone had died here, and that death had been very recent judging by the coppery scent hanging in the air.

She wondered if the blood belonged to Joe or Imogen. Had Huffman caught either one of them and ended their lives right there in the centre of his living room?

She closed her eyes, forcing back the images invading her mind. If the blood had been Joe's or Imogen's, why would Huffman have allowed her to live this long? He wouldn't; he'd have killed her or given her to Rourke or to Larry Bolan to kill for him.

Convincing herself that the blood must belong to someone else, she went towards the doors, skirting the stain in the floor. She heard a creak behind her and realised that it was someone walking along the hall. Probably Rourke on his way back to the room where she'd been imprisoned. She'd hoped that she would've been allowed a little more time to make her escape, but it looked like she was going to be found out in seconds.

She contemplated waiting for Rourke to pass the doorway and putting a bullet in his heart. That's what the sick-headed scumbag deserved. But the sound of gunfire would bring the others running. Better that she get onto the balcony where her options for escape might be higher. At least out there she would get an idea of her surroundings and might be able to find somewhere she could hide.

Grabbing the doors, she pulled one open and went on to the balcony. It spanned the entire length of the building. She hurried to the left. Placing her back against the wall she peered round the door frame back into the room she'd just vacated.

Someone passed the doorway without stopping. She was pretty sure that it was Rourke, but he'd changed his clothing since last she'd seen him. He was now in some sort of paramilitary get-up with a hat pulled down over his hair.

Kate counted the seconds.

When Rourke's shout came she made her move, fleeing along the balcony to the far end. Just round the corner of the building steps led down to the lower level, where there was a second raised porch surrounded by a low railing. She moved down the stairs, watching behind her in case Rourke came charging after her. At the bottom she dropped to a crouch, using the stairs as cover while she surveyed the land to her left. She could see outbuildings. Beyond them was a huge tin shed. She could smell something unpleasant.

In her bare feet she felt vulnerable. More than the fact that her blouse was ripped, revealing a large expanse of her chest, her bare feet made her feel exposed. It was one thing walking on a sandy beach, feeling the sand between your toes, quite another if you had to run over stony ground. But she wasn't going to let that stop her. She quickly slid over the railing, dropping the couple of feet to the floor. She paused, listening for the pursuit that was sure to come. Distantly she heard Rourke's voice raised in anger. Then the thump of feet as people began to respond.

Kate headed for the sheds, jogging gingerly to avoid lacerating her feet, but still coming down on sharp-edged rocks. By the time she reached the first outbuilding she'd already bruised her soles, but at least she wasn't bleeding. Block the pain, she told herself. It's nothing. Keep going.

A bullet struck the wall of the shed, barely missing her. Kate cringed, but turned, lifting her gun. Rourke was on the upper balcony, aiming at her again. He pulled the trigger and the gun barked. Kate jerked to one side. Her return shot made Rourke lunge backwards but otherwise did him no harm.

'She's out here!' he yelled. 'She's heading for the sheds.'

Kate ran. It was her only chance. Put distance between her and her pursuers. She charged along the side of the building, avoiding a third shot from Rourke. Then at the corner she had to throw herself bodily over a wooden fence. She landed heavily on her back, dust rising all around her. Dazed, she peered back the way she'd come. She saw a knot of men boil out of the front of the house. They were indistinct beyond the billow of dust, but she could tell they were rushing her way.

Coming to her feet, she unloaded three rounds at the group. The gun bucked in her hand, more recoil than she was used to and she knew her aim had been too high. It scattered the group, but none of them went down. Ideally she should control her breathing, hold steady, shoot the bastards as they came at her. Instinct made her turn and run again. Guns popped behind her and she felt the tug of one projectile as it skimmed the air next to her left ear. She was passing the open door of the shed. Hulking machinery clustered in the shadows within. She considered putting the machines between her and the men chasing her, but she knew that would only give her momentary respite. They'd simply storm the shed, their greater firepower overwhelming her in seconds.

'Stop running, Kate.' She recognised the voice. Even raised in command, it held a humorous edge.

'Go to hell, Huffman!'

She continued to run.

A second fence barred her way, but she vaulted this one a tad more gracefully than the first. She landed sure-footed, but something sharp jabbed into her sole and this time there was no avoiding the split in her flesh. She grimaced, but kept running.

Another shed presented itself. Beyond it were animal pens and the big tin building. Kate swung to her left, rushing along the front of the building, hidden for the time being from those following. She saw the hulk of an abandoned truck, an old Chevrolet that had been left to rot under the Texan sun. Chickens had colonised the cab at some point. No way that the vehicle was an escape route, but she ducked behind it. Watched and saw movement at the corner of the building. She fired, then glanced over her shoulder. She had to keep moving otherwise the men would split up and some would come at her from behind, bottling her in.

Again she fired at the men at the front of the building, then as they slunk back behind cover she ran and caught the ledge of a window in the shed wall. She pulled herself up and inside the shed within seconds. Instantly her senses were overwhelmed by the stench of scorched metal and aviation fuel. In the darkness she could make out what looked to be parts of an aircraft and two mangled vehicles. They looked like they'd been hidden here very recently as there was still fluid dripping from the wreckage of the helicopter.

She didn't stop to ponder what had caused this devastation, except to conclude that Joe had made an attempt at getting her away after all. The thought gave her comfort. But it was cold comfort at best. Where the hell was he now when she could do with the back-up?

The doors at the front of the shed were shut, so she followed a similar route to the one she'd used to get inside the building. She found a window at the far side. This one was closed. Security wasn't at a maximum though, just a catch that she had to flip open, then she was clambering out into a space full of mud and cow shit. Her feet plunged ankle deep into the filth. She slipped and went down on one knee. Then it was a struggle to gain her footing without giving up her gun. Determined, she pushed through the muck, angling away from the front end of the building where Huffman and the others would inevitably head to.

From within the building she skirted came metallic noises, as if machinery was in motion. A gun cracked behind her and struck the wall of the shed. She thought that the gunman had aimed deliberately high: they wanted to take her alive. That gave her an advantage over her pursuers. She turned, seeking targets, and fired. She hit a man and he went down on his back. She hoped it was Huffman but couldn't be sure because all the men were dressed alike.

Words dashed her hopes.

'This is your last chance, Kate,' Huffman shouted. 'Stop running now or I'll kill you.'

Kate merely ran, went over another fence and then spun round the corner of the big shed.

And ran pell-mell into another figure emerging from a door.

They rebounded, and Kate went down on her back.

Blinking up at the person standing over her, she braced herself for a bullet. But the shot didn't come.

It wasn't one of Huffman's men, but a small dark woman. She was dressed in a blazer and jeans and a white blouse.

She looked like a cop.

Then the reality struck Kate. The woman's white blouse was spattered with blood. So were her hands. She couldn't know it, but Ruth Wicker had been tasked with the job of getting rid of Desmond Molloy and she'd jumped at the opportunity. Wicker was more of a sadist than most of Huffman's hired killers.

Both women realised they were in danger at the exact same second. Kate began to squeeze the trigger of her gun, but she wasn't as keyed in as the small woman. Wicker ducked to the left, then swung her leg, catching

Kate's gun hand, knocking the shot astray. Then Wicker leaned down, grabbed her gun and wrenched it away. She backhanded Kate across the face with a blow like a wedge of steel. Black flashes invaded her vision and she fell backwards.

Wicker reversed the gun in her grip, aimed it between Kate's eyes.

'You're the whore that Joe Hunter wants back,' Wicker said. 'Shame you're going back to him with a hole in your skull, isn't it?'

Kate heard the words with a trickle of relief. Joe was still alive.

Wicker began to exert pressure on the trigger.

'Hold it, Wicker,' Huffman said from behind Kate.

Wicker sighed, lowered the Glock.

Kate craned round to look up at Huffman. He stood over her, a phone to his ear. He was smiling whimsically.

'OK, Hunter,' she heard him say. 'We meet in one hour.'

37

I hung up the phone.

There was a bad taste in my mouth and I felt like spitting. I'd have done so but there was a lady present. Imogen was sitting next to me in the back seat of the Windstar. Rink was in front of her, and Harvey was driving. We were on the move on the streets of Pilot Point so that we didn't present a sitting target if indeed Huffman was trying to vector in on Kate's phone.

'We should bring in the FBI.' It wasn't the first time Imogen had suggested it.

We'd already had this conversation and discarded the idea. But for Imogen's sake, I explained our conclusion.

'I've killed men on your behalf, Imogen. I'd rather see an end to this without facing the rest of my days behind bars.'

'I'd rather go to prison than end up dead,' Imogen huffed.

'Not me.' I left the subject of involving law enforcement at that. Imogen had her part to perform in my plan to get Kate back. It was going to be tricky and carried an element of risk. Imogen could very well die in the execution. But, the way I saw it, she owed her sister that at least.

'Head for Quicksilver Ranch,' I said to Harvey and he nodded.

We followed East Liberty Street out of town, picked up the highway north into Grayson County then took a minor road towards Huffman's place. We were back in semi-rural pastures dotted with trees and bushes. A little further on we'd find the prairie where the earlier ambush had occurred. For the purposes of an exchange for ransom like the one we were on our way to, we'd have normally picked a more public place. That would have cut down on the likelihood of a gun battle. But under these circumstances – and in order for my plan to work – I required the empty prairie. I didn't want any witnesses. None whatsoever.

It was dusk by the time we arrived at our first stop. The drop-off point was as secluded as we could hope for, with only longhorn cattle as witnesses.

Rink and Harvey were out of the Windstar in an instant and both disappeared into the long grass. I climbed into the driving position and set off. Imogen was sitting with her eyes closed. Her face was pale and there was a sheen of sweat on her forehead.

'If everything goes to plan we'll have Kate back within the hour,' I reassured her.

'And if it doesn't?'

'We'll probably all be dead. But I'm not planning on that. Just do as I instructed and everything should be fine.'

'What if Huffman kills me the second he sees me?'

'Then I'll kill him.'

'That's a great consolation,' she muttered.

'He won't shoot you, Imogen, he wants what you recorded on your camera. If he shoots you he'll never get it. He'll be worried about copies and want to check that he has all those accounted for before he does anything to you.'

'He's reckless, Joe. He likes confrontation. I wouldn't be surprised if he shot me just for the hell of it. Just to see how you will react.'

'Then he'll be sorry.'

'You're very sure of yourself,' Imogen said. 'What makes you think you can take him out before he gets you?'

'I was a professional soldier for fourteen years. I've been in similar situations before. Huffman's just a punk who has murdered a few other punks. I'm pretty sure I can handle him.'

My words sounded conceited, but I said them more to give Imogen hope than because I believed them. She snorted. 'Jake was a professional soldier too, Joe. And we both know what happened to him.'

'Yeah. He gave his life for people that he cared for. If it comes to it, so will I.'

Looking in the mirror I saw that Imogen's eyes were now wide open. She was staring back into my reflection. Finally she sighed. She'd caught the hidden meaning in my words.

The rest of our journey was done in silence. But it

wasn't that far, just a mile or so. I brought the Windstar to a halt adjacent to an entrance I hadn't reached that first time on this road. There was a gate, and a copse of trees, and I'd been correct when first I'd spied this place and concluded it was the way to Quicksilver Ranch.

I surveyed the land beyond the gate. Nothing moved. Twilight was setting in and a shadow passed over the prairie. I couldn't see any sign of the ranch itself so it must have been somewhere beyond the horizon. I turned to Imogen. She blinked back at me, tears in her eyes.

'I never intended for any of this to happen.'

'I know.' Reaching over the seat I took one of her hands. 'Keep your chin up, Imogen. Everything'll turn out fine.'

'As long as we get Kate back.'

I was determined that we would. Letting go of her hand, I reached for my SIG, checked it and I was good to go.

'Remember, just do as we agreed.'

'OK.'

No argument from her this time: made me feel a whole lot better about what was to come. I shifted the Windstar into drive, touched the gas and drove through the gate on to Huffman's territory. At the quarter-mile mark, I stopped the vehicle and got out. I opened the rear door and held out my hand to help Imogen out of the car. It was the last time she'd be treated gently before this was over with.

I could hear vehicles approaching.

Without looking for them, I grabbed Imogen by the

collar of her jacket and dragged her to the front of the car. There I threw her down on her knees in a billow of grit and dust. I stood behind her, pulled out my SIG and jammed it tight against the top of her head. Imogen began wailing. Finally I looked up and saw three vehicles approaching in convoy. They stopped a hundred yards short of us and figures began climbing out of the cars. I wasn't surprised to see that one of them towered over all the others: Larry Bolan back where he belonged.

Other than the photos that Harvey had shown me on his laptop, I hadn't ever laid eyes on Robert Huffman. Excluding Bolan, there were five other people who moved to the front of the lead vehicle. They were all dressed in what amounted to pseudo-military gear. One of them was much slighter of build and for a fraction of a second I thought that it could be Kate, but I quickly discarded the notion. It was a woman, but whereas Kate was tall and graceful, this woman held herself with the same masculinity as all the others in the group. Three of the others held guns, while the final man had his hands clasped at his navel as though in prayer. I took that one to be Huffman.

'I've brought Imogen, Huffman,' I yelled at him. 'Show me Kate right now or I put a bullet in her brain.'

I was gratified when the man in a state of prayer shouted back at me. 'What are you doing, Hunter? You don't think I believe you'd kill the woman?'

'It's because of this cheating bitch that I've gone through hell. Believe me: I'd kill her as soon as look at her.'

Huffman came forward and the four with him fanned out. The two on the far sides lifted their rifles and aimed at me.

'I've got a round jacked. Any of your guys get itchy fingers, I might just slip and kill her by accident,' I called.

Huffman waved their guns down.

'Show me Kate. Now!'

It was Larry Bolan who turned back to one of the vehicles. He leaned down, and came out with a squirming bundle that I recognised as Kate. He flung her over his shoulder. Clever, Bolan, using her as a shield. He came to stand next to Huffman. Kate twisted her shoulders to peer back over Bolan and even from that distance I saw her eyes grow big and round. Then she went into a wild frenzy, twisting, trying to get free of Bolan's grip. Beneath the gag her shouts were guttural and I guessed that she was cursing me. I had a gun to her sister's head, so I suppose her reaction was justified.

'Gone home to roost, eh, Bolan?' I shouted. 'I'm not surprised really. You know what they say about shit sticking together.'

Bolan looked at his boss, but it appeared that Huffman hadn't caught the meaning in my words. I wasn't about to make him any the wiser, but it didn't do any harm to place Bolan on the defensive. In return, Bolan lifted his free hand and flipped me the finger.

Right back at you, I thought.

'So how do we play this, Hunter?' Huffman asked.

'You send Kate to me. When she's midway, I set Imogen off from this end.'

'No. We send them at the same time.'

'OK. Just send her.'

'Where's the camera?'

Pulling Imogen's camera out of my jacket pocket I lifted it for him to see. 'You mean this one?'

Before he could answer I lobbed it as hard as I could into the long grass in the field on my right. Hanging on to the damn thing would have guaranteed a volley of shots at both Imogen and me. Better to have Huffman worry that the camera wasn't the one he wanted and have no way of knowing without checking it first. It was a mere distraction, but enough to keep us alive a little longer.

'I take it that you've made copies. How can I be sure that you won't use them against me?'

'Huffman,' I said, as pedantic as I could muster. I did a reasonable impression of a man on the verge of insanity. 'I don't give a shit about you or what you've done in the past. All I'm interested in is getting my woman back. What you do with this bitch or any evidence she has against you is your business. Just get on with it. Send Kate to me so we can make the exchange and I can get out of your hair.'

Huffman stood silently for a moment, deep in contemplation. Finally his chin came up and I saw a smile like that of a shark. He nodded to Bolan and the big man placed Kate on her feet. He leaned in close to her and said something in her ear but I could not hear what it was. Kate turned towards me and there was a mix of hatred and confusion and *something else* in her face when she looked at me.

I pulled Imogen to her feet none too gently. I didn't take the gun from her head.

Then I waited.

When Huffman pushed Kate forward, I did the same to Imogen. Both women took a stumbling step towards each other. I lifted my SIG, aiming it between Imogen's shoulder blades. If Huffman believed that the camera was the one that he wanted, or my denial about copies, he didn't make any sign, so I still held the upper hand while I could threaten Imogen's life.

Mirroring my action, Huffman's sidekicks raised their guns and aimed them at Kate. Bolan pulled out the cannon he'd used to down the chopper earlier in the day, but I noticed him subtly weighing up the others, deciding which one of them was the greatest threat to his personal quest for vengeance. Huffman stood with his hands clasped. He watched the proceedings with his smile fixed in place.

'Remember the plan,' I whispered and Imogen replied by stiffening her shoulders. She sobbed, and this time it wasn't an act.

The women approached each other, their steps short and full of apprehension. I could only see Kate's expression, but I guessed that Imogen's would be the same. Both women were terrified, but full of an overwhelming love for the other.

Just keep walking, Kate, I thought, don't do anything to spoil the plan now. I saw her gaze flicker past her sister and she looked at me. I couldn't show her anything but a stern face; if I did anything else it would spoil everything.

The sisters' steps grew faster as the distance between them lessened. I could hear both of them making wordless noises and I hoped that they wouldn't give in to their urge to run to each other and hug.

'Keep on walking, Kate,' Huffman warned from his end. 'No talking to your sister. No touching either.'

'You heard the man, Imogen. If you want your sister to live, do exactly as he says.' As I shouted those words I saw Kate's face twist. If she'd had her gag removed she'd have been cursing me loud enough for everyone to hear.

Ten feet separated them.

Kate angled towards her sister.

Imogen shook her head savagely, telling her not to come near.

Five feet and Kate held her sister's gaze as though their souls were locked in an embrace.

Three feet.

Two.

One.

I wanted to yell at Imogen, but if I did that the others would fire out of reaction. Instead, I had to wait for the longest second of my life.

In the next instant, Imogen twisted towards Kate, grabbed her as though taking her down in a tackle and both women rolled together to the side of the road and into a shallow gully.

At the same time I rushed forward, firing shots as rapidly as I could squeeze the trigger.

Huffman's people didn't react until a full second and a half after we did.

The two with their rifles raised swung them to find me. I zigzagged, firing back at them. From that distance, and at a run, only a lucky bullet would strike them, but it was enough to make them flinch. Their return shots scorched the air around me. I was still thirty yards short of the women, who were already beginning their crawl in my direction. Another half-second passed and then the remaining man and woman with Huffman and Bolan had their guns up.

'Don't kill Ballard!' I heard Huffman roar.

His command was enough to halt all their bullets as their brains assimilated this new information.

Undeterred, I continued to fire.

My bullets struck the vehicle behind Huffman, and I saw him leap to the side, then scurry backwards to put the vehicle between us. I wasn't concerned about him getting away; I only wanted Kate – and now Imogen – out of there. Angling off the road, I went into the ditch. Rain hadn't fallen lately and the ditch was dry. I pounded along it firing the occasional shot at the group of vehicles.

Huffman's killers were spreading out.

A tall man who looked like he was more used to wrestling steers than firing an assault rifle dropped to one knee and placed the stock of his M16 to his shoulder. He had me in his sights.

Then blood puffed from his head and he went down on his belly, his rifle rolling away from his spasming fingers. A second or so later the crack of a M24 sniper rifle rolled across the prairie.

Thank God, my friends had made it to their positions in time.

'To me,' I yelled at the sisters. 'Keep low, but get here as fast as you can.'

Coming to a halt, I fired a round at another of Huffman's men. He was a muscle-freak but even his overdeveloped pectorals wouldn't stop a jacketed round. He went over backwards, landing on his ass in the road. But then he was rolling to one side, avoiding my second shot. Sitting up quickly, he pulled the trigger on his assault rifle and I had to flatten myself against the ground to avoid the bullets. Kate and Imogen's screams were strident and I blinked up at them, seeing them throw themselves down together.

'Get up,' I shouted at them. 'Stick together. Huffman still wants you alive, Imogen, they won't shoot at you.'

My words of advice weren't true of my own predicament. The muscle man loosed another volley of rounds at me and dirt and blades of grass were kicked into my face. I closed my eyes to avoid being blinded. They were only shut for a second. During that time, I heard the thunder of a sniper rifle and the man's M16 fell silent. When I looked for him he was lying belly down and his head was no longer fully attached to his body.

Then I had to move. Larry Bolan let loose with his Magnum and the noise was like a cannon-roll. Beside him, Huffman's gun also spat fire. Then Rink or Harvey put some Winchester rounds through the vehicle they were standing beside and both men leaped for cover.

Kate's police training was taking over now that she'd

recovered from the initial shock. I saw her haul her sister up and they began running towards me. I covered them, firing at the remaining male stranger. This man looked whip-thin, and he moved sinuously to avoid my bullet. He fired back and I wasn't so quick. The bullet nicked my trapezius muscle and took a chunk of meat with it. Luckily for me it was on my left side so my gun arm was not impeded – that was if I discounted the feeling that I'd just been kicked by a mule and the resulting fire that spread down my chest.

'Get in the car and keep your heads down,' I told Kate as she bundled Imogen towards me. Our eyes met for a fraction of a second and I saw that the hatred there a moment ago was gone. She now appeared full of gratitude and not a little concern at the blood pouring out of my jacket collar. 'I'm OK, just get going.'

'Give me a gun, Joe,' she said. 'I can help.'

'Just help me get Imogen in the car.'

The sinuous man and the woman had dropped to their knees and both had their guns trained on me. However, Imogen and Kate were now in their line of fire and they could not shoot for fear of hitting Imogen. I back-pedalled, keeping up the status quo. I didn't fire on them, merely kept them in my sights. I couldn't see Huffman or Bolan, and guessed both had taken cover when Rink and Harvey had opened up on them.

'It's done, Huffman,' I yelled over the sudden silence. 'Finished. Leave it at that and we'll disappear. You've got the damn camera and the evidence you're worried about. You don't need Imogen any more.'

My words were all bullshit.

I knew that things weren't finished and so must Huffman.

But they were for now.

Kate and Imogen piled in to the Windstar and I was only seconds behind them. Throwing the vehicle into reverse I drove backwards at speed, hit a handbrake turn and then rocketed for the gate. In my rear-view mirror I saw the four remaining figures converge at the front of the lead car. None of them raised their guns.

The last thing I heard from behind was a defiant roar that I put down to Larry Bolan. There was no way things were finished.

38

We had a short wait but Rink and Harvey were back at the same place I'd dropped them off within a few minutes. My friends materialised out of the long grass next to the road, each with his rifle in hand. Harvey clambered in the front while Rink got in with the sisters. Rink stashed both his and Harvey's M24s in the luggage compartment behind the back seats and covered them with a blanket. As soon as that was done, I hit the gas and we took off for our cabin by the lake.

'Jesus Christ,' Harvey said. 'You've been hit, Hunter. Pull over and let me drive.'

'I'll be fine ...' I said through gritted teeth. To be honest the pain was engulfing me and there were shadows at the edges of my vision.

'Pull over, Goddamnit!' Rink said in my ear.

'We'll put some distance between us and Quicksilver Ranch first. The bastards could be following.'

'After you drove off they got back in their vehicles, but they looked like they were heading to the ranch,' Rink said. 'I put a couple bullets their way just to keep 'em moving, but I don't think I hit any of them.'

Kate turned to peer back along the road. It was empty, but that didn't mean that they weren't coming. Our sudden attack had disarrayed them, but they were still capable of fighting back. It was only the threat of the M24s that had stopped them following. Once they realised the hidden snipers had left the scene they would be mounting their pursuit. Huffman wouldn't give up so easily. And neither would Larry Bolan. He'd be royally pissed off that he'd missed his chance at me again.

'We should have dropped them all when we had the chance,' Rink said.

'That wasn't our purpose.'

'I know.' Rink turned to the sisters, saying what I wanted to say. 'Sorry you had to go through that, but there was no other way to get both of you out of there alive.'

'It was terrifying, but it doesn't matter,' Imogen said, looking at her younger sister's face.

'Not now,' Kate agreed and hugged her sister.

They had barely stopped hugging since they'd got into the Windstar. Finally Kate extricated herself from Imogen's arms and leaned forward and touched a point on my neck just above the bullet wound. Her fingers were soft and warm and I trembled.

'Except for one thing, Joe Hunter. You ever do anything like that again and I swear to God I'll kill you myself.'

I'd have responded, except her words were as soft as her touch. I sighed wearily. It had been a long few days since we'd met on the Gulf Coast. My eyes began to close. Not so much fatigue as relief at seeing her alive. Maybe my eyes stayed shut a little too long.

'That's it!' Harvey became animated beside me. 'Pull over now. I'm taking over. Before you do what Huffman couldn't and kill the lot of us.'

I brought the Windstar to a halt and we all shifted position. Harvey drove and Rink took shotgun. I was wedged between the two women in the back. It wasn't a bad place to find myself. Between them they had my shirt undone and they fussed with the wound in my shoulder. I fell asleep with a smile on my lips.

The next time I woke up, I was back at the cabin. Everything was dark and still. My head was a little fuzzy and I thought that at some point someone must have fed me a bucketful of painkillers. My left side was numb, and reaching tentatively with my good hand, I found my shoulder compressed by expertly administered bandages. Sitting up, I found I was on the single bed in the cabin. There was a light on in the bathroom but the door was closed. It sounded empty and I guessed the light had been left on to add some ambient glow without the harsh overhead light waking me. A low buzz of conversation came from outside.

I was naked but for my boxer shorts. I found my jeans and tugged them on, twice falling back on to the bed before I managed to button them up.

My steps were unsteady as I negotiated the room. Opening the door, I saw my friends sitting in a loose group down by the lakeside. They heard the door and all turned to look at me. They had got a fire going and it looked like they were enjoying a late dinner. My stomach did a flip at the greasy smell of burgers and I had to push down the urge to vomit.

Kate and Imogen were so alike in the flickering light from the fire that it took me a second or two to differentiate them. Making matters worse was the fact that Kate was dressed in some of the spare clothing Imogen had brought with her. Kate helped by standing up and moving my way. Imogen, Rink and Harvey watched her approach me, then discreetly returned to their own conversation.

'You're supposed to be sleeping,' Kate said softly.

'You know me, Kate; I never do plan on doing much sleeping. I'll be OK before long.'

'You've been shot, Joe. You're weak and the rest will do you good.'

'I've been shot before. Much worse than this.'

Kate placed a hand on my chest. She traced an old wound just to the left of my sternum. This wasn't a bullet wound but a scar left by a knife that had come very close to ending my life. Tubal Cain – the serial killer who kidnapped my brother last year – had almost killed me, but I'd killed him instead. The other bullet wound I referred to was hidden beneath these latest bandages.

'Back to bed, tough guy,' Kate said, pressing me back into the room.

'There are things to be done . . .'

'Yes, Joe, there are.' Her eyes met mine and even in the dimness I saw her pupils dilate. She pushed me even harder and I stumbled backwards. Kate followed me into the room, pushing until my knees met the bed and I was forced to sit down. Kate stood over me. There were tears in her eyes, and she slowly shook her head.

'At first I thought that you were going to hurt my sister,' Kate said sadly. 'And I hated you for that.'

'It was only a trick . . .'

'I know that now. You risked your life for me and Imogen and you got shot. But at the time . . . God! I don't know! I hated you as much as I hated any of them.'

'But now you know the truth do you still hate me?'

'A little.'

'A little?'

'I hate you for making me hate you,' she said. Then she laughed at the absurdity of her statement.

'I shouldn't have left you alone at that motel.'

'No, you shouldn't have. You should've stayed. You know that's what I wanted, don't you?'

'I did,' I said. 'But there were other things on my mind.'

'Rink explained to me about your ex-wife. That it was your wedding anniversary. You must have loved her a great deal, Joe.'

'I did.'

'You haven't fully let go yet, have you?'

'It wasn't my idea to divorce.'

'Rink said that Diane remarried, that she has a new husband.'

'Yes. Simon. He's a decent man.'

'So don't you think it's time to let her go?'

I couldn't answer. Despite everything there'd always be a place in my heart for my ex-wife.

Kate sat on the edge of the bed. She laid her palm flat on my stomach. She looked incredibly beautiful with the light from the bathroom playing on her skin. 'If you had stayed, things would have been very different.'

'I know and I'm sorry. It must've been awful for you.'

'It was.'

'It's crazy,' I said, 'but everything that's happened since then is because I left you there alone. Makes you wonder about fate, doesn't it?'

Kate eyed me. 'Fate seems to have its own way of sorting out the order of things. If you hadn't gone out when you did, we wouldn't have got this opportunity to get to know each other all over again.'

'You still want to know me?' I leaned up and took one of her hands in mine.

'Now that we've got Imogen back safe and sound, I want that more than anything in the world.'

'Me too.'

I pulled her down beside me and we held each other. Kate kissed me; this time I didn't pull away.

39

Huffman had returned to the living room of his ranch. He was sitting in his wing-backed chair, silently contemplating his next strategy. He held Imogen Ballard's camera in his cupped palms, watching on the small screen as Trent and Larry Bolan beat the sheriff of Little Fork to death. Jim Aitken watched the proceedings, holding his gun levelled at the sheriff's chest so that he couldn't fight back. Not that he'd be able to, not against the Bolans. The horrendous beating culminated in Trent ripping off one of the man's ears. The microphone had picked up Imogen Ballard's sob. She'd tried to restrain herself but failed. Then the picture swept across the forest and came to a halt on a single figure standing watching the proceedings. The picture zoomed in.

'She didn't even get my good side,' Huffman grunted. But there was no mistaking his face. It didn't help matters that he'd lifted a hand and waved at her: pretty incriminating evidence. At that the picture disintegrated into a series of flashes and broken pixels as Imogen fled in panic. He could hear her ragged cries and the pounding of her feet.

A film like this could send him to prison in a heartbeat. There would be copies, despite what Joe Hunter said. It was even more important now that he kill both sisters and their champion. In reality, the sisters had become inconsequential to the feared killer named Quicksilver. He would kill them and that would be that, but with Joe Hunter things would be different. Hunter had embarrassed him in front of the other syndicate enforcers; he would be made to suffer first.

He'd allowed Wicker the pleasure of hacking Desmond Molloy to pieces, but Huffman decided that he personally would take Hunter to the slaughterhouse. Unlike Molloy, Hunter would still be alive when Huffman started cutting.

Huffman turned off the camera.

Larry Bolan was sitting in silence at the far end of the room, lost in his own thoughts. Huffman lifted the camera. 'This is more damaging to you than it is to me,' he told the giant man. 'I'm surprised that you didn't want it back as much as I did.'

'I've never been concerned about the woman or what she filmed,' Larry said. 'What was she going to do, post it on the internet? I've seen more zombie and cannibal shit on YouTube than you can shake a stick at. People don't take any of that stuff seriously. They'd have just put it down to another pile of crap that someone staged.'

'She could've put it into the hands of law enforcement. They'd have taken it seriously enough, particularly when the sheriff failed to turn up for work.'

'We had that covered, boss,' Larry explained. 'He'd have looked like he'd run off with his new woman after stealing money from Judge Wallace.'

Aitken had set that up. He exchanged a filing cabinet drawer from the sheriff's office with the one in Wallace's. There would have been no reason for Devaney's fingerprints to turn up there unless he had broken into the judge's office.

Huffman agreed that the disappearance of the sheriff could be covered by that scenario, but not when there was accompanying footage of the man being beaten to death with him as the overseer. But he let it go. He had the original footage back and copies meant very little without the original. It was as Larry pointed out: these days even an amateur with the most basic computer program could stage a convincing hoax. His lawyers would pull that kind of evidence to pieces.

Huffman put all thoughts of the video away, shelving it as a minor problem to be dealt with later. 'You still want Joe Hunter, Larry?'

'I want him so bad I can taste it.'

'I want him too,' said Huffman. 'But we needn't be enemies over this.'

Larry straightened, causing the chair to creak ominously.

'Since when did we become enemies, boss?'

'Since you shot down my helicopter.' Huffman sat back, folding his hands on his stomach.

'You knew about that?'

'The pilot got a call off before it went down,' Huffman explained. 'He said there was a giant man with a Magnum. Who do you think that sounds like, Larry?'

'But you still asked me back, even though I killed your men?'

'I did, Larry. I understood your motivation. You wanted to be the one to kill Joe Hunter. If killing the others was your way of getting him, so be it.'

Larry stood up. He towered in the shadows of the room, his head almost scraping the ceiling. 'I killed more than those punks.'

'Aitken and Wallace? Yes, I guessed that as well. Aitken's head had been twisted off his shoulders and Wallace had taken a swan dive from the top floor of the restaurant: I didn't think that was Joe Hunter's style.'

'So where does that leave us?'

'It should leave us as enemies. But, like I said, I don't want things to be that way between us.'

Larry laughed. 'Those other assholes you brought in might not have realised that you're using them, but I'm not stupid. They're getting killed one by one. When do you plan for me to die?'

'I'm planning nothing of the sort. The only thing I want is Joe Hunter. He's embarrassed me, Larry.'

'Embarrassed you? The motherfucker murdered my little brother!'

'I want to kill him *personally*.'

Larry shook his head. 'He's mine.'

Huffman stood up, as languid as a cat stretching. Larry tensed. Huffman waved him down. 'Relax,

Larry. I want to kill him, but I don't mind having you along for the ride. We can do this together, but I take the credit.'

'I rip him to pieces but anyone asks and I tell them it was you?' Larry's mouth turned downward as he contemplated Huffman's offer. It was a win-win scenario if ever he'd seen one. He'd get his revenge, but he didn't take the fallout for the man's murder. 'What's not to like about that?'

'No one must ever know the truth, Larry.'

'Who am I going to tell?'

'It will mean killing the others.'

'Grade and Wicker? I don't mind doing them.'

'I mean those Hunter has working with him. Someone was out there with a sniper rifle, could even have been two of them judging by the angles of the shots that dropped Souza and Burton. The women will have to die, too.'

'We'll kill them all.'

'But we keep Hunter for last.'

'Whenever.' Larry nodded towards the floor. 'What about your people downstairs?'

Huffman pondered for the briefest of moments. 'They'll tell anyone exactly what I tell them to say.'

'Whatever.'

Huffman reached out a hand.

Larry eyed him quizzically.

'What's wrong, Larry? Don't we have a deal?'

'We have a deal,' Larry told him. 'I'm just checking where the hell you've got that damn razor.'

Huffman grinned. 'That's why I like you, Larry. Did I ever tell you that you were my favourite?'

'Yeah, boss, you did.'

They shook on their renewed partnership.

40

Pilot Point was deserted as we hit the road in the early hours of the morning. Rink and Harvey were with me in the Windstar, taking up the front seats. Between their large bodies there was little view through the front windscreen. Imogen and Kate were in the back with me, both lost in their own thoughts. Kate had her head on my good shoulder and her soft floral scent made me light-headed. It conjured memories of how we'd spent the last few hours together.

We were heading for DFW Airport to put the women on a plane to Rink's office in Tampa. Rink had organised protection from a couple of ex-cops he occasionally employed. McTeer and Velasquez were good guys I'd shared a beer with on a couple of occasions. They'd agreed to chaperone the sisters on the return flight, then cover them back in Florida. We were meeting them in a couple of hours, then doing a return journey to take Huffman in his lair.

Our time in the cabin had been tender, but when Kate had learned our plans she'd once more become the fiery woman I'd grown to admire. She gave me hell about going after Huffman and the others. I was injured and tired and took the haranguing with a calmness that pissed her off even more. In the end I kissed her again and told her:

'I have to finish this now, Kate. Otherwise none of us will ever be safe. Do you want to go through life constantly watching your back, waiting for someone to turn up and kill you? That's the kind of life I've had to put up with for years . . . it's not something I'd wish on my worst enemy.'

'I'm frightened I won't see you again.'

'I can handle Huffman.'

She'd gently touched my wounded shoulder. 'You were lucky last time; a couple of inches lower and you'd have been dead.'

'That was different. That time I was trying to save lives, not take them.'

The police officer in her had baulked at my final few words.

'They're evil people, Kate.'

'I know.'

'We have to stop them or they'll just keep on coming. Even if we send copies of the tape to the FBI, Huffman has a long reach. If it wasn't him chasing us, it would be someone else. The other syndicates owe him.'

'You expect me to argue,' Kate had said, surprising me, 'but I'm not going to. I've been thinking: other than those at the ranch, there's no one left alive who can identify us. If they were killed, then that would put us in the clear.'

I'd held her gaze and her eyes were calm and clear.

'You've a ruthless streak I didn't know about.'

'Not ruthless, Joe, I'm just being pragmatic.' She'd laughed at the irony. 'It seems like we've spent too much time together. Your way of thinking's beginning to rub off on me.'

'There are still people at Little Fork who know about us. Aitken and the judge.'

'They're both dead.'

'What?'

'I overheard Huffman; he assumed that you were responsible. I guessed otherwise.'

'There were other police with Aitken when he came to try and catch me,' I said. But then I realised that at that time they were unaware of my name. The locals who had been with the Bolans had no idea who I was either. But I wasn't sure what they'd learned about Kate.

It was as if she'd read my mind. 'Aitken didn't know who I was until after he'd handed me over to Huffman. I didn't tell him my name when I first phoned him, only that I needed to speak to him about Imogen Ballard.'

'Imogen's identity is still a problem. The locals know who Huffman was looking for.'

'But they're not going to say anything, are they? Who's going to admit that they were involved with what happened at Little Fork?'

'True. And no one else knows that Imogen ever turned up here. Which means it's even more important that we stop Huffman and the others now.'

Kate had actually convinced herself that my plan was the correct course of action. She'd shaken her head in mock reproof, then she'd held me again. 'Just make sure you don't get yourself killed.'

'I don't plan on that,' I'd reassured her. But it was always a possibility.

We didn't broach the subject again. We just sat next to each other in the Windstar and stayed connected for the journey down to DFW.

McTeer and Velasquez met us. Both men knew we were up against Huffman, but they knew not to ask any questions about what we were planning next. I hugged Imogen goodbye. Then Kate and I shared a private moment before she waved me away. She linked arms with her sister and – flanked by their new bodyguards – they walked together to the departure gate.

'You OK, Joe?' Rink asked. It's not often he addresses me by my given name. I know that when he does he's at his most concerned.

'I've had worse injuries than this,' I told him, working my aching shoulder. The bullet had got skin and a little of the underlying muscle, but it wasn't a debilitating shot. 'It's not going to stop me. Once the adrenalin kicks in, I won't feel a thing.'

'You know that's not what I meant.'

Letting go of Kate was harder than I'd imagined. I'd barely known her a few days, but I had to admit that she had a powerful hold on me.

'I'll be OK.'

Harvey led the way back to the parking lot. Rink and

I walked shoulder to shoulder like we had so many times in the past.

'This is all your fault, you know,' I said.

'How'd you figure that?'

'When we spoke on the phone before Kate went missing, it was you who gave me the kick in the pants I needed.'

'I can live with that.'

'It's a problem, Rink. My lifestyle isn't suited to having a girl along for the ride.'

'Then don't get too serious. Just accept things for what they are. Have a little fun, enjoy yourself for a change.'

'I like her, Rink, but I'm afraid that Kate's the one taking things a bit too seriously.'

'Don't worry, pretty soon she'll see you for the asshole you really are and she'll dump you for someone nicer.'

'Someone like you?'

'Of course.' Rink gave me his face-splitting grin. Then he laid his hand on my shoulder. 'Come on, Casanova. It's time to put all these distractions aside. There'll be time for pretty faces when Huffman's in his grave.'

'Yeah,' I agreed.

Back in the Windstar, I had the back seat to myself and it felt as deserted as an empty hangar. It was difficult getting a certain pretty face out of my mind. In the end, I lay across the seat, snatching a short nap, building my strength for what was to come. I had to be at my best if I ever wanted to see Kate again.

41

'Wicker, I've a job for you,' Huffman said.

The woman had been sipping green tea from a china cup in his kitchen. Her cell phone was lying on the table as though she'd just put it down and Huffman guessed that she'd been reporting back to her employers. She looked at him quizzically. This close, Huffman noticed how dark her eyes were, as though all light had been taken from them, and her pupils had dilated to the maximum. They looked solid black. He wondered if there was something other she'd taken from her DEA days than her skills: she looked high. But then she blinked and the illusion passed.

'I've already got a job, boss. I'm going to kill Joe Hunter for you.'

'There's something else I want from you first.'

Wicker sat back in her chair, splaying her legs in a fashion that wasn't very feminine. She dug her thumbs into her pants pockets and sat looking up at Huffman. 'What could be more important than that?'

'I want Imogen Ballard dead. She could still be a threat to me if she's alive.'

'She's with Hunter. I'll kill her when I get him.'

'I don't think that's the case,' Huffman said. 'In fact, I know it's not.'

Wicker slowly picked up her cell phone and placed it in her breast pocket. Her other tools were either on her person or in the small bag she'd brought with her. She could be on her way with only a moment's notice. 'Tell me what you do know.'

There was much more than he'd relate to her right now. He'd been busy since his conversation with Larry Bolan, thinking it prudent to learn as much about Joe Hunter as he could. He recalled that Kate Piers had arrived in Little Fork by way of a trip to Tampa, Florida. A couple of contacts he had down there had asked around and told him about an Englishman who'd been making waves, and plenty of enemies, in the criminal underworld. It seemed that this man – a cipher by all accounts – was getting quite a reputation as a vigilante. Some people whispered that he was ex-Special Forces. They also said that he moonlighted for a private investigations business run by an ex-soldier named Jared Rington. Jared Rington was out of town, and it didn't take too much imagination to conclude that Rington was one of the snipers who'd helped Hunter earlier. Huffman was of the opinion that neither of the men would be leaving Texas any time soon.

The women were another matter. Hunter would want them out of the way. He was coming back for a showdown, no doubt about it. It was the only route left open to him. The women, Huffman concluded, would be sent back to Tampa where they'd be safe.

'The women boarded a plane out of DFW a couple of hours ago. They used false names, but I don't doubt that it was them. Two men are travelling with them.'

'But not Hunter and his mysterious friend,' Wicker said. 'Someone else is helping them?'

'We were able to check the passenger manifest. Two men arrived on one flight from Tampa, Florida, and then boarded the next flight out. Their names have been put through the IRS database and they came back as being residents of Tampa. Both men are employed as private security consultants. They occasionally subcontract to a company called Rington Investigations.' Huffman placed a slip of paper on the table and Wicker drew it towards her. 'That's their names and the location of their office. Think you can handle this, Wicker?'

'Two rent-a-cops and a couple of women? I'm sure I'm up to the task.' Wicker placed the note alongside her phone in her pocket. 'But why me, boss? Why aren't you sending Grade or that hulking idiot, Bolan?'

'Because I think that you're the best person for the job.'

She smiled. 'For a second there I thought you wanted to protect me from the big bad men that you're going to fight.'

'There is that,' Huffman said. Then he grunted. 'You're as tough as any of the others, Wicker. This isn't a sexist thing: I just thought you'd appreciate another chance at Kate Piers. I stopped you killing her the last time you met.'

'Yeah, you did, boss. And that bitch tried to shoot me, too.'

'So are you up for it?'

She stood up, rocking on her heels and knuckling the small of her back. 'Both sisters, right?'

'Kill Imogen *and* Kate and I'll pay you a bonus,' Huffman promised. He handed her a second slip of paper. 'That's your flight reservation number. Pick your tickets up at the desk I've written on there.'

'How do I get to the airport?'

'Take my car.' He tossed her his keys. 'I'll have it picked up after I'm finished here.'

'I might be back before then,' Wicker said. 'I'll bring it myself.'

Huffman shrugged. He didn't believe that she would be back in time. Hunter would be coming in the next few hours.

42

The biorhythms of the human body and mind are at their lowest ebb between the hours of three and four in the morning, and it's said that more people die during those hours than at any other time of the day. It's certainly true that most people are sound asleep then, a solid reason why police launch early-morning raids on criminals in an attempt to unsettle them and catch them unprepared. When I was actively involved in seek-destroy missions on terrorists, most of my work was done during this dead time.

It would make sense to launch our assault on Huffman but for one fact: Huffman would know that this was when I'd likely be coming for him. He still had some of his killers with him – not to mention Larry Bolan – and he would make sure that they were all alert and ready for the attack. So, I decided to let the bastard sweat, but not for too long.

I couldn't get my head round what Huffman was really all about. This had started with him protecting his investment in an up-and-coming town in Kentucky but now things had changed. It was almost as if the man had taken me on as some form of personal challenge.

I've fought some crazy and dangerous killers in my time. Even after retiring from the unit I have made war against Tubal Cain, a man responsible for taking the bones from dozens of his victims, and also against a contract killer who fancied himself as the fallen angel Dantalion. Both Cain and Dantalion were supremely insane, but to some extent at least I could understand what motivated them. Huffman remained a mystery that I couldn't work out.

It wasn't that he was afraid of me. In fact, judging by the times we'd talked on the phone, he sounded like he was relishing making my acquaintance.

In his own inimitable style, Rink weighed him up better than I did. 'Don't you get it, buddy?' he said in his languid drawl. 'The asshole's playing games. He thinks he's at the centre of some shoot-'em-up video game and he loves every goddamn second of it.'

'You think so?'

We were back at the cabin, sitting out by the fire that Rink had rebuilt, waiting for the sun to cast a finger of light over the lake. The burgers I'd baulked at earlier were now something I looked forward to. Harvey was playing chef. He pointed the tongs he was using to turn the burgers at me. 'Either that or he wants to prove something.'

'Like Cain,' Rink added. 'He wanted you on his list of victims because he thought it'd make him into some sort of big guy.'

'It's different with Huffman, though. He doesn't know who I am. He has my name but nothing about my background.'

'That was before,' Rink pointed out. 'You can bet your sweet cheeks he's been diggin' around and knows exactly who you are now.'

'Wouldn't be surprised if he knows who we all are,' Harvey said, loading a burger into a bun and passing it my way.

I shrugged my shoulders, and remembered that was a bad idea when my wound shrieked in protest. Gritting my teeth, I inspected my late supper, or early breakfast, or whatever. It looked all right. I took a bite and chewed perfunctorily. It tasted better than it looked.

'I don't think he has those kinds of resources,' I said. 'I had Kate's phone with me for a day and a half. If he had connections he'd have been able to trace it. The same kinds of connections would've been able to dig up information on me. He hasn't acted on tracing the phone, and I don't think he's found anything out about me. Nothing about my past anyway.'

'First rule of engagement?' Rink asked.

'Never underestimate your opponent. But that's not what I'm doing. I just can't understand why he would want to face me. What would it achieve?'

Rink wagged a burger-loaded bun at me. 'You're forgettin' what you've accomplished. You've killed half his people; destroyed one of his buildings, fucked up his entire operation in Kentucky and taken Kate back from him. Maybe there's a little grudging respect in him.'

'It's still weird.'

'And the rest of your life has been normal?'

I had to acquiesce.

'Larry Bolan I understand. As far as he's concerned I murdered his brother. If the tables were turned, I'd want me dead too. I just don't get Huffman.'

'So don't bother,' Rink said. 'Let's just go kill the frog-giggin' son of a bitch and get our asses back to Florida.'

Rink's suggestion seemed as good as any other. I chewed on my food as the sun broke over the skyline behind me. It was that false dawn that stretches through the still hours before the rest of the world comes alive. When I'd enough carbohydrates inside me, I washed the greasy taste away with strong coffee. Junk food and caffeine is never the choice of athletes, but I was hoping to get this over with quickly and not run a marathon before my enemies were dead.

Harvey had a mission to perform before we could set off. He'd promised that the M24s would be back with the sergeant at Fort Worth Joint Reserve Base. This time we wouldn't need the rifles, it would be all close stuff. Plus, we had to use guns that would be untraceable on any data base. When Rink and Harvey had fired on the two out at Quicksilver Ranch, we'd relied on the fact that the Winchester bullets would pass through their targets and be lost on the vast prairie. This time there'd be no way to avoid leaving behind incriminating rounds.

Harvey returned within ninety minutes. Meanwhile we had cleaned up the cabin, wiping prints, and ensuring there was no trace of my blood anywhere inside. There was little likelihood that the three supposed-fishermen who'd rented the cabin would be tied to what was to occur in the coming hours, but you could never be too careful. Then we'd prepped our weapons. I had my SIG and a KA-BAR knife, and Rink elected for the Glock 17 and his trusty Mossberg combat shotgun. He too had his knife. I knew that Harvey packed a semi-automatic handgun and he'd be ready to go. We all wore black jackets over T-shirts, jeans and boots: Rink and I looked like doormen from the roughest bar in town, but Harvey still looked sharp.

Before we left Pilot Point for the final time, I had one last task to fulfil. I walked along the shore of the lake while I phoned Kate. Although I told myself that my motive was to check she'd arrived safely at Rink's office, really I wanted to hear her voice again. We hadn't spoken about our time in the cabin and I just wanted to reassure myself that she didn't now regret getting so close. If she didn't want anything further to do with me, it wouldn't change the outcome of my day, except maybe I'd be even more heavy-handed than usual.

'Hi, Joe.' Her voice was low. She sounded tired, but I was relieved to find that it wasn't of me. She had put in a few exhausting days, and I'd woken her from her first sleep in many hours. 'How's your shoulder?'

'It's fine. I'm fine.'

'Let's keep things that way, shall we?'

'You bet,' I said. 'You're back at Rink's place. Are McTeer and Velasquez still with you?'

'They've set up shop in the front: we're using the back room to get a little sleep.'

'Is Imogen OK?'

'She's fine, Joe.'

'I was a little rough on her back there. Tell her that I'm sorry.'

'She's fine. Really.'

'Good. We're about to set off,' I said. 'I just wanted you to know.'

'I'm not going to say goodbye.'

'Me neither.'

'See you later then.'

'Yeah. Try and get some sleep. I'll see you tonight, OK?'

'OK.'

We both rang off before things grew awkward. Then I put the phone away. It was time for my other tools, I thought, and I touched the butt of my gun. When I got back to the cabin, Rink and Harvey were waiting beside the Windstar.

'Ready, Hunter?' Rink asked.

'Let's roll.'

Some people refer to what I do as vigilantism; they assume that I must be some sort of damaged freak raging at the inability of law enforcement to do what needs doing. Often, vigilantes do have a slightly psychotic outlook, so much so that they become exactly what it is they are fighting against. Maybe a small measure of me could be weighed in that context, but it would be very, very small. As a child, I was the one who'd stick up for the little kid who everyone else thought was a loser. I suppose, instead of a vigilante, I should be looked upon as a protector. And the best way I know to protect is to take the fight directly to the threat.

In the past I've been guilty of rushing in and depending on my skills and a huge amount of luck to see me through trouble, but this time it couldn't be so rash. I wanted Huffman dead, but not at the expense of the lives of my friends, Rink and Harvey; they were owed more consideration than that. With that in mind, I decided my plan of attack on the drive to Quicksilver Ranch.

Last time we'd got no further than the entrance to Huffman's land. The ranch itself was over the horizon so we had no idea of the layout of the buildings or the surrounding countryside. But it appeared that Harvey's skill with a computer was up to its usual high standards. While Rink drove the Windstar, Harvey jammed in a mobile broadband connector and brought up aerial images of the ranch. There was little need for spies when you could Google just about anything or anywhere you desired. But Harvey went one further, bringing up the schematics of Huffman's house by digging into planning and construction records held on file in a Grayson County database.

The house was large by anyone's standards, with four storeys if you counted the basement and attic spaces. To me it had the look of a colonial mansion house, with an upper tier serving as the living quarters while the ground floor was given over to kitchen, dining and utility rooms. The house was next to a series of large buildings ending in what looked like livestock pens alongside a large rectangular structure. Then it was just grassland for miles in any direction I chose.

'Won't be easy getting close,' Rink said. 'Not without being seen. We should've kept the M24s and took 'em from a distance.'

This from a man who I'd witnessed crawling to within yards of a terrorist training cell in the Libyan desert to set up close target reconnaissance, then lying undetected, gathering intelligence, until the rest of our unit charged in and wiped them all out.

'The grass will give us cover almost all the way to the house,' Harvey said. 'Unless they have FLIR.'

He was talking about technology that military personnel use to locate enemies lying in ambush. Forward-looking infra-red detectors apply digital thermal imaging to build a picture of anything warmer than the ambient background. Heat leaking from even the best-camouflaged person cannot escape the device.

I didn't think that Huffman had FLIR technology to hand. The people he had working for him came from the criminal underworld and, though they had access to M16 assault rifles, didn't deem the more esoteric equipment necessary. But I could be wrong.

'They won't be looking for us sneaking up on them if I create a diversion,' I said. 'I could draw their fire while you two get into the buildings at the back of the ranch. It's me Huffman wants; they'll concentrate on me and that'll give you the opportunity to come in through the back door.'

'He'll be expecting us, too.' Rink was referring to the fact that we'd shown our hand when launching the ambush yesterday. 'He'll know that there were two shooters out in the grass because of the angles of the shots.'

'But he won't know if you're still working with me or not. If I play the demented vigilante bent on revenge, I think I can hold their attention long enough to make them forget all about you.'

'What's your idea?'

I told them.

Both of my friends shook their heads at the absurdity of my plan.

'Who do you think you are, goddamn Rooster Cogburn?' Rink asked.

Conjuring a picture of John Wayne with his horse's reins between his teeth and a gun in each hand, I grinned. If it was good enough for the Duke, it would be good enough for me.

Fill your hand, Huffman, I thought, *you son of a bitch!*

43

Robert Huffman had any number of places he could have waited for Joe Hunter. He owned several buildings spread across the Midwest. There was an office in Dallas that gave him a view of Reunion Tower and was little more than a stone's throw from the Texas School Book Depository, from where Lee Harvey Oswald purportedly fired the bullets that assassinated John F. Kennedy. His office was perched on the penthouse floor, on a level with the top of the nearby Hyatt, and on the days before the Dallas Stars moved to the American Airlines Center he could hear the cheering of the crowds from the nearby stadium.

But he chose to remain at Quicksilver Ranch because it was the most remote of his properties. Twice now in the past twenty-four hours the sounds of gunfire and exploding vehicles had not raised the interest of the police, and he was counting on the third time being no different. He wanted his war with Hunter to be waged with no outside interference. That wouldn't be the case if they went at it in downtown Dallas.

He waited for Hunter to come to him.

Some of his men were ranged in a skirmish line protecting the approach to the ranch house. They had been out there for hours now. Larry Bolan was somewhere inside preparing himself for Hunter's arrival. He'd allowed Bolan this latitude in order to keep the big man from exploding too soon. His need for revenge on Joe Hunter was like a slowly burning fuse of indeterminate length. Huffman didn't want Bolan's rage let loose until Hunter was no longer a threat. If he had been out there now, the likelihood was that he'd murder Grade and the others in order to ensure he was the only one to get an opportunity to kill Hunter.

He asked himself why he had allowed Bolan to live. His remark that Bolan had always been his favourite was as false as his jovial demeanour. Bolan meant nothing to him other than as a handy tool when it came to doling out violence. But he had become a defective tool. Bolan had murdered six of Huffman's people in his attempt to gain revenge on his brother's killer. He didn't doubt that Bolan would try to kill him if he was perceived as a threat to completing the mission.

Bolan had agreed to give Huffman the glory of killing Hunter, but Huffman didn't believe him. Bolan would want his own legend. He'd sworn to his dead brother, Trent, that he would avenge him. Unless he shouted Hunter's defeat loud and clear, how would Trent hear him all the way from the afterlife?

Bolan would have to die.

There was nothing else for it.

But not yet. Defective tool that he was, Bolan was

still useful. Even a blunt hammer could knock a nail into wood. Once Hunter was dead Larry Bolan would follow him. He could personally tell his wall-eyed, crazy brother all the details when he joined him in hell. He could tell Trent that Robert Huffman, Quicksilver, was the top dog, and he could show his slit throat as proof.

Huffman slid out his razor.

He picked a slip of notepaper off his desk and ran the razor against it, cutting a neat line and allowing the severed portion to flutter to the desktop. The edge was incredibly sharp. Then he turned the blade so that it reflected his eyes. He peered into the depths of the steel, as if the eyes staring back at him were those of a metaphysical being locked within. He wondered if the man in the blade was in fact the real Quicksilver, some elemental spirit that had lain dormant for way too long. Or that a portion of his own soul had been imprisoned within the steel and was demanding release. It had been many years since the razor had tasted blood, but since it had stolen the life from Desmond Molloy, Huffman could almost believe that the blade-being demanded more. All fanciful stuff, he had to accept, because he wasn't one for fantasy. He knew the truth: there was only his own desire for violence. But it did no harm to dream.

'It's time,' he whispered.

44

The sun was a full hand's breadth above the horizon when I drove the Windstar through the gate and on to Quicksilver Ranch. The hire vehicle had been a dependable ally over the last twenty-four hours but it was almost time to say goodbye. Not that I was going to grow all sentimental over it. It was an inanimate object, given the illusion of life by electricity and the combustion of gas. It was simply a tool.

I checked the gas and saw that it was hovering near the empty mark. Maybe I should have put a little more juice in the tank when I'd filled the drum riding on the back seat: I'd look an idiot if the car ran out of fuel before I reached my destination. But I only had a mile to go, and the fuel in the reserve tank would be enough.

Pressing on, I kept steady pressure on the gas pedal. Momentum was my best ally right now. The assault was on. No turning back.

The thought that innocent people might be at the ranch had been a worry, but I didn't think there were any innocents where Robert Huffman was concerned.

He knew I was coming; he wanted impartial witnesses on site as little as I did. If there were any staff employed at the ranch who weren't party to his criminal dealings, they'd have been shunted off by now. I hoped. Because what I planned did not differentiate bad guys from good. It wouldn't be selective. Anyone who got in my way was going to die.

In some respects my tactics weren't the type I'd normally use. Not with any conscience. I'd fought my entire professional career against men who employed these kinds of extremes. Suicide bombers, they're called. In my opinion, driving a moving bomb into a packed marketplace is both crude and cowardly, but it got the job done. In the eyes of the fanatics, these bombers are heroes. I'd always thought of them as the worst kind of scum. And now I'd joined their likes. Nothing would validate my actions except the knowledge that my plan was to save innocent lives. Then there was the fact that I didn't plan on suicide. I was a kamikaze pilot with an ejector seat.

The Windstar roared along the road, picking up speed. I passed the place where I'd rescued Kate. Then I continued, going over the swell in the land and seeing for the first time the lair of my enemy. The house was pale under the wash of the morning sun. It looked archaic in this modern world, and it made me wonder if Huffman was the type to long for past times. But the thought was only fleeting. I saw a man rise up from the side of the road and lift something to his mouth. Radio, I realised, announcing my arrival. Another man materialised from the long grass on the other side of the road and aimed an M16 assault rifle at me. I hadn't seen this bespectacled man before, but Kate had told me about someone called Nixon whom she'd knocked cold when she'd tried to make her own run for freedom. She'd said he was about the most human out of all of Huffman's hired guns.

'Bad judge of character, Kate,' I said.

I gunned the engine, just as the man with the rifle let loose a stream of bullets at the Windstar. Metal tore through the vehicle, sparks and deafening bangs marking their progress, even as I pushed down on the door handle. I felt the tug of a bullet against my jacket, the heat of another passing my nose. Then I jumped for my life. I rolled across the road surface, came to my feet and fired at the man with the radio. My bullet hit him in his throat, cutting off any further words, and he fell over backwards, the radio thrown from his hand when he hit the dirt.

All of three or four seconds had passed since the man with the rifle opened up on the Windstar. I'd gone out the far side, blocked from his view. He was still unloading the remainder of a clip. The vehicle was bucking under the onslaught but hadn't deviated from its target. I had a clear view of the gunman but I let him continue to fire. All part of the plan.

Finally one of his bullets struck the canister in the rear seat and the Windstar went up like a Roman candle. Pieces of steaming metal were cast across the fields, igniting the grass, and the flash of exploding petrol immediately turned to oily black smoke roiling out of the shattered husk of the vehicle. The Windstar's engine died, shredded by the explosion, but the vehicle continued to roll at speed towards the ranch on flaming tyres.

I turned my gun on the man I believed to be Nixon. By now he had seen the devastation his bullets had wrought on the vehicle, but he was still a moment away from realising what the consequences were. His expression turned from one of triumph to one of disbelief as the Windstar continued towards the house.

'Oh, shit!'

'That's about right,' I said under my breath. Then I shot him in the chest. The shot was aimed at centre-mass: it punched his heart out through a hole in his back. At least he was saved from witnessing just how much he'd messed up.

Immediately I started for the house, following in the wake of foul-smelling smoke, dodging puddles of burning fuel that dotted the road. I could have used some of that FLIR technology Harvey had mentioned earlier because I couldn't see a damn thing. But I was happy. I couldn't see them but they couldn't see me: not a bad trade-off.

By the time the Windstar reached the house it was limping on deflated tyres. It wasn't speeding any longer, and it wouldn't be a battering ram the way I'd used Larry Bolan's Dodge Ram back at le Cœur de la Ville. It still hit the front left corner of the house with a solid thump. I could have sworn that the building swayed for a moment, but then smoke wreathed the scene and hid the building from me. I continued running as flames began to lick through the smoke like angry serpents. My rolling incendiary device had achieved the desired result: an unorthodox but explosive method of entry.

There was no time for gloating. I had to keep moving. Show Huffman the true meaning of shock and awe. In my peripheral vision I caught movement off to my left. Another man was running through the grass in my direction, lifting an assault rifle. He fired as he came, but he had about as much danger of hitting me as of winning the lottery. I flinched out of reaction, but not from the bullets whizzing over my head. A living shadow rose up from beside the man and jammed a KA-BAR to the hilt in the man's flesh. It was a savage stab, one that pierced the point just behind the man's clavicle and drove the knife down and into the upper chambers of his heart. He died instantly. Rink grabbed the rifle out of his hands even as he fell dead on the ground. Rink dropped low again and was lost to view.

Three down, but with no idea how many we were up against, I kept running. One thing was for sure, the odds had to be creeping in our favour.

Passing the burning Windstar, I gave it little attention, happy only that the flames from the vehicle had set the tinder-dry building alight. I jumped up on to the porch, my SIG searching for targets. Hearing a thump from above me, I kicked open the front door and quickly rushed inside the building, putting my back to the door frame as I cleared the room before me. I heard the thud of running feet above. Shouts. I also heard gunfire from some distance away and guessed that Rink or Harvey had engaged someone on the far side of the building.

Now it was on for real.

I was going to flush Huffman out of his house so that I could kill him in the clear light of day.

To my left flames were licking through new holes in the wall. Pretty soon this entire corner of the house would be aflame. Then the rest would become an inferno. I could wait to allow the flames to do my job for me, but things had become way too personal between me and Huffman to allow that. I moved through the room, only barely aware that it was a kitchen, and I took a quick glance into a passageway beyond.

Clear.

I went on, my gun seeking targets.

More thumps from above. People were responding to the flames engulfing this part of the building, seeking escape at the far end. I looked for a way up there and noticed a stairway halfway down the passage. There were doors either side of the passage and it would be reckless to head directly for the stairs without first ensuring those rooms were empty. I didn't relish the thought of a bullet in my spine.

Gunfire rattled outside, Rink or Harvey loosing a barrage of bullets. Flames crackled and wood creaked and shifted. There was a dull pop as something inside the Windstar exploded, possibly the remaining fuel in the gas tank. Still no sign of Robert Huffman, though. No Larry Bolan either. For a brief second I was worried that both my enemies had fled the farm and I'd merely engaged in war with their underlings. But, I realised, the underlings had to go. They knew my name and if ever any of us were going to be safe again, they had to die.

Pulling open a door on my right, I swept the interior for targets. The room was a utility area with washing machines and the like, but no people. So I returned my attention to the bottom of the stairs. I could hear the retreat of feet as someone upstairs ran to the back of the house. I was eager to get up there after whoever that was, but it was still important that I left no one behind me.

Pulling open another door, I brought round the SIG.

Something whacked down on my extended wrist. I cursed under my breath as my hand went numb. Desperately I held on to my weapon. If I relinquished it now, that would be the end of me. In reaction I threw up my left arm and caught a blow aimed at my face on my elbow. But then a knee pounded me in the chest and I was pushed back into the passageway. I slammed the far wall, rebounded and immediately I fired. My bullet hit the man coming at me. It stopped him in his tracks, but only fleetingly. In some distant part of my mind I registered the man was wearing a Kevlar vest. The point-blank shot had struck him like a mule kick, but the vest had saved his life. The man came at me, lifting his own gun. I wasn't wearing a vest.

I dodged as the gun fired, barely avoiding the round that punched a hole in the wall next to my head; if he'd aimed at my body instead he'd have got me. There was only a fraction of a second between the realisation that I was still alive and my response. I brought up my gun and fired again, hitting the man in the meat of his left thigh. The bullet took a chunk of his leg, but his forward momentum threw him against me and we both grappled with each other's gun hands like we were engaged in a crazy dance.

I was only vaguely aware of the man trying to kill me. It was the same sinuous son of a bitch who'd survived when I took Kate from Huffman. He was older than me by fifteen years, slim of build, but strong. Even with one leg crippled, the man still had an incredible fluidity to his movement. He flipped my gun hand, turning my gun towards me, trapped my elbow, and then headbutted me in the face. I saw red flashes. But I didn't let the sudden shock stop me. I pivoted on my feet, lifting and looping my trapped elbow so that we disengaged from our chest-to-chest position, then I kicked at the knee of his good leg. The man grunted, but he straightened my elbow out, swung his armpit over it while raising the wrist, then forced his body weight down on the flexed elbow in an effort at snapping it. My gun hand was stretched out aiming away from him, but his gun hand was also tied up as he grappled with my wrist. Neither of us could get off a shot. I released his gun wrist, giving me room to move, and I dropped my centre of balance lower than his, taking pressure off my elbow. It was simply about angles. I turned my elbow a fraction and he no longer had me controlled.

I back-heeled him in his groin. Then I stamped the same foot down his shin, raking the flesh in an effort at tearing it off the bones. But he was a wily son of a bitch. Even as he reacted to the two new points of agony, he struck down with the butt of his gun on my injured shoulder. Pain shrieked throughout my entire body. But it also galvanised me. I butted backwards and my crown smashed against his jaw, knocking him back on his heels. Spinning quickly I thrust my left palm into his face, the heel smacking like a wedge of wood into his philtrum. There are tales that such a blow can kill a man, driving the bones of the nose up and into the brain, though in my opinion it's a fallacy. But I still crushed the cartilage and was showered by a spray of blood.

We pulled apart and there was an instant where we appraised each other.

Then the man spat out a wad of blood and shattered dentures.

You're good, whoever you are, I thought. But you're too old for this game.

Then I powered my foot into his gut. The Kevlar absorbed most of the force, but he couldn't keep his balance. He began to bring up his gun but I was that much faster.

My round hit him in his open mouth and gave him an equally hollow orifice in the back of his skull.

He stood for a second, the spark of shock dim in his eyes. Then it was like some divine puppet master had clipped his strings and he crumpled in a boneless heap.

Testing my face with my fingers, I stared down at him. I'd a nasty welt growing on my left cheek where he'd headbutted me, but was all right otherwise. As for the killers Huffman had brought in against me, another one was now gone.

Our fight had lasted little more than half a minute, but already things had changed dramatically.

Smoke was boiling along the passage. Heat followed it. Either one could kill me as quickly as this man had tried to do.

My attention snapped back to the stairs. I was in a hurry to get up there, but it was more in response to a shout from above.

'Grade! Grade? Did you get him, Grade?'

No, I wanted to shout back, *Grade didn't make the grade*.

I didn't, though; I just started advancing, taking it quietly. I didn't know who was waiting for me, but the voice had not been that of either Huffman or Bolan.

Gunfire erupted at the back of the house and I remembered that my friends were still out there. They could have been fighting my two worst enemies for all I knew, but there was someone else I wanted first. The asshole that Kate told me about: Rourke. He was in need of a lesson.

Muffling my voice with my forearm, I shouted, 'That you, Rourke?'

'Yeah,' he answered. 'Did you get the bastard?'

'Yeah. Got him.'

And now I'm coming for you.

45

It was time for Larry to reappraise his priorities.

Top on his list would never change: Joe Hunter must die. No question about it. But things weren't going the way he imagined. He'd been looking for a grand showdown, some sort of cinematic gladiatorial combat. *Mano a mano.* He certainly hadn't expected to be in the centre of a burning building with no idea if he was going to die of smoke inhalation, roasted like a hog on a spit, or shot dead by any of the anonymous rounds tearing through the rapidly disintegrating building.

He'd agreed to things that had placed him in this awkward position, things that were now getting in the way of his own agenda. What he should have done was told Huffman to go screw himself, shoot the man in the face and then find Joe Hunter himself. Instead Larry was forced to duck and dive for his life with no real assurance that he'd get his shot at the man who'd murdered his brother.

He could hear Trent roaring inside his skull, full of fury that his big brother had lied to him. Trent had always had a big mouth, the bone of contention that made Larry fantasise about killing his sibling. Yet he missed his brother more than he could ever say. And he would do anything to make Trent happy.

'I'm getting to it, Trent,' Larry barked. 'Just give me a chance to get my ass out of here first.'

Trent's admonishments were replaced by the roar of flames as the bedroom wall combusted behind him.

It was a bit weird talking to his dead brother. Trent couldn't hear him, Larry accepted, but speaking the words out loud gave him the surge of resolve to get moving.

He was currently stuck in one of the bedrooms on the upper floor. Larry had been catching a few minutes' sleep. He'd been on the go for the past two days and, despite his desire for action, fatigue had finally caught up with him. The few minutes had slipped into . . . what, a couple of hours or more?

When the car had crashed into the front of the building, turning the house into an inferno, Larry had awakened. Then bullets had cut through the room, someone on the outside trying to force any living person from this end of the house to the far end. He didn't need the bullets to tell him he had to move; the prospect of being burnt alive did that.

He heard the bang of guns from downstairs, more from outside. He pulled open the bedroom door and looked out into an empty passage. Larry felt for the Desert Eagle strapped to his hip. He pulled out the gun and moved into the hall. A man bolted out of a room ahead and Larry almost shot him. Then he recognised the punk called Rourke. Larry considered shooting anyway. He would die either under Larry's gun or under Hunter's later, so why not just get a chore out of the way? But Larry allowed his gun to drop.

Rourke was a punk but he was still a useful punk.

'Rourke?' Rourke spun about, raising his own gun, before recognising Larry. Larry waved his gun down and the man obeyed. 'Where the hell is Huffman?'

'He's at the back of the house.' Rourke's eyes were wide and his face was as pale as the underbelly of a worm. Larry could see his gun trembling.

'Hunter's at the front. What's he doing back there?'

'The same as we should be doing: getting the hell out of here!'

Larry grabbed the man's shirt-front. 'You're being paid to do a job. Not run the fuck away.'

'Yeah, but I didn't sign up to get slaughtered by a goddamn maniac!'

'Do your fuckin' job,' Larry growled at him, 'Or Hunter won't be the only maniac slaughtering you.'

He propelled Rourke towards the head of the stairs.

'Guard those stairs, asshole.'

'Grade's already at the bottom.'

'Hunter will get by him,' Larry said. No question there.

'And you expect *me* to kill him?'

No, I expect you to die, Larry thought. But at least you'll slow him down while I get my ass out of here. Back along the passage, smoke rolled out of the room that he'd just vacated. Larry gave Rourke the eyeball. 'I expect you to at least try, you goddamn coward.'

'What about you?'

Larry put a hand to his chest. 'Me? I'm finding another way down. I *am* going to kill the bastard.'

Then, with Rourke covering his back, Larry charged along the hall towards the furthest rooms. Back there was an exit on to the balcony that ran all the way round the house. As he ran he heard Rourke ask, 'Did you get him, Grade?'

Larry almost stopped. If Grade had indeed got Hunter he'd eat his boots. He heard a reply, but couldn't make it out over the roar of flames. More smoke coiled along the passage hiding Rourke from view. Now he only heard coughing. He continued with his first plan.

'Huffman!' he called as he approached the room at the furthest corner of the house. The door was partially shut and he had no desire to walk in without any announcement. Huffman would probably shoot him out of reaction.

'Boss, it's me, Larry.' He pushed the door open. There were no wildly fired bullets, so he followed the swing of the door and entered the room. He couldn't see the boss man. Caution made him check behind the door. He didn't want the man coming at him from behind: not with that damn razor.

Huffman wasn't waiting to fillet him like a fish.

Larry scanned the room, saw that the door to the balcony was open. He moved quickly across the room and took a peek outside. A man was just disappearing round the corner of the building towards the back. He was dressed in those military fatigues that Huffman had made all his people wear like they were a bunch of yuppies on a paintball adventure. The short grey hair poking below the rim of his ball cap told Larry that it was Huffman.

As Larry stepped out on to the balcony to follow Huffman, a man lunged out from behind the adjacent building and lifted a shotgun. He was a large muscular man with dark hair, tawny skin, hooded eyes and a vivid scar on his chin. He didn't look like he was from around these parts. Larry had a split second to take in the man's appearance before he had to throw himself aside to avoid the buckshot that tore a basketball-sized hole in the wall next to him.

He fired back, his Desert Eagle bucking like a cannon, but the man pulled away, concealing himself behind the outbuilding.

'Who the hell is that?' Larry hadn't been party to Huffman's talk with Ruth Wicker, so did not know that the man shooting at him was Jared Rington.

An M16 rattled from the back of the house.

He saw chips of wood fly from the balcony railing, then a second afterwards Huffman came scrambling back into view, his hands shielding his head as though flesh and bone would be enough to save him from the high velocity rounds making matches of the wood around him. Huffman skidded down on his backside. Larry went towards him, watching over his shoulder for the guy with the shotgun. He grabbed Huffman and pulled him to his feet.

'Things ain't going the way we planned, are they, boss?'

Huffman slammed his shoulders against the house wall, eyes casting round. It was the first time that Larry had seen him looking anything other than mildly amused. He wasn't laughing now.

'There's a black guy out there with a machine gun,' Huffman said. 'The son of a bitch nearly cut me in half.'

Larry shot a thumb over his shoulder. 'There's a Japanese dude over there, as well. The hell's going on?'

Huffman scowled. 'Hunter got three at the get-go. One of those assholes must have killed another. Who does that leave alive, Larry?'

'Only person I've seen is Rourke.' Larry didn't think that Rourke would be around for much longer, though. 'He said that Grade's downstairs.'

'There're four of us against three. We still hold the upper hand.'

Larry did a quick count in his head. 'What about Wicker?'

'I gave her another job.' Huffman shook his head, then pulled the cap off and threw it down. It wasn't much of a disguise now that most of the others were dead. 'In hindsight, that might not have been my best idea.'

Larry blinked.

'Where is she?'

'I sent her to Tampa after the women,' Huffman said. Suddenly he crouched. Larry also dropped low and buckshot tore a wide pattern in the wall above his head.

'Son of a bitch!' Larry shouted.

'We're penned down here, Larry. We have to do something about that.'

'I'm going to kill Joe Hunter.'

'What about those other two bastards?'

'I'll kill them as well.' Larry bobbed his head up for a look and rounds from an M16 stitched a design above him. Larry flattened himself as well as a man of his giant girth could. 'But you're right: we have to get out of here first.'

Larry spied across the intervening space to the next building, then again into the house. Smoke was now billowing into the room they had their backs to.

'Can't see any way out of it,' Larry said. 'We either take the fight to them or we burn to death.'

'I'm not about to give in to these assholes.'

'I'm with you on that one, boss,' Larry told him. 'We're better than them.'

The corner of Huffman's mouth twisted into a facsimile of his usual smile. He racked the slide on his gun, lifted it so it was alongside his jaw as if he was a poster boy for the latest James Bond movie. 'You go first, Larry. I'll cover you.'

Larry looked at Huffman. To think he used to stand guard over this man, watching him suck the meat from a lobster claw and allowing him to disrespect his little brother by making Trent stand outside in the cold. For the first time, he saw Huffman for what he really was: a warped sociopath with delusions of grandeur.

Larry stood up tall, heedless of the men down below.

They'd never been shooting to kill him anyway. They were only there to contain him and Huffman while Joe Hunter came on them from inside.

He looked down at Huffman.

'OK, boss, I'll go get these two,' Larry said.

Then he sprang forward, placed one boot heel on the balcony railing, and vaulted into space.

46

There was a man at the top of the stairs.

Since Kate had told me about Rourke and the degradation he'd put her through, I wanted to kill him almost as much as I did Quicksilver. Kate told me about the way he'd watched as she'd performed intimate and private tasks, forever making lewd suggestions and promises. He had been rough in his treatment of her, and more than once his hands had lingered where it was unnecessary. Rourke hadn't physically raped her, but throughout her ordeal he'd been constantly raping her in his mind. His debasement of Kate required punishment in kind.

It was difficult not to charge up the stairs and pump bullets at him. But instead, I went slow and sure. He thought I was the man that I'd killed downstairs. Grade. Concealed by the thickening tendrils of smoke, he was none the wiser. Taking each step slowly, I groaned as if I was injured, lowering the man's reaction time as I made him wonder what had happened.

'Killed the bastard,' I croaked, 'but he got me good, man.'

'He shot you?'

Rourke's voice was no more than five feet ahead of me now. I kept my head down so that he couldn't get a good look at my face. The smoke helped. Even when I coughed, it sounded like a man who'd been hurt.

'You sure he's dead, Grade?'

'He's dead,' I said, finally reaching the top stair. The man was to my right and he was holding a gun, loosely, like he'd forgotten it was there. I stumbled towards him and raised a hand, as though looking for support. He lifted his own free hand and I wasn't sure if he was trying to help me or to ward me off. Either way, it didn't matter; I immediately plucked his gun out of his grasp.

He knew then who I was. I expected him to put up some kind of fight, but he didn't; he crunched against the wall bringing up his hands in a pleading gesture. Just your typical bully. Not so tough when he was up against someone tougher.

I jammed my SIG under his jaw.

'Grade's dead.'

'Please! Dear God! Don't kill me . . .'

I shook my head slowly. Smoke coiled around me and I could feel a furnace blast of heat pushing through my clothes. For the briefest of moments I felt immeasurably cruel. I wanted to make the man go down on his knees and beg for his life before I sent him into the flames crawling on all fours like a dog. But then I'd be the bully.

'Is your name Rourke?'

At first he wouldn't answer, so I thumbed back the

hammer on my gun. I didn't need to, all I had to do was pull the trigger and it would fire, but it was quite intimidating.

'Yeah, man, I'm Rourke. But I'm nobody!'

'I know that. That's why I'm going to give you a chance.'

'You're going to let me live?'

'Yes. But you won't be a danger to women again.'

In my other hand was the gun I'd just taken off him. It was pointed low, between his thighs. I squeezed off a single round.

Rourke screamed and collapsed at the same time.

'If you can crawl out of here, you'll live,' I told him as I walked away. 'But that's down to you.'

Rourke was too concerned with screaming to crawl.

Flames or smoke or bleeding to death, one of them would most likely finish him, but I'd kept my word. I'd given him a chance at survival, although he wouldn't be raping anyone in future.

In front of me was an open door, and beyond it what looked like a bedroom. Bright light washed the room in total contrast to the rest of the house behind me. Taking a quick glance back over my shoulder, I noticed Rourke was lost to sight. I heard the crash of Rink's Mossberg. Voices were raised in a harsh whisper, but the sound of the disintegrating building made it impossible to hear the actual words. Still, I recognised Larry Bolan's deep baritone and the self-regarding tones of Robert Huffman.

Both my enemies were right there.

I didn't want Larry just yet but Huffman was a necessity.

An M16 rattled and bullets punched into the room. The bullets went high, digging up and into the attic space above. Harvey and Rink had the men cornered at the back of the building just as we'd planned. I moved into the room, lifting my SIG. I had to disable one or other of them immediately: even with my friends watching my back it would be difficult fighting both men.

Then I heard a rumble on the planks, saw through the door a huge shadow hurtle over the balcony. This was followed seconds later by the clatter of shattering glass and I understood that Larry Bolan had jumped for it, throwing himself across the space between the house and the next building and had crashed through a window in an effort to evade capture. The big man was proving more agile than I'd ever have given him credit for.

For now, Larry was out of the picture. Let him run. Rink and Harvey would chase him down between them, but right then I only wanted Huffman. I moved quickly across the room, gauging his position by the sound of muttered curses coming through the open door.

I considered shooting him through the wall. The wood would do no more to stop my bullets than cheesecloth. But that just wasn't satisfying enough. In my present state of mind, I wanted revenge on the punk. I wanted the son of a bitch to know exactly who had killed him.

So slowly, ever so slowly, I edged out of the door and looked down at the man who was on one knee firing at my friends below. I pressed the muzzle of my SIG on the top of his head.

'Drop the gun, asshole.'

Huffman's eyes rolled up at me and he sighed.

'You think this is bad, Huffman? Think again. It's about to get much, much worse.'

47

A man weighing almost twice the average isn't designed for flight. There was nothing graceful about the way Larry threw himself through space, and within a few feet he was losing altitude and speed. Noticing the window on the building opposite as a means of escape from the burning house he'd trusted to momentum to carry him to freedom. It was a bad calculation. He missed the window completely. However, his weight did come with a guarantee: it was a greater force than the wall of the building could withstand. He slammed the building feet first, smashing directly through the boards. He was lucky that there were no hidden support joists as he'd have likely smashed himself flat against them. Instead he went directly through the wood and fell the remaining body length on to hard-packed dirt inside the building. Above him, his demolition work on the wall caused more wood to fall and the window he'd originally aimed for shattered as its frame gave way.

Coming to his feet, Larry felt blood on his face and he probed a shallow gash on his forehead. His feet had taken most of the brunt of the collision but his head hadn't gone unscathed. He didn't recall knocking his head on the window ledge, but that was what must have occurred. When his blood had settled and the adrenalin surge had subsided, his head would likely feel like a punchbag. But that was a consideration for later. Right now he had to keep moving. Two men with guns were too close by for comfort.

He still had no idea who the two dudes were, other than that they'd come here with Joe Hunter. He was pretty sure they wouldn't stand around while he got his shit together and faced Hunter on more stable ground than the rapidly disintegrating ranch house. Man to man he'd kick both their asses, he was pretty sure of that; even together he still thought he could take them. But not when one had a shotgun and the other a machine-gun. They'd flank him and riddle him full of lead. That would spoil his plan for their illustrious leader.

He still clutched the Desert Eagle.

He fired a couple of shots through the wall, just to make the men hold back for a second or two. He needed that time to decide what the hell he was going to do next.

Then he thought, *the crap with this*! Got to move, take the fuckers one at a time.

He charged across the building, dodging round some abandoned agricultural equipment. Towards the front of the building the door stood open, but that would take him dangerously close to the guy with the shotgun before he was ready. He aimed instead for a door in the far side. He didn't wait to check if it was unlocked, he just raised one arm and barrelled directly through it, knocking the door off its hinges. He burst out into daylight tinged with smoke from the burning house, turned immediately to his left and raced along a passageway next to the building where Huffman had stored the wreckage of the chopper shot down the day before.

At the end of the passage he slid to a stop. He poked his head round the corner of the building, looking for the black man. There was no sign of him and Larry ran across rocky earth to where he'd parked Tito's appropriated Cadillac. He leaped in without opening the door, thankful that he'd left the soft top down, and jammed the keys into the ignition. In all those horror or thriller movies cars have a habit of refusing to start first time, adding to the tension as someone sneaks up on the good guy. But the Cadillac burst to life first turn.

He wasn't running away. No, this was all about strengthening his position. Huffman was pure ego. He wanted to be the top dog in everyone's eyes.

Well, crap on you, Huffman, he thought. *You think you're the toughest dude alive: wait till you get a load of me.*

He floored the gas pedal, turning the Cadillac in a wide circle, and headed along a service track that followed a route past the cattle pens. No shots followed his mad flight and he knew that for the moment he'd given the black guy the slip.

Larry swung the Cadillac round the end of the slaughterhouse. The stench of old blood and animal dung displaced the acrid smoke from his nostrils, but he wasn't sure it was a good trade. Then he powered the classic car to the front and stomped on the gas again. Then he'd no time for smells or any other distractions; he had to concentrate on killing the man with the shotgun without him blasting his head from his shoulders.

His size made it difficult to scrunch down in his seat, and he knew that his head still offered a target the size of a basketball, but there was nothing else for it. He powered on, trusting as much to luck as speed to see him through. He whipped by the building containing the chopper. Then he passed the one he'd so recently smashed inside. Next he was passing the gap he'd jumped.

The guy with the shotgun was there, his weapon aimed at the balcony. Larry glanced up and saw Joe Hunter standing with his gun pressed to Huffman's head. Hunter could wait until later. He fired at the Japanese man.

He saw the man spin and go down in the dirt.

Everything had happened too quickly to see how badly he was injured. Maybe he was dead.

Then he was passing the house.

Wind made smoke billow across his vision. Sparks from the fire were like a swarm of burning locusts. The front of the building was already gone. But none of this registered. All that concerned Larry was spinning the wheel and making a return run.

The Cadillac burst through the smoke into clear air. Here the road sloped up to where Nixon and the others had launched their ineffective ambush. Larry used the slope to swing the vehicle on, and he turned back towards the house, giving the big car throttle.

He blasted through the smoke, relying on its cover to put another .357 round through the Japanese dude. Sparks billowed around him and the smoke brought tears to his eyes, but he didn't stop. He didn't see the figure spilling out of the remains of the house. The man was on fire, hair and clothing burning. The man was screaming, but he looked senseless, as though he was merely screaming at the world in general. At the last second he stumbled, turning directly in the path of the Cadillac.

It was too late for Larry to swerve. He just blasted right on into the man. Larry had never liked that coward, Rourke, anyway.

The huge car was more than a match for the fragile human being. It smashed Rourke into the air and his body caromed off the windshield. If the car had had a hard roof, that would have been that, but the soft top was down. Rourke's flailing body spun over the shattered windshield and landed directly in Larry's lap.

Rourke was a fair-sized man, and his body slammed Larry like a battering ram. The shock of the collision, spattering blood and flames, all conspired against Larry and there was nothing he could do to hang on to the Cadillac's steering wheel. The car veered to the left and hit the raised walkway at the front of the house, punching out a couple of support beams to the balcony above. Then, in the next second, the car bounced outwards, flipping in a roll that hurled Larry and Rourke out of the car and on to the rocky earth.

Cognisance left Larry. His mind was full of flashing images and explosions of pain as his body rolled across the floor. Stones dug at him, dust filled his eyes and mouth, something gave in his ribcage with a pop. Then he was lying on his back and the world was spinning and dipping in his vision. Everything was eerily silent.

He lay there for mere seconds.

Then he sat up, blinking and spitting crud from his mouth.

Smoke wreathed across his vision.

Larry groaned, felt for the abnormal shape in his chest and realised that he'd broken a rib. The pain was only one of many similar pains; nothing serious like a shattered spine or crushed skull plagued him.

His hearing came back with a jolt. Trent was screaming at him to get his ass in gear.

He rolled on to his knees, head swimming, then got to his feet where he swayed like a tower in the face of a hurricane.

Superheated wind tore the smoke away from him.

Shit.

Standing directly in front of him was the Jap dude. Blood was apparent only by its absence. Larry had missed the shot and the man was holding a goddamn Mossberg aimed at his gut.

'You have a beef with Joe Hunter,' said the man, 'you have a beef with me.'

48

'Drop the gun, Huffman.'

It's the power a beautiful face has over a man. For the last few days I could have been accused of being led by my heart instead of by my brain. Pretty much everything I'd done had been driven by the rage I felt at Huffman because he'd threatened a woman that I was attracted to. But now I'd hit melting point. Considering everything, my actions weren't the most rational. I'd tried to validate them by telling myself that to defeat Huffman he had to believe that I was a rabid lone wolf who was unmindful of the consequences. My plan seemed to have worked.

But now the madness had to stop.

Here on in I had to get a grip on what I was doing.

'Son of a bitch,' Huffman said under his breath. Then a smile crept on to his lips. It looked too forced to be genuine. 'So you made it by everyone and now it's down to just you and me?'

'Drop the gun, Huffman,' I repeated. 'Or I swear to God I'll kill you now.'

'Then what happens? You shoot me anyway?'

'Maybe you'd prefer to burn to death.' Without taking my gun from his skull, I nodded backwards at the flames behind us. The heat was stinging the exposed flesh on the back of my neck.

'I'd prefer to talk.' Huffman gave me a patronising smile that made me wish I could kill in cold blood.

'We've gone way past talking. Now drop the goddamn gun.'

Huffman allowed the gun to fall from his fingers. I dragged it away from him with my foot and then back-heeled it into the flames.

'I'm worth millions of dollars, Hunter. Name your price.'

'No, Huffman, this wasn't ever about money.'

He twisted his smile. 'You're pissed at me because of the women. OK, I get that. But it wasn't personal. I'm a businessman; I was simply looking after my interests.'

'That's not the way I see it.'

'People have died, yes! But they were all greedy men with their own agendas.'

'You played them as much as you tried to play me, Huffman. It was all a game to you. One you wanted to win. I bet you're the one that's pissed now.'

He gave a shrug as though the destruction of his empire meant nothing. 'You win some, you lose some. That's business.'

Just then I heard the roar of an engine. Larry Bolan drove past us in his Cadillac, firing his gun at Rink. I knew by the way that Rink spun to the ground, then bounced back up again, that he was unhurt. We shared a brief glance before I had to return my attention to a more pressing task.

'Your business partner has the right idea,' I pointed out. 'Looks like Larry's making a run for it.'

'Bolan wasn't my partner,' Huffman sneered, as if such a thing was beneath him. 'Even he has his own agenda.'

'Yeah, I know that. But you were playing him too.'

'You seem to have got my number.' Huffman laughed. 'Yeah, and you've got me. So what now?'

I indicated that he stand, transferring the gun to a point under his jaw.

'We're going to get it on. That was always the idea of your little game.'

'And when I kill you, what's to stop your friends shooting me?'

'Who says you're going to kill me?' I pressed the SIG tightly enough to put pressure on the nerves. He stoically took the pain, but it was all a bluff. I could see it in the way his smile faltered.

Sometimes men are at their most dangerous when they see no way out.

He spun quickly, and I caught the glint of steel flashing from under his sleeve. He pulled away from the gun even as he turned to slash at my exposed throat. He was a second away from opening it right up.

He should have waited, because, unlike the others he'd murdered by this sneak attack, I'd anticipated his move. It's the way to win any game: not by cheating, but by always being one step ahead of your opponent.

I knew that he'd try to cut me. I let him think he was going to. I even let him pull away from my gun because an instantaneous death courtesy of a bullet through his brain was too good for him. Instead I rammed my KA-BAR through the meat of his upper right arm.

Huffman's mouth went wide in a shout of incredulity. His fingers opened reflexively and I saw four inches of gleaming steel hanging useless from a leather strip attached to his wrist. I ripped the KA-BAR out of his bicep, angled it towards his gut.

Then the world tilted.

There was an incredibly loud bang from below us, coupled with the screech of tortured metal; the balcony lurched upwards, and dropped from beneath my feet. In reaction I grabbed at the door frame, dropping my knife, and held on tightly. Out in the open, Huffman skidded away from me across the planks, hit the rail and toppled over. My first thought was that the fire had eaten away at the foundations of the building much sooner than I'd anticipated, but then I recognised the sound as the impact of a vehicle and knew that Larry had never been running away. Whether or not he'd intended to, Larry had just saved Huffman's life.

Not for long, though.

Sparks danced around me as my feet scrabbled for purchase on the sloping balcony. My SIG was still tight in my left hand and I shoved it into my waistband. My knife was gone, probably down on the ground where Huffman had fallen. I couldn't see the bastard, but I did see Rink stalk into the smoke at the front of the house. Rink was going after Larry Bolan, and I wanted to follow him, but first I wanted to make sure that Huffman didn't sneak away.

The heat from within the building stung the flesh of my fingers. I let go of the door frame, sliding on my heels and backside to the edge of the balcony. Striking the base of the wooden rail, I wedged myself there, then started looking out for Huffman. Rink had gone to the right: I quickly scanned left and caught a flash of Huffman lurching out of sight round the corner of the adjacent building.

I went over the railing and dropped to the ground, tucking and rolling the way I'd learned during parachute training, and came back to my feet. Then I went after Huffman. A figure materialised out of the smoke haze to my left. Harvey, an M16 gripped in his hands.

'I'm going to kill Huffman,' I told him. No ifs or buts, just the surety that the bastard would die. 'Rink's gone after Larry. He might need your help.'

There was no need for spoken affirmation; Harvey nodded and we passed each other at a run.

49

'The fuck do you think you are?' Heedless of the Mossberg shotgun aimed at him, Larry Bolan smiled at the man blocking his way.

'The name's Rink.'

Larry rumbled a laugh deep in his chest, ignoring the pain throbbing in his ribs. 'Rink? What kind of pussy *Jap* name is that?'

'It's the name of the man who's gonna kill you.'

'Are you going to shoot me, asshole? Or are you a bigger man than your punk friend?'

'I'm gonna shoot you.'

Larry shook his head. 'No you ain't. If you were going to shoot me, you'd have done it by now.'

'Didn't say I was gonna do it yet.'

'So what you going to do, bore me to death?'

'You're gonna get your giant ass kicked first.'

Larry shook with laughter. He lifted a hand the size of a boxing glove and rubbed at the dirt round his mouth. He appraised the man whose head barely reached Larry's shoulder. 'You think a midget like you can handle me?'

Through the smoke charged a tall black man. He was holding an assault rifle that he immediately lifted and aimed at Larry's chest.

'Shit, how many cockroaches we got around here?' Larry asked.

Rink and the black man shared a glance.

'Hunter wants this asshole,' Rink said.

The black man's lips turned down and he scowled. 'We should just kill the mutha.'

'He'll die,' Rink promised.

Larry grunted scornfully. 'The two of you better make your move; I'm getting kind of sick of standing here.'

Rink waved the shotgun away from the burning building. 'Take a walk.'

'Going to shoot me in the back like a coward?'

'No, when I kill you I'll be smilin' in your face.'

Larry walked.

People like Rink and Joe Hunter and this black dude had an intrinsic flaw in their make-up as killers. They laid too much emphasis on all this honour bullshit. With the roles reversed, Larry would have blasted the fuckers' heads off. Rink especially seemed the kind of man who'd commit ritual *seppuku* before letting anything ignoble get in the way of his code of honour. Larry was kind of counting on that.

He'd only taken three paces when he suddenly stooped low. Neither gun blasted chunks out of him, so he quickly stood back up and spun all in one movement. He was gripping the smoldering corpse of Rourke, and he launched it through the air at the black man. In life Larry had deemed Rourke a pitiful excuse for a human being, but he was worth much more now that he was dead. His charred remains flying through space caused the black guy to step back, his eyes widening in shock, and his intention to shoot forgotten. Larry didn't go after him, he launched himself at Rink.

Rink was caught in a flux of indecision, but he wasn't encumbered by a flailing corpse. He began to bring up the gun so that the butt was aimed at Larry's chin. Even as Larry caromed into him, Rink slammed the wooden stock into his jaw. A jolt like electricity shook Larry, but he'd been hit harder during rough-house play with Trent when they were boys. He snatched at the shotgun, tore it out of Rink's hands and hurled it from him.

In his peripheral vision, he saw the black man leap over Rourke's corpse and bring up the rifle, but there was no way he could shoot without cutting Rink to pieces as well. Larry ignored the black man, swinging a fist into Rink's face.

Rink ducked and Larry's pile-driving punch missed him. Rink swung an elbow that cracked against Larry's ribs. Some of that sneaky Jap karate stuff, Larry thought. Luckily the elbow had struck his uninjured side or Rink could have pushed his broken rib into a lung. As it was, the blow barely registered. Larry hammered downwards, slamming his forearm on Rink's skull. Rink grunted, but his arms grappled Larry's waist.

The black man rushed in, gun lifted club-like.

Larry leaned over and wrapped both arms round

Rink's back, clasping his hands under the man's chest. Then he heaved Rink off his feet. He swung at the black man, even as the assault rifle slammed against his shoulder. Rink's legs knocked the black man away. Then Larry hauled Rink high in the air and slung him down at the floor. Larry wanted to shatter the man's skull, drive the fragments into his neck, but Rink wasn't totally unfamiliar with the move and rounded his shoulders at the last instant to take the brunt of the force. A normal man would have still been shattered, but Rink was more powerfully muscled than the norm. Even so, he was a child in Larry's hands.

Without loosening his grip, Larry dragged Rink up with sheer brute force, intent on repeating the pile-driving move. Rink was limp now. There'd be no avoiding a crushed skull this time.

The black man was fast. Rink's legs had knocked him away, but he came back almost as quickly. He dropped the rifle which was proving an encumbrance this close in, and he hit Larry a flurry of blows directly in the face. Left-right-left: a blur that would put a pro-boxer to shame. Larry's bottom lip split at the third punch. He cursed, his eyes becoming slits as he turned to the black man. The guy got his hands on Rink and held on to him, stopping Larry from slamming him a second time. Upside down, Rink dug his hand between Larry's legs, grabbing for his testicles.

Larry didn't care. He released his grip, thrust out with his chest and powered Rink into his friend. Both men crashed to the floor, Rink now on top of the black

man. They spilled apart, and Rink swung over on to his
back, so that both men lay side by side in the dirt.

Larry stood over them, feeling the raging fire behind
him.

'Welcome to hell, boys.'

50

Huffman seemed to have a destination in mind. He ran adjacent to the buildings and didn't look back. I could have shot him and had done, but I wanted him to hurt more than that. I ran after him.

He charged past the outbuildings, past the animal pens, and then swung to the right towards the large tin shed. I was fleeter than he was and had gained on him when I saw him duck into a doorway in the side of the building.

I didn't want to shoot him dead, but I was otherwise unarmed and there was no way I was entering that building with my gun in my waistband. I drew my SIG, racked the slide, but kept my finger alongside the trigger guard so there was no accidental discharge.

Huffman's right arm was severely wounded, but he could still use that damn razor. Even so, I went after him without concern for the blade. Immediately inside the building, I put my back to the wall and swept the open space with my gun.

It was dim inside the building. The stench was the first thing that hit me, then my gaze registered the swinging chains and steel stockades, and lastly my ears picked out the rattle of metal and the scuff of feet. I couldn't see Huffman, but he couldn't have got too far ahead of me. To my right some of the chains swayed as though pushed aside in his flight. I went after him and the odour of rotting flesh washed over me like a wave.

I'd smelled this charnel house stink before. It was the kind of stench that hung over the village of slaughtered peasants I'd come across in the Indian Ocean or the mass grave I'd discovered in the Balkans. Blood and innards had been spilled here. I was in a goddamn slaughterhouse.

More chains swung slowly on my right, and I veered that way. High up in the walls, just below the corrugated steel roof, were narrow windows. They weren't there to let in light but to ventilate the building. Instead, I saw creeping tendrils of smoke drifting in. The smoke twisted and coiled like serpents and shafts of dim light were all that illuminated the building, ever-changing strobes between the patterns of smoke.

A clink of metal sounded from somewhere ahead of me, like a door latch lifting and falling. Huffman, the son of a bitch, was trying to give me the slip out of another exit. I rushed in that direction and saw a large silver oblong structure barring my way which I knew instinctively was some sort of industrial-sized cold room. Had Huffman gone in there, hoping to hide from me?

Gun in hand I stepped up to the door. The latch was half open. Cocking an ear to the door, I listened, even though it was a fruitless exercise. The structure by its very nature was surrounded by a soundproofed vacuum. There was nothing for it: the only way of clearing the room was to go inside.

Ordinarily the door would emit a sucking noise as the rubber seal was broken and pressure was displaced in the room, but the door opened without sound. It told me the door had been opened recently, or there was no power to the refrigerated room. I decided I was right on both counts. I peeled the door wide and stared into darkness, my gun poised to shoot. The stench wafting over me was rich with fresh blood.

Something rushed me from the darkness.

Despite my desire to make Huffman suffer, I fired a quick volley of shots into the figure coming at me like a phantom out of its tomb.

Even as I fired, I knew that it wasn't Huffman. This body had no arms or legs and was swinging from a large hook jammed through its ribs. It looked like Huffman had been there, though, because there was a huge bloodless gash in its throat.

Though I was only a split second in understanding, that was long enough for Huffman to leap out of the shadows at me. He held the razor loosely in his right hand, but that wasn't my major concern. In his left was a large butcher's hook. He grasped a wooden handle crossways in his palm, while the gleaming steel hook jutted from between his two middle fingers. It was easily a foot long, giving him a far greater reach than I had. I back-pedalled into the open room.

'*Gonna kill you!*'

He slashed at my head and only the barrel of my SIG halted the hook from holing me like a bowling ball.

There was no time for shouting challenges or curses of my own. Huffman was a man possessed by a demon. He rained blows on me with the hook, then slashed at my body with the razor. My gun halted the hook, but there was only a jacket and shirt between me and the razor blade. There was a stinging pain across my abdomen.

I scrambled away, dimly aware that he'd only nicked me. I knew that because my intestines weren't pooling around my feet.

Chains bounced off my shoulders as I dodged, then my lower spine banged up against one of the steel stock-pens. The bars formed a right angle a yard to my left, blocking my way out. Huffman thought he had me penned in like the animals that once died here, but I just flipped over the bars and landed ankle-deep in cow dung. Huffman's hook struck sparks from the metal bar. I lifted my gun, but I was still reluctant to shoot. I powered backwards and Huffman followed me, vaulting the stock-pen bars and landing where I'd just been.

His razor was a silver crescent cutting the air in front of my face. Swerving round it, I slashed the barrel of my gun at his head, but missed. My heel skidded in the crap, and I heard Huffman's exultant shout. He came after me, ripped upwards with the hook and the point caught in the trigger guard of my gun and snatched it out of my hand.

Should have shot the bastard, I told myself. Then it

was too late for self-admonishment: I had to stop him or die.

His arm went up, the wicked point of the hook poised to slam into my skull. I snatched at the dung on the floor and threw a handful of it into his face. He cried out, blinking to clear his eyes, and I rammed a foot into his stomach, throwing him back against the bars.

Huffman shouted wordlessly, just a ragged scream of fury. He slashed the hook one way, the razor the other, arms like a windmill. Blood from his punctured bicep spattered on my face. He swung again, and this time I dodged inside the hook and jammed the sole of my boot into his extended knee. The patella popped and Huffman staggered in pain. Then I drove my stiffened palm into his nose, smashing the cartilage. In the dim light I caught a flash of white and knew that his eyes were rolling up into his skull. But though semi-conscious he wasn't finished. Instinct made him slash at me again with the hook and I'd no recourse but throw out my right arm to avoid disembowelment. The metal bar of the hook slammed against my arm, but luckily it was below the curve. I pushed my numb arm against the bar, jamming it inside the inner curve of the hook, and rammed the hook tight up against Huffman's chest. My headbutt caught him directly in his already smashed nose even as I grappled with him for the razor. I wrapped my hand round his right fist.

Finally I found voice.

'This is for both sisters,' I said. 'You'll hurt neither of them again.'

'I'm . . . better . . . than . . . you . . .'

'No. You're not.'

There was little strength in his damaged arm.

It was easy enough to wrench his hand up and swipe it across his own throat.

I slashed him so deeply that his throat opened like a second mouth. His trachea was exposed and gaping, his veins and arteries pulsed and jetted blood all over me. His eyes finished their roll upwards into his skull. Then he collapsed. My arm was still entangled in the hook and I felt it wrench away from me. I got a new hole in my jacket and a small nick in the meat of my forearm but I was happy enough at that.

Huffman kicked and shuddered a few times, but I paid him no heed. He was dead, just residual shock animating him. I found my gun ten feet away, but it was clogged with animal dung from where it had slid across the floor. I wiped the gun on Huffman's shoulder, but I couldn't trust it to fire without jamming. I stuffed it in my waistband at the small of my back then bent for another weapon.

Just as I did so, an almighty explosion rocked the slaughterhouse on its foundations. All around me the hanging chains rattled like a thousand snare drums.

Larry Bolan was still out there and this wouldn't be finished until he was dead too.

51

The ranch house and the building next to it were engulfed in flames. The third building along was smouldering. Inside was the wreckage of a helicopter and vehicles and there was fuel everywhere. Just as Larry Bolan reached for the dropped M16 the building went nuclear.

Super-heated air blasted him, snatching at his clothing and spiky hair. He felt like he was on fire. But then the initial blast passed and he found that he was still standing: a little singed, but still alive. Smoke boiled all around him, invading his nostrils and lungs and making him cough. Then chunks of wood rained down, thumping to the earth like gargantuan hailstones. He avoided being smashed to pulp by some of the heavy beams that crashed down right beside him. Larry thought he could be blessed. Someone up there's watching over me, he thought. It couldn't be Trent: Trent had gone somewhere much lower down the celestial ladder.

Blinded by the smoke, it didn't stop him reaching for the assault rifle a second time. He found the stock just where he remembered, then hefted it up into his hands.

He'd never fired an assault rifle before, but how difficult could it be? Point and shoot, right?

He also remembered where Rink and the black guy had been lying and he pulled on the trigger, spraying rounds at them. The gun bucked in his hands, rattling out rounds until the magazine was spent.

Some explosions erupt outwards, causing a vacuum of displaced air. After the initial blast, the heat and smoke rush back in to fill the void, before mushrooming up into the sky. Larry felt the wind racing back towards the new implosion, the smoke following it like a thousand tattered banners caught in a slipstream. The air cleared surprisingly quickly, and showed him where he was shooting. It was where both men had been lying, but they weren't there.

'Shit,' Larry growled.

Rink was ten feet to his right, the black guy the same distance to his left. Both men had pulled out sidearms and were aiming directly at his head.

'Fucking pussies,' Larry said to them. 'You're going to shoot me after all this, *you fucking cowards*?'

'No,' Rink said. He nodded over Larry's shoulder. 'We're just keeping you busy till our buddy gets here.'

Larry Bolan turned.

Out of the smoke, covered almost head to foot in blood, walked Joe Hunter. His face was set in stone and his eyes were like slivers of ice. In his hand he held a huge butcher's hook.

Some people would be terrified by the image but Larry only smiled.

52

'You OK, Hunter?'

'I'm fine, Rink.'

'Whose is all the blood?' Harvey asked.

'Huffman's.'

'Hope he didn't have AIDS,' Rink said.

I frowned.

'You want me to drop this piece of shit now?' Rink asked, his gun on Larry Bolan.

'No. We have something to settle.'

'He killed my brother.' Larry dropped his assault rifle on the ground. He looked at Rink and Harvey, challenging them to disagree with him. 'I owe him.'

'Looks like you just tried to kill *my* brothers. I owe you, too.'

Larry lifted his hands to me, wiggled his fingers.

I'd promised Larry Bolan his one on one with me, but I never promised Queensberry Rules. I lifted the hook and ran at him; it kind of evened up our reach. But I wasn't going to use it on him, not how Huffman had with me. I threw it at his head.

Larry ducked and the hook sailed over the top of him. But that was all I needed.

Before he'd straightened up again, I launched myself in the air and drove my knee directly into his face. Usually it would be insane sacrificing my stability to such a move, but when you're fighting a giant what else is there for it? My knee, with the full weight of my body behind it, slammed his jaws shut and rocked him back on his heels. I followed him, punching him in the throat and then whipping an instep into his crotch.

Larry swung blindly at me and I dodged out then came back with another punch to his throat. It was like punching a leather drum. His backhand caught me across the chest and it was like I'd been swatted by King Kong. I staggered back, trying to catch my breath. Larry followed, hands reaching for me. He was limping slightly from the kick in the balls, but he was too full of fury to slow down.

He threw a right at my chest, and I slipped it and drove my fist into his ribs. They felt mushy. Larry grunted in agony. Old wound, I guessed, but then he was coming at me with his own kick. His leg was as powerful as a bull's and if he got a good kick in my guts he'd probably have killed me. I avoided his boot by a fraction of a hair, then, while it was still sweeping upwards, I dropped the point of my elbow into the jumble of nerves on his outer thigh. The force of his kick almost parted my shoulder, but my elbow dug deep, and when he staggered away he was limping even more.

'Son of a bitch,' he snarled, slapping at his thigh to get some life back in it.

While he was still numb and ungainly I swarmed him. I threw a right hook into his middle, a left into his softened ribs. Then I trapped an elbow, striking with the other fist at the side of his neck. Lesser men could be dropped by a shot to the carotid sinus, but Larry was a solid wedge of meat. He threw a hand at me and entangled his fingers in my jacket, hauled me towards him. He was frothing at the mouth and I thought he was going to chew off my face. I headbutted him. Not once but three times in quick succession. With each whack of my forehead I saw stars, but it was much worse for him.

But then Larry's strength became a factor. He got his arms round my back and lifted me in a bear hug. He squeezed, and though I tried not to I roared in agony. My ribs felt like they were in a car crusher, and I knew it was only a matter of seconds before they'd cave in and lacerate my internal organs.

'Hunter . . .'

Rink's concerned shout came distantly to my ears and I knew my friend would be running in to help.

'No, Rink,' I shouted. '*This asshole is mine!*'

Anything goes on a battlefield and this was about one of the most brutal I'd ever found myself on. I leaned in and clamped my teeth on to Larry Bolan's eyebrow. I bit down with all my might.

Larry roared, throwing me away from him.

I landed on my back in the dirt, feeling like I'd just been in a train wreck. Like last time we'd met. I could barely breathe, but then I spat out the chunk of Larry's brow and things got a little easier.

'You dirty . . .' Larry had his right hand clamped over the gushing wound in his face.

What did he expect? Did he want to shame me into defeat?

I struggled on to my knees. Larry was coming again. He launched a kick into my guts and I rolled with it. It still felt like I'd been hit by a runaway train but I gained space from him. There was a smouldering beam of wood thrown here by the exploding shed and I flung myself over it. Larry stooped and grabbed it. It probably weighed more than I did, but he lifted it, heedless of the embers, and hurled it at me. I staggered backwards, followed by a billowing shower of sparks as it crashed down at my feet.

Rink and Harvey were both shouting but their actual words were lost on me.

'Do not shoot him!'

But that wasn't what they were getting at. Our fight had taken us dangerously close to the roaring flames of the ranch and I was too caught up in the adrenalin rush to notice. By the looks of Larry Bolan he didn't care either. Blood poured from the wound in his eyebrow, but his eyes seethed beneath it. His mouth was clamped in a rictus. He charged me, his hands going for my throat.

I ducked beneath his outstretched arms, sweeping them over my head with my forearms, gave him an elbow into his damaged ribs. He bent in pain and I clambered up and on to his back. I clamped my legs round his waist and one hand in his hair and struck repeatedly with the knife-edge of my free hand in the side of his neck. He began to weaken.

Larry Bolan must have known he was going to die. Even if he finished me, it wouldn't matter what I'd said; Rink or Harvey would drop him. But he wanted to take me with him.

'Trent!' he roared. Then he clamped his arms over my legs to stop me pulling free and ran directly at the burning building like we were in a piggy-back race, intending crashing through the wall of flames and into the heart of the inferno. Neither Rink nor Harvey could shoot him for fear of hitting me. I let go of his hair, forgot all about chopping his neck and I did something so terrible that it would come back to haunt me in nightmares.

As Larry charged towards the flames and I felt the skin on my face begin to roast I reached round and jammed my fingers into the corners of his mouth. Then I hauled backwards, as if I was reining in a mad stallion. Larry's face split like an overripe melon and his system failed him with the shock of what I'd done. His arms flopped wide, and I sprawled on my back, chunks of Larry's lips clenched between my fingers.

Maybe what I did was enough to throw him over the precipice of insanity, maybe he had no desire to live any longer with only half a face, but he kept on running and the last I saw of him was a lumbering shadow flailing within the flames.

Next, hands were at my collar and I was dragged unceremoniously away from the building as it crashed down and sealed Larry's fate.

I lay there in stunned silence. Equally quiet were my friends. In the end, Rink said, 'You shoulda let me shoot him, Joe.'

I looked at the filth in my hands and was sickened. But then I recalled the threat Huffman had made to Kate. That he'd allow Larry to rip her apart. Larry wanted to eviscerate me, too. Well, what goes around comes around.

Together we moved past the burning buildings and turned into the road. The entire ranch was now a magnificent pyre from which smoke billowed into the heavens. Beneath a shawl of smoke I saw the crumpled form of a man lying on the road. I knew without checking that the smashed-up body was that of Rourke. I felt no pity. He'd died after all, but it wasn't me who'd killed him. I'd only helped him along in the right direction.

'Is he the last of them?'

'I got a man round back, plus another out in the field that I took the rifle off,' Harvey said.

'Goddamnit,' Rink said. 'I stuck one with my knife, but all I got to shoot at was freakin' walls.'

Harvey grinned. 'That's the only way we could be sure you wouldn't miss.'

'Course, I got to soften Bolan up for you, Joe.'

'Yeah, but it was me who made a start on his lips for you,' Harvey added.

My friends, like many soldiers stuck in desperate

circumstances, were trying to lighten the mood with graveyard humour. I was doing a quick head count. I wasn't sure how many people Huffman had at his disposal, but there was at least one I hadn't come across yet.

'There was a woman. She was with Huffman when we took Kate away from him. Where's she at?'

'I didn't kill any woman,' Harvey said. As it was to me, the very thought of killing a woman – even a mob enforcer like that one – was abhorrent to him.

Rink shrugged expansively. 'Like I said, all I got to do was shoot at walls.'

I experienced slowly creeping dread. 'I've got a horrible idea where she is at.'

53

Rink's office was in downtown Tampa. He had a condominium up near Temple Terrace in the wooded area north-east of the city, but he chose to work from the office. He wasn't one for taking his work home with him. Like Rink, there was nothing fancy about the building. It was simply a solid construction, a bit like the man it served. Rink had inherited his Japanese mother Yukiko's love of minimalism. The walls were white, the desk, computer and chairs enough to satisfy any clients walking in through his doors, but all the other excesses of a modern office space were missing.

A door in the back of the office led to an equally stark room where Rink occasionally bedded down if he was working late and couldn't be bothered facing the drive home. Because of his size, he had installed a double bed. He also had a coffee percolator and a microwave oven. A shower stall and toilet completed the living area, providing all mod cons when the alternative was having nowhere to stay.

Kate wasn't complaining. After being a prisoner in Huffman's house, this place felt like a home from home to her. Imogen grumbled about the cramped living arrangements, but Kate only smiled. Her sister had just spent seven days on a luxury cruise liner; it was about time she felt a little of the discomfort that Kate had endured on her behalf. Not that she wanted her sister to suffer, not really. She loved her dearly and wanted only the best for her.

The sisters had to share the bed. There was nowhere else they could relax, unless they went out in the office with McTeer and Velasquez, and though Kate was grateful for the men's presence they weren't exactly riveting company. Both were taciturn individuals who seemed happy only when they were sharing a common silence. Kate wondered if their time on the force had made them so dour; a reason she was considering quitting her career. If she ended up as miserable and cynical as those two she'd sooner get the hell out now while she still retained a spark of life.

Lying next to Imogen reminded Kate of when they were small children. They'd had to share a room with their older brother, Jake. He'd had the single bed while Kate and Imogen had top-to-toed in the double that their parents had installed. Kate was six years old before Jake got his own room and she'd inherited his bed. But, many times after that, she'd still crawled into the double alongside Imogen when a particularly bad dream had disturbed her or when thunder rumbled outside. Even now she couldn't help throwing her arms around her slumbering sister and snuggling up close.

Imogen was in the midst of a dream. She mumbled

something incomprehensible and her brow creased as though she was perturbed. It wasn't surprising, considering what she'd gone through. Kate gently stroked her sister's forehead, smoothed her sleep-tousled hair and some of the lines relaxed on her face.

'It's OK, Imogen. Everything's OK,' Kate said very quietly.

The words helped soothe her, but they felt false to Kate's own ears.

She was still worried.

She was thinking about Joe.

Why hadn't he called yet? The only possible reason was that he was still engaged in battle with Huffman and his men. Either that or he'd failed. What if he was injured? What if he was dead? No! She wouldn't even contemplate that possibility. Joe was better than Huffman and all the scum he'd gathered around him. In fact, Kate had never known a man the like of Joe Hunter before.

As an officer with the NYPD she'd worked alongside some pretty tough individuals, some intelligent people too, but Joe embodied something that went beyond the norm. His cool exterior concealed a man of deep and complex emotions. He cared about the well-being of others to a point that he'd forfeit his life to make things better for them. There was nothing that he asked in return – apart from the occasional request that she trust him and do as he asked – there was nothing selfish about him. He'd agreed to help her find Imogen, to lay down his life to achieve that, but had never once enquired about payment. He'd agreed to help because he felt that he owed Kate's family a debt. Jake had been killed while saving the lives of his comrades, but Joe had risked his own life in return, carrying Jake out of the war zone. Joe had already paid his debt in that respect.

As a police officer she should have baulked at the extremes that Joe went to, except she understood him. He was working from a different set of rules than the bureaucracy laid down in the police procedural manuals she followed. He worked according to a different ethos, a somewhat old-fashioned creed that harked back to less complicated days. He was like the old-time marshals who patrolled the Wild West relying on their toughness and their sense of right and wrong to bring calm to the chaos of a lawless nation. Like him, she wanted to make the world a better place. It was why she'd enrolled as a police officer. They'd chosen a different route, that was all. She wished she'd had the nerve to do what Joe did. His methods seemed to get results.

Restless, she slid slowly from the bed so that she didn't waken Imogen. She stood by the bedside, pushing her feet into her shoes. She was already fully clothed, had stayed that way since arriving at Rink's office, knowing that they might have to move at a moment's notice. She leaned down to where her purse lay, and pulled out the cell phone that Joe had returned to her. She checked the phone for any messages she might have missed, but the screen was empty. She pushed buttons, finding Joe's number stored in the memory. She hovered over the button, wanting to ring, but knowing she might distract him when he needed that the least. Something else made her pause: what if she dialled him and the phone simply rang and rang and was never answered? How would she feel then?

From the front office she heard the tinkle of a bell as the front door was opened. She heard McTeer greeting someone. She couldn't make out the words, but there was no concern in his voice.

She put the phone back in her purse, took out the Glock 17 that Joe had given her. It wasn't her gun, but one he'd taken from a man at Little Fork. She racked the slide, jacking a bullet into the firing position. She flicked off the safety. Then she went to the door and listened. McTeer said something else, muffled by the intervening door, but then he laughed. Kate almost relaxed her finger on the trigger. Almost, but not quite. She heard a woman laugh in response to McTeer's words.

Kate cracked the door open an inch, peering round the door frame. She could make out McTeer at Rink's desk, reclining in the seat with his fingers linked behind his head. Velasquez wasn't there. He must have gone off on an errand of his own, leaving McTeer to guard the sleeping women. Standing on the other side of the desk was a slim woman with long blond hair. She was wearing glasses and a flowery dress that reached just below her knees. Over the dress was a cardigan buttoned below her ample breasts. The woman had a large purse hanging over one shoulder, and as Kate watched she saw the woman dip a bejewelled hand into the purse.

'I brought identification with me,' the woman said. 'I've got it right here.'

Kate moved without thought.

She stepped fully into the room, lifting her Glock.

The woman caught Kate's movement in her peripheral vision and she began to withdraw her hand from the purse.

'Shit!' McTeer kicked back to put distance between him and the silenced handgun that the woman lifted. McTeer slapped at the gun in his shoulder rig, but it was no use. Too little too late.

A gun spat flame. But this gun did not come with a silencer and the noise of the discharge compressed the eardrums of all three of them in the room.

Kate was deaf to the second and third shots she fired directly into Ruth Wicker.

Struck side-on, Wicker took the bullets in her right ribcage, and she was pushed over on her buckling left knee. Her reactive shot missed McTeer by inches and drilled a hole in the wall behind him. He stood up, bringing out his gun. Wicker ignored him, bringing her gun round at Kate. Her hand was trembling and she jerked on the trigger. Kate saw the flash of fire spit from Wicker's gun, but she didn't hear its retort. She was stuck in a place where only killing her enemy meant anything.

Kate fired again.

This time her bullet hit Wicker in the head, snatching away strands of the blond wig and a large portion of her skull. Wicker went down on her back, her legs splayed in an unladylike way. Her gun fell from lifeless fingers.

McTeer was standing in stunned fascination, his own gun forgotten for the moment. He looked down at the woman lying dead on the office floor.

'Jesus . . .' he hissed. 'How'd you know she was one of Huffman's people?'

'I don't know.' Kate wasn't sure if it was a premonition, or pure luck that she'd come out of the room when she did with her gun ready. Maybe it was simply because she'd been expecting something like this. Whatever, she had Joe Hunter to thank for it. If she'd fumbled with the safety, maybe shouted a cop-like warning, then McTeer would be dead. Perhaps Wicker would be standing over Imogen pumping rounds into her body. But Kate had stopped her.

'Christ,' McTeer said running a hand over his face. 'She almost had the drop on me. You saved my life, Kate. Thanks.'

'It was nothing,' Kate said. Now that Wicker was gone, she hugged her arms round her chest. She felt very weak.

'Nothing, my ass! I was supposed to be protecting you.'

'The disguise didn't work on me.' She looked down on Wicker, and even with the wig, the glasses, the feminine clothing, Kate didn't see anything but the vindictive bitch who'd almost shot her at Quicksilver Ranch.

'Goddamnit!' McTeer said, studying the close grouping of the shots in Wicker's side, the wound in her head. 'That was good shooting!'

Kate felt mildly pleased with the acknowledgement. 'It wasn't that good, McTeer,' she said with a sad smile. 'She was too close to miss.'

Behind her, Imogen came out of the bedroom. She was tentative, holding her breath as she crept close to Kate. Imogen touched her on the shoulder and Kate turned and they hugged close. Then Imogen pulled away, lifting Kate's phone up to her. 'It's Joe,' she said.

Thank God! Kate thought, reaching for the phone, there's still time. 'Joe . . .' she said, her voice barely above a whisper.

Then Imogen saw the blood on Kate's breast.

Kate blinked slowly at her sister. She looked down at the wound in her chest. Imogen let out a sob. After all this, after all that they'd been through, they still hadn't escaped Robert Huffman's reach. When Wicker had fired her last shot, it had cut directly through Kate's body. She had been too close to miss.

'No!' Imogen cried as she reached to support her failing sister. The phone slipped from Kate's fingers, and Joe's warning voice sounded tinny and very distant, and totally overwhelmed by Imogen's grief-stricken scream.

EPILOGUE

I heard the screaming over the phone and knew that I'd failed my prime directive. I felt Kate's death like a solid wedge of ice had been driven through my heart. Maybe in time I'd have come to love her as deeply as I had once loved my wife, but now she was gone. All I had left were the memories of those few hours we'd spent together. Maybe I should have screamed, too, but I couldn't. I only wept silently.

Rink gripped my shoulder, but he didn't say anything. I wiped my face. You can't be a soldier and fight the kind of battles I have if you're going to collapse under the weight of grief. There'd be no grieving yet. Not while there were still things to be done.

Clean-up was the immediate problem we all had to face, and I stepped up to the challenge. Anything to keep my mind off Kate.

Quicksilver Ranch burned like a nuclear reactor in meltdown, the flames fed by a wind that sprang up, and by the fuel we added to the buildings. The building laced with aviation fuel burned almost white-hot. We carried the dead there and flung them on the flames. I wished that Huffman was still alive when I dumped him in the fire.

After cleaning ourselves up, we appropriated a vehicle belonging to one of Huffman's people and it took us as far as the outskirts of Dallas. On a road bridge we tossed our weapons into the river below. There was no ceremony to the action, just good sense. The vehicle made a fire of its own on a deserted parking lot, and we walked away headed for DFW airport.

Little Fork was a major problem, but I was pretty certain that nothing there could be tied to us. The fact that Imogen's house had been burned down and the corpses of men found inside it was the biggest stumbling block. They would in turn be tied to the deaths of Jim Aitken, Judge Wallace and the guy I'd shot on the stairs at the restaurant. But it now looked like Larry Bolan was going to be held responsible for all three of those deaths. It also looked like he'd shot dead his younger brother, Trent, before heading off on the rampage that destroyed Quicksilver Ranch.

Kate's passing was hard on us all. She'd died a hero, but she could never claim that accolade. Her death was put down to a random drive-by shooting that took an awful lot of setting up, but was managed by a man who'd always been in the business of covering the true nature of death. My old CIA contact, William Hayes Conrad IV, had been a great help in the past and he came through once again. I knew he would. When he helped me resolve the issue with the contract killer, Dantalion, he'd told me he couldn't keep on condoning murder. But nothing of what we'd done was construed as such this time. The way things turned out, Walter made it known that a disagreement between factions of the criminal underworld had erupted into all-out war. Many suspected criminals had died in the process when enforcers from various syndicates started killing each other during a power struggle. The media had a ball with it, but as usual the news was only topical for a few days. We wouldn't be earning any medals of commendation for our actions, but at least we were kept out of prison. Ruth Wicker, the enforcer who'd gone after and ultimately murdered Kate, was the only person who connected us to the war that was waged across Kentucky and Texas. But Walter covered that too. He sent in a clean-up crew that made Wicker disappear completely and her name – like Kate's – was never added to the tally of the dead. Kate's death was handled with more dignity, but it was still something that pained us all deeply. Sadly Kate would only be remembered as a statistic of a violent and senseless world, except in the hearts and minds of those who truly cared for her.

Imogen flew back to Maine to be near the Piers family plot where she could be close to Kate. I had failed to keep Kate safe, and now Imogen felt it was down to her to do that. She was still hurting from her loss, but she was buoyed by the knowledge that those responsible for murdering her lover and her sister were all dead.

With Rink and Harvey, I attended Kate's funeral, standing barely six feet from where I had when we'd buried Jake. It was difficult letting her go, but what else could I do? I wondered what life could have been like if she'd survived. She had her career and I had mine, and it wasn't something that could ever have worked. But I sure wished she was still around.

THANKS AND ACKNOWLEDGEMENTS

There are many people who help writers to achieve their dreams of writing and publishing a book. I have so many to thank that it is inevitable I will forget to mention someone. You know who you are, so thanks to you all.

Special thanks go to the following:
Luigi Bonomi, Alison Bonomi, George Lucas, Sue Fletcher, David Highfill, all the team at ILA, Ajda Vucicevic, Jack Barclay, Swati Gamble, Gabe Robinson, Eleni Fostiropoulos, Sharyn Rosenblum, Kelly Edgson-Wright, Alice Wood, a support team beyond comparison.

Adrian Magson, Col Bury, Richard Gnosill, Sheila Quigley, Pauline Rowson, Pat Bertram, and all the gang at ITW debut authors; all writers who have helped in ways they may or may not know.

Jim, Dave, John, Raymond, Jacky, Val, Jordon, Bunny, Geoff, Mandy and last on the list, but first in my heart, Denise.

In loving memory of Megs and Izzy.

JOE HUNTER

BRITAIN'S BEST VIGILANTE V AMERICA'S WORST CRIMINALS

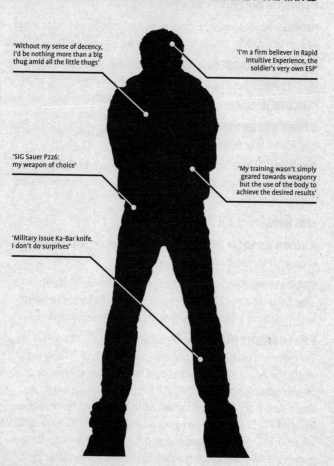

'Without my sense of decency, I'd be nothing more than a big thug amid all the little thugs'

'I'm a firm believer in Rapid Intuitive Experience, the soldier's very own ESP'

'SIG Sauer P226: my weapon of choice'

'My training wasn't simply geared towards weaponry but the use of the body to achieve the desired results'

'Military issue Ka-Bar knife. I don't do surprises'

CURRICULUM VITAE – JOE HUNTER

NAME: Joe Hunter.

DATE OF BIRTH: 8th August 1969.

PLACE OF BIRTH: Manchester, England.

HOME: Manchester, England but in process of relocating to Florida, USA.

MARITAL STATUS: Divorced from Diane, who has now remarried.

CHILDREN: None.

OTHER DEPENDENTS: Two German shepherd dogs, Hector and Paris (currently residing with Diane).

PARENTS: Joe's father died when he was a child and his mother remarried. Both his mother and stepfather reside in Manchester.

SIBLINGS: Half-brother, John Telfer.

KNOWN ASSOCIATES: Jared 'Rink' Rington, Walter Hayes Conrad, Harvey Lucas.

EDUCATION: Secondary school education to 'O' level standard. Joe received further education and underwent self-teaching while in the British Army and Special Forces.

EMPLOYMENT HISTORY: Joined British Army at age 16. Transferred to the Parachute Regiment at age 19 and was drafted into an experimental coalition counterterrorism team code named 'ARROWSAKE' at age 20. As a sergeant, Joe headed his own unit comprising members from various Special Forces teams. Joe retired from 'ARROWSAKE' in 2004 when the unit was disbanded and has since then supported himself by working as a freelance security consultant.

HEIGHT: 5' 11".

WEIGHT: 13 stone.

BUILD: Athletic.

HAIR COLOUR/STYLE: Short brown hair with slight greying.

EYE COLOUR: Blue/brown.

APPEARANCE: Muscular but more lean than bulky, he has the appearance of a competitive athlete. His demeanour is generally calm and unhurried. Due to his background, Joe has the ability to blend with the general public when necessary, but when relaxed he tends to dress casually. He doesn't consider himself handsome, but women find him attractive. His eyes are his most striking feature and the colour appears to change dependent on his mood.

BLOOD TYPE: AB

MEDICAL HISTORY: Childhood complaints include measles and chicken pox. As an adult Joe has had no major medical conditions, but has been wounded on several occasions. Joe carries numerous scars including a bullet wound in his chest and various scars from knife and shrapnel wounds on his arms and legs. He has had various bone breakages, but none that have proven a continued disability.

RELIGION: Joe was raised in a Church of England environment, but is currently non-practising.

POLITICS: Joe has no political preferences and prefers morals and ethics.

CHARACTER: Joe can come over as a little aloof at times. He is a deep thinker who prefers only to speak when he has something important to say. He is very loyal to his family and friends. He dislikes injustice, hates bullies and will stand up to defend others in need of help.

MUSIC: Wide choice of music, but particularly enjoys vintage rhythm and blues.

MOVIES: Joe's favourite movie is 'It's a Wonderful Life'. It is a morality tale that resonates with his belief that a person's actions – good or bad – continually affect those around them.

BOOKS: When he was younger he enjoyed classic fiction by HP Lovecraft, RE Howard and Edgar Allan Poe, but currently reads a wide range of crime and suspense novels.

CIGARETTES: Smoked various brands but gave up.

ALCOHOL: Drinks only moderately and infrequently. Prefers beer to liquor.

DRUGS: Has been subjected to drugs during his military career, but has never personally taken any illegal drugs. Joe hates the influence that drugs have on the world and stands against those producing and supplying them.

HOBBIES: Fitness. Joe works out whenever he can with a combination of running, circuit training and martial arts.

SPECIAL SKILLS: As a soldier Joe gained many skills pertinent to his job, but also specialised in CQB (Close Quarter Battle), Point Shooting, Defensive Driving and in Urban Warfare Tactics. He is particularly adept with the handgun (usually a SIG Sauer P226) and with the knife (usually a military issue KA-BAR).

CURRENT OCCUPATION: Joe describes himself as a security consultant and sometimes PI, but some people call him a vigilante.

CURRENT WHEREABOUTS: USA.

Want to find out what Joe Hunter does next? Here is a taster from Matt Hilton's *Cut and Run*.

I

His first thought was that his sins had caught up with him.

It was a moment of epiphany he'd never have come to without this shocking wake-up call.

Linden Case had always denied that there was anything wrong in the way he treated the whores. He paid them well, even gave them a bonus if they particularly pleased him. By the nature of their trade they allowed him to do to them whatever he desired. But he fully grasped his reason for being here in this dark basement of a building in a less than salubrious district of Tampa, Florida.

Earlier he'd been driving his Mercedes along 7th Avenue in the historic Ybor district. Although the area was famous as a tourist destination where people came to view the colourful architecture, there was also a darker underbelly that appealed to him. Street girls often hung out there, waiting for men like Case to offer them a ride. He had stopped at a red light – ironically, under the circumstances – and checked out a woman standing on the sidewalk while he waited for the light to go green.

She was Seminole; dusky-skinned with jet black hair. On green, he'd driven off. He was only interested in blondes. As he'd waited for a stocky woman to clear the crossing, his passenger door opened and a man slipped in beside him. Case was used to women being so bold, but never men.

'Hey, buddy, I'm not your type, OK?'

'You're exactly my type, Case.'

'How do you know my name?'

The man shoved a handgun into Case's ribs.

'Shut your mouth and drive.'

Case wasn't familiar with handguns. This one was big and black, and it was enough to know that it would kill him. He drove.

The man refused to answer Case's questions. He spoke only to give him directions. They left the Ybor district, heading south over Causeway Boulevard. Case noticed a huge depot with trains parked on sidings, but he was unfamiliar with this area of the city. The man signalled him off the highway into a rundown area made up of derelict buildings. At a warehouse made from preformed concrete sheets, the man made Case get out of the Mercedes. Case had again tried to get the man to answer his questions, but all that earned him was a smack round the head with the butt of the gun.

When Case came round he was inside the derelict warehouse. His hands and feet had been strapped to a chair using electricians' tape. Case strained against his bindings but he wasn't strong enough to break them.

'You're wasting your time.'

Case sat rigid in his chair. The voice had come from in front of him but he couldn't see the man who'd spoken. It was too dark for that.

'Who are you?'

'The name's Joe Hunter.'

'You're a cop?'

'No. I'm a concerned member of the public.'

'Why are you doing this to me?'

'You're a bad man. I'm here to punish you.'

The only light was a faint strip beneath a door at the far end of the room. Case saw movement as a figure passed through it.

'What do you mean? I'm not a bad man!'

'I've been watching you, Case. I've followed you. I know what you did to the women.'

'*I paid them,*' Case shouted. 'They knew what I wanted.'

'You hurt them.' The man's voice had dropped an octave, but the menace in his words had grown exponentially. 'Do you think cash was fair exchange for what you did?'

'Yes. I offered money and they agreed. Every time: it was a done deal!' Case strained at his bindings. The tape stretched, biting into his flesh. He heard footsteps coming towards him. Case readied himself for a blow, but it didn't come. The man walked behind the chair and laid his hands on Case's shoulders.

'I want you to look at something.'

The man dragged him and the chair round so he was facing in the opposite direction. Nothing but blackness.

Then a click as he threw a switch.

A single bulb had been covered with a strip of muslin. The cloth obscured most of the light, but there was enough to see what was directly below it.

The woman strapped to the chair was barely out of her teens. She was just the type that Case usually preferred. Slim with blond hair. She used to be pretty. Now both her eyes were swollen shut, bruises blooming on both cheeks. Her nose had been broken, split across the bridge and leaking blood. Her lips were mashed and blood-flecked drool hung in a string from her chin.

'Is this a done deal, Case?'

Case shuddered at the impotence of his situation.

The woman moaned, but didn't have the strength to move. All she managed was a glance up at Case that spoke of shame. The look condemned Case more than the man's actions ever could.

The man who called himself Hunter balled his fist. 'Is it right that a man beats a woman?'

'*Leave her alone.*'

He turned to face Case.

'So it's OK for you to hurt them, but no one else can? Is that what you're saying, Case?' The man took out a fifty dollar bill and laid it on the woman's thighs. Then he backhanded her across her face. Not hard, but enough so that her head was rocked on her shoulders. 'Does paying her make things right?'

'Goddamnit!' Case again fought against his bindings. He was shuddering so hard he was almost vibrating. 'Leave her alone, you bastard.'

The man took a knife from his belt. In the subdued

light from the muslin-wrapped bulb, the blade looked tarnished. 'You have used your hands on women before, Case. Have you ever used one of these?'

'Nooooo…'

The man placed the blade against the woman's throat.

'Please,' Case cried. 'Not her. Please don't hurt my daughter.'

The man snorted. 'You didn't stop to think about the women you hurt. Why should I care?'

Then he slashed the blade across the woman's throat. Even in the dimness of the basement, Case saw the gout of blood pour down her chest. He screamed.

'An eye for an eye, Case. The women that you hurt were other men's daughters.'

Case had stopped screaming now. Through his tears he watched the final seconds of his daughter's life ebb away.

The man moved towards him.

'Does what I did to your darling Jessica make me a bad man?'

'You bastard. You sick murderous bastard.'

'Yes. That answers the question.' The man lifted the blade. 'But it damns you, as well, Case.'

2

Don't look back or you might find the devil hot on your heels.

It's an idea I subscribe to. An analogy fit for one with a past full of terrible events.

The problem is, by being optimistic and only looking ahead, you can miss the devil gaining ground. Before you know it, he's right there and has rammed his toasting fork through your spine and is dangling you over the flames of hell.

I've made too many enemies not to cast the occasional glance over my shoulder. The practice has served me well and has kept me alive to date.

I parked my Audi A6 at an entrance to the grounds of Tampa University and got out the car while I opened up my phone and went through the motions of taking a call. Looking northwest, Kennedy Boulevard spanned the river and beside it on the eastern shore was the cylindrical Rivergate Tower that's affectionately known to locals as the beer can. It reminded me of the leaning tower of Pisa, after Superman's evil alter-ego pushed it back in line in that cheesy movie. My eyes merely skimmed over the tower, it was a familiar sight to me, and I watched the traffic approaching over the river bridge.

I was looking for the nondescript light grey sedan that had been following me all the way across from Cypress Point Park, where I'd gone for my morning run. It was only a couple of months since Kate Piers died and I missed her. I'd intended clearing my head with a burst of physical effort, the only thing that could shift the troubling thought that Kate died because I'd failed to keep her safe, but that wasn't to be. When I'd arrived at the park the sedan was waiting for me, and had tucked itself in behind me all the way here. Only my unscheduled stop had forced it to continue on by.

Down on the Hillsborough River, birds dived at shoals of fish and I could hear their raucous calls even over the swish of passing traffic. There was a tang of citrus and exhaust fumes on the air, and the sun was hot and still. Sunbeams bounced off the windows of the beer can, sending razors of light back at me. All these things were distractions and, like the memories of Kate Piers, I blocked them out.

The sedan returned within a minute. I leaned against my Audi, and had a full-on argument with my unheeding phone. As the car swept past I allowed my gaze to skim over it. I had all of a second to identify those within the car, but I'd trained myself to snap-shoot a scene and replay it through my mind at my leisure. The car continued on by and already its driver was looking for somewhere to stop.

I got back in my car and set off over the bridge,

heading into downtown Tampa. Behind me, those in the sedan would be frantically searching for somewhere to turn. I could easily have given them the slip at that point, but I wanted to know who these people were. More than that, I wanted to know what they were up to. I drove slowly, giving them an opportunity to catch up.

Four blocks on and I saw the grey sedan in my mirror. I turned right on to Florida Avenue, continued straight ahead until I was stopped by a red light at Whitling Street. The sedan was three cars back behind a Jeep and a Ford and I saw the passenger lean out of the window to get a better look at me. This action was amateurish or it was contrived.

While I waiting for the light to change, I ran the snapshot image I'd shelved through my mind. The driver was a man in his late thirties, muscular build, short dark hair, broken nose. His front seat passenger was a shade older, stocky, but his hair was a tad longer and flecked with grey. Despite the heat, they wore sports jackets over formal shirts, ties knotted at their throats.

Going on green, I followed the road under the Crosstown Expressway as though I was going to head out on to Harbour Island, but at the Garrison Channel I took a left and headed for St Pete Times Forum, a hockey stadium I'd been to a couple of times with my friend, Rink. The sedan followed me on to Ice Palace Drive towards the arena with the benefit of only one car between us. I flicked on my indicators to show I was pulling over into a lay-by adjacent to the public park opposite the stadium.

There was no game today, so the parking lot across the way was almost deserted and nobody was wandering through the park next to the water. It was a good place to get myself killed if the men in the sedan were better than they looked. But I didn't think they were. When weighing up the seclusion against my own needs, it was just the spot I needed to get to the bottom of things.

The grey sedan drove past. As it did, I played at being interested in the park. From under my shirt I pulled out my SIG Sauer P226 and racked the slide. Normally I'm good to go with one in the chamber, but it wasn't a great idea to be driving round with the gun ready to discharge, particularly when my modified gun comes with no safety.

Waiting for the road to clear of traffic, I watched the sedan draw to a halt twenty feet in front of me. As soon as it did, I walked up to the driver's window and slammed it with the butt of my gun. Even as glass sprayed over the driver's legs, I pressed my gun against the man's neck.

'Show me your hands.'

Both men threw their empty hands in the air, stunned by the manner of my arrival.

'OK. Both of you get out of the car now.'

They clambered out. I kept my gun close to the driver and made the other walk round towards me. He did so without lowering his hands. There was a car passing the front of the ice stadium but it was going the other way. I glanced towards the nearby Marriott Hotel, but we were unobserved. I waved them towards the park with a jerk of the gun barrel. Then I concealed my gun beneath my shirtfront: just in case.

They went without argument, as if perhaps they were expecting this from me. I quickly glanced about, searching for any other car I might have missed. There was nothing evident.

Gravel paths wound their way round the park. We followed one until we were at the water. I made them get down on the grass, while I stood over them.

'Sit on your hands. Anyone makes a move without my say-so gets shot. Are we clear?' The men sat on their hands, looking nonplussed by the situation. I had expected fear, anger, and argument. It made me reappraise them. They weren't the amateurs I'd surmised: this was definitely planned. 'So what's the deal?'

The older man gave me a weary smile while the other just sat there. I nodded at the older one.

'We're not your enemies, Hunter,' he said.

'I'll decide that after you tell me why you were following me.'

'We're under orders.'

'You weren't doing a very good job.'

'We weren't hiding.' He smiled again. 'In fact, back there at the lights, I leaned out the car so you could see me.'

We could have gone on like that all day. It was a beautiful day, none of it to be wasted.

'Let's get to the point.'

'I'm Castle, my friend here's Soames. We're cops,' he said, as if that should explain everything. 'Homicide.'

I gave him a slow blink. Maybe that revelation was supposed to make me put my gun away. I'm not the type to be intimidated by the presence of cops, though.

'I already guessed that.'

'So why the gun and games?'

'Not all cops have my best interests at heart.'

'Not any more.' Soames looked at me with hard eyes, challenging me. I could see how he'd earned the broken nose.

I ignored him and asked Castle, 'What do you want from me?'

'If you'd let me get off my ass, that'd be a start.'

'Not yet.'

'Can I show you my badge so you know we're real cops?'

Studying their clothing, I said, 'That's already a given. Keep your hands where they are.'

'We don't want trouble Hunter.'

'What *do* you want?'

'We need you to come in and answer a few questions.'

It wouldn't be the first time I'd been invited to the local precinct house on Franklin, but the manner was a first.

'So why didn't you just approach me in the normal way?'

Castle raised his eyebrows at the barrel of my SIG. 'It was either us, nice and easy like this, or it would've been a SWAT team. Knowing the way Joe Hunter is rumoured to work, our guess was there'd be less blood spilt this way.'

A worm of unease slithered its way through my guts. SWAT team?

'You're saying that I'm under arrest?'

'Prefer it if you came in under your own steam,' Castle said. 'But if you'd rather I Mirandize you and do everything by the book, that's OK, too.'

I put my SIG away. I'm licensed to carry, but that didn't allow me to hold police officers under threat. 'What am I supposed to have done?'

'Assaulted officers and damaged county property for a start,' Soames muttered. The man didn't like me, but he was here under orders to keep his opinions to himself. Castle seemed easier with the situation but even he shot Soames a frown of disapproval.

'We just need to clear up a couple of things,' he said. 'You satisfy us, we'll kick you loose again in an hour.'

There were many things I'd done in the year I'd been living here; I wondered which one of them had come back to haunt me. Nothing obvious came to mind: each and every one of them had been extremely violent – but, in my opinion, justified.

'Is there a parking ticket I've forgotten about?' I moved back, allowing the men to get up. Castle grunted as he helped himself stand with one hand propped on a thigh. Soames swarmed up and he wasn't impressed at my joke.

'You're a fucking piece of work, Hunter.'

It looked for the briefest of moments that Soames would go for his piece, but Castle grabbed his elbow. 'I'm sure it's all a misunderstanding. One we can clear up with Hunter's help.'

There was nothing I'd been involved in during the last couple of weeks that would attract the eye of the local police department, so I was sure that he was right.

'I'll follow you in.'

'Give me your gun,' Soames said.

Shaking my head slowly, I said, 'I'll check it in at the station.'

Soames wavered and I gave him a steady look. Castle cleared his throat, touched his partner on the elbow again. The older detective turned and walked away, but Soames felt he had something to prove.

'You might have fooled Castle, but I know *exactly* what you are.'

I didn't reply. If what he was suggesting was true, then it would have been the Special Response Team – Florida's version of SWAT – who'd come for me, not two detectives on a peace keeping mission.

Grunting a curse, Soames moved quicly after his partner.

And I thought that was that. I'd go along to the station and answer a few questions, put things straight and be back on the street in an hour. It was too lovely a day to be cooped up for long. Maybe there'd still be time to have the jog around the park at Cypress Point that I'd originally planned.

I should have known better.

A volley of bullets took out both cops' brains and they crumpled to the ground.

3

It went without saying that Soames and Castle were dead. Both men had lost a good portion of their skulls and there were twin fans of blood and brain matter spread across the gravel footpath next to them. My gun was up, but anyone studying the scene would notice immediately that the direction of my gun barrel and the spray of blood were at contradictory angles. Not that something so obvious would make a jot of difference. I wasn't going to stand there like a statue and wait for the police investigators to arrive at the scene.

I had to move.

Not to escape justice: I could prove that it wasn't my gun that had fired the killing shots. I had to move because whoever was out there could be adjusting their aim to put a round through my head.

As I raced off the path I was calculating the trajectory of the shots. The Marriott was a high-point to my left, but the blood from the headshots had splashed towards the hotel. We had been hidden by shrubbery and trees from anyone on the road where we'd left our cars. The shots hadn't come from a boat on Garrison Channel behind me. There was only one place left where the shooter could have been stationed in order to take the shots.

Placing a tree bole between me and the gunman, I glanced up at the nearby ice stadium roof. St Pete Times Forum was a huge oblong-shaped building, with glass-fronted galleries on the two sides that I could see. The roof was a shallow arch, and could be negotiated by a nimble person, but it didn't appear to have a walkway or any visible service ducts where a shooter could be positioned. At each corner of the building, forming support bulwarks for the galleries, were squat square towers that had flat roots bordered by low walls. My gaze fell directly on the one nearest to me.

From the corner of this tower came a flash and almost instantaneously a chunk of the tree I was hiding behind was blasted into splinters. The crack of a high-velocity round came to my ears in the next instant. The precise moment I'd seen the flash I'd moved, and the bullet that struck bark from the tree missed me, but I wasn't sure that I'd avoid a second round. The shooter was armed with a sniper rifle, and from this distance it could put a bullet directly through a tree trunk as flimsy as this one.

Dodging to my left, I immediately reversed direction and went right, throwing myself through bushes towards the slope leading down towards the channel. I heard two reports of the rifle, but thankfully no rounds ripped through my body. I scrambled over the embarkment, went down on my belly and placed the swell in the ground between us. He couldn't see me now, but I couldn't see him either.

My mind was racing. The police suspected my involvement in a crime I was innocent of, but now that the officers sent to bring me in were dead, no one would believe me. The man with the sniper rifle had seen to that. It also explained why he hadn't shot to kill. I was being set up.

Someone must have heard the shots – in fact I could hear alarmed voices calling out from the nearby hotel – and the police would be along any minute. The sensible thing would be to wait for the responding emergency vehicles, put down my gun and throw myself on the mercy of the justice system. But I was under no illusions; there was no way I was going to hang round, not when all they'd see was a cop killer. I'd be face down in the dirt, my hands cuffed and surrounded by armed men itching to blow me away long before I could argue my innocence.

There was only one way out of this that I could see.

I had to take down the shooter.

The shoreline was made up of stones and gravel, but gave way within a few yards to tufts of grass. If I stood up, or even crouched, I'd be an easy target. The trees and shrubbery in the park didn't offer much cover from the shooter with his high vantage either, so all I could do was belly crawl along the shore, my knees and elbows propelling me along. I considered crawling into the channel and swimming, but I needed my weapon dry.

Fifty yards on, I quickly raised my eyes over the embankment and saw that the shooter would have to lean out from the tower to get me, now that I'd compromised his position. I didn't think he'd do that. I quickly raced up the embankment and into a small copse of trees. Crouching there, I pulled out my gun.

If I used it now, tests would show that the gun had been fired, I'd have gunshot residue on my skin and clothing: it would mean more questions if the police took me down, it would compound my guilt as a cop killer. But I wasn't going to go against a man with a sniper rifle with only my bare hands.

Distantly I heard the first wail of sirens. The police were on their way. My window of opportunity had just been slammed in my face.

Got to move, I told myself. I have to take down this man or I'll never get the chance again.

I charged across the park towards the road that separated me from the stadium. When no bullets came my way I realised that the shooter had probably abandoned his position and was making his getaway. Apparently I wasn't the only one who could hear the approaching sirens.

My car and that of the dead detectives was way off on my left, but apart from them there were no vehicles on the road. The ice stadium was a huge edifice looming over me. I was in the open, but no bullets were fired at me. Whoever was trying to set me up had many options for escape. If the stadium had been filled with Tampa Bay Lightning fans, the shooter could simply melt amongst the crowds, but this was a day when the hockey team weren't playing; the only people round would be a skeleton crew of staff. But that meant that the gunman could slip out unnoticed by any number of exits from the public areas or via service doors round the back.

I looked for a getaway vehicle.

There was nothing remarkable about the few cars I'd noted in the parking lot – and anyway, they were too exposed to be the choice location for a fleeing murderer to park his car. More likely the killer had his getaway car round the back among the staff's vehicles. I started to angle that way, hoping to cut him off. I'd only got a few paces when I heard the roar of an engine. Reversing direction, I sprinted back towards the front of the building. I couldn't see anything moving on the road that ran parallel with the stadium, and there was nothing on the public parking lot. Coming to a standstill I listened, trying to pinpoint the noise. Beyond the stadium's official parking lot was a second open space, and I guessed that this was used for overspill parking on busy match days. There was still nothing moving. But then I saw a dark blue Ford erupt like a cork from a bottle from a ramp in the second lot. The ramp must have exited from a vehicle park underground, or maybe it was from a loading dock where deliveries were made to the stadium. It didn't really matter, not when the car was over a hundred yards away and speeding away from me.

Futile as it seemed, I ran after it. It would have been a waste of ammunition to fire at the car, so I concentrated on getting as good a look as possible at the car and its driver. The Ford sped off the lot, took a left on the service road, then a right on to Jefferson Street. Then it was gone.

Immediately I ran back the way I'd come, heading for my Audi. Converging sirens were very loud now and I had to get out of there as quickly as possible. As I ran for my car I recited over and over again the Ford's registration number like it was a mantra. And I lodged in my mind the one glance I'd got of the shooter's face. There was something uncannily familiar about that one glimpse, but I couldn't put my finger on it.

Piling into my car, I jammed it into gear and peeled away from the small parking bay. I headed for the ice stadium and swung into the service road towards Jefferson Street. In my mirrors I saw the flashing gumball lights of squad cars screeching to a halt where my car had just been. Then one of the cop cars revved wildly and came after me.

There was still the option of pulling over and explaining to the cops what had really happened. Anyone could see that Castle and Soames had been shot from a distance by a high-velocity rifle and that I was armed only with a 9mm handgun that hadn't been fired. But they'd assume that I had an accomplice who'd taken the shots; I must have led the officers to this trap, otherwise how would the shooter know where we were? I'd probably spend days in a cell awaiting arraignment for murder while the real killer went about his business unhindered. It didn't escape me that he was setting me up to take the fall for his crimes and I wondered what the hell he was planning next.

Giving up wasn't an option. The way I saw it, the only way to prove my innocence was to throw the gunman at their feet. Preferably alive so that he could confess, but under the present circumstances, it was more likely he'd be dead. The killer was planning – or had already executed – something big. And it was down to me to stop him.